The Call of the Wild

The Call of the Wild

BY JACK LONDON

With an Illustrated Reader's Companion

BY DANIEL DYER

UNIVERSITY OF OKLAHOMA PRESS
Norman and London

Published with the assistance of the
National Endowment for the Humanities,
a federal agency which supports the
study of such fields as history,
philosophy, literature, and language.

Library of Congress Cataloging-in-Publication Data

London, Jack, 1876–1916.
The call of the wild / by Jack London ;
with an illustrated Reader's companion by Daniel Dyer.
p.   cm.
Includes bibliographical references and index.
ISBN 0-8061-2757-0 (cloth : alk. paper)
1. Klondike River Valley (Yukon)—Gold discoveries—Fiction.
2. Dogs—Klondike River Valley (Yukon)—Fiction.
I. Dyer, Daniel (Daniel Osborn), 1944–   . II. Title.
PS3523.O46C3   1995
813'.52—dc20   95-15717
CIP

Text design by Trina Stahl.

The paper in this book meets the guidelines for permanence
and durability of the Committee on Production Guidelines for Book Longevity
of the Council on Library Resources, Inc. ⊖

1 2 3 4 5 6 7 8 9 10

For Joyce,

who has always believed

And get the atmosphere. Get the breadth and thickness to your stories. . . . The reader, since it is fiction, doesn't want your dissertations on the subject, your observations, your knowledge as your knowledge, your thoughts about it, your ideas—BUT PUT ALL THOSE THINGS WHICH ARE YOURS INTO THE STORIES, INTO THE TALES, ELIM- INATING YOURSELF. . . . AND THIS WILL BE THE ATMOSPHERE. AND THIS AT- MOSPHERE WILL BE YOU, DON'T YOU UNDERSTAND, YOU! YOU! YOU! And for this, and for this only, will critics praise you, and the public appreciate you, and your work be art. In short, you will then be the artist; do not do it, and you will be the artisan. . . . Don't narrate—paint! draw! build! CREATE!

—JACK LONDON, to Cloudesley Johns, 16 June 1900

Contents

Illustrations

All maps and figures follow page 76.

MAPS

FIGURES

Preface

$\mathcal{A}$LTHOUGH THERE ARE about thirty editions of *The Call of the Wild* currently in print in English alone, there has not ever been available an edition with a wide assortment of photographs and maps from the Gold Rush years; nor has there been one with comprehensive annotations.

The Library of America edition (1990), for instance, has a meticulously accurate text but provides only fifteen footnotes. The maps (reproductions from Pierre Berton's *Klondike Fever*) are helpful but do not show all the places London mentions in the Northland segments of the novel, and there are no maps of the significant California and other West Coast locations. In accordance with standard Library of America format, there are no photographs or other illustrations. The other recent scholarly edition (Oxford University Press, 1990) has an excellent introduction and text and features twenty-five notes and a better map, but, again, there are no photographs or other illustrations.

A new edition is necessary, then, to help contemporary readers enter London's increasingly unfamiliar world. A score of footnotes will no longer suffice. When London wrote the novel, he was correctly confident that most of his readers would be familiar with the Klondike Gold Rush, which had begun only a half-dozen years earlier. Throughout the Rush, the major magazines of the day—month after month—carried lengthy feature stories about the region and its events; metropolitan newspapers provided daily coverage—often with maps and other illustrations. Scores of books and pamphlets on the subject were widely available.

Nearly a century has now passed: The town of Dyea, Alaska, is gone altogether—as are the Whitehorse Rapids; Pullman cars and the sounds of trains arriving at flag-stops are as unfamiliar to today's readers as the ringing of typewriter bells will be to tomorrow's; most readers today could not draw an accurate picture of a Yukon sled, or offer a contemporary equivalent for the slang word *squarehead.* Most do not have in their minds an image of the White Pass or of Dawson City at the height of the Rush.

Readers are certainly free to imagine whatever they wish as they turn the pages of a novel—doing so has always been one of the rewards of reading. But Jack London's realism—in *The Call of the Wild* and in much of his other fiction—did not venture far from reality. He wrote about places and people and situations he knew intimately. It is the aim of this edition to help readers see what Jack London saw, from the "sun-kissed Santa Clara Valley" to the "nightmare" of the Dyea beach to the frozen and brutal "Long Trail" between Dawson City and Skagway.

A Note on the Text: In preparing this new edition of *The Call of the Wild* I have used the first book printing, issued by Macmillan in July 1903. I have retained all of the original spelling and punctuation; in those few instances where doing so creates ambiguity or confusions of other sorts, I have furnished explanations.

A Note on the Reader's Companion: In the annotations, which begin after London's text and the illustrations, I have offered no literary criticism or interpretation (a summary of the principal critical views of the novel may be found in the Introduction). Rather, I have sought to explain the contexts of the novel. When, for example, London refers in the first chapter to "the little flag station known as College Park," he has in his mind's eye a specific Southern Pacific depot between Santa Clara and San Jose, only blocks from the residence of his good friends Ted and Mabel Applegarth. And when in the fourth chapter he mentions "Cassiar Bar," he is surely remembering that, during his own trip to the Klondike in the fall of 1897, he and his companions ran aground on that very sandbar in the Yukon River.

The Call of the Wild is a spare novel—a "prose poem," Maxwell Geismar calls it—and there are many times when a phrase or sentence that was highly evocative in 1903 simply no longer suffices. For example, in the second chapter London writes that Buck's team had "a hard day's run, up the Cañon, through Sheep Camp, past the Scales and the timber line, across glaciers and snowdrifts hundreds of feet deep, and over the great Chilcoot Divide, which stands between the salt water and the fresh and guards forbiddingly the sad and lonely North." With those few words London has condensed one of the most spectacular images of the entire Gold Rush—the scaling of the Chilcoot Pass.

Accordingly, preceding the Reader's Companion I have provided photographs and maps from the Gold Rush era to help readers today see what many in London's day were able to remember. I have also included the perspectives of other Northland writers from the Gold Rush era, at times allowing their long-silent voices to speak at length, for in many, many instances their words are complementary to London's. I have included, as well, relevant passages from London's other Northland stories, where he occasionally paints what he merely sketches in *The Call of the Wild*. Finally, I have shown, where possible, how London's personal experiences in California, Alaska, and the Yukon figure in the novel.

The principal categories of information available in the Reader's Companion include the following:

1. *Place-Names.* London names dozens of communities, rivers, lakes, and other geographical features. All are actual; all can be located on the maps accompanying this edition. At times, I have provided information about the origin of the name (English and, in some cases, American Indian). For places important in the novel, I have included even more detail. Except in direct quotation, I have throughout the Reader's Companion used contemporary spellings of all place-names.

2. *Personal Names.* In much of his work Jack London uses the actual or slightly altered names of family, friends, and acquaintances. His cousin, Ernest Everhard, for example, lends his name to the protagonist of the futuristic novel *The Iron Heel* (1908). Klondike acquaintances Elam Harnish, Merritt Sloper, Del Bishop, "Old Man" Tarwater, and Emil Jensen appear more or less as themselves in other stories. A man named Louis Bondell (Louis Bond was another Yukon acquaintance) appears briefly in "Trust," and London himself is a young sailor by the name of Liverpool in "Like Argus of the Ancient Times."

In his fiction London occasionally includes, as well, the names of actual personalities important in the history of the Gold Rush—for example, "Swiftwater" Bill Gates, Superintendent Charles Constantine of the North-west Mounted Police, Tagish Charley, Arizona Charlie Meadows, Al Mayo, and Jack McQuesten. I have—where confidence permits—pointed out those names with personal or historical significance.

3. *Public Transportation.* Using actual rail, ferry, and steamship schedules from 1897, I have verified London's accounts of travel by public conveyance.

4. *Flora and Fauna.* Except where noted, London was accurate about the plants and animals he mentions in the text. I have not commented about such items unless their significance in the story merits such attention—or unless I believe they would be unfamiliar to the general reader.

5. *Dogs: Breeds, Behavior, and Travel.* I have provided information about unfamiliar breeds, authenticated London's accounts of the behavior of Northland dogs, and explained, where necessary, the techniques of travel by dog-team.

6. *Slang.* I have translated all slang expressions no longer in common usage—for example, "all 'll go well and the goose hang high," an odd expression meaning "all will be well."

7. *Miscellaneous Items.* I have explained London's allusions to Klondike history, American Indians, and to many other items that are either no longer common knowledge (Pullman cars, Hudson's Bay Company) or are vague or arcane ("snubbing" a "poling boat").

Acknowledgments

THE PURSUIT OF materials relating to *The Call of the Wild* has led me to libraries, archives, and historical societies all over the United States and Canada. In virtually every case I was surprised—not by the invariable professionalism I encountered (that I expected) but by the eagerness with which people sought to answer questions which, in some cases, must have seemed awfully insignificant. Space does not permit me to acknowlege the nature of each contribution to this volume, but I do want, at least, to mention those institutions and individuals whose assistance was so crucial to this project: Rose Schreier and India Spartz, Alaska Historical Library, Juneau; Rick Ewig, American Heritage Center, University of Wyoming; the Aurora, Ohio, branch of the Portage County Library; Bancroft Library, University of California, Berkeley; George Miles, Western Americana Collection, Beinecke Rare Book and Manuscript Library, Yale University; Sibylle Zemitis and Kathleen A. Correia, California State Library, Sacramento; Ellen Halteman, California State Railroad Museum, Sacramento; Canada Map Office, Ottawa; Cleveland Public Library; Kimberly J. Murphy, Colt's Manufacturing Company, Inc.; Connecticut State Library, Hartford; Marge Heath, Elmer E. Rasmuson Library, University of Alaska Fairbanks; Carolyn Powell and Jenny Watts, The Henry E. Huntington Library, San Marino, California; Mary Lou Selander and Lisa Johnson, Hiram College Library; Maureen E. Dolyniuk, Archivist, Hudson's Bay Company, Winnipeg; Jack London State Historical

Park, Glen Ellen, California; Marianne Mills, Chief Ranger, Klondike Gold Rush National Historical Park, Seattle; Karl Gurcke, KGRNHP, Skagway; James D. Fox, Knight Library, University of Oregon; Graham Staffen, Leddy Library, University of Windsor, Ontario; Bob Morris, Geography and Maps Division, Library of Congress; the Manuscript Division, the Newspaper and Current Periodical Division, and the Photography Division, Library of Congress; Philip Budlong, Mystic Seaport Museum; Deborah W. Lelansky, National Archives; Denise Rioux, National Archives of Canada, Ottawa; Kathleen T. Baxter, Reference Archivist, National Anthropology Archives, National Museum of Natural History, Washington, D.C.; The Newberry Library, Chicago; Municipal Archives, New York City; New York Public Library; William Sturm, Oakland History Room, Oakland Public Library; Virginia M. Adams, Old Dartmouth Historical Society Whaling Museum, New Bedford, Massachusetts; Margaret Brughera, Public Library of New London, Connecticut; Rick Caldwell and James Mossman, Puget Sound Maritime Historical Society, Seattle; Irene A. Stachura, San Francisco Maritime National Historical Park; San Francisco Public Library; Leslie Masunaga and Jerome Munday, San Jose Historical Museum; John Kensit, California Room, San Jose Public Library; Bea Lichtenstein, Santa Clara Arts and Historical Consortium; Dorothy DeDontney, Santa Clara County Historical and Genealogical Society; Santa Clara Public Library; Helen Kerfoot, Secretariat for Geographical Names, Ottawa; United States Geological Survey; University Microfilms International; Peggy D'Orsay, Yukon Archives, Whitehorse. No librarians were more resourceful than Tom Vince, Jane Spencer, and their colleagues at the nearby Hudson, Ohio, Library and Historical Society.

Various individuals were especially helpful throughout the course of my research: Richard H. Engeman, Photographs and Graphics Librarian, Special Collections and Preservation, University of Washington Libraries; Henry Bender, railroad historian; Beryl C. Gillespie, coauthor of volume 6 of the Smithsonian's *Handbook of North American Indians (Subarctic);* and Ted Wurm, railroad historian.

At the Carmelite Monastery in Santa Clara, Sister Emmanuel, O.C.D., shared with me all the monastery's photographs and information about the old Judge Bond ranch, conducted a tour of the grounds, and has remained a wonderful correspondent since 1992.

To Joachim Altvater, a young German man I met on the Chilkoot Trail during my hike over the mountains in 1993, I owe an enormous debt. When I injured my knee approaching the summit, "Joe" (as he wanted to be called) stayed with me all the way to Lake

Lindeman, making sure I was able to finish what I had begun. He has my eternal gratitude and friendship. I wish to thank as well the two Canadian wardens stationed at Lindeman: Frank James and Debbie Verhalle.

True friends—Claude and Dorothy Steele, Tom and Suzy Sanders, Hans and Lora Farnstrom—welcomed me into their homes while I was conducting research in various parts of the country. Mike and Barb Cassell helped me prepare for the Chilkoot Trail with equipment and reassurance. Bill Appling and Evie Davis have never failed to hearten me.

Some former colleagues have been enthusiastic about the project from its inception: Tom Davis, Jim McClelland, and Eric and Ann Marie Gustavson of Western Reserve Academy. Three of my former professors, Charles McKinley and Abe C. Ravitz of Hiram College and Sanford Marovitz of Kent State University, were unwavering in their support.

Several books were fundamental to my initial research. Pierre Berton's histories of the Gold Rush (*Klondike* and *The Klondike Quest*); Franklin Walker's *Jack London and the Klondike: The Genesis of an American Writer*; Earl Wilcox's *"The Call of the Wild," by Jack London: A Casebook*; Earle Labor's unsurpassed essays on *The Call of the Wild*; and Russ Kingman's monumental volume *Jack London: A Definitive Chronology*.

The principal Jack London scholars and experts were uniformly supportive throughout my research. I. Milo Shepard, Jack London's great-nephew and executor of the Trust of Irving Shepard (Jack London's nephew), has been extremely helpful. I greatly appreciate his granting me access to the Jack and Charmian London materials at the Huntington Library.

The late Sal Noto sent me long letters and information about the College Park depot and helped me establish contact with the Carmelite Monastery and with historians Ted Wurm and Henry Bender. Sal was a thoughtful man—and an avid collector of London materials—and I am sorry he did not live to see the publication of his contributions to this edition.

My appreciation, as well, goes to Clarice Stasz, Susan Nuernberg, and Jacqueline Tavernier-Courbin for words of encouragement whose importance are incalculable.

Earle Labor has been a true mentor. When I first approached him about doing comprehensive annotations for *The Call of the Wild*, he was immediately enthusiastic; in the ensuing years he has answered countless questions, offered piercing criticism, and supplied materials from his vast personal collection. He is a meticulous scholar, a loyal friend, and a man whose generous spirit made this project possible.

The world of Jack London lost its most fiercely devoted citizen when Russ Kingman passed away on 21 December 1993. Russ's advice and criticism were of immense value throughout the course of my research. He answered every letter (and there were many), was willing during my countless phone calls to stay on the line until my questions ended, and sent thick piles of information about London and *The Call of the Wild* from his personal files. Jack London had no finer friend than Russ Kingman. I am happy he was able to see this work in its early drafts—and I am sorry he was not able to help me improve it even more than he did. I hope he would have found it acceptable.

His wife, Winnie, remains a loyal correspondent and a devoted London scholar; she is among the most charitable persons I have ever met.

The National Endowment for the Humanities has twice supported my interest in Jack London and *The Call of the Wild:* first, by selecting me to participate in a Summer Seminar ("Jack London: The Major Works") and second, by choosing me for the NEH–Reader's Digest Teacher-Scholar Award, a grant that helped finance a year-long sabbatical during which I did the major portion of the research for this edition.

My thanks, as well, to the Board of Education, Aurora City Schools, for granting me a sabbatical leave for the 1992 to 1993 academic year and to my inspirational Harmon School colleagues over the years, especially Jerry Brodsky, Andy Kmetz, Mike Lenzo, Eileen Kutinsky, and Bob Luckay. I must also thank my students; they have asked so many questions about *The Call of the Wild* that I have had to write nearly sixty thousand words to answer them all.

Members of my family have contributed in a wide variety of ways throughout the project. My uncles and aunts—John and Juanita Dyer, Clark and Edith Dyer, Ronald and Nola Osborn—have opened their doors and arms whenever I have visited the West on research trips.

Until his death in 1990, Thomas Coyne, my father-in-law, was a steady source of strength. He would have been the first to phone to congratulate me on the publication of this volume, and I will miss receiving that call more than I can possibly express.

I wish to thank Annabelle Coyne, my mother-in-law, for all she has meant to me. To her inexorable enemy, Alzheimer's, she has refused to surrender and she has moved through the deepening darkness of her disease with a dignity that is both poignant and astonishing.

My father, Edward Dyer, has for years fed me stories about my own great-grandfather's year in the Klondike; Dad's careful transcription of Great-Grandpa's Gold Rush diary was an early inspiration for me. My mother, Prudence Dyer, spent a long day in the Connecticut State Library for me, chasing a wisp of information about the steam-yacht *Narwhal* and its owner, Charles Osgood. Moreover, she read an initial draft of this volume and offered far more suggestions than I wanted to hear! For fifty years she has been a powerful model of intellectual integrity, the embodiment of the highest personal and academic standards.

My brothers, Dick and Dave, have always been critics whose voices I have valued and respected. I appreciate, as well, my sister-in-law Janice McCormick, who asks gentle questions with no easy answers. And to Bella and Ricky, my niece and nephew . . . may you enjoy this book one day!

In 1986 my son Steve joined me on my first trek to the Yukon when he was only thirteen. We stood side by side at the Chilkoot trailhead at the old Dyea townsite; we shared sourdough pancakes at the Golden North Hotel in Skagway; we quaked with fear as we bounced along in the ocean air in a single-engine plane back to Juneau. I hope this book will bring back to him the memories of some of our most wonderful hours together.

To my wife, Joyce, must go my deepest gratitude. She has been throughout our quarter-century together a most loving companion—and a critic whose opinions I trust above all others. This volume exists because of her faith in me.

Introduction

FEW AMERICAN NOVELS have enjoyed such enduring popularity as Jack London's *The Call of the Wild*. Nearly thirty different editions are currently in print—some sheared and sanitized for young children, others published for scholars by venerable houses like Oxford University Press and Library of America, still others bowdlerized for use in public schools, where London's tale remains among the most frequently studied novels in America.[1]

Numerous editions for collectors are available as well: In 1960, Heritage Press published a lush, slip-cased text with wash-drawings by Henry Varnum Poor and an introduction by Pierre Berton, dean of Klondike historians; Chatham River Press (1983) has a gilt-edged volume with many of the original 1903 illustrations; and Portland House Illustrated Classics (1987) has published an impressive reissue of the 1912 edition, whose Paul Bransom illustrations London himself termed "splendid."[2] An original 1903 first edition, in dust jacket, brings thousands of dollars at auction.

Jack London would probably be amused to see the transformations *The Call of the Wild* has undergone as it approaches its centennial. *Classics Illustrated* has issued two entirely different comic-book versions of the tale (1952, 1990). In 1987, Chatham Audio Classics produced a slick package of *Wild* materials, including a complete reading of the text on three cassette tapes and a clothbound edition of the novel. There have been six filmed versions of the story featuring among the principal players Clark Gable, Loretta Young, Charlton Heston, and Rick Schroeder. On a CD-ROM (sold by the Clearvue Company in Chicago) are both the complete text of the novel and an "audio-picture-book" version. The Cleveland Public Library has the entire novel "on-line": new generations of readers can now read the novel on their home computers. It will probably not be long before Buck leaps at the head of the pack on an interactive laser disc.[3]

Further indications of the novel's perpetual popularity abound. In Santa Clara, California, a bronze plaque on the wall of the Carmelite Monastery correctly declares that London used the location—formerly a ranch—as "Judge Miller's place," the initial setting for the novel. A mile away, on the wall of a historical home, another bronze plaque incorrectly declares that London wrote the story on the veranda. (He composed the novel at his own home, a bungalow on Blair Avenue in the Piedmont Hills overlooking Oakland.)[4] Each summer, in Dawson City, Yukon, one can hear readings from *The Call of the Wild* at the Jack London Cabin, a reconstruction of the primitive log structure where London spent a few days in January 1898 prospecting on his Henderson Creek claim.

Perhaps the most pervasive—and permanent—influence of the novel has come from its title. Now one of the most common locutions in American English, "the call of the wild" is employed regularly by everyone from cartoonists to copywriters, the latter finding it suitable for products as varied as cologne and camping supplies. It serves as the title of a recent country music album by Aaron Tippin.[5]

Robin Lampson has attempted, unsuccessfully, to determine the origin of the phrase and has speculated somewhat hyperbolically that it is "probably as old as the English language"; as Lampson notes, however, *The Oxford Dictionary of Quotation's* credits London with its creation. London certainly believed that to be so. In a letter to Karl E. Harriman, editor of *Red Book*, he crowed: "The title was a ten-strike. It has become a phrase in the English language."[6]

Oddly, London's correspondence reveals that he did not initially care for the title. In a letter to George P. Brett, president of the Macmillan Company, London wrote on 10 March 1903:

> *I did not like the title,* The Call of the Wild, *and neither did the* Saturday Evening Post *[to whom London had sold the serial rights]. I racked my brains for a better title, & suggested* The Sleeping Wolf. *They, however, if in the meantime they do not*

hit upon a better title, are going to publish it in the Post *under* The Wolf. *This I do not like so well as* The Sleeping Wolf, *which I do not like very much either. There is a good title somewhere, if we can only lay hold of it.*

On 19 March, Brett replied that *The Wolf* seemed to him "a bad title," and *The Sleeping Wolf* was "not a great deal better. . . ." He went on to say that he liked *The Call of the Wild* "pretty well" and that in any case the decision should be London's.

Two weeks later, London was still undecided: "Concerning title," he wrote to Brett, "I must confess to a sneaking preference for *The Call of the Wild.* But, under any circumstance, I want the decision of the title to rest with you. You know the publishing end of it, and the market value of titles, as I could not dream to know."

A week later, the issue of the title was nearly settled. London wrote to Brett once again, this time arguing for *The Call of the Wild* instead of *Call of the Wild.* "Somehow," London contended, "the 'The' seems to give it a different & more definite meaning."[7] In July 1903 the story began its five-week serial life as "The Call of the Wild" in the *Saturday Evening Post.* London awakened "The Sleeping Wolf" a few years later for use as the title of the final chapter of *White Fang.*

The novel enjoyed immediate critical and popular acclaim. "It is a fascinating romance of the frozen North . . . with singular strength of phrase and illuminating vision . . . ," declared the *Philadelphia Press* (July 1903). "It is a story both strong and literary," announced the *Oakland Herald* (July 1903). "It is virile in its handling, natural in its settings, confident and sincere in its language, rising at times to heights which cannot be described as short of poetic." The *San Francisco Chronicle* (August 1903) was no less enthusiastic: "[A] marvelously graphic picture of the great gold rush to the Klondike. . . . Fierce, brutal, splashed with blood, and alive with the crack of whip and blow of club." "It is the best thing the public has had so far from the pen of a young author who . . . has already shown a fresh and vigorous bent in story," offered the *Athenaeum* (August 1903). "[F]ar and away the best book that Mr. Jack London has ever written," added the *Bookman* (October 1903). "[N]ot a pretty story at all, but a very powerful one," offered the more restrained *Atlantic Monthly* (November 1903).[8]

Despite the overwhelmingly positive critical reception for his book, London had to answer charges of plagiarism leveled by L. A. M. Bosworth in the *Independent* (14 February 1907). Noting what he called "striking similarities" between *The Call of the Wild* and

Egerton R. Young's memoir, *My Dogs in the Northland* (1902), Bosworth prepared a side-by-side display of a number of passages from the two books. In the same February 1907 issue the *Independent* granted London space immediately after Bosworth's charges to reply—which he did most aggressively, admitting his debt to Young but arguing that, since *My Dogs in the Northland* was a work of nonfiction, it was no more inappropriate to use factual material from it than to record something he had witnessed or heard about. "Fiction-writers," London asserted, "have always considered actual experiences of life to be a lawful field for exploitation. . . . [And] to charge plagiarism in such a case is to misuse the English language."[9]

London had probably first learned of *My Dogs in the Northland* in the *New York Times Saturday Review of Books and Art*, which had originally reviewed both Young's book and London's *A Daughter of the Snows* on 6 December 1902. Appearing in the same issue was a letter to the editor from William H. Dall ridiculing London's portrayals of American Indians—an attack to which London reacted strongly in a letter to his friend Anna Strunsky. Ironically, the review of Young's book began with a slight reproach to London, who, complained the reviewer, had provided in his fiction only a "slight idea of the dogs which draw his heroines over the snowy distances"; Young's book, by contrast, "fill[ed] in" with the sort of "precise" information about huskies that the reviewer had "long wanted to know."[10]

A few years later came the plagiarism controversy. The *New York Times Saturday Review of Books* published a brief notice of it on 23 February 1907; then on 9 March it ran a letter from Young, who maintained it was not he who had initiated the charges against London: "I absolutely knew nothing of the article in The Independent," wrote Young, "until a copy of it was sent to me." He claimed, however, that he had never received from London a "letter of 'thanks'" for his influence on *The Call of the Wild*. London quickly posted a personal reply, stating that a couple of years earlier he had written to Young in care of his publisher—a communication apparently never received. "I don't care a snap of my fingers for the rest of the world," wrote London, "but I wish personally to vindicate myself to you in this matter."[11]

Having forgotten—or dismissed—the charges of plagiarism, critics have continued to publish uniformly positive reviews of the book. Maxwell Geismar (1960) called the novel a "famous fable," "a handsome parable of buried impulses," and "a beautiful prose poem." Franklin Walker (1960) says that it "belongs on a shelf with *Walden* and *Huckleberry*

Finn." Earle Labor (1967) describes it as "a poem informed by the rhythms of epic and myth," in which we hear "the faint but clear echo of an inner music." Charles Child Walcutt calls it London's "purest book"; Abraham Rothberg (1981), the "most perfectly realized novel he ever wrote." And E. L. Doctorow (1990) labels it a "mordant parable" and "his masterpiece."[12]

Indeed, negative comments of any sort about the novel are rare. John Perry (1981) comes as close as anyone, claiming that the book is not really a novel at all but "seven short stories stitched together by Buck."[13]

Today, it is not hard to find a copy of the novel in just about any bookstore in the country—or, indeed, in the world. The story appears in more than eighty languages (*Der Ruf der Wildnis* is the German title; *L'appel sauvage* and *L'appel de la fôret*, the French); it has surely achieved the status Labor has accorded it: "one of the great books in world literature."[14]

Jack London, who wrote quickly and revised little throughout his career, invested no more time in the composition of *The Call of the Wild* than he did in any other work. "The whole history of this story," he wrote in modest understatement to Brett, "has been very rapid." His own records reveal that he began the work on 1 December 1902, completed it on 31 January 1903, and by April he had an advance copy in hand. (On 1 April, George Brett at Macmillan wrote with only "a few suggested alterations" and characterized the book as "pretty perfect as it is. . . .") One June evening, as Charmian London later recalled, Jack London read aloud "in his musical voice" the entire novel to a "thralled circle."[15]

For his short novel of approximately thirty-two thousand words London received no royalties whatsoever, only two fixed payments. On 3 March 1903, he accepted $750—three cents per word—from the *Saturday Evening Post*, where a shortened *Wild* appeared in five weekly installments between 20 June and 18 July 1903. And on 25 March 1903 London agreed to accept from Macmillan a one-time payment of two thousand dollars.[16]

London himself never expressed any regret for his decision to surrender all rights to his most popular work for $2,750. At the time, he was not well known around the country, and George P. Brett at Macmillan had made an intriguing offer. On 19 March 1903, Brett sent to London a proposal for what he called an "experiment." If London would accept a single payment of the two thousand dollars, Macmillan would publish the book "in a very attractive typographic format" and spend "a very large sum of money . . . in endeavouring to give it a wide circulation and thus assist the sale of not only your already published books but of those still to come. . . ." Brett cautioned London ("Don't let me overpersuade you in the matter."), but London quickly accepted. He wrote to Brett on 25 March, "pushing the book in the manner you mention will be of the utmost value to me, giving me, as you say, an audience for subsequent books."[17]

In a biographical memoir, Joseph Noel, a journalist friend of London's at the time, remembers trying to convince the young author that a royalty contract would be far more profitable, but London was "stubborn," insisting he would in the long run benefit from the deal he had negotiated with Macmillan.[18]

During and immediately after the writing of the novel, London seemed unaware that he had composed a classic. In a letter on 13 March 1903 to his friend Anna Strunsky, he referred to it only as "my dog story." He continued, "I started it as a companion to my other dog story 'Bâtard,' . . . but it got away from me, & Instead of 4000 words it ran 32000 before I could call a halt." And after the novel was published, with an astonishing disregard for the value of his work, he apparently discarded the original manuscript, along with any notes he may have used in its composition.[19]

One would expect a serious writer's most celebrated book to attract commensurate attention from serious scholars. However, although most of the principal London critics have published essays or comments about *The Call of the Wild*, there is only one book-length piece of criticism, Tavernier-Courbin's *The Call of the Wild: A Naturalistic Romance* (1994). Readers interested in critical views of the novel must search for chapters in monographs, or for articles in academic journals, or for whatever introductory material the editor of any particular edition provides.[20]

There are two principal reasons for this inattention. First, because of its canine protagonist and because of its brevity and clarity, the novel was long considered a book for children—more precisely, a book for boys. *Adventures of Huckleberry Finn* suffered for a while from a similar reputation. Second, the very popularity of the tale persuades some of its superficiality. If anyone *can* read it, and if everyone *wants* to read it (so such reasoning goes), then it belongs on the shelf alongside *Old Yeller* and *Lassie*, not works of "serious" fiction. As Labor and Leitz have pointed out, however, "to read the novel on this level is tantamount to reading *Moby-Dick* as a long-winded fisherman's yarn."[21]

From the beginning, readers have recognized that *The Call of the Wild* is a tale that operates on a variety of levels and is therefore open to a variety of interpretations. In the view of nearly every critic, its primary attraction is the power of the narrative itself— "thrilling" and "enthralling" commented some of the first reviewers, "a story of the robust variety which is never the work of any but a strong and original mind." Critics in subsequent years have continued to praise the novel for its entertainment value. Doctorow terms it "well and truly told"; Labor and Leitz call it "a ripping good story—fast-paced, vividly detailed, replete with action and adventure"; and Clifton Fadiman declares it "the most powerful dog story ever written."[22]

Some have argued that this narrative appeal is linked to the novel's "back-to-nature" theme. Kate B. Stillé (1903) said that the book counteracts "the trend of the times, which muzzles and massacres the individual, that touches society with decay. . . ." Carl Sandburg (1906) argued that the novel is not only "the greatest dog story ever written," but it also examines a "curious and profound" issue: "The more civilized we become the deeper is the fear that back in barbarism is something of the beauty and joy of life we have not brought along with us." Later critics have echoed that notion. Tony Tanner (1965) views Buck's story as "a release, a sloughing off of bonds. . . ." Raymond Benoit sees the novel as "a ritual enactment of the American wish to turn back to simplicity." Charles N. Watson points out that Buck shares with Huck Finn the "perennial American dream of escape and freedom associated with the natural world," a world that London believed, says Nash, was "also a *better* world"; Walcutt contends that Buck achieves in the wilderness an "Adamic purity, where man was fresh-minted and society had not bowed him down under its load of falsity"; Lundquist argues that London saw the "redemptive virtues . . . [in] the primitive environment"; and Charles Frey concludes that the "lesson" in the novel is that one should "slough off one's conventional self of civilization and liberate for action one's true savage being."[23]

Another prevalent view is that the appeal of the tale comes from London's accurate and compelling view of the Northland. "[Y]ou realise the bitter sting of the cold," wrote one reviewer in 1903, "and the stretch of the endless miles of Arctic snow." Another early critic applauded London's "marvelously graphic picture of the great gold rush . . . and of the life of the packer and miner in Alaska." Karl-Heinz Wirzberger (1973) likewise praises London's "authentic picture of this gold rush"; Dwight Swain (1986) recognizes that the novel "helps us to understand and be thrilled by a time and place, and events, few of us have ever known"; and Gary Paulsen (1994) believes London captured "the savagery of that time and place, of how it was to live it." He views the novel as "a kind of literal docudrama."[24]

The first critics identified yet another, related strength of the book—its realistic portrayals of Northland dogs. *Atlantic Monthly* praised London for this "single-minded study of animal nature," and Geismar has called London "the poet of Darwinism as the animals themselves understood it."[25] However, a few famous contemporaries of London's, like President Theodore Roosevelt and naturalist John Burroughs, included him among the "nature-fakers"—writers who endowed animals with physical and mental faculties far beyond their actual capacities. London responded testily to the charge, claiming that his "dog-heroes" were "not directed by abstract reasoning, but by instinct, sensation, and emotion, and by simple reasoning." London believed, as he wrote shortly after *The Call of the Wild* was published, that his accounts of dogs' mental and emotional lives were precise: "We may conclude from their actions," he explained to Merle Maddern, an in-law, "what their mental processes might be, and such conclusions may be within the range of possibility."[26]

A number of early reviewers recognized that London's tale was more than a powerful, realistic account of a dog in the Klondike and pointed out Darwinian themes. J. Stewart Doubleday, for instance, saw that the "philosophy of the survival of the fittest runs through every page. . . ." Such comments came as no surprise to London's regular readers. He was an avowed evolutionist, an outspoken admirer of Huxley and Spencer and Darwin—indeed, he had taken with him to the Klondike a copy of *On the Origin of Species*, and he claimed that he always tried to keep his stories "in line with the facts of evolution. . . ."[27] Virtually all of London's later critics have alluded to the Darwinian aspects of the novel.[28]

Many readers have seen in the story any number of immediate and objective autobiographical parallels between the narrative and London's own life. London, in fact, did derive much of *The Call of the Wild* from his experiences in the San Francisco Bay area as well as in Alaska and the Yukon. The tale begins on a Santa Clara ranch he had visited; Buck boards the train at a depot London knew well; the dog-teams traverse terrain London himself had crossed in 1897–98. Other readers have made even more specific connections between the facts in the story and London's personal struggles. Andrew Flink (1974) believes that John Thornton assumed in Buck's life the role that John London (Jack's stepfather) had played in Jack's; he argues later that Buck's sufferings are analogous to

London's during his thirty days of imprisonment in the Erie County (New York) Penitentiary in 1894. Robert Barltrop (1976) maintains that the theme of the "struggle for existence" is traceable to London's experiences in the slums of East End London in 1902 as he conducted research for his sociological study, *The People of the Abyss.* John Seelye (1991) believes that there is, indeed, "a large element of autobiography in much of what London wrote. . . ."[29]

But many have also noted deeper and more subjective autobiographical connections: In this view, "the dominant primordial beast" refers not only to Buck but to Jack London himself. A promotional booklet issued by Macmillan in 1905, for example, contended that London's "sturdy ancestral stock" had enabled him "to prove his mastery over environment, very much as Buck does in *The Call of the Wild.*" Joan London wrote in her 1939 biography of her father that "the story of Buck's triumph was the story of his own fierce struggle." Later commentators have elaborated upon this basic notion. Franklin Walker (1966), for instance, writes that London, like Buck, was "making his effort to be successful, to win in the fight, and to be loved. . . ." Sinclair sees in the novel London's record of "his own childish fears of cold, deprivation, and solitude, as well as his compulsion always to be free and roving, on the hunt to gratify every desire, yet leading his brothers of the wild in the quest of eternal youth." Doctorow adds that it is "perhaps his fatherless life of bitter self-reliance in late nineteenth-century America that he transmutes here." James R. Giles (1994) argues that London, "through Buck's climactic surrender to violence," was finally able to embrace and resolve his own early pain and suffering." And Tavernier-Courbin declares that composing the novel "afforded London an opportunity to transcend his personal, emotional, and intellectual disappointments"; moreover, it enabled him to "lose himself in a world of beauty and purity"—a stark contrast to the impoverished world of his own youth and of the East End of London from which he had so recently returned.[30]

Jack London's daughter wrote that he reacted "with astonishment" to allegorical and autobiographical interpretations. "'I plead guilty,' he admitted, 'but I was unconscious of it at the time. I did not mean to do it.'"[31]

Psychological interpretations of the novel have ranged from these very autobiographical views to notions reflecting the influences of Freud and his followers. In 1923, for example, E. Haldeman-Julius saw that London was writing about "the race-memory preserved in the sub-conscious mind." Watson (1983) argues that Buck's return to the wild was a "countermovement," a "rejection of maternal security. . . ." James McClintock (1975) sees London's Northland as "the uncharted land of the spirit" where all of us seek our identities "by facing death, by participating in life's essential contest for preservation of meaningful selfhood." John S. Mann (1978) agrees that Buck attains a "new identity" and shows how London reveals the changes in Buck by "almost obsessive preoccupations" with "doubling"—that is, with "opposing worlds" and antitheses. Doctorow (1990) puts it more succinctly: Buck, on "a dream-field of wilderness," achieves "a self-realization." And Christopher Gair (1994) claims that Buck is able to survive the harsh conditions he encounters after he is stolen because of his "ability to double" himself—to "assume a new public (and private) face" when conditions demand it.[32]

Richard Fusco presents a sociological perspective, arguing that Buck moves through four "families" in the novel—a process of "socialization." From the carefree, aristocratic world of Judge Miller's ranch, to the drudgery and danger of the various dog-teams, to the love-relationship with John Thornton, and, finally, to the primordial solidarity of the wolf pack, Buck eventually achieves an existence that resembles the "compromise between civilization and primitive man Rousseau described for the individual political state." Seelye (1991) argues that the dogs in the novel "serve as subjective agents of his [London's] protest against economic exploitation." And Kenneth S. Lynn sees London's socialism in the adventures of Buck, who was "initially a member of the false aristocracy of ease and luxury" but eventually becomes "the head of the true competitive aristocracy."[33]

The most powerful and convincing interpretations of *The Call of the Wild*, however, unite the psychology of Carl Jung and the research of Joseph Campbell: The mythic elements of the tale—its connections with the oldest and most universal of all stories—account for the book's enduring appeal, for the struggles of Buck are no less than the struggles of all humanity.[34]

In 1953 Geismar first pointed out both "the underlying structure of dream and myth" in the novel and the relationships to the primitive rituals Frazer cataloged in *The Golden Bough*.[35] Some years later, Labor produced a systematic analysis of *The Call of the Wild* as "a mythic romance"—an ancient and intricate tapestry woven with Jungian threads. Labor argues that Buck has moved by the end of the novel into "a world of the 'collective unconscious,' the primordial world" to which modern man "would return, in dreams, to find his soul." Buck "is no longer a dog . . . but a projection of the reader's essential mythic *self*, a dynamic symbol of libido, *élan vital*, the life force."

Labor then demonstrates how Buck's progress in the novel approximates the generic "monomyth" described by Campbell in *Hero with a Thousand Faces*. Labor shows that the first three chapters of *The Call of the Wild* are "prosaic": They chronicle in realistic fashion the "Call to Adventure"—the experiences of a dog stolen from his life of comfort in the South and taken to the North where he must quickly adapt to new and perilous circumstances. The events of Chapters 4, 5, and 6 require Buck—like Campbell's mythic heroes—to experience the "supreme ordeal": (virtual) death and rebirth. Then, Chapter 7 records his "apotheosis": Buck becomes the "Ghost Dog" of Yeehat Indian legends.

Labor points out how London "modulates both setting and style poetically to enhance Buck's transformation." The precise geography of the first six chapters, for example, disappears in the final pages. Early in the novel London employed dozens of actual place names; none appear after the first page of the last chapter. As Labor shows, Buck leaves the actual world and enters "the timeless landscape of myth" where London's economical, functional language is also transformed, becoming increasingly lyrical in the final pages and paragraphs.[36]

Critics in subsequent years have adopted and adapted these mythic interpretations. Jonathan H. Spinner (1974), for example, compares Buck's abrupt departure from California to Adam's expulsion from Eden; Sinclair (1977) calls the novel "a myth about life and death and nature"; Mann (1978) admires London's ability to "elevate the savage world of Darwin to the pure and terrible world of myth"; Watson (1983) reminds readers of the novel's similarities to the "rites of sacrifice and succession" described in *The Golden Bough*; Donald Pizer (1984) sees London as "essentially a writer of fables and parables"; *The Call of the Wild* is a "beast fable" which reveals London's notion that "the strong, the shrewd, and the cunning shall prevail when . . . life is bestial." Clarice Stasz (1988) believes that London employed the devices of the "mythic fable" in order to present the "philosophical beliefs of the day tempered by romanticism"; Doctorow (1990) views Buck as "not a literal dog but a mythopoetic thesis"; and Tavernier-Courbin (1994) calls the book "one of the world's most romantic novels," not alone for its mythic elements but because of its emphasis on love, beauty, and justice, and because of its appeal to a complete range of emotions . . . and because it dramatizes a human dream of adventure, freedom, and personal fulfillment. . . ."[37]

Literary criticism can provide a set of powerful, adjustable lenses through which we can examine a work of fiction. As we change the lens-settings, and as each new image emerges into focus—emphasizing details, directing our attention, eliminating distractions—we may find the view instructive, perhaps even beautiful. We must recognize, however, that even the most elegant literary theories distort as much as they illuminate, and to the extent that we allow ourselves to adopt any single interpretation of *The Call of the Wild*—or of any literary work—we deny ourselves the mystery of discovery, the loveliness of the whole. Jack London's little novel has endured for nearly one hundred years not because it is a compelling story of the last great gold rush, not because it is a clear portrayal of the life and mind and soul of a splendid dog, not because it is a graceful allegory of the rites of passage we all undergo, not because it enables us to enter an exciting and terrifying world governed by brutal Darwinian principles, not because it provides so many glimpses of the life and mind of its creator—not even because it approximates in power and technique the timeless myths of all humankind. *The Call of the Wild* has remained a classic for *all* these reasons—and for reasons it will take new generations of readers to imagine.

The Call of the Wild

BY JACK LONDON

CHAPTER ONE

Into the Primitive

"Old longings nomadic leap,
Chafing at custom's chain;
Again from its brumal sleep
Wakens the ferine strain."

1   BUCK DID NOT read the newspapers, or he would have known that trouble was brewing, not alone for himself, but for every tide-water dog, strong of muscle and with warm, long hair, from Puget Sound to San Diego. Because men, groping in the Arctic darkness, had found a yellow metal, and because steamship and transportation companies 5   were booming the find, thousands of men were rushing into the Northland. These men wanted dogs, and the dogs they wanted were heavy dogs, with strong muscles by which to toil, and furry coats to protect them from the frost.

Buck lived at a big house in the sun-kissed Santa Clara Valley. Judge Miller's place, it was called. It stood back from the road, half hidden among the trees, through 10   which glimpses could be caught of the wide cool veranda that ran around its four sides. The house was approached by gravelled driveways which wound about through wide-spreading lawns and under the interlacing boughs of tall poplars. At the rear things were on even a more spacious scale than at the front. There were great stables, where a dozen grooms and boys held forth, rows of vine-clad servants' cottages, an endless and 15   orderly array of outhouses, long grape arbors, green pastures, orchards, and berry patches. Then there was the pumping plant for the artesian well, and the big cement tank where Judge Miller's boys took their morning plunge and kept cool in the hot afternoon.

And over this great demesne Buck ruled. Here he was born, and here he had lived the four years of his life. It was true, there were other dogs. There could not but be other dogs on so vast a place, but they did not count. They came and went, resided in the populous kennels, or lived obscurely in the recesses of the house after the fashion of Toots, the Japanese pug, or Ysabel, the Mexican hairless,—strange creatures that rarely put nose out of doors or set foot to ground. On the other hand, there were the fox terriers, a score of them at least, who yelped fearful promises at Toots and Ysabel looking out of the windows at them and protected by a legion of housemaids armed with brooms and mops.

But Buck was neither house-dog nor kennel-dog. The whole realm was his. He plunged into the swimming tank or went hunting with the Judge's sons; he escorted Mollie and Alice, the Judge's daughters, on long twilight or early morning rambles; on wintry nights he lay at the Judge's feet before the roaring library fire; he carried the Judge's grandsons on his back, or rolled them in the grass, and guarded their footsteps through wild adventures down to the fountain in the stable yard, and even beyond, where the paddocks were, and the berry patches. Among the terriers he stalked imperiously, and Toots and Ysabel he utterly ignored, for he was king,—king over all creeping, crawling, flying things of Judge Miller's place, humans included.

His father, Elmo, a huge St. Bernard, had been the Judge's inseparable companion, and Buck bid fair to follow in the way of his father. He was not so large,—he weighed only one hundred and forty pounds,—for his mother, Shep, had been a Scotch shepherd dog. Nevertheless, one hundred and forty pounds, to which was added the dignity that comes of good living and universal respect, enabled him to carry himself in right royal fashion. During the four years since his puppyhood he had lived the life of a sated aristocrat; he had a fine pride in himself, was even a trifle egotistical, as country gentlemen sometimes become because of their insular situation. But he had saved himself by not becoming a mere pampered house-dog. Hunting and kindred outdoor delights had kept down the fat and hardened his muscles; and to him, as to the cold-tubbing races, the love of water had been a tonic and a health preserver.

And this was the manner of dog Buck was in the fall of 1897, when the Klondike strike dragged men from all the world into the frozen North. But Buck did not read the newspapers, and he did not know that Manuel, one of the gardener's helpers, was an undesirable acquaintance. Manuel had one besetting sin. He loved to play Chinese lottery. Also, in his gambling, he had one besetting weakness—faith in a system; and this made his damnation certain. For to play a system requires money, while the wages of a gardener's helper do not lap over the needs of a wife and numerous progeny.

55 The Judge was at a meeting of the Raisin Growers' Association, and the boys were busy organizing an athletic club, on the memorable night of Manuel's treachery. No one saw him and Buck go off through the orchard on what Buck imagined was merely a stroll. And with the exception of a solitary man, no one saw them arrive at the little flag station known as College Park. This man talked with Manuel, and money 60 chinked between them.

"You might wrap up the goods before you deliver 'm," the stranger said gruffly, and Manuel doubled a piece of stout rope around Buck's neck under the collar.

"Twist it, an' you'll choke 'm plentee," said Manuel, and the stranger grunted a ready affirmative.

65 Buck had accepted the rope with quiet dignity. To be sure, it was an unwonted performance: but he had learned to trust in men he knew, and to give them credit for a wisdom that outreached his own. But when the ends of the rope were placed in the stranger's hands, he growled menacingly. He had merely intimated his displeasure, in his pride believing that to intimate was to command. But to his surprise the rope tightened 70 around his neck, shutting off his breath. In quick rage he sprang at the man, who met him halfway, grappled him close by the throat, and with a deft twist threw him over on his back. Then the rope tightened mercilessly, while Buck struggled in a fury, his tongue lolling out of his mouth and his great chest panting futilely. Never in all his life had he been so vilely treated, and never in all his life had he been so angry. But his strength 75 ebbed, his eyes glazed, and he knew nothing when the train was flagged and the two men threw him into the baggage car.

The next he knew, he was dimly aware that his tongue was hurting and that he was being jolted along in some kind of a conveyance. The hoarse shriek of a locomotive whistling a crossing told him where he was. He had travelled too often with the Judge 80 not to know the sensation of riding in a baggage car. He opened his eyes, and into them came the unbridled anger of a kidnapped king. The man sprang for his throat, but Buck was too quick for him. His jaws closed on the hand, nor did they relax till his senses were choked out of him once more.

"Yep, has fits," the man said, hiding his mangled hand from the baggageman, who

85 had been attracted by the sounds of struggle. "I'm takin' 'm up for the boss to 'Frisco. A crack dog-doctor there thinks that he can cure 'm."

Concerning that night's ride, the man spoke most eloquently for himself, in a little shed back of a saloon on the San Francisco water front.

"All I get is fifty for it," he grumbled; "an' I wouldn't do it over for a thousand, 90 cold cash."

His hand was wrapped in a bloody handkerchief, and the right trouser leg was ripped from knee to ankle.

"How much did the other mug get?" the saloon-keeper demanded.

"A hundred," was the reply. "Wouldn't take a sou less, so help me."

95 "That makes a hundred and fifty," the saloon-keeper calculated; "and he's worth it, or I'm a squarehead."

The kidnapper undid the bloody wrappings and looked at his lacerated hand. "If I don't get the hydrophoby—"

"It'll be because you was born to hang," laughed the saloon-keeper. "Here, lend 100 me a hand before you pull your freight," he added.

Dazed, suffering intolerable pain from throat and tongue, with the life half throttled out of him, Buck attempted to face his tormentors. But he was thrown down and choked repeatedly, till they succeeded in filing the heavy brass collar from off his neck. Then the rope was removed, and he was flung into a cagelike crate.

105 There he lay for the remainder of the weary night, nursing his wrath and wounded pride. He could not understand what it all meant. What did they want with him, these strange men? Why were they keeping him pent up in this narrow crate? He did not know why, but he felt oppressed by the vague sense of impending calamity. Several times during the night he sprang to his feet when the shed door rattled open, expecting 110 to see the Judge, or the boys at least. But each time it was the bulging face of the saloon-keeper that peered in at him by the sickly light of a tallow candle. And each time the joyful bark that trembled in Buck's throat was twisted into a savage growl.

But the saloon-keeper let him alone, and in the morning four men entered and picked up the crate. More tormentors, Buck decided, for they were evil-looking 115 creatures, ragged and unkempt; and he stormed and raged at them through the bars. They only laughed and poked sticks at him, which he promptly assailed with his teeth till he realized that that was what they wanted. Whereupon he lay down sullenly and allowed the crate to be lifted into a wagon. Then he, and the crate in which he was imprisoned, began a passage through many hands. Clerks in the express office took charge of him; he was carted about in another wagon; a truck carried him, with an assortment of boxes and parcels, upon a ferry steamer; he was trucked off the steamer into a great railway depot, and finally he was deposited in an express car.

For two days and nights this express car was dragged along at the tail of shrieking locomotives; and for two days and nights Buck neither ate nor drank. In his anger he had met the first advances of the express messengers with growls, and they had retaliated by teasing him. When he flung himself against the bars, quivering and frothing, they laughed at him and taunted him. They growled and barked like detestable dogs, mewed, and flapped their arms and crowed. It was all very silly, he knew; but therefore the more outrage to his dignity, and his anger waxed and waxed. He did not mind the hunger so much, but the lack of water caused him severe suffering and fanned his wrath to fever-pitch. For that matter, high-strung and finely sensitive, the ill treatment had flung him into a fever, which was fed by the inflammation of his parched and swollen throat and tongue.

He was glad for one thing: the rope was off his neck. That had given them an unfair advantage; but now that it was off, he would show them. They would never get another rope around his neck. Upon that he was resolved. For two days and nights he neither ate nor drank, and during those two days and nights of torment, he accumulated a fund of wrath that boded ill for whoever first fell foul of him. His eyes turned bloodshot, and he was metamorphosed into a raging fiend. So changed was he that the Judge himself would not have recognized him; and the express messengers breathed with relief when they bundled him off the train at Seattle.

Four men gingerly carried the crate from the wagon into a small, high-walled back yard. A stout man, with a red sweater that sagged generously at the neck, came out and signed the book for the driver. That was the man, Buck divined, the next tormentor, and he hurled himself savagely against the bars. The man smiled grimly, and brought a hatchet and a club.

"You ain't going to take him out now?" the driver asked.

"Sure," the man replied, driving the hatchet into the crate for a pry.

There was an instantaneous scattering of the four men who had carried it in, and from safe perches on top the wall they prepared to watch the performance.

Buck rushed at the splintering wood, sinking his teeth into it, surging and wrestling with it. Wherever the hatchet fell on the outside, he was there on the inside, snarling and growling, as furiously anxious to get out as the man in the red sweater was calmly intent on getting him out.

155 "Now, you red-eyed devil," he said, when he had made an opening sufficient for the passage of Buck's body. At the same time he dropped the hatchet and shifted the club to his right hand.

And Buck was truly a red-eyed devil, as he drew himself together for the spring, hair bristling, mouth foaming, a mad glitter in his blood-shot eyes. Straight at the man
160 he launched his one hundred and forty pounds of fury, surcharged with the pent passion of two days and nights. In mid air, just as his jaws were about to close on the man, he received a shock that checked his body and brought his teeth together with an agonizing clip. He whirled over, fetching the ground on his back and side. He had never been struck by a club in his life, and did not understand. With a snarl that was part bark and
165 more scream he was again on his feet and launched into the air. And again the shock came and he was brought crushingly to the ground. This time he was aware that it was the club, but his madness knew no caution. A dozen times he charged, and as often the club broke the charge and smashed him down.

After a particularly fierce blow, he crawled to his feet, too dazed to rush. He
170 staggered limply about, the blood flowing from nose and mouth and ears, his beautiful coat sprayed and flecked with bloody slaver. Then the man advanced and deliberately dealt him a frightful blow on the nose. All the pain he had endured was as nothing compared with the exquisite agony of this. With a roar that was almost lionlike in its ferocity, he again hurled himself at the man. But the man, shifting the club from right to
175 left, coolly caught him by the under jaw, at the same time wrenching downward and backward. Buck described a complete circle in the air, and half of another, then crashed to the ground on his head and chest.

For the last time he rushed. The man struck the shrewd blow he had purposely withheld for so long, and Buck crumpled up and went down, knocked utterly senseless.
180 "He's no slouch at dog-breakin', that's wot I say," one of the men on the wall cried enthusiastically.

"Druther break cayuses any day, and twice on Sundays," was the reply of the driver, as he climbed on the wagon and started the horses.

185 Buck's senses came back to him, but not his strength. He lay where he had fallen, and from there he watched the man in the red sweater.

"'Answers to the name of Buck,'" the man soliloquized, quoting from the saloon-keeper's letter which had announced the consignment of the crate and contents. "Well, Buck, my boy," he went on in a genial voice, "we've had our little ruction, and the best thing we can do is to let it go at that. You've learned your place, and I know mine. 190 Be a good dog and all 'll go well and the goose hang high. Be a bad dog, and I'll whale the stuffin' outa you. Understand?"

As he spoke he fearlessly patted the head he had so mercilessly pounded, and though Buck's hair involuntarily bristled at touch of the hand, he endured it without protest. When the man brought him water he drank eagerly, and later bolted a generous 195 meal of raw meat, chunk by chunk, from the man's hand.

He was beaten (he knew that); but he was not broken. He saw, once for all, that he stood no chance against a man with a club. He had learned the lesson, and in all his after life he never forgot it. That club was a revelation. It was his introduction to the reign of primitive law, and he met the introduction half-way. The facts of life took on a 200 fiercer aspect; and while he faced that aspect uncowed, he faced it with all the latent cunning of his nature aroused. As the days went by, other dogs came, in crates and at the ends of ropes, some docilely, and some raging and roaring as he had come; and, one and all, he watched them pass under the dominion of the man in the red sweater. Again and again, as he looked at each brutal performance, the lesson was driven home to Buck: 205 a man with a club was a lawgiver, a master to be obeyed, though not necessarily conciliated. Of this last Buck was never guilty, though he did see beaten dogs that fawned upon the man, and wagged their tails, and licked his hand. Also he saw one dog, that would neither conciliate nor obey, finally killed in the struggle for mastery.

Now and again men came, strangers, who talked excitedly, wheedlingly, and in all 210 kinds of fashions to the man in the red sweater. And at such times that money passed between them the strangers took one or more of the dogs away with them. Buck wondered where they went, for they never came back; but the fear of the future was strong upon him, and he was glad each time when he was not selected.

Yet his time came, in the end, in the form of a little weazened man who spat 215 broken English and many strange and uncouth exclamations which Buck could not understand.

"Sacredam!" he cried, when his eyes lit upon Buck. "Dat one dam bully dog! Eh? How moch?"

"Three hundred, and a present at that," was the prompt reply of the man in the
220 red sweater. "And seein' it's government money, you ain't got no kick coming, eh, Perrault?"

Perrault grinned. Considering that the price of dogs had been boomed skyward by the unwonted demand, it was not an unfair sum for so fine an animal. The Canadian Government would be no loser, nor would its despatches travel the slower. Perrault
225 knew dogs, and when he looked at Buck he knew that he was one in a thousand— "One in ten t'ousand," he commented mentally.

Buck saw money pass between them, and was not surprised when Curly, a good-natured Newfoundland, and he were led away by the little weazened man. That was the last he saw of the man in the red sweater, and as Curly and he looked at
230 receding Seattle from the deck of the *Narwhal*, it was the last he saw of the warm Southland. Curly and he were taken below by Perrault and turned over to a black-faced giant called François. Perrault was a French-Canadian, and swarthy; but François was a French-Canadian half-breed, and twice as swarthy. They were a new kind of men to Buck (of which he was destined to see many more), and while he developed no affection
235 for them, he none the less grew honestly to respect them. He speedily learned that Perrault and François were fair men, calm and impartial in administering justice, and too wise in the way of dogs to be fooled by dogs.

In the 'tween-decks of the *Narwhal*, Buck and Curly joined two other dogs. One of them was a big, snow-white fellow from Spitzbergen who had been brought away by a
240 whaling captain, and who had later accompanied a Geological Survey into the Barrens. He was friendly, in a treacherous sort of way, smiling into one's face the while he meditated some underhand trick, as, for instance, when he stole from Buck's food at the first meal. As Buck sprang to punish him, the lash of François's whip sang through the air, reaching the culprit first; and nothing remained to Buck but to recover the bone.
245 That was fair of François, he decided, and the half-breed began his rise in Buck's estimation.

The other dog made no advances, nor received any; also, he did not attempt to steal from the newcomers. He was a gloomy, morose fellow, and he showed Curly plainly that all he desired was to be left alone, and further, that there would be trouble if

250 he were not left alone. "Dave" he was called, and he ate and slept, or yawned between times, and took interest in nothing, not even when the *Narwhal* crossed Queen Charlotte Sound and rolled and pitched and bucked like a thing possessed. When Buck and Curly grew excited, half wild with fear, he raised his head as though annoyed, favored them with an incurious glance, yawned, and went to sleep again.

255 Day and night the ship throbbed to the tireless pulse of the propeller, and though one day was very like another, it was apparent to Buck that the weather was steadily growing colder. At last, one morning, the propeller was quiet, and the *Narwhal* was pervaded with an atmosphere of excitement. He felt it, as did the other dogs, and knew that a change was at hand. François leashed them and brought them on deck. At the

260 first step upon the cold surface, Buck's feet sank into a white mushy something very like mud. He sprang back with a snort. More of this white stuff was falling through the air. He shook himself, but more of it fell upon him. He sniffed it curiously, then licked some up on his tongue. It bit like fire, and the next instant was gone. This puzzled him. He tried it again, with the same result. The onlookers laughed uproariously, and he felt

265 ashamed, he knew not why, for it was his first snow.

CHAPTER TWO

The Law of Club and Fang

266   BUCK'S FIRST DAY on the Dyea beach was like a nightmare. Every hour was filled with shock and surprise. He had been suddenly jerked from the heart of civilization and flung into the heart of things primordial. No lazy, sun-kissed life was this, with nothing to do but loaf and be bored. Here was neither peace, nor rest, nor a moment's safety. All

270 was confusion and action, and every moment life and limb were in peril. There was imperative need to be constantly alert; for these dogs and men were not town dogs and men. They were savages, all of them, who knew no law but the law of club and fang.

    He had never seen dogs fight as these wolfish creatures fought, and his first experience taught him an unforgetable lesson. It is true, it was a vicarious experience,

275 else he would not have lived to profit by it. Curly was the victim. They were camped near the log store, where she, in her friendly way, made advances to a husky dog the size of a full-grown wolf, though not half so large as she. There was no warning, only a leap in like a flash, a metallic clip of teeth, a leap out equally swift, and Curly's face was ripped open from eye to jaw.

280   It was the wolf manner of fighting, to strike and leap away; but there was more to it than this. Thirty or forty huskies ran to the spot and surrounded the combatants in an intent and silent circle. Buck did not comprehend that silent intentness, nor the eager way with which they were licking their chops. Curly rushed her antagonist, who struck

again and leaped aside. He met her next rush with his chest, in a peculiar fashion that
tumbled her off her feet. She never regained them. This was what the onlooking huskies
had waited for. They closed in upon her, snarling and yelping, and she was buried,
screaming with agony, beneath the bristling mass of bodies.

So sudden was it, and so unexpected, that Buck was taken aback. He saw Spitz
run out his scarlet tongue in a way he had of laughing; and he saw François, swinging an
axe, spring into the mess of dogs. Three men with clubs were helping him to scatter
them. It did not take long. Two minutes from the time Curly went down, the last of her
assailants were clubbed off. But she lay there limp and lifeless in the bloody, trampled
snow, almost literally torn to pieces, the swart half-breed standing over her and cursing
horribly. The scene often came back to Buck to trouble him in his sleep. So that was
the way. No fair play. Once down, that was the end of you. Well, he would see to it
that he never went down. Spitz ran out his tongue and laughed again, and from that
moment Buck hated him with a bitter and deathless hatred.

Before he had recovered from the shock caused by the tragic passing of Curly, he
received another shock. François fastened upon him an arrangement of straps and
buckles. It was a harness, such as he had seen the grooms put on the horses at home.
And as he had seen horses work, so he was set to work, hauling François on a sled to the
forest that fringed the valley, and returning with a load of firewood. Though his dignity
was sorely hurt by thus being made a draught animal, he was too wise to rebel. He
buckled down with a will and did his best, though it was all new and strange. François
was stern, demanding instant obedience, and by virtue of his whip receiving instant
obedience; while Dave, who was an experienced wheeler, nipped Buck's hind quarters
whenever he was in error. Spitz was the leader, likewise experienced, and while he could
not always get at Buck, he growled sharp reproof now and again, or cunningly threw his
weight in the traces to jerk Buck into the way he should go. Buck learned easily, and
under the combined tuition of his two mates and François made remarkable progress.
Ere they returned to camp he knew enough to stop at "ho," to go ahead at "mush," to
swing wide on the bends, and to keep clear of the wheeler when the loaded sled shot
downhill at their heels.

"T'ree vair' good dogs," François told Perrault. "Dat Buck, heem pool lak hell. I
tich heem queek as anyt'ing."

By afternoon, Perrault, who was in a hurry to be on the trail with his despatches, returned with two more dogs. "Billee" and "Joe" he called them, two brothers, and true huskies both. Sons of the one mother though they were, they were as different as day and night. Billee's one fault was his excessive good nature, while Joe was the very opposite, sour and introspective, with a perpetual snarl and a malignant eye. Buck received them in comradely fashion, Dave ignored them, while Spitz proceeded to thrash first one and then the other. Billee wagged his tail appeasingly, turned to run when he saw that appeasement was of no avail, and cried (still appeasingly) when Spitz's sharp teeth scored his flank. But no matter how Spitz circled, Joe whirled around on his heels to face him, mane bristling, ears laid back, lips writhing and snarling, jaws clipping together as fast as he could snap, and eyes diabolically gleaming—the incarnation of belligerent fear. So terrible was his appearance that Spitz was forced to forego disciplining him; but to cover his own discomfiture he turned upon the inoffensive and wailing Billee and drove him to the confines of the camp.

By evening Perrault secured another dog, an old husky, long and lean and gaunt, with a battle-scarred face and a single eye which flashed a warning of prowess that commanded respect. He was called Sol-leks, which means the Angry One. Like Dave, he asked nothing, gave nothing, expected nothing; and when he marched slowly and deliberately into their midst, even Spitz left him alone. He had one peculiarity which Buck was unlucky enough to discover. He did not like to be approached on his blind side. Of this offence Buck was unwittingly guilty, and the first knowledge he had of his indiscretion was when Sol-leks whirled upon him and slashed his shoulder to the bone for three inches up and down. Forever after Buck avoided his blind side, and to the last of their comradeship had no more trouble. His only apparent ambition, like Dave's, was to be left alone; though, as Buck was afterward to learn, each of them possessed one other and even more vital ambition.

That night Buck faced the great problem of sleeping. The tent, illumined by a candle, glowed warmly in the midst of the white plain; and when he, as a matter of course, entered it, both Perrault and François bombarded him with curses and cooking utensils, till he recovered from his consternation and fled ignominiously into the outer cold. A chill wind was blowing that nipped him sharply and bit with especial venom into his wounded shoulder. He lay down on the snow and attempted to sleep, but the frost soon drove him shivering to his feet. Miserable and disconsolate, he wandered about among the many tents, only to find that one place was as cold as another. Here and

350 there savage dogs rushed upon him, but he bristled his neck-hair and snarled (for he was learning fast), and they let him go his way unmolested.

Finally an idea came to him. He would return and see how his own team-mates were making out. To his astonishment, they had disappeared. Again he wandered about through the great camp, looking for them, and again he returned. Were they in the tent?

355 No, that could not be, else he would not have been driven out. Then where could they possibly be? With drooping tail and shivering body, very forlorn indeed, he aimlessly circled the tent. Suddenly the snow gave way beneath his fore legs and he sank down. Something wriggled under his feet. He sprang back, bristling and snarling, fearful of the unseen and unknown. But a friendly little yelp reassured him, and he went back to

360 investigate. A whiff of warm air ascended to his nostrils, and there, curled up under the snow in a snug ball, lay Billee. He whined placatingly, squirmed and wriggled to show his good will and intentions, and even ventured, as a bribe for peace, to lick Buck's face with his warm wet tongue.

Another lesson. So that was the way they did it, eh? Buck confidently selected a

365 spot, and with much fuss and waste effort proceeded to dig a hole for himself. In a trice the heat from his body filled the confined space and he was asleep. The day had been long and arduous, and he slept soundly and comfortably, though he growled and barked and wrestled with bad dreams.

Nor did he open his eyes till roused by the noises of the waking camp. At first he

370 did not know where he was. It had snowed during the night and he was completely buried. The snow walls pressed him on every side, and a great surge of fear swept through him—the fear of the wild thing for the trap. It was a token that he was harking back through his own life to the lives of his forebears; for he was a civilized dog, an unduly civilized dog, and of his own experience knew no trap and so could not of himself

375 fear it. The muscles of his whole body contracted spasmodically and instinctively, the hair on his neck and shoulders stood on end, and with a ferocious snarl he bounded straight up into the blinding day, the snow flying about him in a flashing cloud. Ere he landed on his feet, he saw the white camp spread out before him and knew where he was and remembered all that had passed from the time he went for a stroll with Manuel to

380 the hole he had dug for himself the night before.

A shout from François hailed his appearance. "Wot I say?" the dog-driver cried to Perrault. "Dat Buck for sure learn queek as anyt'ing."

Perrault nodded gravely. As courier for the Canadian Government, bearing important despatches, he was anxious to secure the best dogs, and he was particularly
385 gladdened by the possession of Buck.

Three more huskies were added to the team inside an hour, making a total of nine, and before another quarter of an hour had passed they were in harness and swinging up the trail toward the Dyea Cañon. Buck was glad to be gone, and though the work was hard he found he did not particularly despise it. He was surprised at the
390 eagerness which animated the whole team and which was communicated to him; but still more surprising was the change wrought in Dave and Sol-leks. They were new dogs, utterly transformed by the harness. All passiveness and unconcern had dropped from them. They were alert and active, anxious that the work should go well, and fiercely irritable with whatever, by delay or confusion, retarded that work. The toil of the traces
395 seemed the supreme expression of their being, and all that they lived for and the only thing in which they took delight.

Dave was wheeler or sled dog, pulling in front of him was Buck, then came Sol-leks; the rest of the team was strung out ahead, single file, to the leader, which position was filled by Spitz.
400 Buck had been purposely placed between Dave and Sol-leks so that he might receive instruction. Apt scholar that he was, they were equally apt teachers, never allowing him to linger long in error, and enforcing their teaching with their sharp teeth. Dave was fair and very wise. He never nipped Buck without cause, and he never failed to nip him when he stood in need of it. As François's whip backed him up, Buck found
405 it to be cheaper to mend his ways than to retaliate. Once, during a brief halt, when he got tangled in the traces and delayed the start, both Dave and Sol-leks flew at him and administered a sound trouncing. The resulting tangle was even worse, but Buck took good care to keep the traces clear thereafter; and ere the day was done, so well had he mastered his work, his mates about ceased nagging him. François's whip snapped less
410 frequently, and Perrault even honored Buck by lifting up his feet and carefully examining them.

It was a hard day's run, up the Cañon, through Sheep Camp, past the Scales and the timber line, across glaciers and snowdrifts hundreds of feet deep, and over the great Chilcoot Divide, which stands between the salt water and the fresh and guards
415 forbiddingly the sad and lonely North. They made good time down the chain of lakes

which fills the craters of extinct volcanoes, and late that night pulled into the huge camp at the head of Lake Bennett, where thousands of gold-seekers were building boats against the break-up of the ice in the spring. Buck made his hole in the snow and slept the sleep of the exhausted just, but all too early was routed out in the cold darkness and harnessed with his mates to the sled.

That day they made forty miles, the trail being packed; but the next day, and for many days to follow, they broke their own trail, worked harder, and made poorer time. As a rule, Perrault travelled ahead of the team, packing the snow with webbed shoes to make it easier for them. François, guiding the sled at the gee-pole, sometimes exchanged places with him, but not often. Perrault was in a hurry, and he prided himself on his knowledge of ice, which knowledge was indispensable, for the fall ice was very thin, and where there was swift water, there was no ice at all.

Day after day, for days unending, Buck toiled in the traces. Always, they broke camp in the dark, and the first gray of dawn found them hitting the trail with fresh miles reeled off behind them. And always they pitched camp after dark, eating their bit of fish, and crawling to sleep into the snow. Buck was ravenous. The pound and a half of sun-dried salmon, which was his ration for each day, seemed to go nowhere. He never had enough, and suffered from perpetual hunger pangs. Yet the other dogs, because they weighed less and were born to the life, received a pound only of the fish and managed to keep in good condition.

He swiftly lost the fastidiousness which had characterized his old life. A dainty eater, he found that his mates, finishing first, robbed him of his unfinished ration. There was no defending it. While he was fighting off two or three, it was disappearing down the throats of the others. To remedy this, he ate as fast as they; and, so greatly did hunger compel him, he was not above taking what did not belong to him. He watched and learned. When he saw Pike, one of the new dogs, a clever malingerer and thief, slyly steal a slice of bacon when Perrault's back was turned, he duplicated the performance the following day, getting away with the whole chunk. A great uproar was raised, but he was unsuspected; while Dub, an awkward blunderer who was always getting caught, was punished for Buck's misdeed.

This first theft marked Buck as fit to survive in the hostile Northland environment. It marked his adaptability, his capacity to adjust himself to changing conditions, the lack of which would have meant swift and terrible death. It marked, further, the decay or

going to pieces of his moral nature, a vain thing and a handicap in the ruthless struggle
450 for existence. It was all well enough in the Southland, under the law of love and
fellowship, to respect private property and personal feelings; but in the Northland, under
the law of club and fang, whoso took such things into account was a fool, and in so far as
he observed them he would fail to prosper.

Not that Buck reasoned it out. He was fit, that was all, and unconsciously he
455 accommodated himself to the new mode of life. All his days, no matter what the odds,
he had never run from a fight. But the club of the man in the red sweater had beaten
into him a more fundamental and primitive code. Civilized, he could have died for a
moral consideration, say the defence of Judge Miller's riding-whip; but the completeness
of his decivilization was now evidenced by his ability to flee from the defence of a moral
460 consideration and so save his hide. He did not steal for joy of it, but because of the
clamor of his stomach. He did not rob openly, but stole secretly and cunningly, out of
respect for club and fang. In short, the things he did were done because it was easier to
do them than not to do them.

His development (or retrogression) was rapid. His muscles became hard as iron,
465 and he grew callous to all ordinary pain. He achieved an internal as well as external
economy. He could eat anything, no matter how loathsome or indigestible; and, once
eaten, the juices of his stomach extracted the last least particle of nutriment; and his
blood carried it to the farthest reaches of his body, building it into the toughest and
stoutest of tissues. Sight and scent became remarkably keen, while his hearing developed
470 such acuteness that in his sleep he heard the faintest sound and knew whether it
heralded peace or peril. He learned to bite the ice out with his teeth when it collected
between his toes; and when he was thirsty and there was a thick scum of ice over the
water hole, he would break it by rearing and striking it with stiff fore legs. His most
conspicuous trait was an ability to scent the wind and forecast it a night in advance. No
475 matter how breathless the air when he dug his nest by tree or bank, the wind that later
blew inevitably found him to leeward, sheltered and snug.

And not only did he learn by experience, but instincts long dead became alive
again. The domesticated generations fell from him. In vague ways he remembered back
to the youth of the breed, to the time the wild dogs ranged in packs through the primeval
480 forest and killed their meat as they ran it down. It was no task for him to learn to fight
with cut and slash and the quick wolf snap. In this manner had fought forgotten

ancestors. They quickened the old life within him, and the old tricks which they had stamped into the heredity of the breed were his tricks. They came to him without effort or discovery, as though they had been his always. And when, on the still cold nights, he pointed his nose at a star and howled long and wolflike, it was his ancestors, dead and dust, pointing nose at star and howling down through the centuries and through him. And his cadences were their cadences, the cadences which voiced their woe and what to them was the meaning of the stillness, and the cold, and dark.

Thus, as token of what a puppet thing life is, the ancient song surged through him and he came into his own again; and he came because men had found a yellow metal in the North, and because Manuel was a gardener's helper whose wages did not lap over the needs of his wife and divers small copies of himself.

CHAPTER THREE

The Dominant Primordial Beast

THE DOMINANT PRIMORDIAL beast was strong in Buck, and under the fierce conditions of trail life it grew and grew. Yet it was a secret growth. His new-born
495 cunning gave him poise and control. He was too busy adjusting himself to the new life to feel at ease, and not only did he not pick fights, but he avoided them whenever possible. A certain deliberateness characterized his attitude. He was not prone to rashness and precipitate action; and in the bitter hatred between him and Spitz he betrayed no impatience, shunned all offensive acts.

500   On the other hand, possibly because he divined in Buck a dangerous rival, Spitz never lost an opportunity of showing his teeth. He even went out of his way to bully Buck, striving constantly to start the fight which could end only in the death of one or the other. Early in the trip this might have taken place had it not been for an unwonted accident. At the end of this day they made a bleak and miserable camp on the shore of
505 Lake Le Barge. Driving snow, a wind that cut like a white-hot knife, and darkness had forced them to grope for a camping place. They could hardly have fared worse. At their backs rose a perpendicular wall of rock, and Perrault and François were compelled to make their fire and spread their sleeping robes on the ice of the lake itself. The tent they had discarded at Dyea in order to travel light. A few sticks of driftwood furnished
510 them with a fire that thawed down through the ice and left them to eat supper in the dark.

Close in under the sheltering rock Buck made his nest. So snug and warm was it, that he was loath to leave it when François distributed the fish which he had first thawed over the fire. But when Buck finished his ration and returned, he found his nest

515 occupied. A warning snarl told him that the trespasser was Spitz. Till now Buck had avoided trouble with his enemy, but this was too much. The beast in him roared. He sprang upon Spitz with a fury which surprised them both, and Spitz particularly, for his whole experience with Buck had gone to teach him that his rival was an unusually timid dog, who managed to hold his own only because of his great weight and size.

520 François was surprised, too, when they shot out in a tangle from the disrupted nest and he divined the cause of the trouble. "A-a-ah!" he cried to Buck. "Gif it to heem, by Gar! Gif it to heem, the dirty t'eef!"

Spitz was equally willing. He was crying with sheer rage and eagerness as he circled back and forth for a chance to spring in. Buck was no less eager, and no less

525 cautious, as he likewise circled back and forth for the advantage. But it was then that the unexpected happened, the thing which projected their struggle for supremacy far into the future, past many a weary mile of trail and toil.

An oath from Perrault, the resounding impact of a club upon a bony frame, and a shrill yelp of pain, heralded the breaking forth of pandemonium. The camp was

530 suddenly discovered to be alive with skulking furry forms,—starving huskies, four or five score of them, who had scented the camp from some Indian village. They had crept in while Buck and Spitz were fighting, and when the two men sprang among them with stout clubs they showed their teeth and fought back. They were crazed by the smell of the food. Perrault found one with head buried in the grub-box. His club landed heavily

535 on the gaunt ribs, and the grub-box was capsized on the ground. On the instant a score of the famished brutes were scrambling for the bread and bacon. The clubs fell upon them unheeded. They yelped and howled under the rain of blows, but struggled none the less madly till the last crumb had been devoured.

In the meantime the astonished team-dogs had burst out of their nests only to be

540 set upon by the fierce invaders. Never had Buck seen such dogs. It seemed as though their bones would burst through their skins. They were mere skeletons, draped loosely in draggled hides, with blazing eyes and slavered fangs. But the hunger-madness made them terrifying, irresistible. There was no opposing them. The team-dogs were swept back against the cliff at the first onset. Buck was beset by three huskies, and in a trice

545 his head and shoulders were ripped and slashed. The din was frightful. Billee was crying as usual. Dave and Sol-leks, dripping blood from a score of wounds, were fighting bravely side by side. Joe was snapping like a demon. Once, his teeth closed on the fore leg of a husky, and he crunched down through the bone. Pike, the malingerer, leaped upon the crippled animal, breaking its neck with a quick flash of teeth and a jerk. Buck
550 got a frothing adversary by the throat, and was sprayed with blood when his teeth sank through the jugular. The warm taste of it in his mouth goaded him to greater fierceness. He flung himself upon another, and at the same time felt teeth sink into his own throat. It was Spitz, treacherously attacking from the side.

Perrault and François, having cleaned out their part of the camp, hurried to save
555 their sled-dogs. The wild wave of famished beasts rolled back before them, and Buck shook himself free. But it was only for a moment. The two men were compelled to run back to save the grub, upon which the huskies returned to the attack on the team. Billee, terrified into bravery, sprang through the savage circle and fled away over the ice. Pike and Dub followed on his heels, with the rest of the team behind. As Buck drew
560 himself together to spring after them, out of the tail of his eye he saw Spitz rush upon him with the evident intention of overthrowing him. Once off his feet and under that mass of huskies, there was no hope for him. But he braced himself to the shock of Spitz's charge, then joined the flight out on the lake.

Later, the nine team-dogs gathered together and sought shelter in the forest.
565 Though unpursued, they were in a sorry plight. There was not one who was not wounded in four or five places, while some were wounded grievously. Dub was badly injured in a hind leg; Dolly, the last husky added to the team at Dyea, had a badly torn throat; Joe had lost an eye; while Billee, the good-natured, with an ear chewed and rent to ribbons, cried and whimpered throughout the night. At daybreak they limped warily
570 back to camp, to find the marauders gone and the two men in bad tempers. Fully half their grub supply was gone. The huskies had chewed through the sled lashings and canvas coverings. In fact, nothing, no matter how remotely eatable, had escaped them. They had eaten a pair of Perrault's moose-hide moccasins, chunks out of the leather traces, and even two feet of lash from the end of François's whip. He broke from a
575 mournful contemplation of it to look over his wounded dogs.

"Ah, my frien's," he said softly, "mebbe it mek you mad dog, dose many bites. Mebbe all mad dog, sacredam! Wot you t'ink, eh, Perrault?"

The courier shook his head dubiously. With four hundred miles of trail still between him and Dawson, he could ill afford to have madness break out among his dogs. Two hours of cursing and exertion got the harnesses into shape, and the wound-stiffened team was under way, struggling painfully over the hardest part of the trail they had yet encountered, and for that matter, the hardest between them and Dawson.

The Thirty Mile River was wide open. Its wild water defied the frost, and it was in the eddies only and in the quiet places that the ice held at all. Six days of exhausting toil were required to cover those thirty terrible miles. And terrible they were, for every foot of them was accomplished at the risk of life to dog and man. A dozen times, Perrault, nosing the way, broke through the ice bridges, being saved by the long pole he carried, which he so held that it fell each time across the hole made by his body. But a cold snap was on, the thermometer registering fifty below zero, and each time he broke through he was compelled for very life to build a fire and dry his garments.

Nothing daunted him. It was because nothing daunted him that he had been chosen for government courier. He took all manner of risks, resolutely thrusting his little weazened face into the frost and struggling on from dim dawn to dark. He skirted the frowning shores on rim ice that bent and crackled under foot and upon which they dared not halt. Once, the sled broke through, with Dave and Buck, and they were half-frozen and all but drowned by the time they were dragged out. The usual fire was necessary to save them. They were coated solidly with ice, and the two men kept them on the run around the fire, sweating and thawing, so close that they were singed by the flames.

At another time Spitz went through, dragging the whole team after him up to Buck, who strained backward with all his strength, his fore paws on the slippery edge and the ice quivering and snapping all around. But behind him was Dave, likewise straining backward, and behind the sled was François, pulling till his tendons cracked.

Again, the rim ice broke away before and behind, and there was no escape except up the cliff. Perrault scaled it by a miracle, while François prayed for just that miracle; and with every thong and sled lashing and the last bit of harness rove into a long rope, the dogs were hoisted, one by one, to the cliff crest. François came up last, after the sled and load. Then came the search for a place to descend, which descent was ultimately made by the aid of the rope, and night found them back on the river with a quarter of a mile to the day's credit.

By the time they made the Hootalinqua and good ice, Buck was played out. The

580

585

590

595

600

605

610

rest of the dogs were in like condition; but Perrault, to make up lost time, pushed them late and early. The first day they covered thirty-five miles to the Big Salmon; the next day thirty-five more to the Little Salmon; the third day forty miles, which brought them well up toward the Five Fingers.

615 Buck's feet were not so compact and hard as the feet of the huskies. His had softened during the many generations since the day his last wild ancestor was tamed by a cave-dweller or river man. All day long he limped in agony, and camp once made, lay down like a dead dog. Hungry as he was, he would not move to receive his ration of fish, which François had to bring to him. Also, the dog-driver rubbed Buck's feet for half 620 an hour each night after supper, and sacrificed the tops of his own moccasins to make four moccasins for Buck. This was a great relief, and Buck caused even the weazened face of Perrault to twist itself into a grin one morning, when François forgot the moccasins and Buck lay on his back, his four feet waving appealingly in the air, and refused to budge without them. Later his feet grew hard to the trail, and the worn-out 625 foot-gear was thrown away.

At the Pelly one morning, as they were harnessing up, Dolly, who had never been conspicuous for anything, went suddenly mad. She announced her condition by a long, heart-breaking wolf howl that sent every dog bristling with fear, then sprang straight for Buck. He had never seen a dog go mad, nor did he have any reason to fear madness; 630 yet he knew that here was horror, and fled away from it in a panic. Straight away he raced, with Dolly, panting and frothing, one leap behind; nor could she gain on him, so great was his terror, nor could he leave her, so great was her madness. He plunged through the wooded breast of the island, flew down to the lower end, crossed a back channel filled with rough ice to another island, gained a third island, curved back to the 635 main river, and in desperation started to cross it. And all the time, though he did not look, he could hear her snarling just one leap behind. François called to him a quarter of a mile away and he doubled back, still one leap ahead, gasping painfully for air and putting all his faith in that François would save him. The dog-driver held the axe poised in his hand, and as Buck shot past him the axe crashed down upon mad Dolly's head.

640 Buck staggered over against the sled, exhausted, sobbing for breath, helpless. This was Spitz's opportunity. He sprang upon Buck, and twice his teeth sank into his unresisting foe and ripped and tore the flesh to the bone. Then François's lash descended, and Buck had the satisfaction of watching Spitz receive the worst whipping as yet administered to any of the teams.

645   "One devil, dat Spitz," remarked Perrault. "Some dam day heem keel dat Buck."

"Dat Buck two devils," was François's rejoinder. "All de tam I watch dat Buck I know for sure. Lissen: some dam fine day heem get mad lak hell an' den heem chew dat Spitz all up an' spit heem out on de snow. Sure. I know."

From then on it was war between them. Spitz, as lead-dog and acknowledged
650 master of the team, felt his supremacy threatened by this strange Southland dog. And strange Buck was to him, for of the many Southland dogs he had known, not one had shown up worthily in camp and on trail. They were all too soft, dying under the toil, the frost, and starvation. Buck was the exception. He alone endured and prospered, matching the husky in strength, savagery, and cunning. Then he was a masterful dog, and
655 what made him dangerous was the fact that the club of the man in the red sweater had knocked all blind pluck and rashness out of his desire for mastery. He was preëminently cunning, and could bide his time with a patience that was nothing less than primitive.

It was inevitable that the clash for leadership should come. Buck wanted it. He wanted it because it was his nature, because he had been gripped tight by that nameless,
660 incomprehensible pride of the trail and trace—that pride which holds dogs in the toil to the last gasp, which lures them to die joyfully in the harness, and breaks their hearts if they are cut out of the harness. This was the pride of Dave as wheel-dog, of Sol-leks as he pulled with all his strength; the pride that laid hold of them at break of camp, transforming them from sour and sullen brutes into straining, eager, ambitious creatures;
665 the pride that spurred them on all day and dropped them at pitch of camp at night, letting them fall back into gloomy unrest and uncontent. This was the pride that bore up Spitz and made him thrash the sled-dogs who blundered and shirked in the traces or hid away at harness-up time in the morning. Likewise it was this pride that made him fear Buck as a possible lead-dog. And this was Buck's pride, too.

670   He openly threatened the other's leadership. He came between him and the shirks he should have punished. And he did it deliberately. One night there was a heavy snowfall, and in the morning Pike, the malingerer, did not appear. He was securely hidden in his nest under a foot of snow. François called him and sought him in vain. Spitz was wild with wrath. He raged through the camp, smelling and digging in every
675 likely place, snarling so frightfully that Pike heard and shivered in his hiding-place.

But when he was at last unearthed, and Spitz flew at him to punish him, Buck flew, with equal rage, in between. So unexpected was it, and so shrewdly managed, that Spitz was hurled backward and off his feet. Pike, who had been trembling abjectly, took

heart at this open mutiny, and sprang upon his overthrown leader. Buck, to whom fair
680 play was a forgotten code, likewise sprang upon Spitz. But François, chuckling at the
incident while unswerving in the administration of justice, brought his lash down upon
Buck with all his might. This failed to drive Buck from his prostrate rival, and the butt
of the whip was brought into play. Half-stunned by the blow, Buck was knocked
backward and the lash laid upon him again and again, while Spitz soundly punished the
685 many times offending Pike.

In the days that followed, as Dawson grew closer and closer, Buck still continued
to interfere between Spitz and the culprits; but he did it craftily, when François was not
around. With the covert mutiny of Buck, a general insubordination sprang up and
increased. Dave and Sol-leks were unaffected, but the rest of the team went from bad to
690 worse. Things no longer went right. There was continual bickering and jangling.
Trouble was always afoot, and at the bottom of it was Buck. He kept François busy, for
the dog-driver was in constant apprehension of the life-and-death struggle between the
two which he knew must take place sooner or later; and on more than one night the
sounds of quarrelling and strife among the other dogs turned him out of his sleeping
695 robe, fearful that Buck and Spitz were at it.

But the opportunity did not present itself, and they pulled into Dawson one dreary
afternoon with the great fight still to come. Here were many men, and countless dogs,
and Buck found them all at work. It seemed the ordained order of things that dogs
should work. All day they swung up and down the main street in long teams, and in the
700 night their jingling bells still went by. They hauled cabin logs and firewood, freighted up
to the mines, and did all manner of work that horses did in the Santa Clara Valley. Here
and there Buck met Southland dogs, but in the main they were the wild wolf husky
breed. Every night, regularly, at nine, at twelve, at three, they lifted a nocturnal song, a
weird and eerie chant, in which it was Buck's delight to join.

705 With the aurora borealis flaming coldly overhead, or the stars leaping in the frost
dance, and the land numb and frozen under its pall of snow, this song of the huskies
might have been the defiance of life, only it was pitched in minor key, with long-drawn
wailings and half-sobs, and was more the pleading of life, the articulate travail of
existence. It was an old song, old as the breed itself—one of the first songs of the
710 younger world in a day when songs were sad. It was invested with the woe of
unnumbered generations, this plaint by which Buck was so strangely stirred. When he

moaned and sobbed, it was with the pain of living that was of old the pain of his wild fathers, and the fear and mystery of the cold and dark that was to them fear and mystery. And that he should be stirred by it marked the completeness with which he harked back
715   through the ages of fire and roof to the raw beginnings of life in the howling ages.

Seven days from the time they pulled into Dawson, they dropped down the steep bank by the Barracks to the Yukon Trail, and pulled for Dyea and Salt Water. Perrault was carrying despatches if anything more urgent than those he had brought in; also, the travel pride had gripped him, and he purposed to make the record trip of the year.
720   Several things favored him in this. The week's rest had recuperated the dogs and put them in thorough trim. The trail they had broken into the country was packed hard by later journeyers. And further, the police had arranged in two or three places deposits of grub for dog and man, and he was travelling light.

They made Sixty Mile, which is a fifty-mile run, on the first day; and the second
725   day saw them booming up the Yukon well on their way to Pelly. But such splendid running was achieved not without great trouble and vexation on the part of François. The insidious revolt led by Buck had destroyed the solidarity of the team. It no longer was as one dog leaping in the traces. The encouragement Buck gave the rebels led them into all kinds of petty misdemeanors. No more was Spitz a leader greatly to be feared.
730   The old awe departed, and they grew equal to challenging his authority. Pike robbed him of half a fish one night, and gulped it down under the protection of Buck. Another night Dub and Joe fought Spitz and made him forego the punishment they deserved. And even Billee, the good-natured, was less good-natured, and whined not half so placatingly as in former days. Buck never came near Spitz without snarling and bristling
735   menacingly. In fact, his conduct approached that of a bully, and he was given to swaggering up and down before Spitz's very nose.

The breaking down of discipline likewise affected the dogs in their relations with one another. They quarrelled and bickered more than ever among themselves, till at times the camp was a howling bedlam. Dave and Sol-leks alone were unaltered, though
740   they were made irritable by the unending squabbling. François swore strange barbarous oaths, and stamped the snow in futile rage, and tore his hair. His lash was always singing among the dogs, but it was of small avail. Directly his back was turned they were at it again. He backed up Spitz with his whip, while Buck backed up the remainder of the team. François knew he was behind all the trouble, and Buck knew he knew; but Buck

745 was too clever ever again to be caught red-handed. He worked faithfully in the harness, for the toil had become a delight to him; yet it was a greater delight slyly to precipitate a fight amongst his mates and tangle the traces.

At the mouth of the Tahkeena, one night after supper, Dub turned up a snowshoe rabbit, blundered it, and missed. In a second the whole team was in full cry. A hundred

750 yards away was a camp of the Northwest Police, with fifty dogs, huskies all, who joined the chase. The rabbit sped down the river, turned off into a small creek, up the frozen bed of which it held steadily. It ran lightly on the surface of the snow, while the dogs ploughed through by main strength. Buck led the pack, sixty strong, around bend after bend, but he could not gain. He lay down low to the race, whining eagerly, his splendid

755 body flashing forward, leap by leap, in the wan white moonlight. And leap by leap, like some pale frost wraith, the snowshoe rabbit flashed on ahead.

All that stirring of old instincts which at stated periods drives men out from the sounding cities to forest and plain to kill things by chemically propelled leaden pellets, the blood lust, the joy to kill—all this was Buck's, only it was infinitely more intimate. He

760 was ranging at the head of the pack, running the wild thing down, the living meat, to kill with his own teeth and wash his muzzle to the eyes in warm blood.

There is an ecstasy that marks the summit of life, and beyond which life cannot rise. And such is the paradox of living, this ecstasy comes when one is most alive, and it comes as a complete forgetfulness that one is alive. This ecstasy, this forgetfulness of

765 living, comes to the artist, caught up and out of himself in a sheet of flame; it comes to the soldier, war-mad on a stricken field and refusing quarter; and it came to Buck, leading the pack, sounding the old wolf-cry, straining after the food that was alive and that fled swiftly before him through the moonlight. He was sounding the deeps of his nature, and of the parts of his nature that were deeper than he, going back into the

770 womb of Time. He was mastered by the sheer surging of life, the tidal wave of being, the perfect joy of each separate muscle, joint, and sinew in that it was everything that was not death, that it was aglow and rampant, expressing itself in movement, flying exultantly under the stars and over the face of dead matter that did not move.

But Spitz, cold and calculating even in his supreme moods, left the pack and cut

775 across a narrow neck of land where the creek made a long bend around. Buck did not know of this, and as he rounded the bend, the frost wraith of a rabbit still flitting before him, he saw another and larger frost wraith leap from the overhanging bank into the

immediate path of the rabbit. It was Spitz. The rabbit could not turn, and as the white teeth broke its back in mid air it shrieked as loudly as a stricken man may shriek. At

780 sound of this, the cry of Life plunging down from Life's apex in the grip of Death, the full pack at Buck's heels raised a hell's chorus of delight.

Buck did not cry out. He did not check himself, but drove in upon Spitz, shoulder to shoulder, so hard that he missed the throat. They rolled over and over in the powdery snow. Spitz gained his feet almost as though he had not been overthrown, slashing Buck

785 down the shoulder and leaping clear. Twice his teeth clipped together, like the steel jaws of a trap, as he backed away for better footing, with lean and lifting lips that writhed and snarled.

In a flash Buck knew it. The time had come. It was to the death. As they circled about, snarling, ears laid back, keenly watchful for the advantage, the scene came to

790 Buck with a sense of familiarity. He seemed to remember it all,—the white woods, and earth, and moonlight, and the thrill of battle. Over the whiteness and silence brooded a ghostly calm. There was not the faintest whisper of air—nothing moved, not a leaf quivered, the visible breaths of the dogs rising slowly and lingering in the frosty air. They had made short work of the snowshoe rabbit, these dogs that were ill-tamed wolves; and

795 they were now drawn up in an expectant circle. They, too, were silent, their eyes only gleaming and their breaths drifting slowly upward. To Buck it was nothing new or strange, this scene of old time. It was as though it had always been, the wonted way of things.

Spitz was a practised fighter. From Spitzbergen through the Arctic, and across

800 Canada and the Barrens, he had held his own with all manner of dogs and achieved to mastery over them. Bitter rage was his, but never blind rage. In passion to rend and destroy, he never forgot that his enemy was in like passion to rend and destroy. He never rushed till he was prepared to receive a rush; never attacked till he had first defended that attack.

805 In vain Buck strove to sink his teeth in the neck of the big white dog. Wherever his fangs struck for the softer flesh, they were countered by the fangs of Spitz. Fang clashed fang, and lips were cut and bleeding, but Buck could not penetrate his enemy's guard. Then he warmed up and enveloped Spitz in a whirlwind of rushes. Time and time again he tried for the snow-white throat, where life bubbled near to the surface, and

810 each time and every time Spitz slashed him and got away. Then Buck took to rushing, as

though for the throat, when, suddenly drawing back his head and curving in from the side, he would drive his shoulder at the shoulder of Spitz, as a ram by which to overthrow him. But instead, Buck's shoulder was slashed down each time as Spitz leaped lightly away.

815 Spitz was untouched, while Buck was streaming with blood and panting hard. The fight was growing desperate. And all the while the silent and wolfish circle waited to finish off whichever dog went down. As Buck grew winded, Spitz took to rushing, and he kept him staggering for footing. Once Buck went over, and the whole circle of sixty dogs started up; but he recovered himself, almost in mid air, and the circle sank down again 820 and waited.

But Buck possessed a quality that made for greatness—imagination. He fought by instinct, but he could fight by head as well. He rushed, as though attempting the old shoulder trick, but at the last instant swept low to the snow and in. His teeth closed on Spitz's left fore leg. There was a crunch of breaking bone, and the white dog faced him 825 on three legs. Thrice he tried to knock him over, then repeated the trick and broke the right fore leg. Despite the pain and helplessness, Spitz struggled madly to keep up. He saw the silent circle, with gleaming eyes, lolling tongues, and silvery breaths drifting upward, closing in upon him as he had seen similar circles close in upon beaten antagonists in the past. Only this time he was the one who was beaten.

830 There was no hope for him. Buck was inexorable. Mercy was a thing reserved for gentler climes. He manœuvred for the final rush. The circle had tightened till he could feel the breaths of the huskies on his flanks. He could see them, beyond Spitz and to either side, half crouching for the spring, their eyes fixed upon him. A pause seemed to fall. Every animal was motionless as though turned to stone. Only Spitz quivered and 835 bristled as he staggered back and forth, snarling with horrible menace, as though to frighten off impending death. Then Buck sprang in and out; but while he was in, shoulder had at last squarely met shoulder. The dark circle became a dot on the moon-flooded snow as Spitz disappeared from view. Buck stood and looked on, the successful champion, the dominant primordial beast who had made his kill and found it 840 good.

CHAPTER FOUR

Who Has Won to Mastership

*E*H? WOT I say? I spik true w'en I say dat Buck two devils."

This was François's speech next morning when he discovered Spitz missing and Buck covered with wounds. He drew him to the fire and by its light pointed them out.

"Dat Spitz fight lak hell," said Perrault, as he surveyed the gaping rips and cuts.

845   "An' dat Buck fight lak two hells," was François's answer. "An' now we make good time. No more Spitz, no more trouble, sure."

While Perrault packed the camp outfit and loaded the sled, the dog-driver proceeded to harness the dogs. Buck trotted up to the place Spitz would have occupied as leader; but François, not noticing him, brought Sol-leks to the coveted position. In his

850   judgment, Sol-leks was the best lead-dog left. Buck sprang upon Sol-leks in a fury, driving him back and standing in his place.

"Eh? eh?" François cried, slapping his thighs gleefully. "Look at dat Buck. Heem keel dat Spitz, heem t'ink to take de job."

"Go 'way, Chook!" he cried, but Buck refused to budge.

855   He took Buck by the scruff of the neck, and though the dog growled threateningly, dragged him to one side and replaced Sol-leks. The old dog did not like it, and showed plainly that he was afraid of Buck. François was obdurate, but when he turned his back Buck again displaced Sol-leks, who was not at all unwilling to go.

François was angry. "Now, by Gar, I feex you!" he cried, coming back with a
860 heavy club in his hand.

Buck remembered the man in the red sweater, and retreated slowly; nor did he
attempt to charge in when Sol-leks was once more brought forward. But he circled just
beyond the range of the club, snarling with bitterness and rage; and while he circled he
watched the club so as to dodge it if thrown by François, for he was become wise in the
865 way of clubs.

The driver went about his work, and he called to Buck when he was ready to put
him in his old place in front of Dave. Buck retreated two or three steps. François
followed him up, whereupon he again retreated. After some time of this, François threw
down the club, thinking that Buck feared a thrashing. But Buck was in open revolt. He
870 wanted, not to escape a clubbing, but to have the leadership. It was his by right. He had
earned it, and he would not be content with less.

Perrault took a hand. Between them they ran him about for the better part of an
hour. They threw clubs at him. He dodged. They cursed him, and his fathers and
mothers before him, and all his seed to come after him down to the remotest generation,
875 and every hair on his body and drop of blood in his veins; and he answered curse with
snarl and kept out of their reach. He did not try to run away, but retreated around and
around the camp, advertising plainly that when his desire was met, he would come in and
be good.

François sat down and scratched his head. Perrault looked at his watch and
880 swore. Time was flying, and they should have been on the trail an hour gone. François
scratched his head again. He shook it and grinned sheepishly at the courier, who
shrugged his shoulders in sign that they were beaten. Then François went up to where
Sol-leks stood and called to Buck. Buck laughed, as dogs laugh, yet kept his distance.
François unfastened Sol-leks's traces and put him back in his old place. The team stood
885 harnessed to the sled in an unbroken line, ready for the trail. There was no place for
Buck save at the front. Once more François called, and once more Buck laughed and
kept away.

"T'row down de club," Perrault commanded.

François complied, whereupon Buck trotted in, laughing triumphantly, and swung
890 around into position at the head of the team. His traces were fastened, the sled broken
out, and with both men running they dashed out on to the river trail.

Highly as the dog-driver had forevalued Buck, with his two devils, he found, while the day was yet young, that he had undervalued. At a bound Buck took up the duties of leadership; and where judgment was required, and quick thinking and quick acting, he 895 showed himself the superior even of Spitz, of whom François had never seen an equal.

But it was in giving the law and making his mates live up to it, that Buck excelled. Dave and Sol-leks did not mind the change in leadership. It was none of their business. Their business was to toil, and toil mightily, in the traces. So long as that were not interfered with, they did not care what happened. Billee, the good-natured, could lead 900 for all they cared, so long as he kept order. The rest of the team, however, had grown unruly during the last days of Spitz, and their surprise was great now that Buck proceeded to lick them into shape.

Pike, who pulled at Buck's heels, and who never put an ounce more of his weight against the breast-band than he was compelled to do, was swiftly and repeatedly shaken 905 for loafing; and ere the first day was done he was pulling more than ever before in his life. The first night in camp, Joe, the sour one, was punished roundly—a thing that Spitz had never succeeded in doing. Buck simply smothered him by virtue of superior weight, and cut him up till he ceased snapping and began to whine for mercy.

The general tone of the team picked up immediately. It recovered its old-time 910 solidarity, and once more the dogs leaped as one dog in the traces. At the Rink Rapids two native huskies, Teek and Koona, were added; and the celerity with which Buck broke them in took away François's breath.

"Nevaire such a dog as dat Buck!" he cried. "No, nevaire! Heem worth one t'ousan' dollair, by Gar! Eh? Wot you say, Perrault?"

915 And Perrault nodded. He was ahead of the record then, and gaining day by day. The trail was in excellent condition, well packed and hard, and there was no new-fallen snow with which to contend. It was not too cold. The temperature dropped to fifty below zero and remained there the whole trip. The men rode and ran by turn, and the dogs were kept on the jump, with but infrequent stoppages.

920 The Thirty Mile River was comparatively coated with ice, and they covered in one day going out what had taken them ten days coming in. In one run they made a sixty-mile dash from the foot of Lake Le Barge to the White Horse Rapids. Across Marsh, Tagish, and Bennett (seventy miles of lakes), they flew so fast that the man whose turn it was to run towed behind the sled at the end of a rope. And on the last night of 925 the second week they topped White Pass and dropped down the sea slope with the lights of Skaguay and of the shipping at their feet.

It was a record run. Each day for fourteen days they had averaged forty miles. For three days Perrault and François threw chests up and down the main street of Skaguay and were deluged with invitations to drink, while the team was the constant
930 centre of a worshipful crowd of dog-busters and mushers. Then three or four western bad men aspired to clean out the town, were riddled like pepper-boxes for their pains, and public interest turned to other idols. Next came official orders. François called Buck to him, threw his arms around him, wept over him. And that was the last of François and Perrault. Like other men, they passed out of Buck's life for good.

935   A Scotch half-breed took charge of him and his mates, and in company with a dozen other dog-teams he started back over the weary trail to Dawson. It was no light running now, nor record time, but heavy toil each day, with a heavy load behind; for this was the mail train, carrying word from the world to the men who sought gold under the shadow of the Pole.

940   Buck did not like it, but he bore up well to the work, taking pride in it after the manner of Dave and Sol-leks, and seeing that his mates, whether they prided in it or not, did their fair share. It was a monotonous life, operating with machine-like regularity. One day was very like another. At a certain time each morning the cooks turned out, fires were built, and breakfast was eaten. Then, while some broke camp, others
945 harnessed the dogs, and they were under way an hour or so before the darkness fell which gave warning of dawn. At night, camp was made. Some pitched the flies, others cut firewood and pine boughs for the beds, and still others carried water or ice for the cooks. Also, the dogs were fed. To them, this was the one feature of the day, though it was good to loaf around, after the fish was eaten, for an hour or so with the other dogs,
950 of which there were fivescore and odd. There were fierce fighters among them, but three battles with the fiercest brought Buck to mastery, so that when he bristled and showed his teeth they got out of his way.

Best of all, perhaps, he loved to lie near the fire, hind legs crouched under him, fore legs stretched out in front, head raised, and eyes blinking dreamily at the flames.
955 Sometimes he thought of Judge Miller's big house in the sun-kissed Santa Clara Valley, and of the cement swimming-tank, and Ysabel, the Mexican hairless, and Toots, the Japanese pug; but oftener he remembered the man in the red sweater, the death of Curly, the great fight with Spitz, and the good things he had eaten or would like to eat. He was not homesick. The Sunland was very dim and distant, and such memories had
960 no power over him. Far more potent were the memories of his heredity that gave things

he had never seen before a seeming familiarity; the instincts (which were but the memories of his ancestors become habits) which had lapsed in later days, and still later, in him, quickened and become alive again.

965 Sometimes as he crouched there, blinking dreamily at the flames, it seemed that the flames were of another fire, and that as he crouched by this other fire he saw another and different man from the half-breed cook before him. This other man was shorter of leg and longer of arm, with muscles that were stringy and knotty rather than rounded and swelling. The hair of this man was long and matted, and his head slanted back under it from the eyes. He uttered strange sounds, and seemed very much afraid of

970 the darkness, into which he peered continually, clutching in his hand, which hung midway between knee and foot, a stick with a heavy stone made fast to the end. He was all but naked, a ragged and fire-scorched skin hanging part way down his back, but on his body there was much hair. In some places, across the chest and shoulders and down the outside of the arms and thighs, it was matted into almost a thick fur. He did not stand

975 erect, but with trunk inclined forward from the hips, on legs that bent at the knees. About his body there was a peculiar springiness, or resiliency, almost catlike, and a quick alertness as of one who lived in perpetual fear of things seen and unseen.

At other times this hairy man squatted by the fire with head between his legs and slept. On such occasions his elbows were on his knees, his hands clasped above his head

980 as though to shed rain by the hairy arms. And beyond that fire, in the circling darkness, Buck could see many gleaming coals, two by two, always two by two, which he knew to be the eyes of great beasts of prey. And he could hear the crashing of their bodies through the undergrowth, and the noises they made in the night. And dreaming there by the Yukon bank, with lazy eyes blinking at the fire, these sounds and sights of another

985 world would make the hair to rise along his back and stand on end across his shoulders and up his neck, till he whimpered low and suppressedly, or growled softly, and the half-breed cook shouted at him, "Hey, you Buck, wake up!" Whereupon the other world would vanish and the real world come into his eyes, and he would get up and yawn and stretch as though he had been asleep.

990 It was a hard trip, with the mail behind them, and the heavy work wore them down. They were short of weight and in poor condition when they made Dawson, and should have had a ten days' or a week's rest at least. But in two days' time they dropped down the Yukon bank from the Barracks, loaded with letters for the outside. The dogs were tired, the drivers grumbling, and to make matters worse, it snowed every day. This

995 meant a soft trail, greater friction on the runners, and heavier pulling for the dogs; yet the drivers were fair through it all, and did their best for the animals.

Each night the dogs were attended to first. They ate before the drivers ate, and no man sought his sleeping-robe till he had seen to the feet of the dogs he drove. Still, their strength went down. Since the beginning of the winter they had travelled eighteen
1000 hundred miles, dragging sleds the whole weary distance; and eighteen hundred miles will tell upon life of the toughest. Buck stood it, keeping his mates up to their work and maintaining discipline, though he, too, was very tired. Billee cried and whimpered regularly in his sleep each night. Joe was sourer than ever, and Sol-leks was unapproachable, blind side or other side.

1005 But it was Dave who suffered most of all. Something had gone wrong with him. He became more morose and irritable, and when camp was pitched at once made his nest, where his driver fed him. Once out of the harness and down, he did not get on his feet again till harness-up time in the morning. Sometimes, in the traces, when jerked by a sudden stoppage of the sled, or by straining to start it, he would cry out with pain. The
1010 driver examined him, but could find nothing. All the drivers became interested in his case. They talked it over at meal-time, and over their last pipes before going to bed, and one night they held a consultation. He was brought from his nest to the fire and was pressed and prodded till he cried out many times. Something was wrong inside, but they could locate no broken bones, could not make it out.

1015 By the time Cassiar Bar was reached, he was so weak that he was falling repeatedly in the traces. The Scotch half-breed called a halt and took him out of the team, making the next dog, Sol-leks, fast to the sled. His intention was to rest Dave, letting him run free behind the sled. Sick as he was, Dave resented being taken out, grunting and growling while the traces were unfastened, and whimpering broken-
1020 heartedly when he saw Sol-leks in the position he had held and served so long. For the pride of trace and trail was his, and, sick unto death, he could not bear that another dog should do his work.

When the sled started, he floundered in the soft snow alongside the beaten trail, attacking Sol-leks with his teeth, rushing against him and trying to thrust him off into the
1025 soft snow on the other side, striving to leap inside his traces and get between him and the sled, and all the while whining and yelping and crying with grief and pain. The half-breed tried to drive him away with the whip; but he paid no heed to the stinging lash, and the man had not the heart to strike harder. Dave refused to run quietly on the trail

1030 behind the sled, where the going was easy, but continued to flounder alongside in the soft snow, where the going was most difficult, till exhausted. Then he fell, and lay where he fell, howling lugubriously as the long train of sleds churned by.

With the last remnant of his strength he managed to stagger along behind till the train made another stop, when he floundered past the sleds to his own, where he stood alongside Sol-leks. His driver lingered a moment to get a light for his pipe from the man 1035 behind. Then he returned and started his dogs. They swung out on the trail with remarkable lack of exertion, turned their heads uneasily, and stopped in surprise. The driver was surprised, too; the sled had not moved. He called his comrades to witness the sight. Dave had bitten through both of Sol-leks's traces, and was standing directly in front of the sled in his proper place.

1040 He pleaded with his eyes to remain there. The driver was perplexed. His comrades talked of how a dog could break its heart through being denied the work that killed it, and recalled instances they had known, where dogs, too old for the toil, or injured, had died because they were cut out of the traces. Also, they held it a mercy, since Dave was to die anyway, that he should die in the traces, heart-easy and content. 1045 So he was harnessed in again, and proudly he pulled as of old, though more than once he cried out involuntarily from the bite of his inward hurt. Several times he fell down and was dragged in the traces, and once the sled ran upon him so that he limped thereafter in one of his hind legs.

But he held out till camp was reached, when his driver made a place for him by 1050 the fire. Morning found him too weak to travel. At harness-up time he tried to crawl to his driver. By convulsive efforts he got on his feet, staggered, and fell. Then he wormed his way forward slowly toward where the harnesses were being put on his mates. He would advance his fore legs and drag up his body with a sort of hitching movement, when he would advance his fore legs and hitch ahead again for a few more inches. His 1055 strength left him, and the last his mates saw of him he lay gasping in the snow and yearning toward them. But they could hear him mournfully howling till they passed out of sight behind a belt of river timber.

Here the train was halted. The Scotch half-breed slowly retraced his steps to the camp they had left. The men ceased talking. A revolver-shot rang out. The man came 1060 back hurriedly. The whips snapped, the bells tinkled merrily, the sleds churned along the trail; but Buck knew, and every dog knew, what had taken place behind the belt of river trees.

CHAPTER FIVE

The Toil of Trace and Trail

THIRTY DAYS FROM the time it left Dawson, the Salt Water Mail, with Buck and his mates at the fore, arrived at Skaguay. They were in a wretched state, worn out and worn
1065 down. Buck's one hundred and forty pounds had dwindled to one hundred and fifteen. The rest of his mates, though lighter dogs, had relatively lost more weight than he. Pike, the malingerer, who, in his lifetime of deceit, had often successfully feigned a hurt leg, was now limping in earnest. Sol-leks was limping, and Dub was suffering from a wrenched shoulder-blade.

1070 They were all terribly footsore. No spring or rebound was left in them. Their feet fell heavily on the trail, jarring their bodies and doubling the fatigue of a day's travel. There was nothing the matter with them except that they were dead tired. It was not the dead-tiredness that comes through brief and excessive effort, from which recovery is a matter of hours; but it was the dead-tiredness that comes through the slow and prolonged
1075 strength drainage of months of toil. There was no power of recuperation left, no reserve strength to call upon. It had been all used, the last least bit of it. Every muscle, every fibre, every cell, was tired, dead tired. And there was reason for it. In less than five months they had travelled twenty-five hundred miles, during the last eighteen hundred of which they had had but five days' rest. When they arrived at Skaguay they were
1080 apparently on their last legs. They could barely keep the traces taut, and on the down grades just managed to keep out of the way of the sled.

"Mush on, poor sore feets," the driver encouraged them as they tottered down the main street of Skaguay. "Dis is de las'. Den we get one long res'. Eh? For sure. One bully long res'."

1085 The drivers confidently expected a long stopover. Themselves, they had covered twelve hundred miles with two days' rest, and in the nature of reason and common justice they deserved an interval of loafing. But so many were the men who had rushed into the Klondike, and so many were the sweethearts, wives, and kin that had not rushed in, that the congested mail was taking on Alpine proportions; also, there were official 1090 orders. Fresh batches of Hudson Bay dogs were to take the places of those worthless for the trail. The worthless ones were to be got rid of, and, since dogs count for little against dollars, they were to be sold.

Three days passed, by which time Buck and his mates found how really tired and weak they were. Then, on the morning of the fourth day, two men from the States came 1095 along and bought them, harness and all, for a song. The men addressed each other as "Hal" and "Charles." Charles was a middle-aged, lightish-colored man, with weak and watery eyes and a mustache that twisted fiercely and vigorously up, giving the lie to the limply drooping lip it concealed. Hal was a youngster of nineteen or twenty, with a big Colt's revolver and a hunting-knife strapped about him on a belt that fairly bristled with 1100 cartridges. This belt was the most salient thing about him. It advertised his callowness—a callowness sheer and unutterable. Both men were manifestly out of place, and why such as they should adventure the North is part of the mystery of things that passes understanding.

Buck heard the chaffering, saw the money pass between the man and the 1105 Government agent, and knew that the Scotch half-breed and the mail-train drivers were passing out of his life on the heels of Perrault and François and the others who had gone before. When driven with his mates to the new owners' camp, Buck saw a slipshod and slovenly affair, tent half stretched, dishes unwashed, everything in disorder; also, he saw a woman. "Mercedes" the men called her. She was Charles's wife and Hal's sister—a nice 1110 family party.

Buck watched them apprehensively as they proceeded to take down the tent and load the sled. There was a great deal of effort about their manner, but no businesslike method. The tent was rolled into an awkward bundle three times as large as it should have been. The tin dishes were packed away unwashed. Mercedes continually fluttered

1115 in the way of her men and kept up an unbroken chattering of remonstrance and advice. When they put a clothes-sack on the front of the sled, she suggested it should go on the back; and when they had put it on the back, and covered it over with a couple of other bundles, she discovered overlooked articles which could abide nowhere else but in that very sack, and they unloaded again.

1120 Three men from a neighboring tent came out and looked on, grinning and winking at one another.

"You've got a right smart load as it is," said one of them; "and it's not me should tell you your business, but I wouldn't tote that tent along if I was you."

"Undreamed of!" cried Mercedes, throwing up her hands in dainty dismay.
1125 "However in the world could I manage without a tent?"

"It's springtime, and you won't get any more cold weather," the man replied.

She shook her head decidedly, and Charles and Hal put the last odds and ends on top the mountainous load.

"Think it'll ride?" one of the men asked.

1130 "Why shouldn't it?" Charles demanded rather shortly.

"Oh, that's all right, that's all right," the man hastened meekly to say. "I was just a-wonderin', that is all. It seemed a mite top-heavy."

Charles turned his back and drew the lashings down as well as he could, which was not in the least well.

1135 "An' of course the dogs can hike along all day with that contraption behind them," affirmed a second of the men.

"Certainly," said Hal, with freezing politeness, taking hold of the gee-pole with one hand and swinging his whip from the other. "Mush!" he shouted. "Mush on there!"

The dogs sprang against the breast-bands, strained hard for a few moments, then
1140 relaxed. They were unable to move the sled.

"The lazy brutes, I'll show them," he cried, preparing to lash out at them with the whip.

But Mercedes interfered, crying, "Oh, Hal, you mustn't," as she caught hold of the whip and wrenched it from him. "The poor dears! Now you must promise you won't be
1145 harsh with them for the rest of the trip, or I won't go a step."

"Precious lot you know about dogs," her brother sneered; "and I wish you'd leave me alone. They're lazy, I tell you, and you've got to whip them to get anything out of them. That's their way. You ask any one. Ask one of those men."

1150 Mercedes looked at them imploringly, untold repugnance at sight of pain written in her pretty face.

"They're weak as water, if you want to know," came the reply from one of the men. "Plum tuckered out, that's what's the matter. They need a rest."

"Rest be blanked," said Hal, with his beardless lips; and Mercedes said, "Oh!" in pain and sorrow at the oath.

1155 But she was a clannish creature, and rushed at once to the defence of her brother. "Never mind that man," she said pointedly. "You're driving our dogs, and you do what you think best with them."

Again Hal's whip fell upon the dogs. They threw themselves against the breast-bands, dug their feet into the packed snow, got down low to it, and put forth all 1160 their strength. The sled held as though it were an anchor. After two efforts, they stood still, panting. The whip was whistling savagely, when once more Mercedes interfered. She dropped on her knees before Buck, with tears in her eyes, and put her arms around his neck.

"You poor, poor dears," she cried sympathetically, "why don't you pull hard?—then 1165 you wouldn't be whipped." Buck did not like her, but he was feeling too miserable to resist her, taking it as part of the day's miserable work.

One of the onlookers, who had been clenching his teeth to suppress hot speech, now spoke up:—

"It's not that I care a whoop what becomes of you, but for the dogs' sakes I just 1170 want to tell you, you can help them a mighty lot by breaking out that sled. The runners are froze fast. Throw your weight against the gee-pole, right and left, and break it out."

A third time the attempt was made, but this time, following the advice, Hal broke out the runners which had been frozen to the snow. The overloaded and unwieldy sled forged ahead, Buck and his mates struggling frantically under the rain of blows. A 1175 hundred yards ahead the path turned and sloped steeply into the main street. It would have required an experienced man to keep the top-heavy sled upright, and Hal was not such a man. As they swung on the turn the sled went over, spilling half its load through the loose lashings. The dogs never stopped. The lightened sled bounded on its side behind them. They were angry because of the ill treatment they had received and the 1180 unjust load. Buck was raging. He broke into a run, the team following his lead. Hal cried "Whoa! whoa!" but they gave no heed. He tripped and was pulled off his feet. The capsized sled ground over him, and the dogs dashed on up the street, adding to the gayety of Skaguay as they scattered the remainder of the outfit along its chief thoroughfare.

1185   Kind-hearted citizens caught the dogs and gathered up the scattered belongings. Also, they gave advice. Half the load and twice the dogs, if they ever expected to reach Dawson, was what was said. Hal and his sister and brother-in-law listened unwillingly, pitched tent, and overhauled the outfit. Canned goods were turned out that made men laugh, for canned goods on the Long Trail is a thing to dream about. "Blankets for a
1190 hotel," quoth one of the men who laughed and helped. "Half as many is too much; get rid of them. Throw away that tent, and all those dishes,—who's going to wash them, anyway? Good Lord, do you think you're travelling on a Pullman?"

    And so it went, the inexorable elimination of the superfluous. Mercedes cried when her clothes-bags were dumped on the ground and article after article was thrown
1195 out. She cried in general, and she cried in particular over each discarded thing. She clasped hands about knees, rocking back and forth broken-heartedly. She averred she would not go an inch, not for a dozen Charleses. She appealed to everybody and to everything, finally wiping her eyes and proceeding to cast out even articles of apparel that were imperative necessaries. And in her zeal, when she had finished with her own,
1200 she attacked the belongings of her men and went through them like a tornado.

    This accomplished, the outfit, though cut in half, was still a formidable bulk. Charles and Hal went out in the evening and bought six Outside dogs. These, added to the six of the original team, and Teek and Koona, the huskies obtained at the Rink Rapids on the record trip, brought the team up to fourteen. But the Outside dogs,
1205 though practically broken in since their landing, did not amount to much. Three were short-haired pointers, one was a Newfoundland, and the other two were mongrels of indeterminate breed. They did not seem to know anything, these newcomers. Buck and his comrades looked upon them with disgust, and though he speedily taught them their places and what not to do, he could not teach them what to do. They did not take kindly
1210 to trace and trail. With the exception of the two mongrels, they were bewildered and spirit-broken by the strange savage environment in which they found themselves and by the ill-treatment they had received. The two mongrels were without spirit at all; bones were the only things breakable about them.

    With the newcomers hopeless and forlorn, and the old team worn out by
1215 twenty-five hundred miles of continuous trail, the outlook was anything but bright. The

two men, however, were quite cheerful. And they were proud, too. They were doing the thing in style, with fourteen dogs. They had seen other sleds depart over the Pass for Dawson, or come in from Dawson, but never had they seen a sled with so many as fourteen dogs. In the nature of Arctic travel there was a reason why fourteen dogs

1220 should not drag one sled, and that was that one sled could not carry the food for fourteen dogs. But Charles and Hal did not know this. They had worked the trip out with a pencil, so much to a dog, so many dogs, so many days, Q.E.D. Mercedes looked over their shoulders and nodded comprehensively, it was all so very simple.

Late next morning Buck led the long team up the street. There was nothing lively

1225 about it, no snap or go in him and his fellows. They were starting dead weary. Four times he had covered the distance between Salt Water and Dawson, and the knowledge that, jaded and tired, he was facing the same trail once more, made him bitter. His heart was not in the work, nor was the heart of any dog. The Outsides were timid and frightened, the Insides without confidence in their masters.

1230 Buck felt vaguely that there was no depending upon these two men and the woman. They did not know how to do anything, and as the days went by it became apparent that they could not learn. They were slack in all things, without order or discipline. It took them half the night to pitch a slovenly camp, and half the morning to break that camp and get the sled loaded in fashion so slovenly that for the rest of the

1235 day they were occupied in stopping and rearranging the load. Some days they did not make ten miles. On other days they were unable to get started at all. And on no day did they succeed in making more than half the distance used by the men as a basis in their dog-food computation.

It was inevitable that they should go short on dog-food. But they hastened it by

1240 overfeeding, bringing the day nearer when underfeeding would commence. The Outside dogs, whose digestions had not been trained by chronic famine to make the most of little, had voracious appetites. And when, in addition to this, the worn-out huskies pulled weakly, Hal decided that the orthodox ration was too small. He doubled it. And to cap it all, when Mercedes, with tears in her pretty eyes and a quaver in her throat, could not

1245 cajole him into giving the dogs still more, she stole from the fish-sacks and fed them slyly. But it was not food that Buck and the huskies needed, but rest. And though they were making poor time, the heavy load they dragged sapped their strength severely.

Then came the underfeeding. Hal awoke one day to the fact that his dog-food was half gone and the distance only quarter covered; further, that for love or money no additional dog-food was to be obtained. So he cut down even the orthodox ration and tried to increase the day's travel. His sister and brother-in-law seconded him; but they were frustrated by their heavy outfit and their own incompetence. It was a simple matter to give the dogs less food; but it was impossible to make the dogs travel faster, while their own inability to get under way earlier in the morning prevented them from travelling longer hours. Not only did they not know how to work dogs, but they did not know how to work themselves.

The first to go was Dub. Poor blundering thief that he was, always getting caught and punished, he had none the less been a faithful worker. His wrenched shoulder-blade, untreated and unrested, went from bad to worse, till finally Hal shot him with the big Colt's revolver. It is a saying of the country that an Outside dog starves to death on the ration of the husky, so the six Outside dogs under Buck could do no less than die on half the ration of the husky. The Newfoundland went first, followed by the three short-haired pointers, the two mongrels hanging more grittily on to life, but going in the end.

By this time all the amenities and gentlenesses of the Southland had fallen away from the three people. Shorn of its glamour and romance, Arctic travel became to them a reality too harsh for their manhood and womanhood. Mercedes ceased weeping over the dogs, being too occupied with weeping over herself and with quarrelling with her husband and brother. To quarrel was the one thing they were never too weary to do. Their irritability arose out of their misery, increased with it, doubled upon it, outdistanced it. The wonderful patience of the trail which comes to men who toil hard and suffer sore, and remain sweet of speech and kindly, did not come to these two men and the woman. They had no inkling of such a patience. They were stiff and in pain; their muscles ached, their bones ached, their very hearts ached; and because of this they became sharp of speech, and hard words were first on their lips in the morning and last at night.

Charles and Hal wrangled whenever Mercedes gave them a chance. It was the cherished belief of each that he did more than his share of the work, and neither forbore to speak this belief at every opportunity. Sometimes Mercedes sided with her husband, sometimes with her brother. The result was a beautiful and unending family quarrel. Starting from a dispute as to which should chop a few sticks for the fire (a dispute which concerned only Charles and Hal), presently would be lugged in the rest of the family, fathers, mothers, uncles, cousins, people thousands of miles away, and some of them dead. That Hal's views on art, or the sort of society plays his mother's brother wrote, should have anything to do with the chopping of a few sticks of firewood, passes

1285 comprehension; nevertheless the quarrel was as likely to tend in that direction as in the direction of Charles's political prejudices. And that Charles's sister's tale-bearing tongue should be relevant to the building of a Yukon fire, was apparent only to Mercedes, who disburdened herself of copious opinions upon that topic, and incidentally upon a few other traits unpleasantly peculiar to her husband's family. In the meantime the fire

1290 remained unbuilt, the camp half pitched, and the dogs unfed.

Mercedes nursed a special grievance—the grievance of sex. She was pretty and soft, and had been chivalrously treated all her days. But the present treatment by her husband and brother was everything save chivalrous. It was her custom to be helpless. They complained. Upon which impeachment of what to her was her most essential

1295 sex-prerogative, she made their lives unendurable. She no longer considered the dogs, and because she was sore and tired, she persisted in riding on the sled. She was pretty and soft, but she weighed one hundred and twenty pounds—a lusty last straw to the load dragged by the weak and starving animals. She rode for days, till they fell in the traces and the sled stood still. Charles and Hal begged her to get off and walk, pleaded with

1300 her, entreated, the while she wept and importuned Heaven with a recital of their brutality.

On one occasion they took her off the sled by main strength. They never did it again. She let her legs go limp like a spoiled child, and sat down on the trail. They went on their way, but she did not move. After they had travelled three miles they unloaded

1305 the sled, came back for her, and by main strength put her on the sled again.

In the excess of their own misery they were callous to the suffering of their animals. Hal's theory, which he practised on others, was that one must get hardened. He had started out preaching it to his sister and brother-in-law. Failing there, he hammered it into the dogs with a club. At the Five Fingers the dog-food gave out, and a

1310 toothless old squaw offered to trade them a few pounds of frozen horse-hide for the Colt's revolver that kept the big hunting-knife company at Hal's hip. A poor substitute for food was this hide, just as it had been stripped from the starved horses of the cattlemen six months back. In its frozen state it was more like strips of galvanized iron, and when a dog wrestled it into his stomach it thawed into thin and innutritious leathery

1315 strings and into a mass of short hair, irritating and indigestible.

And through it all Buck staggered along at the head of the team as in a nightmare. He pulled when he could; when he could no longer pull, he fell down and remained down till blows from whip or club drove him to his feet again. All the stiffness and gloss had gone out of his beautiful furry coat. The hair hung down, limp and 1320 draggled, or matted with dried blood where Hal's club had bruised him. His muscles had wasted away to knotty strings, and the flesh pads had disappeared, so that each rib and every bone in his frame were outlined cleanly through the loose hide that was wrinkled in folds of emptiness. It was heartbreaking, only Buck's heart was unbreakable. The man in the red sweater had proved that.

1325   As it was with Buck, so was it with his mates. They were perambulating skeletons. There were seven all together, including him. In their very great misery they had become insensible to the bite of the lash or the bruise of the club. The pain of the beating was dull and distant, just as the things their eyes saw and their ears heard seemed dull and distant. They were not half living, or quarter living. They were simply so many bags of 1330 bones in which sparks of life fluttered faintly. When a halt was made, they dropped down in the traces like dead dogs, and the spark dimmed and paled and seemed to go out. And when the club or whip fell upon them, the spark fluttered feebly up, and they tottered to their feet and staggered on.

There came a day when Billee, the good-natured, fell and could not rise. Hal had 1335 traded off his revolver, so he took the axe and knocked Billee on the head as he lay in the traces, then cut the carcass out of the harness and dragged it to one side. Buck saw, and his mates saw, and they knew that this thing was very close to them. On the next day Koona went, and but five of them remained: Joe, too far gone to be malignant; Pike, crippled and limping, only half conscious and not conscious enough longer to malinger; 1340 Sol-leks, the one-eyed, still faithful to the toil of trace and trail, and mournful in that he had so little strength with which to pull; Teek, who had not travelled so far that winter and who was now beaten more than the others because he was fresher; and Buck, still at the head of the team, but no longer enforcing discipline or striving to enforce it, blind with weakness half the time and keeping the trail by the loom of it and by the dim feel of 1345 his feet.

It was beautiful spring weather, but neither dogs nor humans were aware of it. Each day the sun rose earlier and set later. It was dawn by three in the morning, and twilight lingered till nine at night. The whole long day was a blaze of sunshine. The ghostly winter silence had given way to the great spring murmur of awakening life. This

1350 murmur arose from all the land, fraught with the joy of living. It came from the things that lived and moved again, things which had been as dead and which had not moved during the long months of frost. The sap was rising in the pines. The willows and aspens were bursting out in young buds. Shrubs and vines were putting on fresh garbs of green. Crickets sang in the nights, and in the days all manner of creeping, crawling things rustled

1355 forth into the sun. Partridges and woodpeckers were booming and knocking in the forest. Squirrels were chattering, birds singing, and overhead honked the wild-fowl driving up from the south in cunning wedges that split the air.

From every hill slope came the trickle of running water, the music of unseen fountains. All things were thawing, bending, snapping. The Yukon was straining to

1360 break loose the ice that bound it down. It ate away from beneath; the sun ate from above. Air-holes formed, fissures sprang and spread apart, while thin sections of ice fell through bodily into the river. And amid all this bursting, rending, throbbing of awakening life, under the blazing sun and through the soft-sighing breezes, like wayfarers to death, staggered the two men, the woman, and the huskies.

1365 With the dogs falling, Mercedes weeping and riding, Hal swearing innocuously, and Charles's eyes wistfully watering, they staggered into John Thornton's camp at the mouth of White River. When they halted, the dogs dropped down as though they had all been struck dead. Mercedes dried her eyes and looked at John Thornton. Charles sat down on a log to rest. He sat down very slowly and painstakingly what of his great

1370 stiffness. Hal did the talking. John Thornton was whittling the last touches on an axe-handle he had made from a stick of birch. He whittled and listened, gave monosyllabic replies, and, when it was asked, terse advice. He knew the breed, and he gave his advice in the certainty that it would not be followed.

"They told us up above that the bottom was dropping out of the trail and that the

1375 best thing for us to do was to lay over," Hal said in response to Thornton's warning to take no more chances on the rotten ice. "They told us we couldn't make White River, and here we are." This last with a sneering ring of triumph in it.

"And they told you true," John Thornton answered. "The bottom's likely to drop out at any moment. Only fools, with the blind luck of fools, could have made it. I tell

1380 you straight, I wouldn't risk my carcass on that ice for all the gold in Alaska."

"That's because you're not a fool, I suppose," said Hal. "All the same, we'll go on to Dawson." He uncoiled his whip. "Get up there, Buck! Hi! Get up there! Mush on!"

Thornton went on whittling. It was idle, he knew, to get between a fool and his folly; while two or three fools more or less would not alter the scheme of things.

1385   But the team did not get up at the command. It had long since passed into the stage where blows were required to rouse it. The whip flashed out, here and there, on its merciless errands. John Thornton compressed his lips. Sol-leks was the first to crawl to his feet. Teek followed. Joe came next, yelping with pain. Pike made painful efforts. Twice he fell over, when half up, and on the third attempt managed to rise. Buck made

1390   no effort. He lay quietly where he had fallen. The lash bit into him again and again, but he neither whined nor struggled. Several times Thornton started, as though to speak, but changed his mind. A moisture came into his eyes, and, as the whipping continued, he arose and walked irresolutely up and down.

This was the first time Buck had failed, in itself a sufficient reason to drive Hal

1395   into a rage. He exchanged the whip for the customary club. Buck refused to move under the rain of heavier blows which now fell upon him. Like his mates, he was barely able to get up, but, unlike them, he had made up his mind not to get up. He had a vague feeling of impending doom. This had been strong upon him when he pulled in to the bank, and it had not departed from him. What of the thin and rotten ice he had felt

1400   under his feet all day, it seemed that he sensed disaster close at hand, out there ahead on the ice where his master was trying to drive him. He refused to stir. So greatly had he suffered, and so far gone was he, that the blows did not hurt much. And as they continued to fall upon him, the spark of life within flickered and went down. It was nearly out. He felt strangely numb. As though from a great distance, he was aware that

1405   he was being beaten. The last sensations of pain left him. He no longer felt anything, though very faintly he could hear the impact of the club upon his body. But it was no longer his body, it seemed so far away.

And then, suddenly, without warning, uttering a cry that was inarticulate and more like the cry of an animal, John Thornton sprang upon the man who wielded the club.

1410   Hal was hurled backward, as though struck by a falling tree. Mercedes screamed. Charles looked on wistfully, wiped his watery eyes, but did not get up because of his stiffness.

John Thornton stood over Buck, struggling to control himself, too convulsed with rage to speak.

1415   "If you strike that dog again, I'll kill you," he at last managed to say in a choking voice.

"It's my dog," Hal replied, wiping the blood from his mouth as he came back. "Get out of my way, or I'll fix you. I'm going to Dawson."

1420 Thornton stood between him and Buck, and evinced no intention of getting out of the way. Hal drew his long hunting-knife. Mercedes screamed, cried, laughed, and manifested the chaotic abandonment of hysteria. Thornton rapped Hal's knuckles with the axe-handle, knocking the knife to the ground. He rapped his knuckles again as he tried to pick it up. Then he stooped, picked it up himself, and with two strokes cut Buck's traces.

1425 Hal had no fight left in him. Besides, his hands were full with his sister, or his arms, rather; while Buck was too near dead to be of further use in hauling the sled. A few minutes later they pulled out from the bank and down the river. Buck heard them go and raised his head to see. Pike was leading, Sol-leks was at the wheel, and between were Joe and Teek. They were limping and staggering. Mercedes was riding the loaded
1430 sled. Hal guided at the gee-pole, and Charles stumbled along in the rear.

As Buck watched them, Thornton knelt beside him and with rough, kindly hands searched for broken bones. By the time his search had disclosed nothing more than many bruises and a state of terrible starvation, the sled was a quarter of a mile away. Dog and man watched it crawling along over the ice. Suddenly, they saw its back end
1435 drop down, as into a rut, and the gee-pole, with Hal clinging to it, jerk into the air. Mercedes's scream came to their ears. They saw Charles turn and make one step to run back, and then a whole section of ice give way and dogs and humans disappear. A yawning hole was all that was to be seen. The bottom had dropped out of the trail.

John Thornton and Buck looked at each other.

1440 "You poor devil," said John Thornton, and Buck licked his hand.

CHAPTER SIX

For the Love of a Man

WHEN JOHN THORNTON froze his feet in the previous December, his partners had made him comfortable and left him to get well, going on themselves up the river to get out a raft of saw-logs for Dawson. He was still limping slightly at the time he rescued Buck, but with the continued warm weather even the slight limp left him. And here, lying by the river bank through the long spring days, watching the running water, listening lazily to the songs of birds and the hum of nature, Buck slowly won back his strength.

A rest comes very good after one has travelled three thousand miles, and it must be confessed that Buck waxed lazy as his wounds healed, his muscles swelled out, and the flesh came back to cover his bones. For that matter, they were all loafing,—Buck, John Thornton, and Skeet and Nig,—waiting for the raft to come that was to carry them down to Dawson. Skeet was a little Irish setter who early made friends with Buck, who, in a dying condition, was unable to resent her first advances. She had the doctor trait which some dogs possess; and as a mother cat washes her kittens, so she washed and cleansed Buck's wounds. Regularly, each morning after he had finished his breakfast, she performed her self-appointed task, till he came to look for her ministrations as much as he did for Thornton's. Nig, equally friendly, though less demonstrative, was a huge black dog, half bloodhound and half deerhound, with eyes that laughed and a boundless good nature.

To Buck's surprise these dogs manifested no jealousy toward him. They seemed
1460 to share the kindliness and largeness of John Thornton. As Buck grew stronger they
enticed him into all sorts of ridiculous games, in which Thornton himself could not
forbear to join; and in this fashion Buck romped through his convalescence and into a
new existence. Love, genuine passionate love, was his for the first time. This he had
never experienced at Judge Miller's down in the sun-kissed Santa Clara Valley. With the
1465 Judge's sons, hunting and tramping, it had been a working partnership; with the Judge's
grandsons, a sort of pompous guardianship; and with the Judge himself, a stately and
dignified friendship. But love that was feverish and burning, that was adoration, that was
madness, it had taken John Thornton to arouse.

This man had saved his life, which was something; but, further, he was the ideal
1470 master. Other men saw to the welfare of their dogs from a sense of duty and business
expediency; he saw to the welfare of his as if they were his own children, because he
could not help it. And he saw further. He never forgot a kindly greeting or a cheering
word, and to sit down for a long talk with them ("gas" he called it) was as much his
delight as theirs. He had a way of taking Buck's head roughly between his hands, and
1475 resting his own head upon Buck's, of shaking him back and forth, the while calling him ill
names that to Buck were love names. Buck knew no greater joy than that rough
embrace and the sound of murmured oaths, and at each jerk back and forth it seemed
that his heart would be shaken out of his body so great was its ecstasy. And when,
released, he sprang to his feet, his mouth laughing, his eyes eloquent, his throat vibrant
1480 with unuttered sound, and in that fashion remained without movement, John Thornton
would reverently exclaim, "God! you can all but speak!"

Buck had a trick of love expression that was akin to hurt. He would often seize
Thornton's hand in his mouth and close so fiercely that the flesh bore the impress of his
teeth for some time afterward. And as Buck understood the oaths to be love words, so
1485 the man understood this feigned bite for a caress.

For the most part, however, Buck's love was expressed in adoration. While he
went wild with happiness when Thornton touched him or spoke to him, he did not seek
these tokens. Unlike Skeet, who was wont to shove her nose under Thornton's hand and
nudge and nudge till petted, or Nig, who would stalk up and rest his great head on
1490 Thornton's knee, Buck was content to adore at a distance. He would lie by the hour,
eager, alert, at Thornton's feet, looking up into his face, dwelling upon it, studying it,

following with keenest interest each fleeting expression, every movement or change of feature. Or, as chance might have it, he would lie farther away, to the side or rear, watching the outlines of the man and the occasional movements of his body. And often, such was the communion in which they lived, the strength of Buck's gaze would draw John Thornton's head around, and he would return the gaze, without speech, his heart shining out of his eyes as Buck's heart shone out.

For a long time after his rescue, Buck did not like Thornton to get out of his sight. From the moment he left the tent to when he entered it again, Buck would follow at his heels. His transient masters since he had come into the Northland had bred in him a fear that no master could be permanent. He was afraid that Thornton would pass out of his life as Perrault and François and the Scotch half-breed had passed out. Even in the night, in his dreams, he was haunted by this fear. At such times he would shake off sleep and creep through the chill to the flap of the tent, where he would stand and listen to the sound of his master's breathing.

But in spite of this great love he bore John Thornton, which seemed to bespeak the soft civilizing influence, the strain of the primitive, which the Northland had aroused in him, remained alive and active. Faithfulness and devotion, things born of fire and roof, were his; yet he retained his wildness and wiliness. He was a thing of the wild, come in from the wild to sit by John Thornton's fire, rather than a dog of the soft Southland stamped with the marks of generations of civilization. Because of his very great love, he could not steal from this man, but from any other man, in any other camp, he did not hesitate an instant; while the cunning with which he stole enabled him to escape detection.

His face and body were scored by the teeth of many dogs, and he fought as fiercely as ever and more shrewdly. Skeet and Nig were too good-natured for quarrelling,—besides, they belonged to John Thornton; but the strange dog, no matter what the breed or valor, swiftly acknowledged Buck's supremacy or found himself struggling for life with a terrible antagonist. And Buck was merciless. He had learned well the law of club and fang, and he never forewent an advantage or drew back from a foe he had started on the way to Death. He had lessoned from Spitz, and from the chief fighting dogs of the police and mail, and knew there was no middle course. He must master or be mastered; while to show mercy was a weakness. Mercy did not exist in the primordial life. It was misunderstood for fear, and such misunderstandings made for

1525   death. Kill or be killed, eat or be eaten, was the law; and this mandate, down out of the depths of Time, he obeyed.

    He was older than the days he had seen and the breaths he had drawn. He linked the past with the present, and the eternity behind him throbbed through him in a mighty rhythm to which he swayed as the tides and seasons swayed. He sat by John Thornton's

1530   fire, a broad-breasted dog, white-fanged and long-furred; but behind him were the shades of all manner of dogs, half-wolves and wild wolves, urgent and prompting, tasting the savor of the meat he ate, thirsting for the water he drank, scenting the wind with him, listening with him and telling him the sounds made by the wild life in the forest, dictating his moods, directing his actions, lying down to sleep with him when he lay down, and

1535   dreaming with him and beyond him and becoming themselves the stuff of his dreams.

    So peremptorily did these shades beckon him, that each day mankind and the claims of mankind slipped farther from him. Deep in the forest a call was sounding, and as often as he heard this call, mysteriously thrilling and luring, he felt compelled to turn his back upon the fire and the beaten earth around it, and to plunge into the forest, and

1540   on and on, he knew not where or why; nor did he wonder where or why, the call sounding imperiously, deep in the forest. But as often as he gained the soft unbroken earth and the green shade, the love for John Thornton drew him back to the fire again.

    Thornton alone held him. The rest of mankind was as nothing. Chance travellers might praise or pet him; but he was cold under it all, and from a too demonstrative man

1545   he would get up and walk away. When Thornton's partners, Hans and Pete, arrived on the long-expected raft, Buck refused to notice them till he learned they were close to Thornton; after that he tolerated them in a passive sort of way, accepting favors from them as though he favored them by accepting. They were of the same large type as Thornton, living close to the earth, thinking simply and seeing clearly; and ere they swung

1550   the raft into the big eddy by the saw-mill at Dawson, they understood Buck and his ways, and did not insist upon an intimacy such as obtained with Skeet and Nig.

    For Thornton, however, his love seemed to grow and grow. He, alone among men, could put a pack upon Buck's back in the summer travelling. Nothing was too great for Buck to do, when Thornton commanded. One day (they had grub-staked

1555   themselves from the proceeds of the raft and left Dawson for the head-waters of the Tanana) the men and dogs were sitting on the crest of a cliff which fell away, straight down, to naked bed-rock three hundred feet below. John Thornton was sitting near the

edge, Buck at his shoulder. A thoughtless whim seized Thornton, and he drew the attention of Hans and Pete to the experiment he had in mind. "Jump, Buck!" he
1560 commanded, sweeping his arm out and over the chasm. The next instant he was grappling with Buck on the extreme edge, while Hans and Pete were dragging them back into safety.

"It's uncanny," Pete said, after it was over and they had caught their speech.

Thornton shook his head. "No, it is splendid, and it is terrible, too. Do you know,
1565 it sometimes makes me afraid."

"I'm not hankering to be the man that lays hands on you while he's around," Pete announced conclusively, nodding his head toward Buck.

"Py Jingo!" was Hans's contribution. "Not mineself either."

It was at Circle City, ere the year was out, that Pete's apprehensions were
1570 realized. "Black" Burton, a man evil-tempered and malicious, had been picking a quarrel with a tenderfoot at the bar, when Thornton stepped good-naturedly between. Buck, as was his custom, was lying in a corner, head on paws, watching his master's every action. Burton struck out, without warning, straight from the shoulder. Thornton was sent spinning, and saved himself from falling only by clutching the rail of the bar.

1575 Those who were looking on heard what was neither bark nor yelp, but a something which is best described as a roar, and they saw Buck's body rise up in the air as he left the floor for Burton's throat. The man saved his life by instinctively throwing out his arm, but was hurled backward to the floor with Buck on top of him. Buck loosed his teeth from the flesh of the arm and drove in again for the throat. This time the man
1580 succeeded only in partly blocking, and his throat was torn open. Then the crowd was upon Buck, and he was driven off; but while a surgeon checked the bleeding, he prowled up and down, growling furiously, attempting to rush in, and being forced back by an array of hostile clubs. A "miners' meeting," called on the spot, decided that the dog had sufficient provocation, and Buck was discharged. But his reputation was made, and from
1585 that day his name spread through every camp in Alaska.

Later on, in the fall of the year, he saved John Thornton's life in quite another fashion. The three partners were lining a long and narrow poling-boat down a bad stretch of rapids on the Forty-Mile Creek. Hans and Pete moved along the bank, snubbing with a thin Manila rope from tree to tree, while Thornton remained in the boat,
1590 helping its descent by means of a pole, and shouting directions to the shore. Buck, on the bank, worried and anxious, kept abreast of the boat, his eyes never off his master.

At a particularly bad spot, where a ledge of barely submerged rocks jutted out into the river, Hans cast off the rope, and, while Thornton poled the boat out into the stream, ran down the bank with the end in his hand to snub the boat when it had cleared

1595 the ledge. This it did, and was flying down-stream in a current as swift as a mill-race, when Hans checked it with the rope and checked too suddenly. The boat flirted over and snubbed in to the bank bottom up, while Thornton, flung sheer out of it, was carried down-stream toward the worst part of the rapids, a stretch of wild water in which no swimmer could live.

1600 Buck had sprung in on the instant; and at the end of three hundred yards, amid a mad swirl of water, he overhauled Thornton. When he felt him grasp his tail, Buck headed for the bank, swimming with all his splendid strength. But the progress shoreward was slow; the progress down-stream amazingly rapid. From below came the fatal roaring where the wild current went wilder and was rent in shreds and spray by the

1605 rocks which thrust through like the teeth of an enormous comb. The suck of the water as it took the beginning of the last steep pitch was frightful, and Thornton knew that the shore was impossible. He scraped furiously over a rock, bruised across a second, and struck a third with crushing force. He clutched its slippery top with both hands, releasing Buck, and above the roar of the churning water shouted: "Go, Buck! Go!"

1610 Buck could not hold his own, and swept on down-stream, struggling desperately, but unable to win back. When he heard Thornton's command repeated, he partly reared out of the water, throwing his head high, as though for a last look, then turned obediently toward the bank. He swam powerfully and was dragged ashore by Pete and Hans at the very point where swimming ceased to be possible and destruction began.

1615 They knew that the time a man could cling to a slippery rock in the face of that driving current was a matter of minutes, and they ran as fast as they could up the bank to a point far above where Thornton was hanging on. They attached the line with which they had been snubbing the boat to Buck's neck and shoulders, being careful that it should neither strangle him nor impede his swimming, and launched him into the stream.

1620 He struck out boldly, but not straight enough into the stream. He discovered the mistake too late, when Thornton was abreast of him and a bare half-dozen strokes away while he was being carried helplessly past.

Hans promptly snubbed with the rope, as though Buck were a boat. The rope thus tightening on him in the sweep of the current, he was jerked under the surface, and

1625 under the surface he remained till his body struck against the bank and he was hauled out. He was half drowned, and Hans and Pete threw themselves upon him, pounding the breath into him and the water out of him. He staggered to his feet and fell down. The faint sound of Thornton's voice came to them, and though they could not make out the words of it, they knew that he was in his extremity. His master's voice acted on Buck like an electric shock. He sprang to his feet and ran up the bank ahead of the men to the point of his previous departure.

Again the rope was attached and he was launched, and again he struck out, but this time straight into the stream. He had miscalculated once, but he would not be guilty of it a second time. Hans paid out the rope, permitting no slack, while Pete kept it clear of coils. Buck held on till he was on a line straight above Thornton; then he turned, and with the speed of an express train headed down upon him. Thornton saw him coming, and, as Buck struck him like a battering ram, with the whole force of the current behind him, he reached up and closed with both arms around the shaggy neck. Hans snubbed the rope around the tree, and Buck and Thornton were jerked under the water. Strangling, suffocating, sometimes one uppermost and sometimes the other, dragging over the jagged bottom, smashing against rocks and snags, they veered in to the bank.

Thornton came to, belly downward and being violently propelled back and forth across a drift log by Hans and Pete. His first glance was for Buck, over whose limp and apparently lifeless body Nig was setting up a howl, while Skeet was licking the wet face and closed eyes. Thornton was himself bruised and battered, and he went carefully over Buck's body, when he had been brought around, finding three broken ribs.

"That settles it," he announced. "We camp right here." And camp they did, till Buck's ribs knitted and he was able to travel.

That winter, at Dawson, Buck performed another exploit, not so heroic, perhaps, but one that put his name many notches higher on the totem-pole of Alaskan fame. This exploit was particularly gratifying to the three men; for they stood in need of the outfit which it furnished, and were enabled to make a long-desired trip into the virgin East, where miners had not yet appeared. It was brought about by a conversation in the Eldorado Saloon, in which men waxed boastful of their favorite dogs. Buck, because of his record, was the target for these men, and Thornton was driven stoutly to defend him. At the end of half an hour one man stated that his dog could start a sled with five hundred pounds and walk off with it; a second bragged six hundred for his dog; and a third, seven hundred.

"Pooh! pooh!" said John Thornton; "Buck can start a thousand pounds."

1660   "And break it out? and walk off with it for a hundred yards?" demanded Matthewson, a Bonanza King, he of the seven hundred vaunt.

"And break it out, and walk off with it for a hundred yards," John Thornton said coolly.

"Well," Matthewson said, slowly and deliberately, so that all could hear, "I've got a

1665   thousand dollars that says he can't. And there it is." So saying, he slammed a sack of gold dust of the size of a bologna sausage down upon the bar.

Nobody spoke. Thornton's bluff, if bluff it was, had been called. He could feel a flush of warm blood creeping up his face. His tongue had tricked him. He did not know whether Buck could start a thousand pounds. Half a ton! The enormousness of it

1670   appalled him. He had great faith in Buck's strength and had often thought him capable of starting such a load; but never, as now, had he faced the possibility of it, the eyes of a dozen men fixed upon him, silent and waiting. Further, he had no thousand dollars; nor had Hans or Pete.

"I've got a sled standing outside now, with twenty fifty-pound sacks of flour on it,"

1675   Matthewson went on with brutal directness; "so don't let that hinder you."

Thornton did not reply. He did not know what to say. He glanced from face to face in the absent way of a man who has lost the power of thought and is seeking somewhere to find the thing that will start it going again. The face of Jim O'Brien, a Mastodon King and old-time comrade, caught his eyes. It was as a cue to him, seeming

1680   to rouse him to do what he would never have dreamed of doing.

"Can you lend me a thousand?" he asked, almost in a whisper.

"Sure," answered O'Brien, thumping down a plethoric sack by the side of Matthewson's. "Though it's little faith I'm having, John, that the beast can do the trick."

The Eldorado emptied its occupants into the street to see the test. The tables

1685   were deserted, and the dealers and gamekeepers came forth to see the outcome of the wager and to lay odds. Several hundred men, furred and mittened, banked around the sled within easy distance. Matthewson's sled, loaded with a thousand pounds of flour, had been standing for a couple of hours, and in the intense cold (it was sixty below zero) the runners had frozen fast to the hard-packed snow. Men offered odds of two to one

1690   that Buck could not budge the sled. A quibble arose concerning the phrase "break out." O'Brien contended it was Thornton's privilege to knock the runners loose, leaving Buck

to "break it out" from a dead standstill. Matthewson insisted that the phrase included breaking the runners from the frozen grip of the snow. A majority of the men who had witnessed the making of the bet decided in his favor, whereat the odds went up to three
1695 to one against Buck.

There were no takers. Not a man believed him capable of the feat. Thornton had been hurried into the wager, heavy with doubt; and now that he looked at the sled itself, the concrete fact, with the regular team of ten dogs curled up in the snow before it, the more impossible the task appeared. Matthewson waxed jubilant.

1700 "Three to one!" he proclaimed. "I'll lay you another thousand at that figure, Thornton. What d'ye say?"

Thornton's doubt was strong in his face, but his fighting spirit was aroused—the fighting spirit that soars above odds, fails to recognize the impossible, and is deaf to all save the clamor for battle. He called Hans and Pete to him. Their sacks were slim, and
1705 with his own the three partners could rake together only two hundred dollars. In the ebb of their fortunes, this sum was their total capital; yet they laid it unhesitatingly against Matthewson's six hundred.

The team of ten dogs was unhitched, and Buck, with his own harness, was put into the sled. He had caught the contagion of the excitement, and he felt that in some way
1710 he must do a great thing for John Thornton. Murmurs of admiration at his splendid appearance went up. He was in perfect condition, without an ounce of superfluous flesh, and the one hundred and fifty pounds that he weighed were so many pounds of grit and virility. His furry coat shone with the sheen of silk. Down the neck and across the shoulders, his mane, in repose as it was, half bristled and seemed to lift with every
1715 movement, as though excess of vigor made each particular hair alive and active. The great breast and heavy fore legs were no more than in proportion with the rest of the body, where the muscles showed in tight rolls underneath the skin. Men felt these muscles and proclaimed them hard as iron, and the odds went down to two to one.

"Gad, sir! Gad, sir!" stuttered a member of the latest dynasty, a king of the
1720 Skookum Benches. "I offer you eight hundred for him, sir, before the test, sir; eight hundred just as he stands."

Thornton shook his head and stepped to Buck's side.

"You must stand off from him," Matthewson protested. "Free play and plenty of room."

1725   The crowd fell silent; only could be heard the voices of the gamblers vainly offering two to one. Everybody acknowledged Buck a magnificent animal, but twenty fifty-pound sacks of flour bulked too large in their eyes for them to loosen their pouch-strings.

       Thornton knelt down by Buck's side. He took his head in his two hands and
1730   rested cheek on cheek. He did not playfully shake him, as was his wont, or murmur soft love curses; but he whispered in his ear. "As you love me, Buck. As you love me," was what he whispered. Buck whined with suppressed eagerness.

       The crowd was watching curiously. The affair was growing mysterious. It seemed like a conjuration. As Thornton got to his feet, Buck seized his mittened hand between
1735   his jaws, pressing in with his teeth and releasing slowly, half-reluctantly. It was the answer, in terms, not of speech, but of love. Thornton stepped well back.

       "Now, Buck," he said.

       Buck tightened the traces, then slacked them for a matter of several inches. It was the way he had learned.

1740   "Gee!" Thornton's voice rang out, sharp in the tense silence.

       Buck swung to the right, ending the movement in a plunge that took up the slack and with a sudden jerk arrested his one hundred and fifty pounds. The load quivered, and from under the runners arose a crisp crackling.

       "Haw!" Thornton commanded.

1745   Buck duplicated the manœuvre, this time to the left. The crackling turned into a snapping, the sled pivoting and the runners slipping and grating several inches to the side. The sled was broken out. Men were holding their breaths, intensely unconscious of the fact.

       "Now, MUSH!"

1750   Thornton's command cracked out like a pistol-shot. Buck threw himself forward, tightening the traces with a jarring lunge. His whole body was gathered compactly together in the tremendous effort, the muscles writhing and knotting like live things under the silky fur. His great chest was low to the ground, his head forward and down, while his feet were flying like mad, the claws scarring the hard-packed snow in parallel
1755   grooves. The sled swayed and trembled, half-started forward. One of his feet slipped, and one man groaned aloud. Then the sled lurched ahead in what appeared a rapid succession of jerks, though it never really came to a dead stop again . . . half

an inch . . . an inch . . . two inches. . . . The jerks perceptibly diminished; as the sled gained momentum, he caught them up, till it was moving steadily along.

1760   Men gasped and began to breathe again, unaware that for a moment they had ceased to breathe. Thornton was running behind, encouraging Buck with short, cheery words. The distance had been measured off, and as he neared the pile of firewood which marked the end of the hundred yards, a cheer began to grow and grow, which burst into a roar as he passed the firewood and halted at command. Every man was

1765 tearing himself loose, even Matthewson. Hats and mittens were flying in the air. Men were shaking hands, it did not matter with whom, and bubbling over in a general incoherent babel.

    But Thornton fell on his knees beside Buck. Head was against head, and he was shaking him back and forth. Those who hurried up heard him cursing Buck, and he

1770 cursed him long and fervently, and softly and lovingly.

    "Gad, sir! Gad, sir!" spluttered the Skookum Bench king. "I'll give you a thousand for him, sir, a thousand, sir—twelve hundred, sir."

    Thornton rose to his feet. His eyes were wet. The tears were streaming frankly down his cheeks. "Sir," he said to the Skookum Bench king, "no, sir. You can go to hell,

1775 sir. It's the best I can do for you, sir."

    Buck seized Thornton's hand in his teeth. Thornton shook him back and forth. As though animated by a common impulse, the onlookers drew back to a respectful distance; nor were they again indiscreet enough to interrupt.

CHAPTER SEVEN

The Sounding of the Call

WHEN BUCK EARNED sixteen hundred dollars in five minutes for John Thornton, he
1780 made it possible for his master to pay off certain debts and to journey with his partners
into the East after a fabled lost mine, the history of which was as old as the history of the
country. Many men had sought it; few had found it; and more than a few there were
who had never returned from the quest. This lost mine was steeped in tragedy and
shrouded in mystery. No one knew of the first man. The oldest tradition stopped before
1785 it got back to him. From the beginning there had been an ancient and ramshackle cabin.
Dying men had sworn to it, and to the mine the site of which it marked, clinching their
testimony with nuggets that were unlike any known grade of gold in the Northland.

But no living man had looted this treasure house, and the dead were dead;
wherefore John Thornton and Pete and Hans, with Buck and half a dozen other dogs,
1790 faced into the East on an unknown trail to achieve where men and dogs as good as
themselves had failed. They sledded seventy miles up the Yukon, swung to the left into
the Stewart River, passed the Mayo and the McQuestion, and held on until the Stewart
itself became a streamlet, threading the upstanding peaks which marked the backbone of
the continent.

1795 John Thornton asked little of man or nature. He was unafraid of the wild. With
a handful of salt and a rifle he could plunge into the wilderness and fare wherever he

61

pleased and as long as he pleased. Being in no haste, Indian fashion, he hunted his dinner in the course of the day's travel; and if he failed to find it, like the Indian, he kept on travelling, secure in the knowledge that sooner or later he would come to it. So, on this great journey into the East, straight meat was the bill of fare, ammunition and tools principally made up the load on the sled, and the time-card was drawn upon the limitless future.

To Buck it was boundless delight, this hunting, fishing, and indefinite wandering through strange places. For weeks at a time they would hold on steadily, day after day; and for weeks upon end they would camp, here and there, the dogs loafing and the men burning holes through frozen muck and gravel and washing countless pans of dirt by the heat of the fire. Sometimes they went hungry, sometimes they feasted riotously, all according to the abundance of game and the fortune of hunting. Summer arrived, and dogs and men packed on their backs, rafted across blue mountain lakes, and descended or ascended unknown rivers in slender boats whipsawed from the standing forest.

The months came and went, and back and forth they twisted through the uncharted vastness, where no men were and yet where men had been if the Lost Cabin were true. They went across divides in summer blizzards, shivered under the midnight sun on naked mountains between the timber line and the eternal snows, dropped into summer valleys amid swarming gnats and flies, and in the shadows of glaciers picked strawberries and flowers as ripe and fair as any the Southland could boast. In the fall of the year they penetrated a weird lake country, sad and silent, where wild-fowl had been, but where then there was no life nor sign of life—only the blowing of chill winds, the forming of ice in sheltered places, and the melancholy rippling of waves on lonely beaches.

And through another winter they wandered on the obliterated trails of men who had gone before. Once, they came upon a path blazed through the forest, an ancient path, and the Lost Cabin seemed very near. But the path began nowhere and ended nowhere, and it remained mystery, as the man who made it and the reason he made it remained mystery. Another time they chanced upon the time-graven wreckage of a hunting lodge, and amid the shreds of rotted blankets John Thornton found a long-barrelled flint-lock. He knew it for a Hudson Bay Company gun of the young days in the Northwest, when such a gun was worth its height in beaver skins packed flat. And that was all—no hint as to the man who in an early day had reared the lodge and left the gun among the blankets.

Spring came on once more, and at the end of all their wandering they found, not the Lost Cabin, but a shallow placer in a broad valley where the gold showed like yellow butter across the bottom of the washing-pan. They sought no farther. Each day they worked earned them thousands of dollars in clean dust and nuggets, and they worked 1835 every day. The gold was sacked in moose-hide bags, fifty pounds to the bag, and piled like so much firewood outside the spruce-bough lodge. Like giants they toiled, days flashing on the heels of days like dreams as they heaped the treasure up.

There was nothing for the dogs to do, save the hauling in of meat now and again that Thornton killed, and Buck spent long hours musing by the fire. The vision of the 1840 short-legged hairy man came to him more frequently, now that there was little work to be done; and often, blinking by the fire, Buck wandered with him in that other world which he remembered.

The salient thing of this other world seemed fear. When he watched the hairy man sleeping by the fire, head between his knees and hands clasped above, Buck saw 1845 that he slept restlessly, with many starts and awakenings, at which times he would peer fearfully into the darkness and fling more wood upon the fire. Did they walk by the beach of a sea, where the hairy man gathered shell-fish and ate them as he gathered, it was with eyes that roved everywhere for hidden danger and with legs prepared to run like the wind at its first appearance. Through the forest they crept noiselessly, Buck at 1850 the hairy man's heels; and they were alert and vigilant, the pair of them, ears twitching and moving and nostrils quivering, for the man heard and smelled as keenly as Buck. The hairy man could spring up into the trees and travel ahead as fast as on the ground, swinging by the arms from limb to limb, sometimes a dozen feet apart, letting go and catching, never falling, never missing his grip. In fact, he seemed as much at home 1855 among the trees as on the ground; and Buck had memories of nights of vigil spent beneath trees wherein the hairy man roosted, holding on tightly as he slept.

And closely akin to the visions of the hairy man was the call still sounding in the depths of the forest. It filled him with a great unrest and strange desires. It caused him to feel a vague, sweet gladness, and he was aware of wild yearnings and stirrings for he 1860 knew not what. Sometimes he pursued the call into the forest, looking for it as though it were a tangible thing, barking softly or defiantly, as the mood might dictate. He would thrust his nose into the cool wood moss, or into the black soil where long grasses grew, and snort with joy at the fat earth smells; or he would crouch for hours, as if in concealment, behind fungus-covered trunks of fallen trees, wide-eyed and wide-eared to

1865 all that moved and sounded about him. It might be, lying thus, that he hoped to surprise this call he could not understand. But he did not know why he did these various things. He was impelled to do them, and did not reason about them at all.

Irresistible impulses seized him. He would be lying in camp, dozing lazily in the heat of the day, when suddenly his head would lift and his ears cock up, intent and 1870 listening, and he would spring to his feet and dash away, and on and on, for hours, through the forest aisles and across the open spaces where the niggerheads bunched. He loved to run down dry watercourses, and to creep and spy upon the bird life in the woods. For a day at a time he would lie in the underbrush where he could watch the partridges drumming and strutting up and down. But especially he loved to run in the 1875 dim twilight of the summer midnights, listening to the subdued and sleepy murmurs of the forest, reading signs and sounds as man may read a book, and seeking for the mysterious something that called—called, waking or sleeping, at all times, for him to come.

One night he sprang from sleep with a start, eager-eyed, nostrils quivering and 1880 scenting, his mane bristling in recurrent waves. From the forest came the call (or one note of it, for the call was many noted), distinct and definite as never before,—a long-drawn howl, like, yet unlike, any noise made by husky dog. And he knew it, in the old familiar way, as a sound heard before. He sprang through the sleeping camp and in swift silence dashed through the woods. As he drew closer to the cry he went more 1885 slowly, with caution in every movement, till he came to an open place among the trees, and looking out saw, erect on haunches, with nose pointed to the sky, a long, lean, timber wolf.

He had made no noise, yet it ceased from its howling and tried to sense his presence. Buck stalked into the open, half crouching, body gathered compactly together, 1890 tail straight and stiff, feet falling with unwonted care. Every movement advertised commingled threatening and overture of friendliness. It was the menacing truce that marks the meeting of wild beasts that prey. But the wolf fled at sight of him. He followed, with wild leapings, in a frenzy to overtake. He ran him into a blind channel, in the bed of the creek, where a timber jam barred the way. The wolf whirled about, 1895 pivoting on his hind legs after the fashion of Joe and of all cornered husky dogs, snarling and bristling, clipping his teeth together in a continuous and rapid succession of snaps.

Buck did not attack, but circled him about and hedged him in with friendly advances. The wolf was suspicious and afraid; for Buck made three of him in weight, while his head barely reached Buck's shoulder. Watching his chance, he darted away, and the chase was resumed. Time and again he was cornered, and the thing repeated, though he was in poor condition, or Buck could not so easily have overtaken him. He would run till Buck's head was even with his flank, when he would whirl around at bay, only to dash away again at the first opportunity.

But in the end Buck's pertinacity was rewarded; for the wolf, finding that no harm was intended, finally sniffed noses with him. Then they became friendly, and played about in the nervous, half-coy way with which fierce beasts belie their fierceness. After some time of this the wolf started off at an easy lope in a manner that plainly showed he was going somewhere. He made it clear to Buck that he was to come, and they ran side by side through the sombre twilight, straight up the creek bed, into the gorge from which it issued, and across the bleak divide where it took its rise.

On the opposite slope of the watershed they came down into a level country where were great stretches of forest and many streams, and through these great stretches they ran steadily, hour after hour, the sun rising higher and the day growing warmer. Buck was wildly glad. He knew he was at last answering the call, running by the side of his wood brother toward the place from where the call surely came. Old memories were coming upon him fast, and he was stirring to them as of old he stirred to the realities of which they were the shadows. He had done this thing before, somewhere in that other and dimly remembered world, and he was doing it again, now, running free in the open, the unpacked earth underfoot, the wide sky overhead.

They stopped by a running stream to drink, and, stopping, Buck remembered John Thornton. He sat down. The wolf started on toward the place from where the call surely came, then returned to him, sniffing noses and making actions as though to encourage him. But Buck turned about and started slowly on the back track. For the better part of an hour the wild brother ran by his side, whining softly. Then he sat down, pointed his nose upward, and howled. It was a mournful howl, and as Buck held steadily on his way he heard it grow faint and fainter until it was lost in the distance.

John Thornton was eating dinner when Buck dashed into camp and sprang upon him in a frenzy of affection, overturning him, scrambling upon him, licking his face, biting his hand—"playing the general tom-fool," as John Thornton characterized it, the while he shook Buck back and forth and cursed him lovingly.

For two days and nights Buck never left camp, never let Thornton out of his sight. He followed him about at his work, watched him while he ate, saw him into his blankets at night and out of them in the morning. But after two days the call in the forest began to sound more imperiously than ever. Buck's restlessness came back on him, and he was haunted by recollections of the wild brother, and of the smiling land beyond the divide and the run side by side through the wide forest stretches. Once again he took to wandering in the woods, but the wild brother came no more; and though he listened through long vigils, the mournful howl was never raised.

He began to sleep out at night, staying away from the camp for days at a time; and once he crossed the divide at the head of the creek and went down into the land of timber and streams. There he wandered for a week, seeking vainly for fresh sign of the wild brother, killing his meat as he travelled and travelling with the long, easy lope that seems never to tire. He fished for salmon in a broad stream that emptied somewhere into the sea, and by this stream he killed a large black bear, blinded by the mosquitoes while likewise fishing, and raging through the forest helpless and terrible. Even so, it was a hard fight, and it aroused the last latent remnants of Buck's ferocity. And two days later, when he returned to his kill and found a dozen wolverines quarrelling over the spoil, he scattered them like chaff; and those that fled left two behind who would quarrel no more.

The blood-longing became stronger than ever before. He was a killer, a thing that preyed, living on the things that lived, unaided, alone, by virtue of his own strength and prowess, surviving triumphantly in a hostile environment where only the strong survived. Because of all this he became possessed of a great pride in himself, which communicated itself like a contagion to his physical being. It advertised itself in all his movements, was apparent in the play of every muscle, spoke plainly as speech in the way he carried himself, and made his glorious furry coat if anything more glorious. But for the stray brown on his muzzle and above his eyes, and for the splash of white hair that ran midmost down his chest, he might well have been mistaken for a gigantic wolf, larger than the largest of the breed. From his St. Bernard father he had inherited size and weight, but it was his shepherd mother who had given shape to that size and weight. His muzzle was the long wolf muzzle, save that it was larger than the muzzle of any wolf; and his head, somewhat broader, was the wolf head on a massive scale.

His cunning was wolf cunning, and wild cunning; his intelligence, shepherd intelligence and St. Bernard intelligence; and all this, plus an experience gained in the

1965 fiercest of schools, made him as formidable a creature as any that roamed the wild. A carnivorous animal, living on a straight meat diet, he was in full flower, at the high tide of his life, overspilling with vigor and virility. When Thornton passed a caressing hand along his back, a snapping and crackling followed the hand, each hair discharging its pent magnetism at the contact. Every part, brain and body, nerve tissue and fibre, was keyed

1970 to the most exquisite pitch; and between all the parts there was a perfect equilibrium or adjustment. To sights and sounds and events which required action, he responded with lightning-like rapidity. Quickly as a husky dog could leap to defend from attack or to attack, he could leap twice as quickly. He saw the movement, or heard sound, and responded in less time than another dog required to compass the mere seeing or hearing.

1975 He perceived and determined and responded in the same instant. In point of fact the three actions of perceiving, determining, and responding were sequential; but so infinitesimal were the intervals of time between them that they appeared simultaneous. His muscles were surcharged with vitality, and snapped into play sharply, like steel springs. Life streamed through him in splendid flood, glad and rampant, until it seemed

1980 that it would burst him asunder in sheer ecstasy and pour forth generously over the world.

"Never was there such a dog," said John Thornton one day, as the partners watched Buck marching out of camp.

"When he was made, the mould was broke," said Pete.

1985 "Py jingo! I t'ink so mineself," Hans affirmed.

They saw him marching out of camp, but they did not see the instant and terrible transformation which took place as soon as he was within the secrecy of the forest. He no longer marched. At once he became a thing of the wild, stealing along softly, cat-footed, a passing shadow that appeared and disappeared among the shadows. He

1990 knew how to take advantage of every cover, to crawl on his belly like a snake, and like a snake to leap and strike. He could take a ptarmigan from its nest, kill a rabbit as it slept, and snap in mid air the little chipmunks fleeing a second too late for the trees. Fish, in open pools, were not too quick for him; nor were beaver, mending their dams, too wary. He killed to eat, not from wantonness; but he preferred to eat what he killed

1995 himself. So a lurking humor ran through his deeds, and it was his delight to steal upon the squirrels, and, when he all but had them, to let them go, chattering in mortal fear to the tree-tops.

As the fall of the year came on, the moose appeared in greater abundance, moving slowly down to meet the winter in the lower and less rigorous valleys. Buck had already dragged down a stray part-grown calf; but he wished strongly for larger and more formidable quarry, and he came upon it one day on the divide at the head of the creek. A band of twenty moose had crossed over from the land of streams and timber, and chief among them was a great bull. He was in a savage temper, and, standing over six feet from the ground, was as formidable an antagonist as even Buck could desire. Back and forth the bull tossed his great palmated antlers, branching to fourteen points and embracing seven feet within the tips. His small eyes burned with a vicious and bitter light, while he roared with fury at sight of Buck.

From the bull's side, just forward of the flank, protruded a feathered arrow-end, which accounted for his savageness. Guided by that instinct which came from the old hunting days of the primordial world, Buck proceeded to cut the bull out from the herd. It was no slight task. He would bark and dance about in front of the bull, just out of reach of the great antlers and of the terrible splay hoofs which could have stamped his life out with a single blow. Unable to turn his back on the fanged danger and go on, the bull would be driven into paroxysms of rage. At such moments he charged Buck, who retreated craftily, luring him on by a simulated inability to escape. But when he was thus separated from his fellows, two or three of the younger bulls would charge back upon Buck and enable the wounded bull to rejoin the herd.

There is a patience of the wild—dogged, tireless, persistent as life itself—that holds motionless for endless hours the spider in its web, the snake in its coils, the panther in its ambuscade; this patience belongs peculiarly to life when it hunts its living food; and it belonged to Buck as he clung to the flank of the herd, retarding its march, irritating the young bulls, worrying the cows with their half-grown calves, and driving the wounded bull mad with helpless rage. For half a day this continued. Buck multiplied himself, attacking from all sides, enveloping the herd in a whirlwind of menace, cutting out his victim as fast as it could rejoin its mates, wearing out the patience of creatures preyed upon, which is a lesser patience than that of creatures preying.

As the day wore along and the sun dropped to its bed in the northwest (the darkness had come back and the fall nights were six hours long), the young bulls retraced their steps more and more reluctantly to the aid of their beset leader. The down-coming winter was harrying them on to the lower levels, and it seemed they could never shake off this tireless creature that held them back. Besides, it was not the life of the herd, or of the young bulls, that was threatened. The life of only one member was demanded, which was a remoter interest than their lives, and in the end they were content to pay the toll.

2035   As twilight fell the old bull stood with lowered head, watching his mates—the cows he had known, the calves he had fathered, the bulls he had mastered—as they shambled on at a rapid pace through the fading light. He could not follow, for before his nose leaped the merciless fanged terror that would not let him go. Three hundredweight more than half a ton he weighed; he had lived a long, strong life, full of fight and struggle, and

2040 at the end he faced death at the teeth of a creature whose head did not reach beyond his great knuckled knees.

    From then on, night and day, Buck never left his prey, never gave it a moment's rest, never permitted it to browse the leaves of trees or the shoots of young birch and willow. Nor did he give the wounded bull opportunity to slake his burning thirst in the

2045 slender trickling streams they crossed. Often, in desperation, he burst into long stretches of flight. At such times Buck did not attempt to stay him, but loped easily at his heels, satisfied with the way the game was played, lying down when the moose stood still, attacking him fiercely when he strove to eat or drink.

    The great head drooped more and more under its tree of horns, and the

2050 shambling trot grew weak and weaker. He took to standing for long periods, with nose to the ground and dejected ears dropped limply; and Buck found more time in which to get water for himself and in which to rest. At such moments, panting with red lolling tongue and with eyes fixed upon the big bull, it appeared to Buck that a change was coming over the face of things. He could feel a new stir in the land. As the moose were

2055 coming into the land, other kinds of life were coming in. Forest and stream and air seemed palpitant with their presence. The news of it was borne in upon him, not by sight, or sound, or smell, but by some other and subtler sense. He heard nothing, saw nothing, yet knew that the land was somehow different; that through it strange things were afoot and ranging; and he resolved to investigate after he had finished the business

2060 in hand.

    At last, at the end of the fourth day, he pulled the great moose down. For a day and a night he remained by the kill, eating and sleeping, turn and turn about. Then, rested, refreshed and strong, he turned his face toward camp and John Thornton. He broke into the long easy lope, and went on, hour after hour, never at loss for the tangled

2065 way, heading straight home through strange country with a certitude of direction that put man and his magnetic needle to shame.

As he held on he became more and more conscious of the new stir in the land. There was life abroad in it different from the life which had been there throughout the summer. No longer was this fact borne in upon him in some subtle, mysterious way.

2070 The birds talked of it, the squirrels chattered about it, the very breeze whispered of it. Several times he stopped and drew in the fresh morning air in great sniffs, reading a message which made him leap on with greater speed. He was oppressed with a sense of calamity happening, if it were not calamity already happened; and as he crossed the last watershed and dropped down into the valley toward camp, he proceeded with greater

2075 caution.

Three miles away he came upon a fresh trail that sent his neck hair rippling and bristling. It led straight toward camp and John Thornton. Buck hurried on, swiftly and stealthily, every nerve straining and tense, alert to the multitudinous details which told a story—all but the end. His nose gave him a varying description of the passage of the life

2080 on the heels of which he was travelling. He remarked the pregnant silence of the forest. The bird life had flitted. The squirrels were in hiding. One only he saw,—a sleek gray fellow, flattened against a gray dead limb so that he seemed a part of it, a woody excrescence upon the wood itself.

As Buck slid along with the obscureness of a gliding shadow, his nose was jerked

2085 suddenly to the side as though a positive force had gripped and pulled it. He followed the new scent into a thicket and found Nig. He was lying on his side, dead where he had dragged himself, an arrow protruding, head and feathers, from either side of his body.

A hundred yards farther on, Buck came upon one of the sled-dogs Thornton had bought in Dawson. This dog was thrashing about in a death-struggle, directly on the trail,

2090 and Buck passed around him without stopping. From the camp came the faint sound of many voices, rising and falling in a sing-song chant. Bellying forward to the edge of the clearing, he found Hans, lying on his face, feathered with arrows like a porcupine. At the same instant Buck peered out where the spruce-bough lodge had been and saw what made his hair leap straight up on his neck and shoulders. A gust of overpowering rage

2095 swept over him. He did not know that he growled, but he growled aloud with a terrible ferocity. For the last time in his life he allowed passion to usurp cunning and reason, and it was because of his great love for John Thornton that he lost his head.

The Yeehats were dancing about the wreckage of the spruce-bough lodge when they heard a fearful roaring and saw rushing upon them an animal the like of which they had never seen before. It was Buck, a live hurricane of fury, hurling himself upon them in a frenzy to destroy. He sprang at the foremost man (it was the chief of the Yeehats), ripping the throat wide open till the rent jugular spouted a fountain of blood. He did not pause to worry the victim, but ripped in passing, with the next bound tearing wide the throat of a second man. There was no withstanding him. He plunged about in their very midst, tearing, rending, destroying, in constant and terrific motion which defied the arrows they discharged at him. In fact, so inconceivably rapid were his movements, and so closely were the Indians tangled together, that they shot one another with the arrows; and one young hunter, hurling a spear at Buck in mid air, drove it through the chest of another hunter with such force that the point broke through the skin of the back and stood out beyond. Then a panic seized the Yeehats, and they fled in terror to the woods, proclaiming as they fled the advent of the Evil Spirit.

And truly Buck was the Fiend incarnate, raging at their heels and dragging them down like deer as they raced through the trees. It was a fateful day for the Yeehats. They scattered far and wide over the country, and it was not till a week later that the last of the survivors gathered together in a lower valley and counted their losses. As for Buck, wearying of the pursuit, he returned to the desolated camp. He found Pete where he had been killed in his blankets in the first moment of surprise. Thornton's desperate struggle was fresh-written on the earth, and Buck scented every detail of it down to the edge of a deep pool. By the edge, head and fore feet in the water, lay Skeet, faithful to the last. The pool itself, muddy and discolored from the sluice boxes, effectually hid what it contained, and it contained John Thornton; for Buck followed his trace into the water, from which no trace led away.

All day Buck brooded by the pool or roamed restlessly about the camp. Death, as a cessation of movement, as a passing out and away from the lives of the living, he knew, and he knew John Thornton was dead. It left a great void in him, somewhat akin to hunger, but a void which ached and ached, and which food could not fill. At times, when he paused to contemplate the carcasses of the Yeehats, he forgot the pain of it; and at such times he was aware of a great pride in himself,—a pride greater than any he had yet experienced. He had killed man, the noblest game of all, and he had killed in the face of the law of club and fang. He sniffed the bodies curiously. They had died so easily. It was harder to kill a husky dog than them. They were no match at all, were it not for their arrows and spears and clubs. Thenceforward he would be unafraid of them except when they bore in their hands their arrows, spears, and clubs.

2135 Night came on, and a full moon rose high over the trees into the sky, lighting the land till it lay bathed in ghostly day. And with the coming of the night, brooding and mourning by the pool, Buck became alive to a stirring of the new life in the forest other than that which the Yeehats had made. He stood up, listening and scenting. From far away drifted a faint, sharp yelp, followed by a chorus of similar sharp yelps. As the moments passed the yelps grew closer and louder. Again Buck knew them as things

2140 heard in that other world which persisted in his memory. He walked to the centre of the open space and listened. It was the call, the many-noted call, sounding more luringly and compellingly than ever before. And as never before, he was ready to obey. John Thornton was dead. The last tie was broken. Man and the claims of man no longer bound him.

2145 Hunting their living meat, as the Yeehats were hunting it, on the flanks of the migrating moose, the wolf pack had at last crossed over from the land of streams and timber and invaded Buck's valley. Into the clearing where the moonlight streamed, they poured in a silvery flood; and in the centre of the clearing stood Buck, motionless as a statue, waiting their coming. They were awed, so still and large he stood, and a

2150 moment's pause fell, till the boldest one leaped straight for him. Like a flash Buck struck, breaking the neck. Then he stood, without movement, as before, the stricken wolf rolling in agony behind him. Three others tried it in sharp succession; and one after the other they drew back, streaming blood from slashed throats or shoulders.

This was sufficient to fling the whole pack forward, pell-mell, crowded together,

2155 blocked and confused by its eagerness to pull down the prey. Buck's marvelous quickness and agility stood him in good stead. Pivoting on his hind legs, and snapping and gashing, he was everywhere at once, presenting a front which was apparently unbroken so swiftly did he whirl and guard from side to side. But to prevent them from getting behind him, he was forced back, down past the pool and into the creek bed, till

2160 he brought up against a high gravel bank. He worked along to a right angle in the bank which the men had made in the course of mining, and in this angle he came to bay, protected on three sides and with nothing to do but face the front.

And so well did he face it, that at the end of half an hour the wolves drew back

discomfited. The tongues of all were out and lolling, the white fangs showing cruelly
2165 white in the moonlight. Some were lying down with heads raised and ears pricked
forward; others stood on their feet, watching him; and still others were lapping water
from the pool. One wolf, long and lean and gray, advanced cautiously, in a friendly
manner, and Buck recognized the wild brother with whom he had run for a night and a
day. He was whining softly, and, as Buck whined, they touched noses.
2170 Then an old wolf, gaunt and battle-scarred, came forward. Buck writhed his lips
into the preliminary of a snarl, but sniffed noses with him. Whereupon the old wolf sat
down, pointed nose at the moon, and broke out the long wolf howl. The others sat down
and howled. And now the call came to Buck in unmistakable accents. He, too, sat down
and howled. This over, he came out of his angle and the pack crowded around him,
2175 sniffing in half-friendly, half-savage manner. The leaders lifted the yelp of the pack and
sprang away into the woods. The wolves swung in behind, yelping in chorus. And Buck
ran with them, side by side with the wild brother, yelping as he ran.

And here may well end the story of Buck. The years were not many when the
Yeehats noted a change in the breed of timber wolves; for some were seen with splashes
2180 of brown on head and muzzle, and with a rift of white centring down the chest. But
more remarkable than this, the Yeehats tell of a Ghost Dog that runs at the head of the
pack. They are afraid of this Ghost Dog, for it has cunning greater than they, stealing
from their camps in fierce winters, robbing their traps, slaying their dogs, and defying
their bravest hunters.
2185 Nay, the tale grows worse. Hunters there are who fail to return to the camp, and
hunters there have been whom their tribesmen found with throats slashed cruelly open
and with wolf prints about them in the snow greater than the prints of any wolf. Each
fall, when the Yeehats follow the movement of the moose, there is a certain valley which
they never enter. And women there are who become sad when the word goes over the
2190 fire of how the Evil Spirit came to select that valley for an abiding-place.
In the summers there is one visitor, however, to that valley, of which the Yeehats
do not know. It is a great, gloriously coated wolf, like, and yet unlike, all other wolves.
He crosses alone from the smiling timber land and comes down into an open space
among the trees. Here a yellow stream flows from rotted moose-hide sacks and sinks
2195 into the ground, with long grasses growing through it and vegetable mould overrunning it

and hiding its yellow from the sun; and here he muses for a time, howling once, long and mournfully, ere he departs.

But he is not always alone. When the long winter nights come on and the wolves follow their meat into the lower valleys, he may be seen running at the head of the pack through the pale moonlight or glimmering borealis, leaping gigantic above his fellows, his great throat a-bellow as he sings a song of the younger world, which is the song of the pack.

FINIS

A Reader's Companion

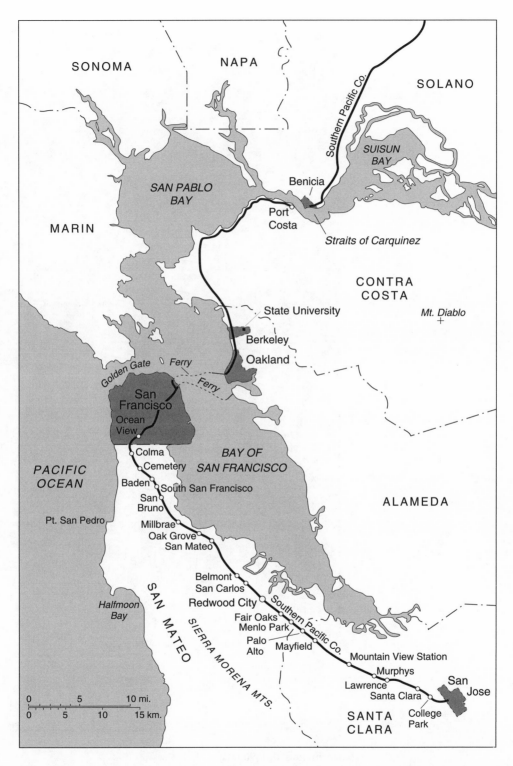

SONOMA
NAPA
SOLANO

SUISUN BAY

Benicia

SAN PABLO BAY

MARIN

Port Costa

Straits of Carquinez

Southern Pacific Co.

CONTRA COSTA

Mt. Diablo

State University

Berkeley

Oakland

Golden Gate   Ferry

Ferry

San Francisco

Ocean View

PACIFIC OCEAN

Colma

Cemetery

Baden South San Francisco

San Bruno

Pt. San Pedro

Millbrae

Oak Grove

San Mateo

BAY OF SAN FRANCISCO

ALAMEDA

Belmont

San Carlos

Redwood City

Fair Oaks

Menlo Park

Palo Alto

Mayfield

Halfmoon Bay

SAN MATEO

SIERRA MORENA MTS.

Southern Pacific Co.

Mountain View Station

Murphys

Lawrence

Santa Clara

San Jose

College Park

SANTA CLARA

0   5   10 mi.

0   5   10   15 km.

San Francisco and Vicinity, 1898 (Adapted from *Rand McNally & Company's Indexed Atlas of the World* [Chicago: Rand McNally, 1898], 357. Map © 1994 by Rand McNally, R. L. 94-5-233. Geography and Maps Division, Library of Congress)

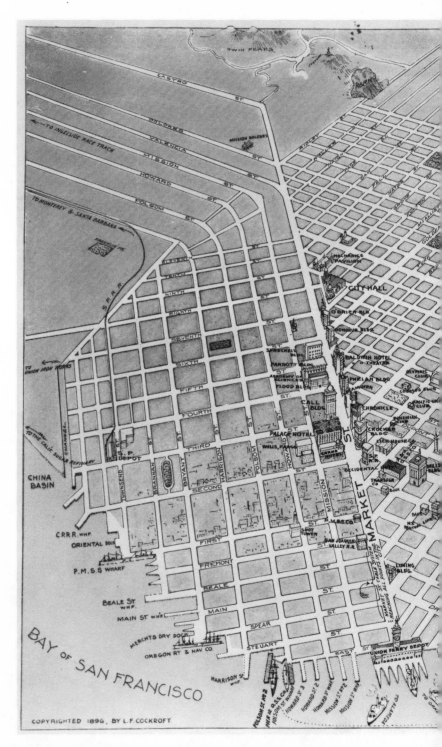

San Francisco, 1896 (Map by L. F. Cockroft.
Geography and Maps Division, Library of Congress)

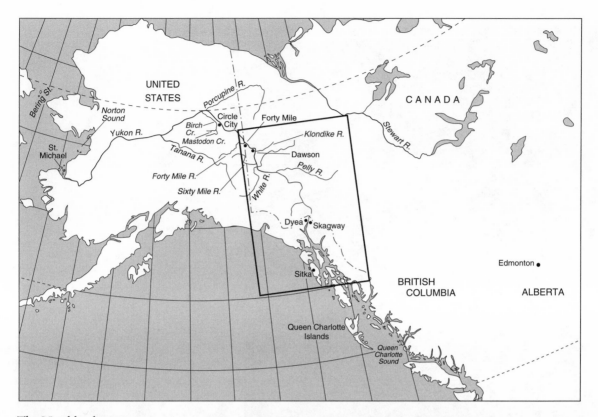

The Northland, 1897 (Adapted from map, The Province Publishing Company, 1897. Geography and Maps Division, Library of Congress)

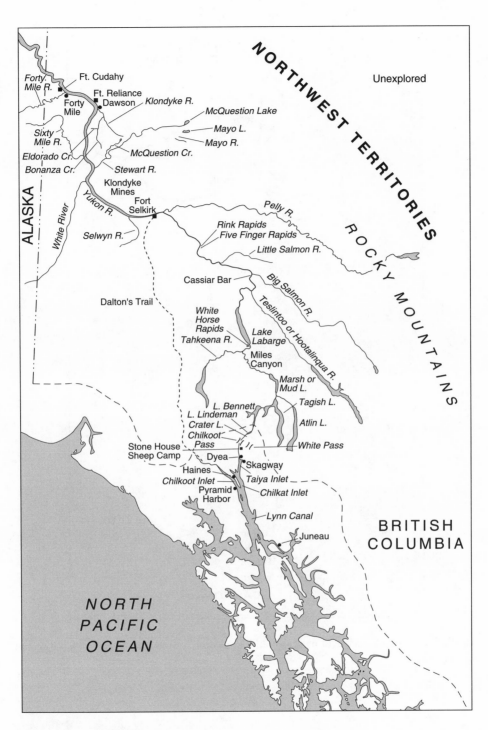

Detail from the Northland, 1897

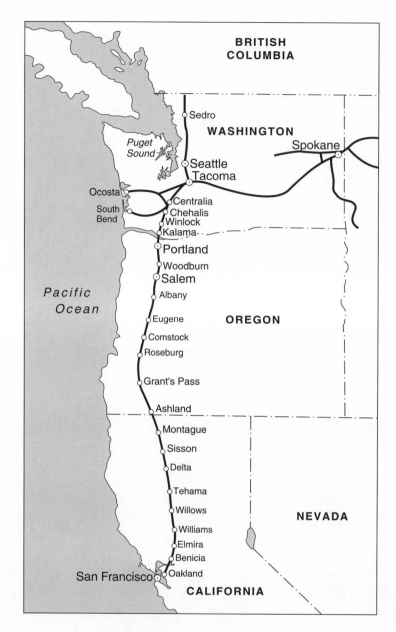

Northern Pacific Railway and Connections (Adapted from *Standard Time Schedules* 10 [May 1897]. California State Railroad Museum Library)

LEFT: John Myers O'Hara (1874–1944). Surprised to learn that the initial quatrain of his poem "Atavism" was the epigraph to *The Call of the Wild*, O'Hara (pictured here in 1919) nonetheless claimed repeatedly thereafter that his poem had inspired London to write the book. O'Hara corresponded occasionally with both Jack and Charmian London, and the trio once met in New York City for dinner. (Photo Courtesy of The Case Collection, The Newberry Library)

RIGHT: Judge Hiram Gilbert Bond ("Judge Miller"). London based his fictional Judge Miller upon an actual judge, Hiram Gilbert Bond (1838–1906), whose sons (Louis and Marshall) London had met in the Klondike. Judge Bond—an entrepreneur and speculator, an organizer of fruit-growers in the Santa Clara Valley, the founder of a bank, and a leading citizen in whatever community he lived— died in Seattle after falling from his horse. (Photo Courtesy of The Huntington Library, San Marino, California)

Golden News in the *Seattle Post-Intelligencer*. When the steamer *Portland* arrived in Seattle from Alaska on 17 July 1897, it brought not only rich miners but news of an incredible strike in the Klondike region of the Canadian Yukon. Seattle began advertising to the world its advantages for gold-seekers—its northern location and its accessibility by rail via the Northern Pacific—and for several years the city enjoyed a period of enormous growth and prosperity resulting from the tens of thousands of people swarming northward.
(Photo Courtesy of the Special Collections Division, University of Washington Libraries, Negative No.: UW 4093)

ABOVE: New Park ("Judge Miller's Place"). In 1895 Judge Bond purchased New Park and established himself as a powerful force in California's Santa Clara Valley. An 1892 drawing from the *San Jose Daily Mercury* shows the large house, the vast orchards, and the grape arbors—all mentioned in the novel by London, who had visited the Bonds in Santa Clara in the middle of October 1901. Visible at the left are the artesian well and cement swimming tank where Buck and "Judge Miller's boys took their morning plunges. . . ." (*San Jose Daily Mercury*, 15 May 1892. Photo Courtesy of the California State Library, California Section, Sacramento, California)

BELOW: Judge Bond's House. This twenty-five-room mansion, with its "wide, cool veranda," "wide-spreading lawns," and "gravelled driveways," was built in the 1850s by William M. Lent. Inside, Buck could indeed have lain "at the Judge's feet before the roaring library fire," for the home did have a spacious library—with fireplace. In 1913, the Carmelites obtained the property through the generosity of Senator James E. Phelan, whose sister had belonged to the order; the house was razed in 1917 to make way for a new monastery building. (Photo Courtesy of The Huntington Library, San Marino, California)

ABOVE: Marshall and Louis Bond with Their Dog Jack ("Buck"). In the fall of 1897, Marshall and Louis Bond moved into this cabin in Dawson City, Yukon, where they spent a year prospecting for gold. In October, Jack London arrived in Dawson City and camped near the brothers. They quickly became friends, and London became an admirer of another Jack, the large dog at the left, which was part St. Bernard and part shepherd. London acknowledged in a letter to Marshall Bond that Jack was the model for Buck.

Left to right are Marshall Bond, Oliver H. P. La Farge, Lyman Colt, and Stanley Pearce. Lying at the right is the Bonds' other dog, Pat, whom Marshall Bond described in his diary as a "shirk." (Photo Courtesy of The Huntington Library, San Marino, California)

BELOW: College Park Shelter Shed (circa 1912). College Park, a tract of land midway between San Jose and Santa Clara, California, was the original home of the University of the Pacific. In 1897, the College Park shelter shed was a stop for the Southern Pacific trains on the San Francisco/Monterey route. London knew the spot well, since his friends Ted and Mabel Applegarth lived only a few blocks away. The shed still stands today, now serving Caltrain's commuter passengers. (Photo Courtesy of Southern Pacific Railroad, Henry E. Bender, Jr., Collection)

ABOVE: Ferry *Oakland* with San Francisco Ferry Building (circa 1898). The *Oakland* was one of the Southern Pacific ferries steaming back and forth on the twenty-to-thirty minute run between San Francisco and Oakland. Just such a vessel would have transported Buck across the San Francisco Bay the morning after he was stolen. (Photo Courtesy of the Moebus Collection, San Francisco Maritime National Historical Park)

BELOW: Yukon Mining School, Seattle (circa 1897). Throughout the Queen City of Seattle, such enterprises as these mushroomed during the Gold Rush years. Note the odd assortment of animals in the team—all varieties were taken to the Yukon to toil in the traces. (Photo Courtesy of the Special Collections Division, University of Washington Libraries, Negative No.: UW 2087)

ABOVE: The Dyea Beach, Dyea, Alaska (circa 1897). Exhausted prospectors stand guard over their supplies on the beach at Dyea. The harbor was extremely shallow, and because incoming ships could not approach very closely, flatboats carried supplies to the beach, then returned to the mother ships for more (miners paid by the pound). Newcomers then had to scramble to move their goods before the incoming tide washed them out to sea. (Photo Courtesy of the Special Collections Division, University of Washington Libraries, Negative No.: Hegg 58)

BELOW: Healy & Wilson's Store, Dyea, Alaska (circa 1897). Outside this store Curly met her fate beneath a pile of snarling huskies. Erected by John J. Healy in 1884, the store was the only permanent structure in the Chilkat-Tlingit fishing camp of Dyea before the Gold Rush. (Photo Courtesy of the Yukon Archives/Vogee Collection, No. 103)

ABOVE: Trail Street, Dyea, Alaska, 1897. Never a prepossessing settlement, Dyea enjoyed only an ephemeral existence. Its principal virtue was its proximity to the Chilkoot Pass, which for a while was the favored route over the Coastal Mountains. Nearby Skagway, however, featured a deep harbor, and by 1898 had a wagon road over the mountains; by 1899 the White Pass and Yukon Railroad traversed the mountains. By 1903, only a half-dozen people remained in Dyea; today it is wilderness once again. (Photo Courtesy of the Special Collections Division, University of Washington Libraries, Negative No.: Hegg 52)

LEFT: "Half-Breed Dog-Driver." François might have looked like this man, "drawn from life by Arthur Heming." His dog-whip, however, would more likely have been the thirty-foot variety preferred by Klondike mushers. (Tyrrell, *Across the Sub-Arctics of Canada*, facing 229. Photo Courtesy of The Newberry Library)

LEFT: Advertisement: Moose Hide Moccasins. François fashioned Buck's booties from "the tops of his own moccasins," which would have been the high-topped variety here advertised. Such ads for Klondike-related products appeared in many American magazines and newspapers throughout the Rush. (*All About the Gold Fields*, 109. Photo Courtesy of The Everett D. Graff Collection, The Newberry Library)

BELOW: Dog Team and Sled with Gee-Pole. The type of Klondike sled that Buck and his mates pulled was generally seven feet long, sixteen inches wide, and six inches high. The mushers used the gee-pole, extending from the right (or "gee") front of the sled, for steering and for breaking out frozen runners. A second person would travel ahead of the dogs, tramping down a trail with snowshoes. (Photo Courtesy of the Special Collections Division, University of Washington Libraries, Negative No.: Goetzman 3013)

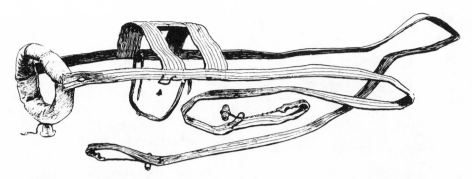

ABOVE: "Klondike Indian Dog Harness." This drawing by *Harper's Weekly* correspondent Edwin Tappan Adney illustrates the type of harness Buck would have worn. This design permitted the reins to pass more comfortably alongside the dog rather than between its legs. (Adney, *Klondike Stampede*, Photo Courtesy of The Edward E. Ayer Collection, The Newberry Library)

BELOW: Dyea Canyon, Alaska. Between Dyea and the headwaters of the Yukon River lie the Coastal Mountains. The trail to the summit follows the Taiya River as it tumbles down from the peaks that loom over Dyea. One of the more tortuous portions of the trail is the canyon of the Taiya River, which, even when frozen, presents deadly perils to the traveler. (Photo Courtesy of the Special Collections Division, University of Washington Libraries, Negative No.: Hegg 80)

LEFT: Chilkoot and Petterson Passes. This is perhaps the best-known photograph from the entire Gold Rush. At left is the Chilkoot Pass (named for the American Indians who discovered and controlled it) with the endless line of miners carrying supplies to the top, a quarter of a mile away. Miners hacked stairs in the ice and dubbed this portion of the trail the "Golden Stairs." To the right is the wider, less precipitous Petterson Trail used by pack and draft animals like Buck. (Photo Courtesy of the Special Collections Division, University of Washington Libraries, Negative No.: Hegg 101)

BELOW: Boat-Building at Lake Bennett. At Lake Bennett, about sixteen miles beyond the Chilkoot summit, the gold-seekers paused to build boats and await the break-up of the ice. From here, they would travel the five hundred or so miles to Dawson City by water. When the ice broke in late May 1898, more than seven thousand boats set off for Dawson. (Photo Courtesy of the Special Collections Division, University of Washington Libraries, Negative No.: Hegg 266)

ABOVE: "Over the Bench Ice of Thirty Mile River." Emerging from Lake Laberge is a rough and pictur-esque thirty-mile stretch of the Yukon River. As winter draws close, the ice of the river freezes from the shore toward the center; adventurous travelers would journey on this "bench-ice" to save time. In just this fashion did François and Perrault proceed over this portion of the river. (Palmer, *In the Klondike*, facing 26. Photo Courtesy of The Everett D. Graff Collection, The Newberry Library)

BELOW: Whitehorse Rapids. These dangerous rapids claimed 150 boats and five lives in the early days of the Rush. Eventually, the North-west Mounted Police took over the river at the site and employed experi-enced white-water navigators to guide vessels through the danger. Today, a nearby dam has formed Lake Schwatka, which has submerged the rapids. (Photo Courtesy of the Special Collections Division, University of Washing-ton Libraries, Negative No.: Hegg 712)

ABOVE: The Shore of Lake Laberge. Immortalized by poet Robert Service in his poem "The Cremation of Sam McGee," the rocky "marge of Lake Laberge" was the campsite where Buck and his mates were attacked by the "four or five score" starving huskies from some "nearby Indian village." Official reports of the North-west Mounted Police reveal that there was indeed near Laberge an encampment of impoverished American Indians. (Photo Courtesy of the Prints and Photographs Division, Library of Congress)

BELOW: Dawson City, Yukon (circa 1897). The population of Dawson City, which is located at the conflu- ence of the Yukon and Klondike rivers, swelled to about thirty thousand at the height of the Rush in 1897– 98. The Yukon is the large river at the right; the smaller Klondike enters faintly from the left, just in front of the small rise in the background. (Photo Courtesy of the Special Collections Division, University of Washington Libraries, Negative No.: Hegg 742)

"Gold Miners at Work." Miners had to burn their way down through the permafrost to bedrock, where the gold, if there was any, would be found. A fire roars in one shaft while the miners clear the other. (Bramble, *Klondike: A Manual*, facing 208. Photo Courtesy of The Edward E. Ayer Collection, The Newberry Library)

RIGHT: Hardy-Hall Arms Co. Advertisement. The "big Colt's revolver" carried by Hal may have been the sort of Colt's Navy .38 or .41 calibre here advertised. Throughout the Rush, weapons manufacturers warned the gold-seekers not to go unarmed into the northern wilderness. (Wilson, *Guide to the Yukon Gold Fields*, Juneau Business Directory in back of volume, 8. Photo Courtesy of The Everett D. Graff Collection, The Newberry Library)

BELOW: Waterfront, Skagway, Alaska (circa 1898). Only about nine miles from Dyea, Skagway eventually won the competition with its neighbor for Gold Rush business because of its deep harbor, accommodating wharves, and wagon and rail roads over the mountains. Today, Skagway is a stop for many Alaskan cruise ships during the summer months. The White Pass and Yukon railroad continues to carry sightseers the forty-one miles to Lake Bennett. (Photo Courtesy of the Prints and Photographs Division, Library of Congress)

ABOVE: Waterfront, Circle City, Alaska (circa 1897). Named because of its location on the Arctic Circle (it is in fact about fifty miles south of it), Circle City was the commercial center for the nearby Birch Creek mining district. Circle's population of about twelve hundred dropped dramatically when gold was discovered on the far-richer Klondike; today, fewer than one hundred people reside in Circle. (Photo Courtesy of the Special Collections Division, University of Washington Libraries, Negative No.: A. Curtis 29122)

BELOW: Poling Boat. Travelers throughout the Yukon used these long, narrow craft. From just such a boat John Thornton fell into the rapids of the Fortymile River. (Photo Courtesy of The Charles Bunnell Collection, Charles E. Bunnell Album #1, #58-1026-166 9N, Archives, Alaska and Polar Regions Department, University of Alaska Fairbanks)

ABOVE: "Looking Down the Canyon, Fortymile River." Jack London never saw these rapids, located about eight miles from the mouth of the Fortymile River, but he must have heard of them: They very nearly claim the lives of John Thornton and Buck. (Sola, *Klondyke: Truth and Facts,* facing 2. Photo Courtesy of The Edward E. Ayer Collection, The Newberry Library)

BELOW: Chilkat Dancers (1895). Jack London invented the "Yeehats," the American Indians who kill Thornton and the others in the novel. During his year in the Northland, however, London had seen many of the coastal Chilkat-Tlingit people, a group of whom are pictured here in ceremonial dress. In the fall of 1897, some of them had taken him by canoe from Juneau to Dyea (a trip of about twelve hours), and he had admired the strength and prowess of the Chilkat packers on the Chilkoot Trail. (Photo Courtesy of the Special Collections Division, University of Washington Libraries, Negative No.: Winter and Pond 209)

CHAPTER ONE

"Into the Primitive"

Epigraph: "Old longings nomadic leap . . ."

This is the first quatrain of "Atavism," by John Myers O'Hara, a poem originally published in the *Bookman* only a month before London began writing *The Call of the Wild*.

ATAVISM

Old longings nomadic leap,
*   Chafing at custom's chain;*
Again from its brumal sleep
*   Wakens the ferine strain.*

Helots of houses no more,
*   Let us be out, be free;*
Fragrance through window and door
*   Wafts from the woods, the sea.*

After the torpor of will,
*   Morbid with inner strife,*

Welcome the animal thrill,
  Lending a zest to life.

Banish the volumes revered,
  Sever from centuries dead;
Ceilings the lamp flicker cheered
  Barter for stars instead.

Temple thy dreams with the trees,
  Nature thy god alone;
Worship the sun and the breeze,
  Altars where none atone.

Voices of solitude call,
  Whisper of sedge and stream;
Loosen the fetters that gall,
  Back to the primal scheme.

Feel the great throbbing terrene
  Pulse in thy body beat,
Conscious again of the green
  Verdure beneath the feet.

Callous to pain as the rose,
  Breathe with instinct's delight;
Live the existence that goes
  Soulless into the night.[1]

O'Hara (1874–1944) graduated from Northwestern University Law School, then practiced law briefly in Chicago before moving to New York City where he became a stockbroker, an investor in race horses, a collector of rare books and works of art, and an amateur poet whose half-dozen collections of verse were published by minor presses in very small runs.

Although O'Hara was not an important poet, he was a man of considerable learning, a polyglot who translated Greek (with a special interest in Sappho), Aztec, Latin, Arabic,

Javanese, Tahitian, and Chinese. His translations of French poems earned him a medal from the *Académie française* in 1935. Nine volumes of his unpublished verse—mostly translations—are in the Manuscripts Division of the Library of Congress.

In an immodest letter to Jack London, O'Hara claimed that he was "esteemed as one of the greatest speculative geniuses that ever stepped into Wall Street"; nonetheless, the crash of 1929 ruined him, forcing him to sell at auction his valuable collections, including many inscribed first editions of London's works, and to move to a bleak residence hotel where, in miserable poverty, he died on 16 November 1944 of what his death certificate termed "natural causes."[2]

O'Hara's personal relationship with Jack London began closely after the publication of *The Call of the Wild* in 1903. When O'Hara learned that the initial lines from "Atavism" had appeared as an unattributed epigraph to a new best-seller, he twice wrote to London, identifying himself as the poet. Apparently, London did not receive the first letter, but when he responded to O'Hara's second, he claimed that he never "knew who wrote" the lines, that he "ran across . . . [them] in a detached fragment" and "never knew the rest of the poem." He then turned to flattery: "Of all the poetry I know, there were no four lines within a hundred million miles as appropriate for the key to *The Call of the Wild* as were those four lines that I used."[3]

London's plea of ignorance is a bit dubious: The 1902 issue of the *Bookman* in which "Atavism" appears also contains notice of publication of two of London's books, *The Cruise of the Dazzler* and *Children of the Frost*. London, who read literary magazines voraciously and maintained extensive files of clippings, certainly would have checked the major journals of the day for information about his forthcoming books. Moreover, he had published two pieces of his own in the *Bookman* in 1902.[4]

Nevertheless, O'Hara must have been satisfied, for in 1909 he dedicated to London a collection of verse, *Songs of the Open*; the first poem is "Atavism." O'Hara sent London a copy, inscribed as follows: "My dear London; This book owes, in large measure, its inspiration to yourself and your immortal classic of the open, *The Call of the Wild*. Therefore, I have taken the honor to myself of dedicating these poems to you not only as a tribute of admiration for your genius, but [as] a token of sincere friendship."[5]

And inside the flyleaf of a presentation copy of another of his collections, *Pagan Sonnets* (1910), he inscribed a sonnet to London:

Ave, Victor!
  I mark you from a rabble-circled space
Emerge as some great gladiator would,
  Triumphant from the combat, with the blood
And dust of the arena in his face;
  Behind, the roar of thousands that abase
Themselves before such prowess as withstood,
  Herculean to meet a multitude,
Onslaught of rabid beast and savage race.
Dear Genius of "Wake-Robin Lodge!"
  Dear Friend!
A sonnett-call [sic] across the continent;
  An answer to the cordial one you sent
in Martin Eden! *May you, to the end,*
  In single-handed battle never err,
And die beside your sword, a conqueror![6]

Over the years, O'Hara occasionally corresponded with Jack London and his wife, Charmian, and in 1909 Jack sent O'Hara a remarkable gift—with a cover letter that subsequently appeared in the *Chicago Evening Post* (13 August 1909):

Dear O'Hara:—Here is my desk copy of "The Call of the Wild." It cruised with 'The Snark' for two years all over the South Seas. And now, in sickness, I am saying farewell to that wonderful cruise, and, sad at heart, I depart for my own land in the hope of getting well.

   Your four lines head this yarn. They epitomize what I have written in 250 pages. I found your lines in the sea of fugitive newspaper verse, and never dreamed at the time to call their author "friend."

   Affectionately yours,
   Jack London[7]

On one occasion (1 February 1912), O'Hara met the Londons in New York City for dinner and an evening at Brady's Playhouse to see *Bought and Paid For*. Afterwards,

Charmian commented in her diary: "O'Hara a character."[8] But O'Hara was never able to accept the Londons' invitations to visit in California.

Near the end of O'Hara's obituary in the *New York Times* is an odd item: "Mr. O'Hara often said it was a poem he wrote which inspired Jack London to write his 'Call of the Wild.'"[9] O'Hara was fond of making this unfounded claim: It appears repeatedly in his scrapbooks. However, none of the editions of *The Call of the Wild* published during London's lifetime give O'Hara credit even for the epigraph.

Line 1—Buck:

On 22 July 1897, Marshall Bond, a young man from Santa Clara, California, was in Seattle, en route to the Klondike. Before boarding his ship to Alaska, he purchased some supplies. "Also bought two big dogs," he commented in his diary. One, named Jack, was a mixed breed—St. Bernard and some kind of collie or shepherd.[10]

When Jack London arrived in Dawson City, Yukon, on 18 October 1897, he camped near the cabin of Marshall Bond and his brother Louis. Although London had not known the Bonds back in the Bay area, he soon discovered the connection and occasionally visited the brothers in their cabin. He was very impressed with the dog Jack, and in a letter to Marshall Bond he admitted: "Yes, Buck was based upon your dog at Dawson." And in Louis Bond's copy of *The Call of the Wild*, London wrote: "Here is the book that never would have been written if you had not gone to Klondike in 1897 and taken Buck along with you."[11]

On 28 May 1906, Louis Bond wrote to London, offering him a photograph of the dog Jack. London apparently asked for a dozen copies, for in a subsequent letter Bond confirmed that he was sending that many. The dozen did not last long. Charmian London soon wrote from Honolulu, asking for more.[12]

The Bonds' dog never returned from the Klondike. Unable to take the animal aboard his ship to Seattle, Louis Bond paid for his passage on another, but he did not arrive. The Bonds never discovered what had happened to him. "Presumably it was sold by a dishonest shipping clerk," Marshall Bond, Jr., surmised in his biography of his father.[13]

One can only speculate about London's reasons for choosing the name "Buck"— Marshall Bond, Jr., believed London simply did not want to use his own name "for a dog hero." In a letter dated 28 August 1903 to Merle Maddern, the niece of his first wife, London offers a different explanation: "The only reason I named him Buck was that years before I had filed away among my notes as appropriate dog names, 'Buck & Bright.' I had thought of using them some time on a pair of dogs. But when I looked over my list of dog-names for a good one for my hero, I chose Buck—I guess because it was stronger than Bright."[14]

Buck appears briefly in another London story, "Jan the Unrepentant." Bright is in both "Flush of Gold" and *Smoke Bellew*. In the former, he breaks his shoulder blade and is shot; in the latter, he is Smoke's lead-dog.[15]

Lines 1–2: "trouble was brewing, not alone for himself, but for every tide-water dog ... from Puget Sound to San Diego"

Puget Sound—named for Lt. Peter Puget, a participant in George Vancouver's 1792 Northwest exploration—is an inlet of the Pacific Ocean north of Seattle in northwest Washington; San Diego is at the southernmost tip of California. Because of the demand in the Klondike, dogs of all varieties along the entire length of the West Coast were stolen and shipped to the Northland. Kathryn Winslow called the situation a "mass canine kidnap-ping," and one gold-seeker warned every dog owner to "lock his pooch up in the base-ment and keep it there."[16]

An official report of the North-west Mounted Police in January 1898 reveals the principal reason for the thefts—profit: Dogs were commanding "a fabulous price, ranging from $150 to $250 each. . . ."[17]

Lines 3–5: "because men, groping in the Arctic darkness, had found a yellow metal ... thousands of men were rushing into the Northland"

The Call of the Wild deals with the so-called "Klondike Gold Rush" (or "Yukon Gold Rush" or "Alaska Gold Rush") of 1897—what Morris Zaslow calls "the most important single event in the history of the Canadian North. . . ." Prospectors had been in the North for nearly thirty years before 1897, however, working the rivers and creeks of Alaska, the Yukon, British Columbia, and the Northwest Territories, looking for the "yellow metal." William Bronson and Richard Reinhardt estimate that there were fifteen hundred "out-siders" in the Yukon valley by the summer of 1896.[18]

The following were the principal Northland discoveries antedating the Klondike strike:

    1870   Sumdum Bay (southeastern Alaska)
    1871   Cassiar District (British Columbia)

1872	Stewart Mine (Sitka, Alaska)
1880	Juneau (Alaska)
1886	Fortymile and Cassiar Bar (Yukon Territory)
1888	Kenai Peninsula (Alaska)
1893	Birch Creek (Circle City, Alaska); Rampart (Alaska)[19]

On 17 August 1896 George Carmack and some American Indian relatives, acting on advice from Robert Henderson, another prospector, staked gold claims on Rabbit Creek, near the confluence of the Yukon and Klondike rivers in the Yukon Territory. Rabbit Creek was thick with gold, as were many of the creek beds of the Klondike's other principal tributaries. Two weeks after the Carmack strike on Rabbit Creek—now called "Bonanza Creek"—Antone Stander and his companions staked nearby Eldorado Creek, which was to become the richest placer gold strike in the world, and the last great gold rush was on.

The first to charge into the region were prospectors from the other mining camps in the Northland, primarily Birch Creek, with its center in Circle City, Alaska, several hundred miles to the west, and Fortymile, only about fifty miles down the Yukon River from the mouth of the Klondike. Stanley, a witness to the stampede from Fortymile, recorded his impressions of what he called a "wild, mad rush":

> *It was a motley procession. On rafts and in boats of every description were people taking with them everything moveable. . . . Nearly every living thing that had previously called Forty Mile "home" was in line. Men who had been in a drunken stupor for weeks were stowed in the bottom of boats and taken along to locate claims. All classes of humanity were there. Honest, hard-working miners, saloon keepers and their attaches and hangers-on, the female followers of mining camps, and, in fact, every human being save the attendants of the trading post.*[20]

In July 1897—nearly a year after the strike on Bonanza—news finally reached the "outside," precipitating one of the greatest acts in the pageant of human folly. Pierre Berton estimates that "at the very least" one hundred thousand people, from all walks of life, left their homes in search of fortune. A hailstorm of requests for information pounded the Chamber of Commerce in Seattle, among them queries from teachers, doctors, lawyers, laborers, secretaries, sales representatives, the Director of the New Jersey School for Feeble-Minded Children, a surveyor for the City of Boston, the owners of the Sunnyside

Shetland Pony Farm in Monmouth, Illinois, and the owner of the Baines Cycle Company in Syracuse, New York.[21]

Newspapers around the country were full of stories about the travel plans of local people—not all of whom exercised good judgment. A bartender in New York City stole and sold the fixtures from the saloon where he worked to outfit himself, his wife, and his child; he was apprehended before departure. A pair of thirteen-year-old boys from Long Island "told their playmates on July 24 that they were going to the Klondike to get some of its gold," reported the *New York Times*. "They would stop at Central Park, they said, to see the animals."[22]

Although there were a number of routes to the Klondike—none via Central Park—most people headed for Skagway and Dyea, two new towns on the southeastern Alaska coast a hundred miles north of Juneau. From there, the argonauts (as newspapers of the era termed them) had to scale the Coastal Mountains, then navigate hundreds of miles of frigid lakes and the mighty Yukon River to reach the goldfields near Dawson City, Yukon.

A few voices urged caution. In the earliest days of the Rush, *The Wave*, a San Francisco weekly, warned that "the Clondyke [*sic*] district has all been practically taken up, so far as original claims are concerned, and anyone going there now to work on his own account would therefore be forced to lease his ground." Hamlin Garland wrote that the Yukon was "a grim and terrible country" and "no place for weak men, lazy men, or cowards." And William H. Dall, a veteran explorer in the region, warned of "serious hardships, and even probable starvation" which would "confront the rash and foolhardy, who push forward without proper supplies into a region whose limitations they do not realize."[23]

Tens of thousands of people, however, ignored the warnings and charged northward—after all, printed alongside the warnings were such encouraging words as these from Josiah Spurr, an Arctic expert: "There is plenty of room for many more prospectors and miners. . . ."[24]

Although London refers in these lines to "the Arctic darkness," no major gold discoveries in Alaska or the Canadian Yukon were made above the Arctic Circle. The Klondike mining region lies a couple of hundred miles south of the Circle.

Lines 4–5: "steamship and transportation companies were booming the find"

Early in the Rush, Henry Tyrrell wrote: "Klondike is the magic word that has thrilled first Seattle, then the entire United States, and finally the whole civilized world. It stands for millions of gold, and it is a synonym for the advancement, after unspeakable suffering, of hundreds of miners from poverty to affluence in the brief period of a few months."[25]

Virtually every major newspaper and magazine published ads for Klondike-related products and services. In December 1897, for example, the Pacific Coast Steamship Company ran a half-page ad in the San Francisco–based *Overland Monthly*, making this claim: "This well equipped company has been running a regular line of steamers from the port of San Francisco to Alaska for over twenty years. . . ." The ad listed books, pamphlets, and maps the company would send for the cost of postage only—for example, "How to Reach the Gold Fields of Alaska," and "How to Reach the Klondike." Two months later, the same journal noted that the most conspicuous symptom of gold fever was the ubiquity of signs, "in every color and variety of lettering," bearing the words "'Alaskan or Klondike Outfits Sold Here.'"[26]

Not all were intelligent enterprises; not all were honest. The Snow and Ice Transportation Company of Chicago, for example, was collecting money for, but not actually providing, the service it advertised. Moreover, all sorts of bogus contraptions were manufactured to sell to the eager and the naive. One, the so-called "Klondike bicycle," was given serious treatment in *The Official Guide to the Klondyke Country and Gold Fields of Alaska*: "Devices for packing large quantities of material are attached to the handle bars and rear forks, and the machine, it is estimated, will carry 500 pounds. The plan is to load it with half the miner's equipment and drag it on four wheels ten miles or so. Then the rider will fold up the side wheels, ride it back as a bicycle, and bring on the rest of the load." A. C. Harris sneered at the device, calling it "absurd" and "practically useless" in the rugged alpine terrain, but he noted that "some 'tenderfeet' have been seen in Seattle armed and equipped with just that thing." And Harry DeWindt was alarmed to see some of the bicycles on the streets of Dyea.[27]

Line 8: "the Santa Clara Valley"

Just south of San Francisco lies the enormous Santa Clara Valley—"larger than the entire state of Rhode Island," gushed *Sunshine, Fruit, and Flowers*, a promotional book from the 1890s. In 1896, Santa Clara County had a population of 56,396 scattered across its 1,250 square miles—indeed, thirty-six square miles larger than Rhode Island. A special section of the *San Jose Daily Mercury* devoted to the region (15 May 1892) presented the county as rivaling the Biblical Canaan in its possibilities: It is a "country rich in orchards, vineyards, gardens and seed farms. The soil is unsurpassed for fertility, and the climate . . . is one which never fails to ripen to perfection every fruit and flower planted in the soil." In the same section of the newspaper, the town of Santa Clara—population about 3,700 at the time—enjoyed similar treatment: "[N]o town in the State has so great a historic charm combined with so many attractions of beauty and location as this community that has . . . retained all the best influences and fairest aspects of the Arcadian days of the valley."[28]

Line 8: "Judge Miller"

For the surname "Miller" London had to look no farther than his own household, for ten-year-old Johnny Miller, son of London's step-sister, Ida, was living with the Londons when Jack wrote *The Call of the Wild*. (Another, less likely, possibility is the poet Joaquin Miller, a friend of London's at the time.)

London based "Judge Miller" upon an actual judge, Hiram Gilbert Bond (1838–1906), whose sons Marshall and Louis London had met in the Klondike. Judge Bond had a distinguished and varied career. After the Civil War he served on a federal bench at Orange Court House, Virginia, and then accepted an appointment from President Grant to a position in Richmond, Virginia, as U.S. Commissioner, a job requiring him to process bankruptcy suits during Reconstruction. Judge Bond later moved to California, where he opened the Citizens' Bank of Santa Clara, bought and operated a sizable ranch, and continued the sorts of investments and financial speculations practiced by wealthy entrepreneurs at the turn of the century. In 1906, Judge Bond moved to Seattle, where he died on 30 March after a fall from a horse. His obituary mentioned that he was "dragged a considerable distance" and immediately thereafter "suffered a fatal stroke of apoplexy."[29]

Lines 8–31: "Judge Miller's place, it was called. . . . [I]t [the house] stood back from the road, half hidden among the trees . . . the wide cool veranda . . . gravelled driveways which wound through wide-spreading lawns and under the interlacing boughs of tall poplars . . . great stables . . . servants' cottages, an endless and orderly array of outhouses, long grape arbors, green pastures, orchards, and berry patches. . . . pumping plant . . . big cement tank where Judge Miller's boys took their morning plunge . . . library . . ."

In 1895, Judge Bond paid twenty-five thousand dollars for a magnificent home and thirty-four rich acres comprising forty blocks in downtown Santa Clara. The prior owner, James Pieronnet Pierce, had named it "New Park" after the English country home of his grandfather. According to the *San Jose Daily Mercury*, New Park in 1892 featured sixty acres of vineyards, twenty-five of orchards, and, in addition to the main house, had a winery, distillery, stables, servants' quarters, and ornamental grounds. Among the crops were Bartlett pears, French prunes, cherries and apricots.[30]

After Bond acquired the property, he leased some additional adjoining land, increasing the dimensions of the ranch to about three hundred acres. Eleven years later (1906), preparing to move to Seattle, he sold the ranch to Henry Brace for forty thousand dollars. The house survived until 1917, when it was razed to make way for a new monastery for the Carmelite sisters, who had obtained the house and ten acres in 1913 through the generosity of Sen. James D. Phelan, whose sister was a member of the order.[31]

Today, the Carmelites continue to maintain the property and its lovely grounds. Only the old carriage house, a water tower, the arbors, and a gazebo, however, remind the visitor of its former identity. One of the original artesian wells continues to provide water for the monastery gardens. The "wide cool veranda," removed as the house was razed, is now attached to the Jamison-Brown house on the grounds of the Triton Museum in Santa Clara.

Jack London had been a guest of the Bonds' at New Park in the middle of October 1901, and there is little doubt that the ranch was in his memory and imagination as he composed these lines. Not only did he acknowledge as much in a letter to Marshall Bond—"And of course Judge Miller's place was Judge Bond's. . . ."—but as nineteenth-century photographs and drawings of the property reveal, there is a very close correlation between the features of Judge Bond's actual and Judge Miller's fictional estates.[32]

Line 16: "artesian well"

Santa Clara County had many such wells. The *Historical Atlas Map of Santa Clara County, California* (1876) identifies as one of "the greatest blessings" of the area its "abundant supply of wholesome water, drawn . . . by means of the artesian wells." The city of Santa Clara obtained its own water from four artesian wells, one of which was so powerful that when first drilled, it flooded the streets with a stream four feet wide and six inches deep for six weeks before it could be capped.[33]

Line 17: "Judge Miller's boys"

Though unnamed in the novel, the "boys" are based on Judge Bond's actual sons, Louis (1865–1908) and Marshall (1867–1941).

Lines 23–25: "Toots, the Japanese pug . . . Ysabel, the Mexican hairless . . . fox terriers"

The pug originated in China, not Japan. There is a black variety, however, that was originally brought to the United States from Japan around the turn of the century.[34]

"Ysabel" is a Spanish variation of "Isabel." In eastern Santa Clara County near Lick Observatory are Isabel Creek, Isabel Valley, and Isabel Mountain—all named for St. Isabel (Santa Ysabel), mother of John the Baptist. Perhaps London selected the name for its geographical significance.

Resembling a Chihuahua, the Mexican hairless is aptly named: It has tufts of hair only on the skull and at the end of the tail. It stands about twelve inches high at the shoulder and weighs about fifteen pounds. Colors are usually black, brown, gray, or pink.

Line 30: "Mollie and Alice, the Judge's daughters"

On a photocopy of a letter from Jack London to Marshall Bond at the Huntington Library, Marshall Bond, Jr., penciled in some information about these names: "He [London] should have said Molly and Amy, the Judge's daughters-in-law." Amy Burnett was the wife of Marshall Bond; Mary Hyde Wilson (known also as "Molly" and "Mollie") married Louis Bond.[35]

Lines 31–32: "the Judge's grandsons"

Judge Bond did have grandsons. Marshall and Amy had two sons (Richard and Marshall, Jr.); Louis and Molly had two sons (Marshall Gilbert and Edward) and a daughter (Kate). All of these grandchildren, however, were born after the publication of *The Call of the Wild*.

Lines 39–40: "Shep . . . a Scotch shepherd dog"

This name is of course an abbreviation of "shepherd," the variety of dog, but it has a greater significance: Shep was the name of one of London's own boyhood dogs. In an unpublished memoir, Frank Atherton, a boyhood friend of London's, remembers that Shep was a cross between a collie and shepherd. Atherton relates how London once saved the dog from a near-drowning or suffocation in a mud hole on the Alameda marsh. Later, the dog was apparently stolen by "some wandering sheep herder," and advertisements in newspapers asking for information about her whereabouts "proved futile."[36]

"Scotch shepherd dog" is not the name of any recognized breed. However, in a book that London consulted for his dog stories (*Anecdotes of Dogs*), collies are referred to as

"The Colley or Shepherd's Dog," so London probably meant some variety of collie—also from Scotland, also herding-dogs.[37]

Another Shep appears briefly in London's story "Where the Trail Forks," and is identified only as a "shepherd dog."[38]

Line 48: "the fall of 1897"

It was actually early summer, on 15 July 1897, that the steamer *Excelsior*, loaded with Klondike gold and miners with tales to tell, docked at San Francisco; two days later, the *Portland* arrived in Seattle, bearing a similar cargo, and the Klondike Gold Rush was on, continuing throughout that summer, fall, and the following winter and spring.

Line 48: "Klondike"

The word *Klondike* is generally considered to be an American Indian word (*Throndiuck*) whose pronunciation is so difficult for speakers of English that the easier "Klondike" was soon substituted. Variously spelled *Klondyke* and *Clondyke*, the word supposedly means "hammer-water"—a reference to the sounds of American Indians hammering their fishing nets into the banks of this small but salmon-rich river.[39]

Hamilton, however, disputes the meaning, citing as evidence none other than George Mercer Dawson, a Canadian government geologist for whom Dawson City was named: "'I am by no means satisfied,'" wrote Dawson, "'that we actually know either its correct Indian pronunciation or meaning.'"[40]

All controversy would have been avoided if cartographers had simply adopted the name recorded in 1883 by explorer Frederick Schwatka: Deer River. Schwatka wrote that the river was "so clear that it tempted some of our party to get out their fishing gear again. . . . This the traders call the Deer River, from the large number of caribou that congregate in its valley during certain seasons of the year." Schwatka moved on, unaware that he had camped near some of the richest placer gold deposits in the world.[41]

London knew the river's prior name, for in "A Relic of the Pliocene" a character refers to the Klondike as "Reindeer River."[42]

Line 50: "Manuel"

Walter G. Manuel was a councilman of the third ward in Oakland, California, during the 1890s. Although London, an Oakland resident much of his early life, never lived in

Manuel's ward, it is likely he would have known of Councilman Manuel, whom the *Oakland Enquirer* identified as "one of the most popular young business men in the city."[43]

During London's teenage years, Councilman Manuel was a prominent opponent of the Chinese lottery, proposing legislation that would have made it a misdemeanor even to have lottery tickets in one's possession. Perhaps London selected this name as an in-joke for his Bay area readers: The lottery opponent metamorphoses into the lottery addict whose passions precipitate Buck's journey to the Yukon.[44]

Lines 51–52: "Chinese lottery"

The "Chinese lottery," which Chinese immigrants brought with them to this country, was known as *puk kop piu* ("white pigeon ticket"), a numbers game that required the gambler to guess which Chinese characters would be selected in each night's drawing. In the game there were eighty characters possible—the first eighty in a well-known Chinese book called the *Thousand Character Classic*. The *Classic*, which contains exactly one thousand characters—no two alike—is so well known in China, writes Stewart Culin, that the characters are occasionally used for the numerals from one to one thousand.

Operators of the lottery drew twenty of the eighty characters each night. For one dollar, players could purchase ten characters, the winnings based upon the number of correct guesses:

5 winning characters	=	$2
6	=	20
7	=	200
8	=	1,000
9	=	1,500
10	=	3,000[45]

Jack London knew firsthand about the seductions—and frustrations—of the lottery. His mother was "susceptible to the lure of Chinese lottery tickets . . . [but] was unlucky."[46]

Line 55: "the Judge was at a meeting of the Raisin Growers' Association"

In a letter to Marshall Bond, London acknowledged that he had based this fictional absence of the Judge's upon an actual event: "And don't you remember that your father was attending a meeting of the Fruitgrowers Association the night I visited you. . . ." On the evening of London's visit to the Bond ranch (15 October 1901), Judge Bond, who was founder and president of the California Cured Fruit Association, addressed a meeting of prune growers in an effort to persuade them to join the organization he and others had founded on 25 January 1900.[47]

Although the text of *The Call of the Wild* refers to raisins, it was prunes, not raisins— or the grapes from which they are formed—that were the principal crop in the Santa Clara Valley. Publicists for the valley boasted it was "the prune-growing center of the world," a claim bolstered by the vast orchards throughout the region—by one count, there were 6,495 prune trees in the county in 1876.[48]

When he arrived in California, Judge Bond found the prune industry "unduly chaotic" and so, wrote his grandson, had "developed a marketing program in which the larger prunes were sold in the east and the smaller ones in Germany." The Judge signed up thirty-eight hundred growers in the Santa Clara Valley, built a warehouse for their produce, and established prices. Unfortunately for Bond and the Association, prices fell dramatically because of record crops in 1900 and 1901, and the group disintegrated. This failure dogged the Judge even to his death, his obituary in the *San Jose Herald* noting the "brief and troublesome existence" of the organization.[49]

Lines 55–56: "the boys were busy organizing an athletic club"

In a letter to Marshall Bond, London recalled that Louis Bond had been "organizing an athletic club" during London's visit to the Bond ranch in October 1901. Clubs of this sort were very popular at the time. Some sponsored cycling events, or boxing matches, or competitions with other clubs, or social events of various kinds. Local newspapers of the day mention, among others, the Pacific Union Club, the Western Athletic Club, and the San Francisco Wheelmen.

At the time of London's visit to the ranch, both Louis Bond and his father were members of the newly formed Garden City Athletic Club in San Jose. Louis was also president of the club and a member of its board of directors. On 6 October 1901 (about a week before London's visit) the *San Jose Daily Mercury* published a lengthy feature about the club and its new facilities at 40 North First Street—"far and away ahead of any similar organization ever attempted in San Jose," claimed the newspaper.

During the week of London's visit, the club was sponsoring a handball tournament and holding meetings to figure out ways to raise "enough funds with which to liquidate the debts of the club." Fund-raising efforts must have failed, however, for the *San Jose City Directory* lists the club's address for the final time in 1904, only three years after its founding.[50]

Line 59: "flag station known as College Park"

At a "flag station," trains do not stop unless signaled. Passengers can ask to be discharged; persons waiting for a train can indicate a desire to board by waving. If the station is large enough to employ personnel, an attendant may alert the train with an actual flag or with some other prearranged signal.

Located midway between San Jose and Santa Clara, College Park was a 432-acre tract of land purchased in 1866 by the trustees of the University of the Pacific for about seventy-two thousand dollars. Part of the land was set aside for the university, the rest sold in lots to raise capital. Originally, the school was called California Wesleyan University, but the name was changed one month later to University of the Pacific. In 1924, the grounds were sold to the University of Santa Clara, and the University of the Pacific moved to Stockton, California, its present location. Currently, Bellarmine College Preparatory School occupies the old university grounds. None of the original buildings survive.[51]

For more than a century, there has been near College Park a train depot—a "shelter shed," in railroad terminology—a fourteen-by-twenty-one-foot structure, open on three sides, with a wall on the west side. During Jack London's day, it was a stop on the Southern Pacific line; now, Caltrain uses the shelter, which closely resembles the original shed. From College Park—which, according to published Southern Pacific timetables from 1897, was a regularly scheduled stop, not a flag station—passengers could travel the fifty miles to San Francisco, where a ferry ride across the Bay would connect them with trains heading east and north. The shed is about three miles from "Judge Miller's place" in Santa Clara.

London was familiar with College Park because two of his Oakland friends, Ted and Mabel Applegarth (brother and sister), had moved to the area and lived on the corner of Elm and Asbury, only three blocks from the depot. London occasionally visited the Applegarths in the years before he wrote the novel.

Line 87: "Concerning that night's ride"

Standard Time Schedules (May 1897) shows that the last Southern Pacific weekday train left College Park at 4:32 P.M. and arrived in San Francisco at 6:30 P.M. The final

Saturday train left College Park at 6:02 P.M. and arrived in San Francisco at 7:45 P.M. A few months later (December 1897), the *Traveler's Official Railroad Guide* shows the last College Park train arriving in San Francisco at 7:30 P.M.[52]

The *San Jose Daily Mercury* in the summer and fall of 1897 shows schedule changes occurring on 1 July, 1 August, and 27 September. Between 1 and 27 August, the latest trains arrived in College Park at 5:37 P.M. on weekdays, 6:52 P.M. on Saturdays. Since the trip to San Francisco, depending on the number of stops, took from one and three-quarters to two hours, Buck would have arrived between 7:30 and 9:00 P.M., depending on the day he was stolen.

Line 88: "a saloon on the San Francisco water front"

Buck and the unnamed kidnapper are spending the night in San Francisco, waiting to ride a morning ferry across the Bay. The Southern Pacific train depot was on Third Street in San Francisco, about two miles from the ferry slips at the Market Street Wharf.

London knew the waterfront well—as an amateur sailor, as a frequent passenger on Oakland–San Francisco ferries, and as an occasional patron of some of the many saloons in the area.

Line 94: "sou"

A French coin of small value. The expression "not a sou," which dates from the early nineteenth century, means "not the slightest bit."

Line 96: "squarehead"

A derogatory term for a Scandinavian. Because of their difficulties with English, Scandinavians in the Yukon—all referred to as "Swedes"—were considered gullible and foolish.

One of the most ironic incidents emerging from the Klondike Gold Rush is the story that someone had blazed the following words on a tree near an unexplored and little-regarded creek: "Reserved for Swedes and cheechakos [newcomers]." That nameless stream turned out to be Eldorado Creek, the richest gold creek ever discovered. London uses this episode as the centerpiece of his story "Too Much Gold."[53]

Line 100: "pull your freight"

A railway expression, meaning "to depart."

Lines 118–122: *wagons and trucks*

Because the Southern Pacific depot was about two miles from the ferry slips, Buck—confined in a crate—would have traveled by horse and wagon to the waterfront. The "truck" is today more commonly called a dolly or a hand-truck.

Line 121: *"ferry steamer"*

In the years before the great bridges were erected, ferryboats conveyed freight and passengers from San Francisco to points across the Bay. At the time of the Gold Rush, the train traffic would have gone by ferries operated by the Southern Pacific Company, which was enjoying a virtual monopoly. The trip cost ten cents and took twenty to thirty minutes.[54]

Buck's journey out of the Bay Area required one additional ferry trip that London does not mention: across the Straits of Carquinez, from Port Costa to Benicia, aboard the largest ferry steamer in the world, the *Solano*. On its deck were four tracks of a length sufficient to accommodate an entire passenger train. Built in 1879, this enormous side-wheeler was in continuous service until 1930, when the Southern Pacific completed a bridge over the straits.[55]

Charmian London notes in her biography of Jack that he had many times seen the *Solano* (bearing its cargo of "transcontinental trains of imposing railway carriages, with their leviathan locomotives") on his sailing excursions up the Sacramento River.[56] And in his autobiographical works *John Barleycorn* and *Tales of the Fish Patrol*, London several times mentions the vessel by name.

Line 122: *"a great railway depot"*

The "Oakland Mole"—a pier built near the Long Wharf, Oakland's first seaport terminal—was erected on a rock-fill out into the Bay at a promontory once known as Gibbons' Point. The pier was 285 feet wide, sufficient to accommodate four rail lines and a parallel wagon road. Begun early in 1880, the Mole took two years to complete and, according to Ford, included a "Victorian-styled" train shed that "spanned a total of fourteen tracks"; inside were "offices, a large waiting room, and the multitude of other facilities that go with a busy train terminal."[57]

London knew the Mole well: It was only a short distance from one of his boyhood homes on Pine Street, and he referred to it by name in a journal he kept of his "hobo" experiences in 1894.[58]

Line 123: "For two days and nights this express car was dragged along"

According to timetables from 1897, the trip by train from Oakland to Seattle, Washington, the next step in Buck's journey, took almost exactly that amount of time. The Oregon Express, the only through-train at the time, departed Oakland Pier at 8:30 in the evening. The trip to Portland, Oregon, where passengers and freight transferred to the Northern Pacific, consumed approximately a day and a half. Trains departing Oakland Pier at 8:30 P.M. on Monday would arrive at 9:30 A.M. on Wednesday in Portland. The Northern Pacific would then depart from Portland at 11:00 A.M. and arrive in Seattle at 4:00 P.M., just four and a half hours short of two days and nights.[59]

Line 141: "they bundled him off the train at Seattle"

The American Indian name for Seattle was *Tzee-tzee-lal-tic* ("little place where one crosses over"). Among the early white arrivals in the area was Dr. David Swinton Maynard, a man who combined his skills as a physician with a financial interest in the salmon-packing industry. In 1851, Maynard named the new city for his friend and fishing companion Noah Sealth, chief of the Suquamps and allied tribes.[60]

In 1890, 42,837 people lived in Seattle. Ten years later—enlarged by Gold Rush business and traffic from the newly completed Northern Pacific line—the population had nearly doubled to 80,671. When Dietz arrived at the height of the Rush in the winter of 1897–98 this is what he witnessed:

> . . . *a maelstrom of raving humanity driven half insane by the desire for gold.* . . . *Money was plentiful and fabulous prices were asked for everything. Every scheme, legal and illegal, mostly illegal, ever devised by mortal to separate a man from his money was run "wide open." Unspeakable dives, houses of ill-fame existed on every block in the business section and women under the protection of the police solicited business everywhere.* . . . *Many pick-pockets, professional gamblers and gunmen collected about these places like flies about a cider jug, and would not stop at murder—to say nothing of lesser crimes.*
>
> *Everything imaginable for use in gold mining and arctic expeditions was offered*

for sale. Fakers filled the streets and hawked their wares which consisted of com-passes, mercury, worthless contraptions for locating and testing gold and a thousand and one things which were found to be absolutely worthless.[61]

The Seattle waterfront was frenzied with activity as well. Mrs. George Black, who had left her timorous husband to pursue her Klondike Eldorado, remembered years later the hustle and bustle: "Over its wharves surged jostling eager crowds of miners, prospectors, traders, trappers, and adventurers, all dressed in the clothes of the trail—hideous red-and-yellow plaid mackinaws, overalls tucked into high boots, and caps of all descriptions. Everywhere were piles of "outfits"—camp supplies, sleds, carts, harness, which, together with dogs, horses, cattle, and oxen, were being loaded into the various boats, sailing almost every hour."[62]

The merchants in Seattle, led by Erastus Brainerd, made a tremendous effort to sup-plant San Francisco as the principal West Coast outfitter and point of departure for the gold-seekers. Seattle advertised heavily in newspapers and magazines all over the country—by one estimate placing five times more ads than any other competitor—and sent copies of a special Klondike issue of the *Seattle Post-Intelligencer* to one hundred thousand loca-tions. As one contemporary observer noted in December 1897: "The war between Greece and Troy was a petty squabble in comparison with the conflict which is now breaking out between San Francisco and Seattle for the coming trade with Alaska."[63]

The efforts of Brainerd and the Seattle merchants were complemented by such publica-tions as a pamphlet from the North American Transportation and Trading Company (with heavy investments in Seattle), coaxing readers to embark from that city: "It will be seen by a glance at the map that Seattle is clearly the gateway to the Alaskan country, as it is also an admirable place to procure their necessary outfit."[64]

Arguing the case for San Francisco was the Alaska Commercial Company, whose own pamphlet in 1898 contained the claim that the city was "the principal . . . commercial city of this coast," that it would "naturally [be] to the interest of any intending traveler to start from this point." Gold-seekers would be wise, the company continued, to board one of its steamers in San Francisco and take the all-water route to the Klondike, thereby avoiding the "[t]errors of the Chilcoot Pass and of the dread Skaguay Trail. . . ."[65]

The *San Francisco Chronicle* contributed a page or so of Klondike coverage virtually every day in the initial months of the Rush, often pointing to the advantages of outfitting in and departing from San Francisco. One headline, for example, claimed: "KLONDIKE AND SAN FRANCISCO, Great Revival Predicted That Will Create a Rival to New York."[66]

Line 143: "a stout man, with a red sweater"

This unidentified man who introduces Buck to "the law of the club" is based upon the many dog-trainers who flourished in Seattle during the Rush. There were at least four "dog schools" in the city, and one of the trainers, E. J. Crandall, calling himself "the Dog King of Seattle," positioned himself every day outside the Butler Hotel and tried to sell the "gaggle of yapping, whining dogs he had bought or stolen. . . ."[67]

Lines 142–95: Buck's training session

One of London's principal sources for his novel was Egerton R. Young's *My Dogs in the Northland* (1902). In one lengthy passage, Young describes a "training" session that very closely resembles Buck's. One of Young's dogs (Rover II) arrived in a "large box-like case"; for three days he had received "neither food nor drink," a condition that had made him "simply furious with his confinement and neglect." The four expressmen who delivered the crate "took their position on the top of the wall" to watch Young open the crate, which he accomplished with an axe: "At every blow struck on the outside of the box, he would spring at the place inside. . . ." Unlike the "man in the red sweater," however, Young does not beat the dog, but quickly supplies him with food and water.

Earlier in his book, however, Young does describe a beating similar to Buck's of one of his other dogs: With an axe handle Young repeatedly smashed the recalcitrant dog (which raged "like a caged lion"). "Again and again he came for me," Young wrote, "but in every instance I was thus able to throw him over. At length he began to lose heart in his rushes, and then, after receiving a specially ugly clip on the jaw, his opposition ceased and all the fight seemed suddenly to go out of him, and there the great big fellow lay sprawled out on the ground and coolly looking at me."[68]

Line 182: "cayuses"

The word *cayuse*, meaning "horse" (often, a "wild horse"), originated in the American West and was in common use during the Rush. The term is derived from the Oregon tribe of American Indians, the Cayuse.

Line 188: "ruction"

Slang for a disturbance or loud quarrel, probably from "insurrection."

Line 190: "all 'll go well and the goose hang high"

A curious expression meaning "things will be all right"—perhaps originally "the goose honks high" because migrating wild geese supposedly fly higher in good weather. Yet another explanation is that the expression is an allusion to "gander-pulling," a nineteenth-century activity requiring a horseback rider to snatch a plucked and well-greased goose dangling by its feet from the branch of a tree.[69]

Line 217: "Sacredam"

This is Perrault's broken-English equivalent of "holy damn" or "goddamn." Black Leclère also uses the term a couple of times in "Bâtard." In a letter to London on 1 April 1903, George Brett at Macmillan expressed some concerns about the "two or three cases of profanity" in the novel. Brett wanted the tale to retain the "virility which is now one of its distinguishing marks," but he worried that the presence of such language would adversely affect the book's sales to schools and libraries. "Do not remove the profanity if it will spoil the book in any way from your standpoint," wrote Brett, "but if it can *safely* be done please leave the profanity out."

In his reply to Brett on 10 April, London argued for the retention of several of the "less vigorous" oaths—"if possible, I pray you leave me two or three," he implored.[70]

Line 219: "three hundred, and a present at that"

Three hundred dollars was not an outrageous price for a fine dog during the Rush. Many participants—and other writers—noted the inflated prices for pack and work animals of all kinds. The *Dyea Trail* commented that good dogs were worth two hundred dollars to four hundred dollars apiece, and in the winter of 1897–98 journalist E. Hazard Wells paid three hundred dollars for a husky named Billick at Dawson City, Yukon, observing that even "[c]ommon curs cost two hundred dollars."[71]

Lines 223–24: "Canadian Government . . . despatches"

The Canadian government was concerned that an uncontrolled rush to the Yukon could be catastrophic. There was no food in the interior during the winter, and officials feared mass starvation. So government agents like Perrault did, in fact, carry crucial dispatches to and from the coast and Dawson City. In January 1898, Superintendent Constantine of the North-west Mounted Police described the contents of one of those dispatches in his annual report: "Relief can only come down the river, and it is necessary that the Government should take immediate action and ship supplies in over the summit. . . ."[72]

Line 227: "Curly"

It is likely that London derived Curly's name from Young's "Cuffy," also a Newfoundland, in *My Dogs in the Northland*. Young describes her as an animal whose "every curl . . . seemed absolutely perfect" and who, like London's Curly, was "affectionate and docile in every way. . . ."[73]

Line 228: "Newfoundland"

One of London's sources (Edward Jesse's *Anecdotes of Dogs*) commends the Newfoundland—a large, black breed—for its "docility" and "affectionate disposition"—Curly's principal traits.[74]

Line 230: "the deck of the Narwhal"

During the Rush there were only two vessels named *Narwhal* operating in American waters—but neither one put in or departed from Seattle in 1897–98. The first, a luxury steam-yacht, was owned by C. H. Osgood of New London, Connecticut, and did not participate in the Rush. The second, a steam-whaler from San Francisco, was hunting in the Arctic throughout most of 1897 and 1898.[75] Accordingly, London either invented the name, or he mistakenly selected the name of a ship that he had most likely seen in San Francisco Bay, home port for the whaler.

Whatever the ship, it would have been crammed with cargo, animals, and passengers. Frank Norris, writing at the time for *The Wave*, described a mad scene on a wharf in San Francisco as the *Excelsior* departed for the Northland:

[T]wenty thousand people thronged about her, packed sardine fashion on the wharves, crowding upon roofs and ships and even into the rigging of near-by masts and yards. Every class and rank and grade was represented in that crowd, from girls in smart frocks who came down from Pacific avenue in their own coupes, to stevedores and

city front touts, who stood about, thumbs in belt, nodding curt farewells to grub-staked "pals," who, with blanket roll and haversack huddled on the afterdeck. There was laughter and tears, sobs and smiles, shouts of encouragement and sighs of regret.[76]

Mrs. George Black, a passenger aboard the ill-named *Utopia* in the spring of 1898, described her ship as "dirty, and loaded to the gunwales with passengers, animals, and freight. Men slept on the floor of the saloon and in every corner." Drinking and gambling, she wrote, were so prevalent—even among the ship's crew—that "our safe arrival in Skagway was due probably to the Guiding Hand that looks after children, fools, and drunken men."[77]

R. W. Roberts complained about the presence of other animals aboard the *Mexico* in May 1897: "On board we have 24 head of cattle, 50 head of sheep and 10 head of hogs. They are quite close to our dining room. You can imagine the rest. None of the stalls have been cleaned since we left shore." And on 28 August 1897, Seattle's *News-Advertiser* printed the grievances of an unhappy passenger aboard the *Willamette*: "[T]he surroundings are filthy, the floors are sprinkled with shavings, and the beef in quarters is hung up on two sides of the room so that one cannot get to one side of the table without rubbing against it. The stench is almost unbearable." Many of the people aboard became so ill that they could not emerge from their bunks below, "and the result was revolting beyond belief. The stench that arose from the forecastle, where they men lay huddled together, permeated every part of the boat and was unbearable."[78]

Line 232: "François"

London based the characters of François and Perrault on Louis Savard, a French-Canadian whom he had known during his winter in the Klondike. (London calls him "French Louis" in *A Daughter of the Snows*, *Burning Daylight*, and *Smoke Bellew*.) In her biography of her husband, Charmian London quoted another of Jack's Yukon acquaintances, Bert Hargrave, on the subject of Louis Savard: "'He had a pronounced French-Canadian accent, the drollness of which so delighted London that he never ceased in his attempts to draw Louis into conversation.'" "François" appears in a list of four French names in one of London's notebooks.[79]

Named only as "a government courier and a half-breed voyageur," François with Perrault, makes a brief appearance in another London tale, "The One Thousand Dozen."[80]

Line 233: "half-breed"

This derogatory expression for a person of mixed ancestry—generally American Indian and Caucasian—can be found throughout the scores of books and articles about the North published in the nineteenth and early twentieth centuries. In fact, the term was so common that it became one of the official categories of prisoners established by the North-west Mounted Police for their annual reports in the late 1890s: Civilians, Indians, Lunatics, and Half-breeds.

There were many offspring of white and American Indian parents living in the Northland. Peter C. Newman notes that these relationships were "vital to the fur trade" because the women acted as "interpreters, mentors and, through their kinship links, vital conduits into Indian society."[81]

Line 238: "the 'tween-decks"

Any space between the decks of a ship—for example, the space below the main deck.

Line 239: "a big, snow-white fellow from Spitzbergen"

"Spitzbergen" is a group of islands in the Arctic Ocean north of Norway—called on some maps "Svalbard," its Norwegian name. Many of the dogs on the islands, wrote Frederick Palmer in 1899, "are so white that when they are on a background of snow you know of their presence only by the black spots for their eyes and a bigger black spot for their noses."[82]

Line 240: "a Geological Survey into the Barrens"

Also known as the "Barren Grounds" or the "Barren Lands" or the "Great Barrens," the Barrens are a desolate region of tundra due west of Hudson Bay. Though rocky and generally treeless, the Barrens have many streams, rivers, and lakes.

London is referring here to the Geological Survey of Canada, established in 1842 to aid the Canadian mining industry by mapping the country. In his history of the Geological Survey, Morris Zaslow observes that the surveyors not only mapped the geology but also "collected materials from every phase of life they encountered—samples of rocks and minerals, plants, animals, fishes, birds, Indian and Eskimo artifacts, even languages and legends."[83]

In 1894 and 1895, Joseph Burr Tyrrell led two expeditions into the Barrens for the Geological Survey, bringing back what Farley Mowat says was "the first really accurate and detailed description of the interior of the Barren Grounds."[84] According to Alex Inglis (Tyrrell's biographer), North American newspapers hailed Tyrrell as a "hero," so London would certainly have known of him—and perhaps had even read the account of the first expedition written by Tyrrell's brother James: *Across the Sub-Arctics of Canada* (1898).

London's use of the Tyrrell expedition helps establish the white dog Spitz's credentials as a worthy opponent for Buck. Inglis notes, "Any dog that could have survived with Tyrrell in the Barrens was immediately recognizable as a remarkably tough creature. To overcome such an enemy Buck would indeed have to be something special."[85]

There is little doubt that London knew about the Barrens and the Geological Survey. He mentions them elsewhere in his fiction, most notably in his short story "In the Forests of the North": "The Barrens—well, they are the Barrens, the bad lands of the Arctic, the deserts of the Circle, the bleak and winter home of the musk-ox and the lean plains wolf. So Avery Van Brunt [an explorer for the Geological Survey] found them, treeless and cheerless, sparsely clothed with moss and lichens and altogether uninviting." Later in the story, London mentions the Thelon River, which Tyrrell had charted for the Geological Survey in 1893.[86]

Lines 251–52: "Queen Charlotte Sound"

In an expedition to the Pacific Northwest in 1786, Captains Nathanial Portlock and George Dixon—commanding, respectively, the *King George* and the vessel named for the king's spouse, the *Queen Charlotte*—named many of the geographical features along the coast, including this spot on the Inside Passage where the Pacific Ocean pounds the shore without any interference from the islands that protect much of the rest of the coast between Puget Sound and Alaska.[87]

Many travelers on the Inside Passage during the Rush commented upon the rough water encountered in the sound. In her memoir of her trip to the goldfields, Alice Edna Berry remembered it as the only "rough" part of the passage. William B. Haskell provides more detail: "At Queen Charlotte Sound . . . the swell of the outer ocean is felt. Those subject to *mal de mar* [sea-sickness] disappear for a time. . . ." And Josiah Edward Spurr describes a similar experience: Passengers appeared at the meal table "with the pale face and defiant look which mark the unfortunate who has newly committed the crime of seasickness."[88]

On 1 August 1897, London crossed the sound aboard the *Umatilla* en route to Alaska.[89]

Lines 252–53: "Buck and Curly grew excited, half wild with fear"

Humans and beasts alike were alarmed by the occasional ferocity of the sea. In her history of the Alaska Steamship Company, Lucile McDonald tells how four dogs aboard the *Willapa* "got loose, panicked, jumped overboard and were lost." A passenger aboard the *Amur* early in 1897 complained about "the ceaseless snarling, fighting, yelping, barking, yapping, snapping, and growling of a pack of dogs. . . . They were omnipresent, on the decks, in the staterooms and cabins, the steerage, the cook's galleys, the lifeboats, everywhere but the rigging. Some were tied, but most were running loose and always under foot." And aboard the hastily outfitted *Blakely*, outward bound from Seattle, the dogs "howled and whined piteously; their imploring cries rose above the creaking and clattering of the boat and the swish of the waters as we bowled along. It produced a pandemonium that was most distressing."[90]

Lines 255–56: "Day and night the ship throbbed to the tireless pulse of the propeller, and . . . one day was very like another"

A variety of personal accounts and published steamship timetables reveal that the nine-hundred-mile voyage from Seattle to Juneau, Alaska, took anywhere from four to seven days. *Klondike and Yukon Guide*, 1898, stated bluntly: 884 miles in four days.[91] The remaining one hundred miles from Juneau to Skagway or nearby Dyea required, under good conditions, another twelve hours or so.

As passengers aboard the plethora of cruise ships operating today along the Inside Passage today can testify, the voyage is one of surpassing beauty. "Mighty forests of huge trees," wrote Addison Mizner, "marched down to the edge of the water on both sides." Charles C. Osborne, a magazine correspondent, wrote in September 1900 that he doubted "if there be any sea-journey of over eight hundred miles where the landscape is more uniformly interesting, or at times more impressive in its wild beauty and desolate grandeur." Mrs. George Black described "some peaks so high that they disappeared into the draping clouds. There were others crested with the snow of ages, which, as it shifted slowly down the mountain-side, transformed itself into many hanging glaciers—great beds of blue-green ice that cracked from time to time and set adrift small icebergs into the sea."[92]

The price of passage from Seattle to Juneau, which could have been booked for seventeen to thirty-two dollars early in the Rush, soon skyrocketed with the demand. On 3 August 1897, the *San Francisco Chronicle* reported that the *Humboldt* would charge each individual three hundred dollars, then add a freight charge of ten cents per pound beyond the permitted 150 pounds—that meant a total fare of about three hundred eighty-five dollars. Pierre Berton reports that some were so desperate for tickets that they paid as much as fifteen hundred dollars—and that by "midwinter the fare settled down to a straight one thousand."[93]

Line 265: "it was his first snow"

This would very likely have been true. In 1896, *Sunshine, Fruit, and Flowers* reported that snow had fallen only twice in the Santa Clara Valley in the previous twenty years.[94]

CHAPTER TWO

"The Law of Club and Fang"

Line 266: "the Dyea beach"

Dyea, Alaska—one hundred miles north of Juneau—was originally a Chilkat-Tlingit Indian village. Although once a permanent site, Dyea had become by the time of the Rush a seasonal fishing camp for the Chilkat near the spot where the Taiya River empties into a sixty-mile-long finger of ocean called the Lynn Canal. Robert C. Kirk, an early visitor, described the inlet as "a beautiful sheet of water that lay crowded in between massive mountains covered with perpetual snow-fields and serpentine glaciers." Aboard a ship from Juneau, Mizner marveled at the "turquoise blue glaciers, high up between cliffs, urging their way to the sea, [as they] caught the slanting rays of the noonday sun."[1]

Most authorities agree that the word *Dyea* (pronounced die-EE) is a Tlingit word meaning "carrying place." Spellings varied considerably, however, and the word appeared as "Ty-a," "Dayay" and "Taiya" on early maps and in Gold Rush–era publications— indeed the river remains the "Taiya." "Carrying place" is an appropriate name because Dyea lay at the foot of the Chilkoot Pass, one of the principal trade routes over the Coastal Mountains to the interior of the Yukon. For generations, the coastal Chilkat traded fish and their by-products for furs and copper with the Tagish and other bands of inland American Indians. During the Rush the Chilkat carried supplies for miners, sometimes charging as much as a dollar a pound for the ton of goods required for each traveler by the

North-west Mounted Police, who maintained a customs post at the top of the mountain passes and would not permit those with inadequate provisions to continue into the Yukon.[2]

Dyea's history was brief but colorful. When Frederick Schwatka arrived at the mouth of the Taiya River in 1883, he saw only "a series of low swampy mud flats and a very miry delta" and was not enticed to linger long. A year later, John J. Healy established a trading post at the site, and for the next dozen years, after Edgar Wilson joined the business, Healy & Wilson's was the sole permanently occupied structure in what would become the town of Dyea. Arthur Treadwell Walden, a Yukon veteran, remembered that when he had first arrived in Dyea in March 1896, it consisted only of the trading post and "a dozen or more Indian shacks."[3]

At the height of the Rush, however, Dyea burgeoned into a bustling town, whose population, according to one of its two newspapers, was ten thousand. By June, Dyea was civilized enough to support both a literary society and a baseball team—which played against the nearby Skagway nine. Julius M. Price, a journalist visiting from England, however, was not impressed, describing Dyea in the spring of 1898 as "one long, dusty, straggling street of wooden and canvas shanties. . . ."[4]

Eventually, Dyea lost its competition for the Gold Rush trade with nearby Skagway, which boasted a deeper harbor and the White Pass and Yukon Railroad, which opened its transmountain service on 20 February 1899. Today, Dyea once again is wilderness, and only a few pilings from the old wharf remind the visitor of its former significance in the history of the North. Fire, flood, storm, foragers, and vandals have claimed all the buildings. In February 1978, much of the old townsite was purchased by the National Park Service.[5]

According to Fred Thompson's diary, London and his party arrived in Dyea on 7 August 1897.[6]

Lines 269–70: "all was confusion and action"

In the early days of the Rush, the Chilkoot Pass was the favored route over the mountains, and Dyea flourished. But when the scores of ships arrived at Dyea, the eager argonauts found not a well-organized port with many wharves and piers, but a beach and one unfinished wharf, appropriately dubbed "Long Wharf" because it extended a mile and a half out into the Lynn Canal. It was not finished until May 1898—and within a year was unusable because of storm damage and shoddy construction. And even when available for service, the wharf presented a problem: The planking was at times so icy that occasionally "landing pilgrims slipped from it into the sea," wrote Harwood Steele, "and were fished out with clothes frozen solid—and pneumonia."[7]

Because of the shallow water large ships could not approach Dyea, so the prospectors and their gear had to float ashore on flatboats—"lighters"—operated by a variety of profit-seekers eager to make as many trips back and forth to the ship as possible. Flat-boaters dumped goods and supplies unceremoniously on the beach, forcing the gold-seekers to scramble frantically to retrieve all their belongings before the tide returned and washed them out to sea. One Gold Rush manual recommended—with no detectable irony—that passengers exercise "haste . . . in the sorting of outfits and getting them above tide water."[8]

Few scenes were so well recorded by the chroniclers of the Gold Rush as what London called elsewhere "the madness of the Dyea beach." The *Dyea Trail* termed it "one of the most animated scenes that can be imagined." Robert C. Kirk complained about the "confusion when tons and tons of boxes and sacks and barrels came ashore, where no steamship people were waiting to receive them, and where each one of the eight hundred passengers [aboard his ship] was hurrying about looking for the goods that bore his private brand."[9]

In his first novel, *A Daughter of the Snows* (1902), London provided more details about the wild scene:

> *Everybody was in everybody else's way; nor was there one who failed to proclaim it at the top of his lungs. A thousand gold-seekers were clamoring for the immediate landing of their outfits. Each hatchway gaped wide open, and from the lower depths the shrieking donkey-engines were hurrying the misassorted outfits skyward. On either side of the steamer, rows of scows received the flying cargo, and on each of these scows a sweating mob of men charged the descending slings and heaved bales and boxes about in frantic search. Men waved shipping receipts and shouted over the steamer-rails to them. Sometimes two and three identified the same article, and war arose. The "two-circle" and the "circle-and-dot" brands caused endless jangling, while every whipsaw discovered a dozen claimants.*[10]

In his diary, Thompson recorded very little about what London saw on the Dyea beach—other than to mention that the steamer *George W. Elder* was unloading—but since he remained in town for a day and a half, it is fair to speculate that he actually witnessed much of what he elsewhere called the "screaming bedlam" of the Dyea beach.[11]

Line 274: "unforgetable"

This word is spelled with one *t* in both the first serial and first book editions.

Line 276: "the log store"

The store is probably Healy & Wilson's trading post, a business so important to travelers in the North that "Healy's Store" appeared instead of "Dyea" on some Gold Rush maps. Although London does not ever give the precise name of this store in his fiction, he does allude to it. In *A Daughter of the Snows*, for example, he calls it "the log store by the Dyea River." And in his essay "Gold Hunters of the North"—published in *Atlantic* in July 1903, the same month and year as *The Call of the Wild*—he does refer to it as "the store of Captain John Healy at Dyea."[12]

As photographs reveal, Healy & Wilson's was actually at least two structures, one of which appears to be frame. The other, however—most likely the storehouse—is clearly log in construction. Because London had spent only a day and a half at Dyea on his way into the Yukon, his memory of the structure may not have been clear. But he was not the only observer who remembered it as log. J. Bernard Moore, who kept a journal between 1887 and 1896, referred to the "hewn logs of the store building." And Spurr, who passed through the region in 1896, wrote of "a log house used as a store for trading with the natives, and known by the name of Healy's Post." Perhaps the log building antedated the frame dwelling, which, in any case, was destroyed by fire sometime before 1920.[13]

Line 276: "a husky dog"

"Husky" is a generic name for any of several northern breeds used for sled work. The American Kennel Club recognizes the Alaskan Malamute, the Samoyed, and the Siberian Husky—all of which could be termed "husky" in the North. In general, huskies weigh about sixty pounds and stand about twenty-two inches at the shoulder. The Alaskan Malamute is somewhat larger: eighty-five pounds and twenty-five inches.[14]

Lines 281–82: "thirty or forty huskies ran to the spot and surrounded the combatants in an intent and silent circle"

Many nineteenth-century visitors to the Northland commented upon the pugnaciousness of the native dogs. Johan Adrian Jacobsen, a Norwegian explorer in the early 1880s, described a "bloody fight" among his animals: "[O]ne of the dogs was thrown against the tent, and the cotton material . . . gave way, flinging the dog directly onto my stomach." On a trip to the region in 1883, Schwatka saw two huskies who fought until they were so exhausted "they had to lean up against each other to rest."[15]

A review of Northland writings reveals only one author who describes the phenomenon of dogs forming a circle to watch two others fight: Jack London. In a short essay in *Harper's Weekly* antedating *The Call of the Wild*, London mentions it for the first time: "The onlooking huskies merely crowd interestedly around, ready, however, for the first slip." And in the short story "Bâtard," a "snarling circle"—a "ring of grinning wolf-dogs"—surrounds the battling Black Leclère and Bâtard, awaiting the outcome. And White Fang, after knocking a dog off its feet would stand by and watch the "stricken dog . . . in the dirt . . . pounced upon and torn to pieces by the pack of Indian dogs that waited."[16]

The closest confirmation of London's descriptions comes from Fridtjof Nansen, a Norwegian who made an assault on the North Pole just prior to the Gold Rush. In his two-volume account of his expedition, Nansen writes: "There is not a trace of chivalry about these curs. When there is a fight, the whole pack rush like wild beasts on the loser."[17]

During his year in the Yukon, London had surely seen fighting huskies—in the notes he kept as he left the Klondike he recorded having seen "dogs fighting" at an encampment of Tanana Indians on 14 June 1898—so perhaps he had actually witnessed such a "circle-and-wait" incident.[18]

Lines 286–87: "They closed in upon her, snarling and yelping, and she was buried, screaming with agony, beneath the bristling mass of bodies."

Although the canine behavior of circling and awaiting the outcome of a battle was not recorded by any Northland writer other than London, the destruction of one dog by a pack of others was—many times. Jeremiah Lynch observed in St. Michael, Alaska, "a dog severely bitten in the ear by another until the blood flowed, and instantly he was worried, bitten, and harried by the other dogs. . . ." Scotty Allan, a dog-driver during the Rush, wrote that it "is a dog's nature to gang the one that is down." Edwin Tappan Adney described a wild fight he saw among thirty or more dogs in the streets of Dawson: "Woe to the under dog in an impromptu melee," he commented; "he has no friend." And in Fairbanks, Alaska, the carcasses of the losers of the regular free-for-alls among the dogs were dumped on the ice of the Tanana River, to be swept away when the ice broke in the spring.[19]

London wrote elsewhere of the ferociousness—and voraciousness—of huskies in a frenzy to destroy. In "The White Silence," the other dogs turn on one of their own—Carmen, the weakest—and, ignoring the blows delivered by Malemute Kid, refuse to "scatter till the last wretched bit had disappeared,—bones, hide, hair, everything." And in "That Spot," London—showing a flash of humor—describes a dog named Spot caught in just such a situation: "I've seen him go down in a dog-fight on the main street with fifty dogs on top of him, and when they were separated, he'd appear on all his four legs, unharmed, while two of the dogs that had been on top of him would be lying dead."[20]

Line 288: Spitz

"Spitz" is a generic term for dogs with stocky bodies, thick coats, tails curved up and over the back, and pointed ears (*spitz* is German for "pointed"). Based on the description of Spitz in the first chapter as "a big, snow-white fellow," it is likely that he was a Samoyed, a white-furred breed weighing approximately fifty pounds and standing twenty-one inches at the shoulder.

Lines 288–89: "He saw Spitz run out his scarlet tongue in a way he had of laughing"

Darwin discusses the phenomenon of dogs "laughing" in *The Expression of the Emotions in Man and Animals*. He uses for one example a "Spitz" dog: "A pleasurable and excited state of mind, associated, with affection, is exhibited by some dogs in a very peculiar manner; namely, by grinning. . . . I have also seen it in a Spitz and in a sheep-dog. . . . The upper lip during the act of grinning is retracted, as in snarling, so that the canines are exposed, and the ears are drawn backwards; but the general appearance of the animal clearly shows that anger is not felt." In *Winterdance* (1994), Gary Paulsen insists that his sled dogs smile to express humor and satisfaction.[21]

Lines 299–300: "an arrangement of straps and buckles . . . a harness"

Adney's *Klondike Stampede*, which was part of London's personal library, contains a description and drawing of the sort of harness London is here referring to:

> In the Upper Yukon the harness used by both Indians and white men is a collar, with side-traces and back-band, and, if more than one dog is used, they are hitched tandem, the traces of the dog ahead being fastened to the traces of the one behind, either close to

the collar or at a point behind the back strap. One sort of collar is made of harness leather stuffed with hair and stiffened with quarter-inch iron wire, serving as hames [two curved pieces lying upon the collar in the harness of an animal, to which the traces are fastened], but part of the collar itself; the back-strap and belly-strap are also leather, and the harness is fitted with metal snaps, the traces being of webbing.[22]

Marshall Bond's dog Jack, the dog upon which Buck was based, also had problems adjusting to the harness for the first time, as Bond wrote in his diary: "Hitched Jack to a sledge & started for El Dorado [Creek]. Downtown [Dawson] put Fox's dog in team, too, but both were novices. . . ."[23] Two days before this happened, London and his party had arrived and camped near the Bond brothers' cabin, so London may actually have witnessed this event.

Line 301: "a sled"

Many of the contemporary accounts of the Rush included descriptions of the sorts of sleds common in the Yukon. Most agreed that the standard size was seven feet long, sixteen inches wide, and about six inches high. Adney, as usual, was more specific: "The bow is slightly upturned, and the top, of four longitudinal pine slats, rests upon four cross-frames of ash, with ash runners shod with two-inch shoes." The sleds weighed about eighty pounds. Adney recorded that the sleds generally cost seven dollars on the "outside" and forty dollars in Dawson. In her account of her journey to Dawson, "An American Girl's Trip to the Klondike," Esther Lyons noted that she paid fourteen dollars for her sled in Seattle in March 1897.[24]

In *Burning Daylight* London briefly describes Daylight's sled—the very sort Buck is learning to pull: It was "a long, narrow affair, sixteen inches wide and seven and a half feet in length, its slatted bottom raised six inches above the steel-shod runners. On it, lashed with thongs of moose-hide, were the food and gear for dogs and men."[25]

Line 305: "whip"

"The whip I used," wrote Bramble in 1897, "had a handle nine inches long and a lash of thirty feet, and it weighed four pounds. The lash was of folded and plaited seal hide, and for five feet from the handle measured five inches round, then for fourteen feet it gradually tapered off, ending in a single thong half an inch thick and eleven feet long." He warned that the whip required "a skillful hand," for an inexperienced driver would be "sure to half-strangle himself, or to hurt his own face with the business end of the lash."[26]

London knew about the design of such a dog-team whip. In *White Fang* he mentions a "whip of cariboo-gut [*sic*] with its biting thirty-foot lash."[27]

Line 306: "Dave . . . was an experienced wheeler"

The so-called "wheeler" or "wheel dog"—generally the strongest member of the team—is placed closest to the sled. The term was originally applied to teams of horses, the "wheel horse" being the one closest to the wheels of a carriage or wagon. The dog in this position is referred to by some Northland writers as the "sled dog" or "sleigh dog"—or even a "steer-dog."[28]

Line 307: "the leader"

Kirk maintained that a good lead dog was as valuable to the driver as "any two dogs in the team." He went on: "A good leader will turn instantly to the right or to the left as the driver shouts . . . , and when an extra effort is needed to draw the sled over an obstruction, a word from the driver puts an energy and life into the leader that are instantly imitated by every other dog in the team."[29]

Line 309: "the traces"

Traces (or reins) were variously fashioned from cloth, leather, caribou intestine, moose hide, or seal hide. In his 1890s journeys, Nansen was alarmed to see that many of the Eskimo dogs he observed had been castrated in order to accommodate the passage of the traces between their front and rear legs, a custom obviated by the development of the collar-harness that Adney describes above.[30]

Line 310: "under the combined tuition of his two mates and François made remarkable progress"

Young's lead dog, Jack, was accomplished at "breaking in obstinate young dogs."[31]

Line 311: "to stop at 'ho,' to go ahead at 'mush'"

"Ho" is a variation of "whoa," a common command to stop for a horse; "mush" derives from the French-Canadian *mouche*, "to make haste." Lynch observed that "ho" and "mush"—along with "gee" and "ha"—"comprise the full extent of a good driver's vocabulary, with perhaps a few minor words as adjuncts." Following his visit to the region, Osborne reported that he had heard "mush" in a variety of situations: "There is something contagious in the sound of it. Dogs are made to *mush-on*; *mush-on* is shouted at the horses; and men never walk, but always *mush-on*."[32]

Lines 312–13: *"to keep clear of the wheeler when the loaded sled shot downhill at their heels"*

Placed in the team just in front of the wheeler, Buck would indeed have had to scamper out of the way whenever the sled raced downhill just behind him. E. Hazard Wells wrote an amusing account of the difficulties of his own dogs in this situation: "Down the declivity we went at terrific speed, the snow flying up in my face in clouds as I hung desperately on to the rope in my hands. Almost by a miracle, we landed safely at the bottom without mishap more serious than running over two dogs which could not keep out of the way. They were not injured except in their feelings."[33]

Line 317: *"Billee"*

There is no way to determine for certain the origin of London's selection of this name—or the unusual spelling—but there are, given London's fondness for using the actual names of Klondike notables, two intriguing possibilities. The candidates are two men, father and son, both named Billie Moore, both among the best known men in the Northland. The elder Billie was the founder of Skagway, Alaska; the younger, whom London met on his way home to California, captained steamboats up and down the Yukon River for many years.[34]

Line 317: *"Joe"*

When *The Call of the Wild* was serialized in *The Saturday Evening Post* in the summer of 1903, this name, with a single exception, was spelled "Jo" throughout.

Lines 330–36: *"an old husky . . . with a battle-scarred face and a single eye . . . called Sol-leks, which means the Angry One. . . . did not like to be approached on his blind side"*

"Sol-leks" does mean "angry" or "angry one" in Chinook Jargon, the trade language of the Northland. In 1896 Warburton Pike wrote that the Jargon, originating with the Chinook Indians of Oregon, developed into a "common language" among the various tribes, then spread northward and was employed by white traders and miners in their encounters with Northland Indians.[35] London knew about Chinook Jargon, referring to it by name elsewhere in his fiction—for example, in "The Wife of a King," "Siwash," "Where the Trail Forks," and "A Relic of the Pliocene."

It is likely that London based Sol-leks on another one-eyed dog, Voyageur, one of Young's animals in *My Dogs in the Northland*. Like Sol-leks, Voyageur was "morose and unsociable," resented "being silently approached on his blind side," and, "once harnessed," displayed a "great transformation," becoming a tireless worker.[36]

Although Sol-leks had apparently lost his eye in battle, Voyageur had lost his to an errant stroke of a whip—a fairly common accident. *Klondike: The Chicago Record's Book for Gold Seekers* (1897) mentions that when "a dog is beaten over the body and head with a chain it is pretty brutal, and many a dog has had ribs and legs broken and eyes knocked out."[37]

Line 365: "proceeded to dig a hole for himself"
Young's dogs likewise "had to dig holes in the snow and sleep there as best they could." And Lynch described a dog "pawing a hole in the snow in which to lie comfortably."[38]

Lines 370–71: "it had snowed during the night and he was completely buried"
Young described a similar instance of what was an occurrence common enough to earn mention in a number of books about the Northland. Haskell tells how, while "[k]icking about in some mounds in the drifted snow," he found three of his dogs, "sleeping as peacefully and snugly as possible." Wells, writing of his beloved husky Billick, told a similar tale: "Often in the morning I have only been able to tell where he was by a little white mound, the falling snow having covered him up completely in the night and acting as a blanket. The moment I called him he'd jump out of his bed, shake himself, and frisk about as gayly as though he had enjoyed the most luxurious sleeping quarters." More recently, Elizabeth Marshall Thomas (1993) wrote how, after a snowfall, she would call to her dogs "in an apparently empty yard, only to see them erupt from the snowdrifts where they had buried themselves."[39]

Line 383: "courier for the Canadian Government"
The North-west Mounted Police employed civilians to carry messages throughout their jurisdiction. In "The Scorn of Women," London mentions one by name, "Devereaux, the official courier, bearing despatches from the Governor."[40]

Line 388: "Dyea Cañon"

About eight miles from the mouth of the Taiya River, the Dyea Canyon presented the first real difficulty for travelers on the trail to Dawson City—a "crevice in the mountains about two miles long and fifty feet wide," wrote Haskell, "with a raging river at the bottom. . . . Great boulders are piled in confused heaps, and the snow-laden stumps of trees and upturned roots stick out in fantastic shapes." At the head of the canyon a small community formed—Canyon City—but as the English journalist Price described it, the "city" was really nothing more than "a small collection of rough wooden shanties and tents."[41]

In a pamphlet published during the Rush, H. Eustace Mitton recorded his own harrowing experience in the canyon in the winter of 1891:

Through this narrow defile the stream ran with great swiftness, and there was open water in numerous places. We made a footpath in the snow on the sides of the can[y]on, and placed our outfit on our backs. We continually came upon small crevasses in the snow, which stopped further progress on that side; we then had to cut down a pine trunk, so that it might fall across the can[y]on, and over this slender bridge we crawled with a load on our backs, all the time knowing that one slip meant precipitation into the rushing torrent below, coupled with certain death.

. . . [I]t took us seven days to get through, a great number of bridges having to be made, and in some places footholes having to be cut in the solid ice, whilst huge boulders of frozen snow continually came crashing down from above.[42]

Thompson noted in his diary entry for 16 August 1897 that the London party regarded the canyon as "a tough proposition," causing all to "get very tired and foot sore."[43]

Line 398: "single file"

Tandem-style was the usual arrangement for Yukon dog teams; coastal Eskimos employed a fan-shaped system.

Lines 405–8: "he got tangled in the traces . . . but Buck took good care to keep the traces clear thereafter"

Anyone who has ever observed a dog hopelessly snarled in a chain or leash must wonder if London has departed from reality here. But Young stoutly maintained that his dogs were "wonderfully clever" at straightening out "mixups." And Paulsen describes how his team "lined out and untangled themselves—they had been running trapline and knew how to do such things. . . ." Palmer was less sanguine about his own dogs, noting that his blunt strategy was "to club them into insensibility, and cut the leather harness. . . ."[44]

Lines 412–15: "it was a hard day's run, up the Cañon, through Sheep Camp, past the Scales . . . and over the great Chilcoot Divide, which stands between the salt water and the fresh and guards forbiddingly the sad and lonely North"

There has been some disagreement about the origin of the name for "Sheep Camp," which lies about five miles beyond the Dyea Canyon. Some say it had once been head-quarters for hunters of mountain sheep; others state just as confidently that there "were no sheep at Sheep Camp, and never had been."[45]

Whatever the origin of the name, the spot became a last campsite before the final assault on the summit of the Chilcoot Pass, which loomed straight ahead about three and a half miles. When he passed through in late December 1897, Mizner saw "two or three shacks and a couple of hundred tents straggled along the floor of the gorge, and that was Sheep Camp. Nothing with more brains than a sheep would ever have camped there." It was, indeed, not a site for the faint of heart—or the incautious. According to an official re-port of the North-west Mounted Police in February 1898, "neither law nor order prevailed in that section, [so] murder, robbery and petty theft were of common occurrence. . . ."[46]

Alice Berry, however, was struck by at least one aspect of the camp: a dance hall run by two women situated very near where Berry and her husband had pitched their tent. "They [the two women] could dance, sing, swear, play roulette, shake dice, and play poker," wrote Berry; "in fact, they could do almost anything, and as I had never seen anybody like that before, I kept my eyes over on their dance hall every minute."[47]

London's party passed through Sheep Camp on 21 August 1897, and in his diary Thompson describes it as "a very tough hole and we camped above about 300 yards." Robert B. Medill, who traveled through at approximately the same time, was more specific in his own diary about just how "tough" it was: He claimed to have seen two hundred dead horses on the arduous, rock-strewn, three-mile trail between Sheep Camp and the foot of the pass. "We were sometimes obliged," he wrote, "to step on one where it lay in a hole on the trail with a bullet hole in its head."[48]

About three miles past Sheep Camp is a gravel ledge known as the Scales. Loose rocks and boulders of all shapes and sizes clutter the trail, forcing travelers at times to proceed hand over hand. As is the case with a number of Northland locations, the origin of the name is debatable. Adney said the spot was named "from having been in former years a weighing-place for goods hoisted or packed over." Although many historians of the Rush agree with Adney, Esther Lyons repeated a somewhat different story told to her by one of her Chilkat packers, who claimed an early traveler had "grown weary" of carrying scales and had abandoned them at the spot, where "they remained for many years. . . ." Lyons believed that story was "more likely" than the traditional explanation.[49]

The "great Chilcoot Divide," known today as the Chilkoot Pass and jointly maintained as part of the Chilkoot Trail by the U.S. National Park Service and Parks Canada, presented a formidable challenge to the gold-seekers. Named for the Chilkoot-Tlingit Indians—closely related to the Chilkat—the pass had for generations been used by the coastal American Indians on their trading expeditions to the interior. An earlier name, Roy Minter reports, was "Vlekuk" (unfortunately, he does not provide a translation), but Mary Lee Davis says that the Chilkoot had called it the "Grease Trail" because they had carried across it "the precious oolakan fish-oil, which was one of their staples of barter with the tribes of the Interior." During his crossing in 1883, explorer Frederick Schwatka named the pass after Colonel J. Perrier of the French Geographical Society, but the name "Perrier Pass" never caught on with the prospectors.[50]

The trail to the summit is only about a half-mile from the Scales, but at a forty-five degree incline. The climb is difficult enough for recreational hikers today—some take several hours to maneuver among and clamber over the boulders that are the "trail"—but the gold-seekers had to pack a year's supplies to the top; otherwise, the North-west Mounted Police stationed at the top would turn them back. This meant repeated trips back and forth—often one a day was all that was possible. Haskell, for example, climbed to the summit forty times.[51]

In the winter of 1897–98, the miners hacked footsteps in the ice and dubbed the final ascent the "Golden Stairs." The most well known photographs of the entire Gold Rush era are those of miners scaling the pass, single-file, in long dark lines etched against the brilliant white snow that fell that winter to depths of seventy feet at the summit. Printed in newspapers and magazines all over the country, those images so inspired filmmaker Charlie Chaplin that he used the scaling of the Chilkoot as the opening sequence in his silent classic *The Gold Rush* (1925).

Photographs reveal that there was more than one way over the pass. The wider and less steep way to the right was called, for unknown reasons, the Petterson Trail; it would have been the way Buck and his teammates traveled, for it was easier for pack animals to negotiate.[52]

The way back down was much quicker—and undoubtedly much more fun, as well, as Mont Hawthorne recalls in his sourdough vernacular:

Off to the side a piece was the shoot, that's where the men had wore down places, as deep as the walls of a room is high, sliding back down again to the bottom. The packers would jump into the shoot, kick out their feet from under them, set down fast, and slide clean to the bottom of the pass. You never seen a man coming down the shoot. All you ever seen was a ball of snow until he crawled out down at the bottom. A man sliding down had to jump up and get out of the shoot fast or the fellow sliding down back of him would land feet first on top of his head.[53]

Black packed over the pass in 1898 and forty years later remembered her ordeal in agonizing detail:

As the day advanced the trail became steeper, the air warmer, and footholds without support impossible. I shed my sealskin jacket. I cursed my hot, high, buckram collar, my tight heavily boned corsets, my long corduroy skirt, my full bloomers which I had to hitch up with every step. We clung to stunted pines, spruce roots, jutting rocks. In some places the path was so narrow that, to move at all, we had to use our feet tandem fashion. Above, only the granite walls. Below, death leering at us.

But soon, too soon, I was straining every nerve, every ounce of physical endurance in that ever upward climb. There were moments when, with sweating forehead, pounding heart, and panting breath, I felt I could go no farther. At such times we dropped out of line and rested in the little snow dug-outs along the way. But such a few moments of rest! Then on with that cursing procession of men and dogs and horses, pulling sleds or toting packs.

Mush on . . . Mush on. . . . It beat into my brain. . . . Cracking of whips. . . . Wild screams of too heavily loaded pack horses which lost their footing and were dashed to the rocks below . . . stumbling . . . staggering . . . crawling. . . . God pity me![54]

London made about a dozen trips up the pass between 27 and 31 August 1897,[55] an experience that no doubt equipped him to describe the climb in some of his most evocative prose:

The mid-day sun beat down upon the stone "Scales." The forest had given up the struggle, and the dizzying heat recoiled from the unclothed rock. On either hand rose the ice-marred ribs of earth, naked and strenuous in their nakedness. Above towered storm-beaten Chilcoot. Up its gaunt and ragged front crawled a slender string of men. But it was an endless string. It came out of the last fringe of dwarfed shrub below, drew a black line across a dazzling stretch of ice, and filed . . . on, up the pitch of the steep, growing fainter and fainter, till it squirmed and twisted like a column of ants and vanished over the crest of the pass.[56]

Lines 415–16: "down the chain of lakes which fills the craters of extinct volcanoes"

Following his 1883 visit, Schwatka was the first to publish the notion that the lakes that lie just over the Chilcoot summit are volcanic in origin. "This small lake," he wrote, referring to Crater Lake, "abruptly walled in, greatly resembled an extinct crater, and such it may well have been." Crater Lake does indeed appear to be what Berton terms it in his *Klondike*—"a cupful of frozen water in an old volcanic hollow." But Dawson and Spurr, both geologists, state that the lakes are glacial rather than volcanic in origin.[57]

Whatever their origin, the lakes presented challenges to travelers. In summer, the trail around them traversed terrain almost lunar in its rugged appearance—and the streams connecting the small lakes were deadly, roaring over jagged rocks, splitting narrow canyons with tumultuous violence. In winter, the instability of the ice was a constant threat to those who ventured on it.

London crossed Crater Lake on 31 August 1897 and later, in *A Daughter of the Snows*, offered a brief description of it, as Frona Welse paused beside "the volcanic ruin of Chilcoot's mighty father, and stood on the bleak edge of the lake which filled the edge of the crater." In *Smoke Bellew*, London describes Deep Lake, a few miles from Crater, as "another volcanic pit filled with glacial water."[58]

Lines 416–18: "the huge camp at the head of Lake Bennett, where thousands of gold-seekers were building boats against the break-up of the ice in the spring"

About sixteen miles from the Chilcoot Summit, Lake Bennett—named by Schwatka for James Gordon Bennett, publisher of the *New York Herald*—is twenty-six miles long and one of the major lakes from whose waters the Yukon River eventually forms. The American Indian word for the lake was *Kusooa*, which means "narrow lake" in Tlingit.[59] From Bennett, the gold-seekers could travel the remaining 530 or so miles to Dawson City by water. During the eight or nine months when the lake is frozen, dog teams can travel across its surface, as Buck and his team-mates are doing here.

During the Gold Rush, thousands of prospectors paused at Bennett to build boats in anticipation of the break-up of the ice; in their zeal, they cut down every tree for miles around the lake, fashioning from them vessels which ranged in quality from adequate to suicidal. Davis gives a clear indication of the enormous effort the boat-building enterprise at Lake Bennett required:

> *Yet to snake huge logs out through the woods with block and tackle, peel and mark them with the charcoal snap-strings [to indicate a path for the saw], hoist them on high saw-pits and then cut them with the heavy rip-saw into twenty- or thirty-foot boards—to saw and plane straight edges on the planks, place them so they would not warp, carry them in the long distance to our camp, build, calk [sic], and launch two boats neither of them small, rig masts and sails and make a half dozen good oars— was all hard work. And yet, somehow, it all seemed sport, and every little cove was a baby shipyard.*[60]

The community of transients and entrepreneurs that grew up around the lake greatly impressed Price, who was surprised to find "almost everything—hot baths, barbers' shops, restaurants, drinking saloons; whilst in the main thoroughfares, mining-agents, land-agents, solicitors, doctors, dentists, company promoters, rubbed elbows with unkempt and dirty Indian packers, brawny, bearded miners, and eager, newly-arrived fortune-seekers. . . ."[61]

The ice finally broke on 29 May 1898, and more than seven thousand homemade boats commenced a wild river race to Dawson.

London and his party built their boat at Lake Lindeman, which is connected to Bennett by a one-mile rapids so dangerous that it required a portage. In a race against freeze-up, they sailed out onto Bennett on 22 September 1897.[62]

Lines 421–23: "That day they made forty miles, the trail being packed; but . . . for many days to follow, they broke their own trail . . . and made poorer time. . . . Perrault travelled ahead of the team, packing the snow with webbed shoes"

Any number of Northland writers verify that forty miles per day is within the normal range on a packed trail. Another proposition altogether is traveling through deep snow, the most physically draining aspect of which, for humans, is "breaking trail" for the dogs— jogging ahead of the team in order to pack the snow so that the short-legged animals do not exhaust themselves floundering through drifts. Frederick Whymper wrote in 1868 that while traveling in deep snow he frequently had to go over the ground three times to prepare it adequately for his dogs.[63]

London described the practice in "The White Silence":

At every step the great webbed shoe sinks till the snow is level with the knee. Then up, straight up, the deviation of a fraction of an inch being a certain precursor of disaster, the snowshoe must be lifted till the surface is cleared; then forward, down, and the other foot is raised perpendicularly for the matter of half a yard. He who tries this for the first time, if haply he avoids bringing his shoes in dangerous propinquity and measures not his length on the treacherous footing, will give up exhausted at the end of a hundred yards; he who can keep out of the way of the dogs for a whole day may well crawl into his sleeping-bag with a clear conscience and a pride which passeth all understanding; and he who travels twenty sleeps on the Long Trail is a man whom the gods may envy.[64]

In order to "break trail" efficiently, snowshoes were a necessity—"webbed shoes," as London calls them here. There were a variety of styles worn by various Northland travelers, some more effective than others. One North-west Mounted Policeman complained in an 1898 report that the shoes issued by the government "are not suitable for this country, being too wide, too heavy, and flat at the toe, [so] I am glad to take those made by the natives."[65]

Line 424: "guiding the sled at the gee-pole"

Extending from the right—or "gee"—front of a Yukon sled was a stout pole used for steering and control. The device was about six feet long, three inches thick, and reached to a person's shoulder. It was useful, wrote Walden, "to break the sled out when frozen in by swinging it from side to side, and to hold back on when going down small hills." He went on to relate how a man with a runaway sled "was killed by the gee-pole breaking and the stub running through his body."⁶⁶

Lines 426–27: "the fall ice was very thin, and where there was swift water, there was no ice at all"

Although London mentions no place-names here, travelers would, after Lake Bennett, cross Lakes Tagish and Marsh and then enter a stretch of water—in London's day called the Fifty Mile River—that included some of the most dangerous rapids on the entire Yukon: Miles (or "Box" or "Grand") Canyon and the Whitehorse and Squaw rapids.

Schwatka named the high-walled canyon for General George Miles, an Indian fighter. "Through this narrow sheet of corrugated rock," Schwatka wrote later, "the wild waters of the great river rush in a perfect mass of milk-like foam, with a reverberation that is audible for a considerable distance, the roar being intensified by the rocky walls which act like so many sounding boards."⁶⁷

Traveling through the five-mile length of the canyon before freeze-up, as Buck and his mates are doing, was an extremely risky proposition, requiring the sled to remain close to the high granite walls of the canyon where the ice formed first. J. Bernard Moore, who traversed the canyon in early fall—just as Buck is doing—wrote that he and his party "found a shelf of ice about ten feet in width frozen on to the [Miles] canyon walls. We took the righthand side. The middle of the canyon was very swift running water with large whirlpools, running at the rate of about fifteen miles per hour or more. . . . [T]aking this route through the canyon on this ledge of ice was a great risk, but it saved us much heavy work in avoiding the route over the hill."⁶⁸

London knew the canyon well, for on 25 September 1897 he and his companions challenged the rapids in an incident so exciting that Thompson reflected upon it at length:

[We] shot [Box Canyon] after taking a look at it with everything in our boat—Jack at stern, Sloper at bow, Jim and myself at the oars—The ride was a swift one as the river at the point narrows to about 30 feet and the water dashes and rolls through this narrow box with walls from 50 to 100 feet hight [sic] at a great speed making it rather dangerous to enter, but as our boat was large and strong we did not feel

alarmed to make the run, and as it was we made the run in 3 minutes otherwise it would have taken us 4 days to pack around. . . .[69]

Two years later, London wrote his own account of those three minutes—although he reduced the time to "two minutes by the watch":

I caught a glimpse of the spectators fringing the brink of the cliffs above, and another glimpse of the rock walls dashing by like twin lightning express trains; then my whole energy was concentrated in keeping to the Ridge. This was serrated with stiff waves, which the boat, dead with weight, could not mount, being forced to jab her nose through at every lunge. . . . The next instant we fell off the Ridge. The water came inboard in all directions, and the boat, caught in a transverse current, threatened to twist broadside. This would mean destruction. I threw myself against the sweep till I could hear it cracking, while Sloper snapped his paddle short off.

And all this time we were flying down the gutter, less than two yards from the wall. Several times it seemed all up with us; but finally, mounting the Ridge almost sidewise, we took a header through a tremendous comber and shot into the whirlpool of the great circular court.

Ordering out the oars for steerage-way, and keeping a close eye on the split currents, I caught one free breath before we flew into the second half of the canyon. Though we crossed the Ridge from left to right and back again, it was merely a repetition of the first half. A moment later the Yukon Belle *rubbed softly against the bank.*[70]

London's most detailed fictional account of the Miles (Box) Canyon rapids is in *Smoke Bellew*:

The Box Canyon was adequately named. It was a box, a trap. Once in it, the only way out was through. On either side arose perpendicular walls of rock. The river narrowed to a fraction of its width and roared through this gloomy passage in a madness of motion that heaped the water in the center into a ridge fully eight feet higher than at the rocky sides. This ridge, in turn, was crested with stiff, upstanding waves that curled over yet remained each in its unvarying place. The canyon was well feared, for it had collected its toll of dead from the passing gold-rushers.[71]

Lines 431–32: "pound and a half of sun-dried salmon, which was his ration"

On his trip out of the Yukon, London raved about the salmon—"cold, firm-fleshed and, above all, delicious," he wrote. These large Chinook salmon, which can grow to be nearly five feet long and 126 pounds, swim up the Yukon River to spawn each year and served as the principal protein in the diet of most of the American Indians along the entire length of the river. Throughout the short sub-Arctic summer, they caught and dried salmon to eat—and with which to feed their dogs. Schwatka complained about the taste, characterizing it as merely "tolerable, ranking somewhere between Limburger cheese and walrus hide." Dall, who led an expedition along the river thirty years before the Rush, wrote that the salmon "is dried in the sun without smoke or salt" on great drying racks set up in every river-side community—a practice whose aesthetic values were not lost on John Sidney Webb, who, in 1898, described the fish "hanging in red strips, burnished with copper tinges in the sun."[72]

Lines 436–37: "A dainty eater, he found that his mates, finishing first, robbed him of his unfinished ration."

This is a well-documented characteristic of Northland dogs. Will H. Chase wrote that "the howling and fighting was fierce" at feeding time. Jacobsen noted that "care must be taken to . . . see that the dog that finishes first does not rob the others of their food. Some gulp their food in seconds and then attack the younger animals." In *My Dogs in the Northland*, Young wrote that one of his dogs, Rover I, was a "dainty, slow eater," and that it was typical of "powerful and greedy dogs" to "rob the weaker ones."[73]

Lines 441 and 444: Pike and Dub

These two are among the more aptly named dogs on the team. Pike is indeed a "piker"—slang for one who shirks responsibilities—and Dub is surely what the slang meaning of his name suggests: one who does things awkwardly or stupidly.

It is possible that London based the behavior of Pike on "Pat," another of Marshall Bond's dogs in the Klondike. In a letter to his mother from Dawson City, Bond wrote that Pat was "a shirk; he lets the lead dog pull him."[74] The lead dog was "Jack," upon whom Buck was based.

Line 446: "This first theft marked Buck as fit to survive in the hostile Northland environment."

Perhaps no quality of Northland dogs has been so universally celebrated—and condemned—as their pilfering prowess. A sampling of opinion:

1. "[T]hey will steal anything in the shape of food. . . ."
2. "[I]f they are not natural born thieves, they are nothing."
3. "[C]lever as a man and quick as an express train."
4. "[A] terrible thief . . . will carry off anything, from a piece of bacon to a pair of boots."
5. "[B]orn thieves."
6. "All husky dogs are thieves. Some will take a pot off its stove by the handle and hide it safely out of sight in the snow while they wait for its contents to cool to their taste."
7. "And the Malamute is the King of all thieves. He will pull your leather boots off your feet while you sleep and eat them for a midnight supper; he delights to eat up his seal-hide harness; he has learned to open a wooden box and will devour canned food, opening any tin can made with his sharp fangs, quicker than a steel can-opener."
8. "[The huskies] did not seem to have any sense of 'dog honor' whatever and were always sneaking about attempting to steal something."
9. "Nothing but the sleight of hand of a conjurer could equal the mystery of their stealing."[75]

Lines 471–74: "He learned to bite the ice out with his teeth when it collected between his toes; and when he was thirsty and there was a thick scum of ice over the water hole, he would break it by rearing and striking it with stiff fore legs. His most conspicuous trait was an ability to scent the wind and forecast it a night in advance."

Young's dogs bite away ice from between their toes in *My Dogs in the Northland*. H. A. Cody's dogs, too, would "pick out the snow and ice with their teeth." Elsewhere in his fiction, London has dogs do this: In "To Build a Fire," for instance, the dog "dropped down in the snow and began to bite out the ice that had formed between the toes. This was a matter of instinct."[76]

The only confirmation of dogs "rearing and striking" ice to obtain drinking water comes from London himself, who declared in an essay that it was "a very common sight." Like Buck, Young's dog Rover I had the ability to "forecast" the weather, invariably selecting "his camping place on the lee side so accurately that when, as it often happened some hours after, the wind rose, it never caught him sleeping in an exposed place."[77]

Lines 477–78: "instincts long dead became alive again"

London is describing a phenomenon that he had read about and that many writers on the natural history of canines have confirmed—the ability of domesticated dogs to regain the instincts of wolves, their wild ancestors. In the early nineteenth century, for example, G. I. Davydov found on Kodiak Island "wild dogs, which have bred from those escaping from the settlements." He noted that they "roam around in large packs."[78]

Hamilton asserts that the "probable impetus" for *The Call of the Wild* came from a similar passage in John Charles Fremont's *Memoirs of My Life*, in which London had marked the following in his copy: "Scores of wild dogs followed, looking like troops of wolves, and having, in fact, but very little of the dog in their composition." The incident occurred near an Arapaho village on 7 July 1841.[79]

In an apparent effort to establish the verisimilitude of *The Call of the Wild*, London had sent to Macmillan a newspaper clipping on the subject, and in a return letter Herbert P. Williams, an editor, thanked London "for the paragraph about the shepherd dogs which ran wild."[80]

Lines 484–85: "he pointed his nose at a star and howled long and wolflike"

Desmond Morris writes that the function of a wolf howl is to "synchronize and assemble the pack for action"—primarily just before their hunting expeditions in the early morning and evening. He adds that the howl also conveys information about the "precise mood" of the wolves and may be territorial in character.[81]

Many Northland writers described the howling of huskies and other dogs. "They never bark," wrote Webb, "but howl, day and night, in a sad, disheartening way." Not everyone shared Webb's empathy. The *Skaguay News* saw no romance in the situation and editorialized against howling: "The half hundred or more dogs that have been tied in the Humbert-Yukon corral for the past few days should either be fed occasionally or turned loose. They howl in relays of twenty-five or thirty each, and a college yell is not to be compared with the commotion they create."[82]

CHAPTER THREE

"The Dominant Primordial Beast"

Line 505: "Lake Le Barge"

In the entire Northland this may be the place-name with the most variant spellings: "Labarge," "Lebarge," and "La Barge" are among the most common. Dall named the lake in 1870 for Michael Laberge (the correct spelling), who had probably never seen the lake, but who had participated in an attempt by the Western Union Telegraph Company in 1865 to string a line across Alaska and the Bering Strait—the so-called "Russian-American Telegraph Expedition." When Schwatka saw the lake in 1883, he was not sure what he had found: "[T]his may be the Lake Labarge of some books," he wrote—so he retained in his nomenclature the original untranslated Chilkat name, *Kluk-tas-si*.[1]

Laberge is thirty miles long and is probably the best known of all Yukon lakes because of the opening lines of Robert Service's poem, "The Cremation of Sam McGee":

> *The Northern Lights have seen queer sights*
> *But the queerest they ever did see*
> *Was that night on the marge of Lake Lebarge*
> *I cremated Sam McGee.*[2]

London and his party arrived at the lake on 26 September 1897 and, because of inclement weather, camped for several days "on the marge."[3]

Line 505: "a wind that cut like a white-hot knife"

Laberge is notorious for its fierce, unpredictable winds. On his way to the Klondike, Addison Clark Dyer recorded in his diary on 16 September 1898 that the "wind got pretty rough" and the waves "ran high." Virtually every other writer who crossed the lake registered a similar reaction. Schwatka wrote that the winds were "raging in a gale"; Walden described winds that "constantly blew up . . . or down the lake"; and Thomas Magee called them "exceedingly wild" and complained of "waves so high that our boat could not have lived in them." London's party had a rough time on the lake, too, and on 30 September 1897 had to pull into a cove to avoid destruction by the ferocious gale blowing at the time.[4]

Lines 506–7: "At their backs rose a perpendicular wall of rock"

Schwatka observed "great towering red rocks" on the western bank of Laberge, and Veazie Wilson described "very marked and singular" limestone formations that "rise abruptly from the water in some places. . . ."[5]

Young mentions a similar campsite—though on a different lake—where "the bold, high banks rose up perpendicularly from the water. . . ."[6]

Line 510: "a fire that thawed down through the ice"

This happens, as well, in *My Dogs in the Northland*: "[T]he instant the fire burnt down through its foundation of logs, the steam from the melting ice would extinguish it."[7]

Lines 514–15: "he found his nest occupied"

This repeatedly happens to Rover I in *My Dogs in the Northland*, and he is no more pleased by the circumstance than is Buck: "He was in no humour to be thus deprived of his choicely selected and laboriously prepared nest. It was most amusing to watch his efforts to get the intruder out."[8]

Line 522: "'by Gar!'"

"Gar" is an Anglo-French corruption of "God." Charmian London writes that Louis Savard, Jack's Klondike companion, used the expression. And elsewhere in his fiction, London has other French-Canadians employ it as well.[9]

London is not consistent in his transcription of the "broken English" of his French Canadians. In this line, for example, François is unable to manage the "th" in "thief" but handles the one in "the" quite well.

Line 531: "some Indian village"

Many travelers during the Rush mentioned a small encampment of Tagish Indians near Lake Laberge. In 1896, Spurr noticed "a few Indians in a summer camp on Lake Labarge." In 1897, on his way in with the first huge wave of gold-seekers, Mont Hawthorne saw a "whole slew of Indians" whose fires "showed plain on the [Laberge] shore." And in 1898, "Indians from a neighbouring village" visited the Laberge camp of Julius M. Price.[10]

A report of the North-west Mounted Police in November 1898 records some details about the Tagish camp—and some common racial attitudes: "They are a worthless lot and very lazy, dressing like whites but looking more like Japs than Indians. They are fairly well armed but have neither horses or cattle and travel in canoes and by dog train."[11]

Other visitors expressed similar views. Haskell called the Tagish "exceedingly filthy and degraded creatures, who will bargain almost anything they have for a little whisky. . . ." And Osborne described them as "light in colour, short, thickly built, with somewhat almond-shaped eyes, straight black hair, high cheekbones, flat features, round heads, small hands and feet"; and then, engaging in a bit of fanciful ethnology, he speculated that "they are probably the direct descendants of pure Malays."[12]

The impoverished condition of the Tagish who camped at Laberge is confirmed by the police report, which recorded that "several families" had "applied for food on account of the men being laid up and unable to hunt, fish or pack."[13]

Although Thompson does not mention the camp in his diary, the London party must have seen it, for Marshall Bond, who passed through the area at approximately the same time—September 1897—alludes to it in an unpublished memoir: "[We] camped that night on the shore of Lake LaBarge near some Indians. They had been catching fish and were camped under roughly devised, little lean-tos, in front of which blazed fires to give them the reflected warmth their scanty bedding could not furnish, for the nights were cold." Nearly one hundred years later, John Hildebrand (1988) poked through the "abandoned Indian village" at Lower Laberge, finding a few relics of interest.[14]

London briefly mentions the people elsewhere. In *A Daughter of the Snows*, for example, he calls them "Lake Le Barge Sticks," using the Chinook Jargon term for the people of the sylvan Yukon Interior ("Stick" suggesting "tree").[15]

Lines 529–63: the attack of the starving huskies

London derived this scene from Young's *My Dogs in the Northland*, in which Young and his party camp on the surface of a frozen lake, build a fire on the ice, and are suddenly and unexpectedly visited by "half a dozen wild looking Indians accompanied by over a dozen of vicious, half-starved Huskie dogs." Young's narrative continues: "The wolfish dogs . . . did not have the politeness to greet us, but after a sudden fierce attack upon my hired dogs, whom they drove away from the fire, they at once set up and began to devour everything eatable, in which they could fasten their teeth."[16]

Such scenes were not uncommon in this vast landscape, frozen much of the year. Acquiring sufficient food was a problem for humans and beasts alike, and when little food was available, the dogs would frequently go without—or become food themselves. Visitors to the region routinely commented on the poor condition of dogs. M. H. E. Hayne described the native dogs as "thin, gaunt ghoulish-looking mongrels, with very long legs, and a general air of starvation." And one Klondike handbook noted—with customary insensitivity—that the dogs "subsist almost entirely on refuse, as the natives at all times are either too hard up or too indifferent to give their dogs any food that a human being can eat."[17]

But American Indians were not the only ones in the Northland to maltreat their animals. Ernest Ingersoll (1897) reported that in the sizable mining camp at Circle City, Alaska, there "were so many [dogs] that no attempt was made to feed them all, and as a result, in their foraging for food, they became a nuisance."[18]

London creates analogous scenes involving humans in at least two other Northland tales. In a segment of *Smoke Bellew* entitled "The Hanging of Cultus George," for example, Smoke and his partner, Shorty, come upon a band of starving American Indians:

> *It was famine unmistakable. Their faces, hollow-cheeked and skin-stretched, were so many death's-heads. . . . Bucks and squaws and children tottered and swayed on shaking legs and continued to urge in, their mad eyes swimming with weakness and burning with ravenous desire. . . . The whole mass pressed in upon them, and the fight was on.*
>
> *At first Smoke and Shorty shoved and thrust and threw back. Then they used the butt of the dog-whip and their fists on the food-mad crowd. And all this against a background of moaning and wailing women and children. Here and there, in a dozen places, the sled-lashings were cut. Men crawled in on their bellies, regardless of a rain of kicks and blows, and tried to drag out the grub. These had to be picked up bodily and flung back. And such was their weakness that they fell continually, under the slightest pressures or shoves.*[19]

Lines 536–37: "the clubs fell on them unheeded"

Voracious dogs did indeed ignore clubs and whips. Joseph Grinnell (1901) was shocked when he first witnessed the resolution—and resilience—of dogs being beaten: "Ordinary animals would have died of broken bones," he wrote, "but it took a 'sore chastisement' to bring these dogs to their senses." And in a similar scene in *My Dogs in the Northland* Young wrote that starving dogs "cared not for the calls sounding in front of them, or the clubs and execrations hurled at them. . . ."[20]

Line 567: Dolly

Jesse finds praiseworthy qualities in a spaniel named "Doll" in *Anecdotes of Dogs*, one of London's sources.[21]

Lines 571–74: "The huskies had chewed through the sled lashings and canvas coverings. . . . nothing, no matter how remotely eatable, had escaped them. . . . a pair of Perrault's moose-hide moccasins, chunks out of the leather traces, and even two feet of lash from the end of François's whip."

Writers who visited the Northland recorded with patent awe the materials and substances that hungry huskies were willing to ingest—harnesses, skin boat covers, fur clothing, a boot, a sealskin sack, the straw that boats were lined with, moccasins, an old leather shirt, a whip, a fur cap, soap, candles, flour sacks, a dishrag, a pair of large gauntlet gloves, the leather of a snowshoe, the leather strap on a gun case, a hairbrush.[22]

The only sure protection, wrote A. W. Greely (1886) for "anything which a dog can eat is to be secured in the field . . . by keeping it under one's head or body." Agnes Deans Cameron related a particularly gruesome tale about the lengths to which starving dogs would go. A fur-clad American Indian boy fell on the ice, was swarmed over by "hungry dogs," and was "killed and partly devoured before anyone had missed him from the camps."[23]

Lines 578–79: "four hundred miles of trail still between him and Dawson"

The distance is approximately correct. Because of London's reference to the now-abandoned Tagish village—located in "Lower Laberge," near the head of the lake—it is possible to estimate the distance to Dawson City, Yukon, at about 420 miles.

Located at the confluence of the Yukon and Klondike rivers, Dawson City is today one of only two towns of any size in the entire Yukon; the other is Whitehorse, the capital. In August 1896, Joe Ladue, an enterprising Northland veteran—that is, a "sourdough"—who had been in the region since 1882, guessed that a strike on the Klondike would bring a large population of miners to the area; he laid out lots on the frozen swamp he had selected for the town-site, established a sawmill, and named the town for George Mercer Dawson (1841–1901), a Canadian geologist, who, despite some physical disabilities (he was a dwarf and hump-backed), was among the most respected men in the North.[24]

A year later, Dawson had a population of thirty thousand, billed itself as "The Paris of the North," and became, until 1951, the capital of the Yukon. Early visitors to the newest city in North America were astonished by its size—and its primitive conditions: "very filthy . . . a regular mud-hole of a place," "a squalid collection of log huts," and "ribbon of mud for a main street" were typical comments."[25]

Webb published more detailed impressions of his arrival by steamboat at 4:00 A.M.:

> [W]e came up to that collection of forty large log cabins and five hundred tents, sprawled at the foot of Moose-skin mountain, named Dawson City. Helter-skelter, in a marsh, lies this collection of odds and ends of houses and habitations, the warehouses of the two companies [Alaska Commercial Company, North American Trading and Transportation Company] cheek by jowl with the cabins and tents. A row of bar-rooms called Front Street; the side streets deep in mud; the river bank a mass of miners' boats, Indian canoes, and logs; the screeching of the sawmill; the dismal, tuneless scraping of the violin of the dance-halls, still wide-open; the dogs everywhere, fighting and snarling; the men either whooping it up or working with the greatest rapidity to unload the precious freight we had brought—all of this rustling and bustling made the scene more like the outside of a circus-tent, including the smell of the saw-dust, than anything else in the world. . . . Dawson City seems like a joke.[26]

Perhaps the most odious feature of life in Dawson was the lack of proper sanitation. Because of the permafrost—the subsoil, which remains frozen year-round—it was impossible to dig satisfactory latrines even during the hottest days of summer. In the winter, miners disposed of their wastes in truly Elizabethan fashion: outside their cabins in piles that froze almost immediately and were then washed into the creeks and rivers during the spring thaw. Samuel Steele, the commander of the Dawson unit of the North-west Mounted

Police, was offended by the ordure, remarking in his annual report that "deposits of every imaginable kind of filth" became visible in the spring.[27]

London and his party arrived in Dawson on 18 October 1897, an event that Thompson mentions in his diary without elaboration of any kind. But London himself, in an article published two years later, characterized the Paris of the North in June 1898 as "dreary, desolate . . . built in a swamp, flooded to the second story, populated by dogs, mosquitoes and gold-seekers."[28]

Lines 583–604: "The Thirty Mile River was wide open. . . . Six days of exhausting toil were required to cover those thirty terrible miles. . . . A dozen times, Perrault, nosing the way, broke through the ice bridges, being saved by the long pole he carried. . . . He skirted the frowning shores on rim ice. . . . Once, the sled broke through. . . . there was no escape except up the cliff"

Some of the rivers in the Yukon, like Fortymile and Sixtymile, are named not for their length but for their distance from a given landmark. The Thirtymile, however—now officially considered a part of the Yukon River—is in fact a rough stretch of water approximately thirty miles long that leads out of Lake Laberge and continues until it merges with the Teslin (or Hootalinqua) River. As Schwatka observed in 1885, the Thirtymile is "quite swift, and so shallow in many places as almost to deserve the name of rapids."[29]

Because of its current, the Thirtymile is slow to freeze, forcing sled-teams to undergo exactly what London is describing here: to move carefully along the "rim ice" (the ice that forms in the shallow water next to the shore, also called "shore-ice" or "bench-ice"), cross "ice bridges" (solid pieces spanning the entire river), and, when the rim or bridge ice does not hold, to scale what Schwatka called "high precipitous banks of clay, forty to sixty feet above," then travel on land high over the torrent. London himself described the cliffs as "precipitous bluffs, rising out of deep water. . . ."[30]

Traveling on rim ice is extremely precarious, as Haskell discovered. At Miles Canyon on his trip out of the Yukon, he and his partner, Joe, confronted a difficult choice—the same choice François and Perrault must make, a choice that had a dreadful consequence:

The waters were roaring with that thunder tone . . . , and along the walls was an uneven shelf of ice which the dashing spray had formed. It seemed sufficiently wide and strong at first, but it gradually narrowed and at times brought us very near the angry water. Joe was ahead and picking his way very carefully. Finally, he came to a place where the shelf of ice was very slanting and he stepped to the outside edge so as to push the sled along and steady it, to prevent it from sliding into the water.

I was preparing to do the same thing when I heard a sharp cry from Joe, and, looking up, I saw him slip, then slide over the edge of the shelf into the raging rapids. His hand clutched the rope of the sled, and, quick as a flash, I sprang forward to catch it. But it was too late. Over went the sled into the misty foam and sank at once, for it was heavily loaded.

As I stood almost rigid with fright, I saw Joe struggling bravely in the waters, but being swept rapidly down, and I knew he was no swimmer. I started and ran, but just then he was drawn under the ice shelf, and that was the last I saw of Joe. The whole thing was over almost in an instant.

Overpowered with horror and grief, I dropped down upon the ice in the midst of that roaring can[y]on and cried like a child.[31]

The treacherous Thirtymile figures in a number of other of London's tales, most strikingly in "The One Thousand Dozen." In a paragraph that provides some details missing in *The Call of the Wild* London recounts an incident involving David Rasmunsen and his American Indian drivers:

On the Thirty Mile river he [Rasmunsen] found much open water, spanned by precarious ice bridges and fringed with narrow rim ice, tricky and uncertain. The rim ice was impossible to reckon on, and he dared it without reckoning, falling back on his revolver when his drivers demurred. But on the ice bridges, covered with snow as they were, precautions could be taken. These they crossed on their snow-shoes, with long poles, held crosswise in their hands, to which to cling in case of accident. Once over, the dogs were called to follow. And on such a bridge, where the absence of the centre ice was masked by the snow, one of the Indians met his end. He went through as quickly and neatly as a knife through thin cream, and the current swept him from view down under the stream ice.[32]

London knew about the Thirtymile and the dangers of bench-ice. He had traveled on it; he had read about it. In his diary, Thompson recorded that the London party reached the Thirtymile at 3:00 P.M. on 2 October 1897: "This river is very swift," he wrote, "and filled with many rocks which make it very dangerous to run. . . ."[33]

Note: By "nosing the way," London meant that Perrault was in the lead, testing the ice with the long pole that Walden said was "more or less customary" for dog-drivers to carry."[34]

Line 610: *"the Hootalinqua and good ice"*

"Hootalinqua," an American Indian word ("where the two big waters meet"), is the older name for the river that contemporary maps call the "Teslin" ("long, narrow water"). An even earlier American Indian name was "Nas-A-Thane" ("no salmon").[35] During the Rush, there was a small settlement at the mouth of the Hootalinqua, for it marked the end of the overland Ashcroft and Stikine trails and was the point at which travelers on those routes would join on the river those—like Buck and his mates—who had come from Lake Bennett.

Many commentators agreed that "good ice"—often unavailable on the Thirtymile— was generally reliable from the Hootalinqua on. Palmer observed that "[n]ear the Hootalinqua the current slackens, and we crossed where the stream was completely frozen over." London's party reached the Hootalinqua on 3 October 1897.[36]

Lines 612–14: *"thirty-five miles to the Big Salmon . . . thirty-five more to the Little Salmon . . . forty miles [more], which brought them well up toward the Five Fingers"*

The mouth of the Big Salmon River is exactly thirty-five river miles from the mouth of the Hootalinqua; the mouth of the Little Salmon is exactly thirty-five more; forty more would have put the team only about twenty-four miles short of Five Finger Rapids.[37]

The names of both the Big and Little Salmon rivers are English translations of Tagish words meaning, naturally, big and little salmon—names that refer not to the size of the rivers but to the fish they contain. Neither river is very large: Big Salmon is 136 miles long; Little Salmon, 116. There had once been a populous American Indian village near the mouth of the Little Salmon, but a flu epidemic decimated the population in 1917.[38]

Five Finger Rapids was the last spot of real danger on the float downriver to Dawson City. "Here the river is caught between two cliffs," writes Pierre Berton, "its passage apparently barred by a wall of broken rock. Through this barrier, the water has torn five narrow channels or 'fingers.'" In his diary, Marshall Bond called the rapids "a spectacular freak. A string of rocks crossing the stream like so many large box cars on a siding." Skagway's *Daily Alaskan* told a grisly story of misadventure at the site, as a man aptly named John Kill attempted to shoot the rapids on barges bearing 504 head of sheep. In the spectacular wreck that ensued, all but fifty of the sheep died, "their bodies scattered along the banks all the way to Dawson."[39]

When Schwatka shot the rapids in 1883, he dubbed them "Rink Rapids" in honor of Dr. Henry Rink, an authority on Greenland, but—no doubt because of the appearance of rocks in the river—travelers continued to use "Five Fingers," the name first given it by W. B. Moore in 1882.[40]

Thompson must have been in an expansive mood the day he shot the rapids with Jack London, for the entry for 5 October 1897 is one of the longest in his entire diary:

> *Up bright and early and started down river again,—came to the Five Finger Rapids at 3 o'clock P.M. and passed them OK. between the bank and first finger on the right hand side of river [the recommended strategy]. These rapids are so distinguished on account of 5 immense rocks towering up and out of the water about 50 feet high and somewhat resembling the fingers of a hand—these fingers are nearly in a straight line from bank to bank and divides [sic] the river at this point into 6 separate channels, the right hand channel being quite easy to run, but all the other channels dangerous on account of large rocks being hidden under the water. In approaching these rapids the river runs for several miles in almost a circle and in case one is not posted will come upon the rapids before he is aware of it. The large rocks towering above the river forming the 5 fingers, as one approaches, look like sentinels, warning one of coming danger. The water here dashes through the fingers at a good speed. . . .*[41]

Lines 620–23: "sacrificed the tops of his own moccasins to make four moccasins for Buck . . . [who] lay on his back, his four feet waving appealingly in the air"

The moccasins worn in the North were not the low-cut variety that many people wear today as bedroom slippers. They were ankle- or calf-high footwear, generally fashioned from moose hide—"large outdoor moccasins," London called them in *Scorn of Women*.[42]

Most Northland writers describe the sorts of moccasins used to protect the feet of sled dogs. Peter C. Newman wrote about the Hudson's Bay Company voyageurs using "tiny deerskin booties" to protect their dogs' feet. And Harris mentioned the dog moccasins in

1897, adding that once "the tenderness is gone from their feet the dogs will bite and tear the moccasins off."[43]

Young writes of using them for his dogs as well in *My Dogs in the Northland*: "The shoes were shaped very much like a man's mitten without the thumb. They were of various sizes so as to fit snugly to the injured foot, whether large or small." And, like Buck, Young's Rover lay on his back and pled to be shod, "eloquently even if mutely. . . ."[44]

Occasionally, starving travelers were forced to boil and eat the tops of their moccasins—a practice London refers to in several tales. Given the prevalence of such stories, it is conceivable that Charlie Chaplin derived from one of them the idea for his famous shoe-eating scene in *The Gold Rush*.[45]

Lines 626–34: "At the Pelly one morning . . . Dolly . . . went suddenly mad. . . . [Buck] plunged through the wooded breast of the island . . . crossed a back channel filled with rough ice to another island, gained a third island"

One of the largest of the Yukon tributaries—457 miles long and draining more than twenty thousand square miles—the Pelly River was named in 1840 by Hudson's Bay Company employee Robert Campbell for Sir John Henry Pelly, who had been the company's British governor for thirty years. Newman adds that "no other HBC Governor is so amply commemorated on the Canadian landscape." Indeed, the name "Pelly" can be found on a river, a bay, two islands, a lake, a mountain, and a point.[46]

In 1848 the Hudson's Bay Company established at the mouth of the Pelly River a trading post and fort, Fort Selkirk (named for Lord Selkirk). Chief Kho-Klux and some of his Chilkat warriors, worried about this threat to the trade monopoly they had long enjoyed, burned the fort on 19 August 1852, and the HBC did not bother to rebuild.[47] For years, travelers noted the ruins of the old HBC post as they passed: Schwatka included in his *Summer in Alaska* a full-page engraving of three lonely chimneys, about all that remained in 1883. During the Gold Rush, the North-west Mounted Police had a post there. Today, the tiny community of Selkirk is gone: The Klondike highway—now the principal route in and out of the Yukon—crosses the Pelly about twenty-five miles east of old Fort Selkirk, and a new community has arisen, Pelly Crossing.

The mouth of the Pelly is about 220 miles—and a week's time by dog-team—away from the spot on Lake Laberge where the team-dogs had been attacked by the starving huskies, some of whom, to judge by their "slavered fangs," must have been suffering from rabies. The incubation period is generally one to two months—though there are rare cases that have appeared in as few as five days: Dolly, who is exhibiting the aggressive and violent symptoms of the second stage of the disease, has contracted rabies in near-record time.

There are indeed many islands near the mouth of the Pelly, so many in fact that Schwatka commented that in many places he "could hardly see both banks at a time." Traveling with Jack London, Thompson observed that "the river is very wide and filled with many islands."[48]

Line 644: "teams"

The *Saturday Evening Post* edition has "team" here, the correct word. "Teams" is a typographical error.

Lines 654–56: *"Then he was a masterful dog, and what made him dangerous was the fact that the club of the man in the red sweater had knocked all blind pluck and rashness out of his desire for mastery."*

In *The Hidden Life of Dogs* Thomas observes that, among wolves and dogs, "high rank can mean life." She asserts as well that much of a dog's behavior can be explained by this "desire for mastery"—the determination to sit atop a hierarchy within which all animals in the territory can coexist comfortably. "Dogs like their societies to be well ordered," she argues; they "rank themselves as if on the rungs of a ladder. . . ."[49]

Lines 672–73: *"Pike, the malingerer, did not appear. He was securely hidden in his nest under a foot of snow."*

Young wrote about how his dogs were prone to do this—and about how his lead dog, Jack, would help the men find his teammates, "some of whom were buried under several feet of snow, and persisted in there remaining in their comfortable retreats in spite of importunate calls, until they had to be literally dug out with snowshoes. . . ."[50]

Lines 699–700: *"in the night their jingling bells still went by"*

Providing dogs with "gaudy belled harnesses" was a practice of the Hudson's Bay Company voyageurs dating back to the eighteenth century. Writers at the time of the Rush described the jingling sounds as well. Young believed his dogs were "very fond" of the "ribbons and little musical bells" that adorned his team, and maintained that they "always seemed to travel better and be in greater spirits when they could dash along in unison with their tinkling."[51]

Line 703: "*Every night, regularly, at nine, at twelve, at three, they [the dogs] lifted a nocturnal song*"

The customary nighttime howling of dogs in Northland communities is well documented. London no doubt derived the precise timing of this outbreak from Young, whose dogs also performed at nine, twelve, and three. David Goodman Mandelbaum observed a similar occurrence among the Plains Cree dogs, which "would howl three times, at sundown, about midnight, toward dawn."[52]

London, who spent some nights in Dawson City, surely heard the "nocturnal song" many times. There were certainly an adequate number of performers—Adney estimated there were fifteen hundred dogs in town, about one to every three to four people. The combined efforts of so many canines would have been impressive—and London does write about it at length in other stories, most notably "The Wife of a King": "Far below, a solitary dog gave tongue. . . . The sound multiplied. Dog after dog took up the strain till the full-throated chorus swayed the night. To him who hears for the first time this weird song, is told the first and greatest secret of the Northland; to him who has heard it often, it is the solemn knell of lost endeavor. It is the plaint of tortured souls, for in it is invested the heritage of the North, the suffering of countless generations—the warning and the requiem to the world's estrays."[53]

Line 705: "*the aurora borealis flaming coldly overhead*"

Aurora borealis is the scientific name for the northern lights. Aurora was the Roman goddess of dawn; *borealis* is from the Latin, meaning "northern"—so the northern lights are, literally, the "northern dawn." Virtually every visitor to Dawson wrote about the spectacular celestial display, which Angelo Heilprin said "never failed to attract the attention of the loiterers on the street."[54]

London himself was fascinated by the displays, sometimes referring to them only briefly: "[T]he colored bars of the aurora borealis were shooting like great searchlights"; "a greenish vapor of pulsing aurora borealis." In "A Daughter of the Aurora," however, and in the following passage from *A Daughter of the Snows* he pauses for lengthy description:

[T]he land was bathed in a soft, diffused flood of light which found its source not in the stars, nor yet in the moon, which was somewhere over on the other side of the world. From the southeast to the northwest a pale-greenish glow fringed the rim of the heavens, and it was from this the dim radiance was exhaled.

Suddenly, like the ray of a search-light, a band of white light ploughed overhead. Night turned to ghostly day on the instant, then blacker night descended. But to the southeast a noiseless commotion was apparent. The glowing greenish gauze was in a ferment, bubbling, uprearing, downfalling, and tentatively thrusting huge bodiless hands into the upper ether. Once more a cyclopean rocket twisted its fiery way across the sky, from horizon to zenith, and on, and on, in tremendous flight, to horizon again. But the span could not hold, and in its wake the black night brooded. And yet again, broader, stronger, deeper, lavishly spilling streamers to right and left, it flaunted the midmost zenith with its gorgeous flare, and passed on and down to the further edge of the world. Heaven was bridged at last, and the bridge endured! . . . [T]ogether they watched the burning vault wherein the stars dimmed and vanished. Ebbing, flowing, pulsing to some tremendous rhythm, the prism colors hurled themselves in luminous deluge across the firmament. Then the canopy of heaven became a mighty loom, wherein imperial purple and deep sea-green blended, wove and interwove, with blazing woof and flashing warp, till the most delicate of tulles, fluorescent and bewildering, was daintily and airily shaken in the face of the astonished night.

Without warning the span was sundered by an arrogant arm of black. The arch dissolved in blushing confusion. Chasms of blackness yawned, grew, and rushed together. Broken masses of strayed color and fading fire stole timidly towards the sky-line. Then the dome of night towered imponderable, immense, and the stars came back one by one. . . .[55]

Lines 716–17: "they dropped down the steep bank by the Barracks to the Yukon Trail, and pulled for Dyea and Salt Water"

Historians and geographers concur that "Yukon" (also spelled "Youcon" in the early days) is an American Indian word meaning "the greatest" or "greatest river." Eskimos called it "Kwikpak"; some American Indians (the Tanana), "Niga-to"—both also meaning "great river." The Yukon is about 2,000 miles long, drains 325,000 square miles, and was, according to Melody Webb, "the last major river system to be discovered."[56]

The Barracks were the headquarters of the North-west Mounted Police, built on the riverbanks at the lower end of Dawson, near the confluence of the Yukon and Klondike rivers. The bank was indeed steep—sixteen feet high above the surface of the river near the Barracks.[57]

At Dawson, the police had erected Fort Herchmer and named it in honor of W. M. Herchmer, one of the original officers of the force, and his son, L. W. Herchmer, the first commissioner of the police brought in from outside the force. An official NWMP report from the period records the details: "A reserve of forty acres was applied for at the junction of the Klondike river with the Yukon for police and other Government purposes; . . . On this reserve the post was built, consisting of nine buildings. With the exception of the storehouse, the buildings are as usual of logs. . . ."[58]

The Yukon Trail was the frozen highway of the north, two thousand miles or so of river surface used for a sled trail in the winter. Upriver, the trail led to Dyea or Skagway and the ocean ("Salt Water"). The surface, however, was not smooth and glassy, but cluttered with unevenly frozen chunks of ice, fallen limbs, and snowdrifts. London well knew the trail, for he had traveled it himself—and had listened to the stories of dog-mushers all winter as he lay encamped near the mouth of the Stewart River.

In a number of tales, London briefly mentions the trail: "a slender sunken line, eighteen inches wide and two thousand miles in length . . . ," he wrote in "The Man with the Gash." But in "To Build a Fire" he provides his most eloquent view of it:

> *The Yukon lay a mile wide and hidden under three feet of ice. On top of this ice were as many feet of snow. It was all pure white, rolling in gentle, [sic] undulations where the ice-jams of the freeze-up had formed. North and south, as far as his eye could see, it was unbroken white, save for a dark hair-line that curved and twisted away into the north, where it disappeared behind another spruce-covered island. This dark hair-line was the trail—the main trail—that led south five hundred miles to the Chilcoot Pass, Dyea, and salt water; and that led north seventy miles to Dawson, and still on to the north a thousand miles to Nulato, and finally to St. Michael on Bering Sea, a thousand miles and half a thousand more.*[59]

London made a slight error here: The team is heading to Skagway, not Dyea.

Lines 717–18: "Perrault was carrying despatches if anything more urgent than those he had brought in"

The messages Perrault carried to Dawson would surely have informed the authorities about the masses of people swarming northward; the return messages would have warned that food and supplies were scarce, and that starvation was probable for those without adequate reserves. The report of Superintendent Charles Constantine, Commander of the Yukon District on 18 January 1898, contained a section, "Food Supplies and Rations," which cautioned that the "outlook for the coming summer is most serious, as no quantity of food can possibly arrive here until nearly the end of July. . . ." He urged the government to "take immediate action and ship supplies in over the summit, which must be freighted over the ice to the foot of Lake Labarge, scows built there and the provisions brought down by the first water, so that we may receive them not later than the 1st June, when our present stock will be entirely exhausted"[60]

Line 721: "the country"

This is a term referring to the Northland. John McPhee wrote about the origins of the expression in his book *Coming into the Country*: "With a clannish sense of place characteristic of the bush, people in the region of the upper Yukon refer to their part of Alaska as 'the country.' A stranger appearing among them is said to have 'come into the country'"— a phrase London uses verbatim in "The Story of Jees Uck."[61]

Lines 722–23: "the police had arranged in two or three places deposits of grub for dog and man"

The North-west Mounted Police was the administrator and enforcer of Canadian law in the Yukon. The name of the service has changed over the years:

1. pre-1904:   North-west Mounted Police (NWMP.)
2. 1904–19:   Royal North-West Mounted Police (RNWMP)
3. post-1919:   Royal Canadian Mounted Police (RCMP)[62]

The force was established by an act of parliament in May 1873 (An Act Respecting the Administration of Justice; and for the Establishment of a Police Force in the North West Territories) and first entered the Yukon in August 1894 in order to establish control over the rowdy mining community of Fortymile.[63]

Once the Klondike Rush commenced, more and more police were dispatched to the Yukon. According to Arthur Lincoln Haydon, there were only eight officers and eighty-eight men in the entire territory at the end of 1897, but within a year the force had grown to two superintendents, eight inspectors, two assistant surgeons, and 254 noncommissioned officers and men—numbers confirmed by official police reports.[64]

The duties of the police were many and varied in the Northland. They inspected road houses, assisted tax collectors, served as deputy clerks-of-court and postmasters, inspected stands of timber, repaired telegraph lines, served summonses and subpoenas, and guarded gold shipments. During the Rush, the police also controlled access to the Yukon—a service Webb called their "most important" task. Moreover, they conducted regular patrols by dog-team, the last of which occurred in 1969, by which time airplanes and snowmobiles had replaced all the teams.[65]

London admired the police, portraying them favorably in a number of tales. Perhaps his greatest flattery occurs in "The League of Old Men," in which he describes a policeman who, except for his height, resembles London himself: "He was a stalwart young fellow, broad-shouldered, deep-chested, legs cleanly built and stretched wide apart, and tall though Imber was, he towered above him by half a head. His eyes were cool, and gray, and steady, and he carried himself with the peculiar confidence of power that is bred of blood and tradition. His splendid masculinity was emphasized by his excessive boyishness,—he was a mere lad,—and his smooth cheek promised a blush as willingly as the cheek of a maid."[66]

The police did, indeed, arrange "deposits of grub for dog and man" along the Yukon Trail—although the completion of this complicated task occurred somewhat later than London suggests. Harwood Steele—son of Samuel Steele, a policeman who was involved in the project—wrote in 1936 that it was early in September 1898 when his father "selected sites for additional detachments along the whole course of the Yukon, thirty miles apart." Each post had "men, dog-trains, dog-feed, canoes, and supplies to last a year." Adney records that in the late winter and early spring of 1898, relief stations had been completed at Whitehorse Rapids, Lake Laberge, Hootalinqua, Big Salmon, Freeman's Point, and Little Salmon—but Buck and his mates are starting down the trail early in the winter of 1897–98.

The list of completed posts published on 11 July 1898 in the *Daily Alaskan* included Dawson, Ainslie, Sixtymile, Stewart River, Meat Raft, Pelly River, Five Finger Rapids, Little Salmon, Big Salmon, Hootalinqua, the foot of Lake Laberge, the head of Lake Laberge, Whitehorse, the foot of Lake Marsh, Tagish Lake, and the head of Lake Bennett.[67]

Because London's winter camp was at the mouth of the Stewart, the site of one of the relief posts, he surely witnessed the police beginning the process; he no doubt heard of the others from dog-drivers pausing at the Stewart before venturing the final seventy miles to Dawson.

Line 724: *"they made Sixty Mile, which is a fifty-mile run"*

The Sixtymile, which is eighty-three miles long, earned its name because it is sixty miles up the Yukon River from Fort Reliance, a trading post established in 1874 by Arthur Harper and LeRoy McQuesten. On 16 October 1897, London's party passed the mouth of the Sixtymile River, where, Thompson noted "a good many empty cabins, a post store, with nothing to sell and a good many boats headed for Dawson." Forty-seven river miles separate Sixtymile and Dawson City.[68]

Line 748: *"at the mouth of the Tahkeena"*

Takhini is Tagish for "mosquito river." DeWindt, suffering from repeated assaults by the insects, commented that the river was "aptly named." The Takhini is not large—only 105 miles long—but its current enters powerfully, writes Hildebrand, "briefly clouding the pale green Yukon with silt." Moore noted in his journal that the river "has confined banks with no islands or sand bars at its mouth."[69]

As Donald Pizer first noted, London here made a rare mistake in Northland geography: The Takhini is about four hundred miles upriver from the Sixtymile, but the next place-name London mentions *after* "Tahkeena" is Rink Rapids, only 183 miles from the Sixtymile. So, unless the team backtracked 217 miles, we must assume that London had some other river in mind.[70] An appropriate alternative would be the Selwyn—named for Dr. Alfred Richard Cecil Selwyn, director of the Geological Survey of Canada, 1869–95—which is about midway between Sixtymile and Rink.[71]

Lines 748–49: *"a snowshoe rabbit"*

The snowshoe hare (*Lepus americanus*) was named because of its large hind feet, which can measure nearly six inches long, and its widely spread toes. The hares can reach speeds of thirty miles per hour, can leap twelve feet, and, when flushed, tend to run in a several-acre circle. The hares are dark brown in summer but don a protective white coat in winter.[72]

Lines 749–51: "a hundred yards away was a camp of the Northwest Police, with fifty dogs, huskies all, who joined the chase"

In 1897–98, the NWMP post nearest to the mouth of the Takhini was at Marsh Lake, dozens of miles away. It would have been unlikely, however, that this particular detachment would have had fifty dogs. An official NWMP report from 1898 establishes that there were only about 130 in the entire Yukon at this time, so it is doubtful that more than a third of them would have been at the mouth of the Takhini. A year later, the NWMP brought in 150 Labradors ("for mail carrying"), but survival was a problem for them: The *Skaguay News* reported on 9 December 1898 that "[s]ixty-seven of the one hundred and forty dogs brought here two weeks ago from Labrador for use by the Northwest Mounted Police, have died since their arrival. . . ."[73]

In *My Dogs in the Northland*, Young's dogs one day chase a black fox, and while in camp, his animals frequently pursued rabbits. The "chase instinct" is strong among dogs, and Mandelbaum reported that the dogs of the Cree "were always eager to give chase. When a hunt was in progress near them, laden dogs had to be held, lest they run after the fleeing buffalo and so spoil their burdens." Amundsen described how his team-dogs would occasionally take off after a hare: "When the dogs got scent of such a tit-bit [*sic*] they started off at full speed; of course it was only the first who got the prey, but this never taught the others anything. They rushed ahead each time with unabated energy and renewed hope."[74]

Incidentally, there was a police detachment at the mouth of the Selwyn River, making it—again—a more likely site for these incidents than Takhini.

Lines 774–75: "But Spitz . . . cut across a narrow neck of land where the creek made a long bend around."

Topographical maps reveal no creek with a "long bend" near the mouth of the Takhini. However, the Takhini itself makes such a bend near the mouth, so in this case the imagination of London—who had never been up the river—coincides at least partially with reality.

The ability of a dog to forecast the moves of a fleeing prey may seem dubious, but one of London's sources (*Anecdotes of Dogs*) relates a tale of an "Esquimaux dog" that chases a hare along a hedgerow, anticipates the hare's next turn, and cuts it off at a spot farther along the hedge.[75] (The hare escapes.)

Lines 778–79: "The rabbit . . . shrieked as loudly as a stricken man may shriek."

Darwin wrote in *The Expression of the Emotions in Man and Animals* that "[h]ares and rabbits for instance, never, I believe, use their vocal organs except in the extremity of suffering. . . ."[76]

Lines 837–38: "the dark circle became a dot on the moon-flooded snow"

In "The Law of Life" (1900) London used a similar image to describe a moose surrounded by a pack of wolves: "And he saw the inexorable circle close in till it became a dark point in the midst of the stamped snow."[77]

CHAPTER FOUR

"Who Has Won to Mastership"

Line 849: "the coveted position"

London derived some of the incident that follows from Young, who, when he tried to replace Voyageur as leader of his team, discovered that the dog was guilty of "cutting off the traces of the dog" that Young had had the "audacity to put in front of him!" Young eventually relented and permitted Voyageur to return to "his coveted place as the leader."[1]

Line 854: "Chook!"

London uses this imperative in a number of other places in his Northland tales—including "The Wife of a King," "The Man with the Gash," "Grit of Women," "Where the Trail Forks," "A Hyperborean Brew," and "Bâtard." In every instance, the person employing it is commanding dogs—or people—to leave or hurry up. In "Bâtard," for instance, Webster Shaw yells "Hi, ya! *Chook!* you Spawn of Hell" in an attempt to get the dog to release its death grip on Black Leclère. In "Where the Trail Forks," the context makes the meaning evident: "At her shrill 'Chook!' the maddened brutes [sled dogs] shot ahead. . . ." London's "chook" is probably the Tlingit word that Aurel Krause and G. I. Davydov transcribe, respectively, as *djuk* and *chaiuk*, meaning "go away" or "quick!"[2]

Lines 876–77: "He did not try to run away, but retreated around and around the camp"

Young's dogs would not come to him when he was angry with them: "They would sit up on their haunches and let me come within about a hundred feet of them, but 'No nearer, thank you,' they seemed to say. Clever fellows. . . ."[3]

Line 910: "Rink Rapids"

To the entire series of rapids near and including Five Finger Rapids, which lie about fifty miles upstream from the mouth of the Pelly River, Schwatka had given the name "Rink"—for Dr. Henry Rink, an authority on Greenland. But the name "Rink" is now applied only to a set of less formidable rapids six miles downstream from Five Finger.

Price wrote that Rink consisted of a "wide tumbling bay, formed by a ledge of rocks extending almost across the entire width of the river." On the right hand the current was "very swift," but, Price declared, it could be managed "without any special risk by cool-headed men." Within a few years, however, Territorial Engineer P. E. Mercier had dynamited the rocks in the rapids, making their passage today little more than a pleasantly swift ride—"no trouble at all," wrote Berton after shooting them in 1971.[4]

Line 911: "two native huskies, Teek and Koona"

One of Young's dogs was named Koona, which, Young writes, is a Cree Indian word meaning "snow." "Teek" is the English spelling of the Tlingit word for ice. London has found fitting names for his two native huskies: Ice and Snow.[5]

Lines 917–18: "The temperature dropped to fifty below zero"

Extreme temperatures are not unusual in the Yukon winter. Robinson notes that −67° F. has been recorded three times—with even lower temperatures likely in the mountains. Hayne reported low temperatures at Fortymile ranging from −50° to −73° F between 1895 and 1897. The old sourdoughs, wrote Adney, applied an informal system of determining low temperatures: "Mercury freezes at −40; coal oil (kerosene) freezes at from −35 to −55, according to grades; 'pain-killer' freezes at −72; 'St. Jacob's Oil' freezes at −75; best Hudson's Bay rum freezes at −80."[6]

Lines 921–22: "In one run they made a sixty-mile dash from the foot of Lake Le Barge to the White Horse Rapids."

Northland writers agree that the rapids—called "Klil-has" ("very bad") by the American Indians in the region—were named "Whitehorse" because the waters resembled "the

flying manes of a regiment of white horses making a charge."[7] The Whitehorse Rapids—
which did lie sixty miles from Lower Laberge—no longer exist: A nearby hydroelectric
dam drowned them in the newly formed Schwatka Lake.

The rapids were terrifyingly beautiful to behold—in fact, Hawthorne thought they
were "the prettiest sight I ever seen in all my life. The river was a real deep blue, and all
over the top of it was big, high, white waves, tossing their heads." And Davis maintained
that the "raging water named itself," for no one could "look down on those galloping
tossed waves and not imagine a stampeding herd of wild and cream-white horses delight-
ing in their strength, racing through the rock-walled chute of the grand canyon of the
Yukon, milling madly in the treacherous corral of the whirlpool, and pouring out at last
into the full-pastured Yukon valley lying beyond."[8]

The Whitehorse and nearby Squaw Rapids were the bane of river travelers. When
Schwatka first saw them in 1883, he judged them to be "ten times more dangerous" than
Miles Canyon. And Ingersoll issued a blunt warning that they "should never be attempted." In the rush for riches, however, caution was an early casualty, and during the
first few days of the Rush in the spring of 1898, 150 boats were lost and five men drowned.
The NWMP quickly took charge of the river and would not permit the inexperienced to
shoot the rapids; before long, a system of cables was installed to haul craft through the
danger. The settlement that grew there eventually became the city of Whitehorse, now the
capital of the Yukon.[9]

When Osborne saw the rapids in the spring of 1898, he observed a wild scene: "The banks
were lined with hundreds of spectators, who, like myself, had experienced the excitement of
the voyage, and watched the fortune of their fellows with eager eyes and absorbing interest....
[I]t thrilled the spectators, who watched for each result with bated breath, breaking into
wild cheers for the successful, and rushing to render practical aid to the unfortunate."[10]

With a thousand people watching from the shore, London and his companions shot the
rapids on 25 September 1897, an event that London describes in his article, "Through the
Rapids on the Way to the Klondike":

*The dangerous point in these rapids is at the tail end, called the "Mane of the Horse,"
from a succession of foamy, mountainous waves. Extending three-quarters of the
way across, a rocky reef throws the whole river against the right bank; then comes
the hump, and it is thrown back to the left, forming another whirlpool, more risky
by far than that of the Box [Miles Canyon].*

When we struck the "Mane," the Yukon Belle *[a name London and his party had given to one of their boats] forgot her heavy load, taking a series of leaps almost clear of the water, alternating with as many burials in the troughs. To this day I cannot see how it happened, but I lost control. A cross current caught our stern and we began to swing broadside. Then we jumped into the whirlpool, though I did not guess it at the time. Sloper [a companion] snapped a second paddle and received another ducking.*

It must be remembered that we were traveling at racehorse speed, and that things happened in a tithe of the time taken to tell them. From every quarter the water came aboard, threatening to swamp us. The Yukon Belle *headed directly for the jagged left bank, and though I was up against the steering sweep till it cracked, I could not turn her nose downstream. Onlookers from the shore tried to snapshot us, but failed to gauge our speed or get more than a wild view of angry waters and flying foam.*

The bank was alarmingly close, but the boat still had the bit in her teeth. It was all happening so quickly, that I for the first time realized I was trying to buck the whirlpool. Like a flash I was bearing against the opposite side of the sweep. The boat answered, at the same time following the bent of the whirlpool, and headed upstream. But the shave was so close that Sloper leaped to the top of a rock. Then, on seeing we had missed by a couple of inches, he pluckily tumbled aboard, all in a heap, like a man boarding a comet.

Though tearing like mad through a whirlpool, we breathed freer. Completing the circle, we were thrown into the "Mane," which we shot a second time and safely landed in a friendly eddy below.[11]

It should be noted that one of the most persistent canards about Jack London is the story that he lingered a few days at the Whitehorse Rapids and accumulated a small fortune. In *Sailor on Horseback*, Irving Stone wrote that after Jack successfully shot the rapids he was "deluged with offers to take other boats through. He charged twenty-five dollars a boat, remained for several days, and earned three thousand dollars for his party. There was another five thousand dollars to be had, but it was already mid-September."[12]

This story has been reported as fact by Winslow (*Big Pan-Out*), Shannon Garst (*Jack London: Magnet for Adventure*), and many others—including Pierre Berton.[13] Yet both

Thompson's diary and London's own published account mention only a second trip—to help an apprehensive husband and wife. Since London was not reluctant about advertising his physical accomplishments—and piloting 120 boats without incident through the Whitehorse Rapids would surely qualify as a Herculean feat—one must infer that Stone fabricated the episode, probably for its dramatic value.

London took the precise wording of this passage from a newspaper article about a record run made by Dick Heath: "In one day they made a sixty-mile dash from the foot of Lake Labarge to White Horse Rapids."[14]

London's spelling—"White Horse"—was the accepted one until 1957, when the Geographic Board of Canada standardized spellings in the region, transforming many two-word place-names into one word (Fortymile, Sixtymile, Whitehorse).[15]

Line 923: "Marsh, Tagish, and Bennett (seventy miles of lakes)"

The distance from Marsh Lake to the settlement at Bennett is approximately seventy miles. Miner Bruce's *Alaska*, a volume London took with him to the Klondike, quotes sizes for these lakes that total sixty-two miles. Other volumes from the era give various other totals, ranging from Bruce's low of sixty-two to a high of seventy-six (Schwatka).[16]

Schwatka named Marsh Lake—called "Mud Lake" by the miners—for Professor Othniel Charles Marsh (1831–99), who taught paleontology for many years at Yale University and also worked for the United States Geological Survey. In this case, the appearance of the lake and its name make happy companions, for, as Kirk observed, the "shores of this lake are flat and marshy, a fact suggesting its name. . . ."[17]

Tagish Lake was named by and for the indigenous people of the region, the Tagish Indians, a subdivision of the Tlingit. *Taku*, from which the Anglicized "Tagish" derives, is a contraction of the Tlingit word *tak-wakh-tha-ku*, which means "place where the geese sit down." Lyons wrote that its waters were so clear that "many fragments of pink and white marble that cover the bottom may be seen at a depth of ten feet."[18]

Line 925: "White Pass"

The Chilkoot Pass was one principal route over the Coastal Mountains to the Yukon headwaters; the White Pass, the other. Named by Dominion Land Surveyor William Ogilvie for Sir Thomas White, Canadian Minister of the Interior, the pass was surveyed in 1887 by William "Billie" Moore, who first crossed it on 6 June 1887 with his Tagish companion, Skookum Jim Mason. Moore, who would establish a town-site at the foot of the mountains, was hoping to profit from the pass, and in a government report on 6 January 1888, he claimed that an "easy grade can be obtained" along the route.[19]

The trail was one of surpassing beauty, as Osborne recorded:

The scenery was magnificent, wild and rugged beyond description. The black frown-ing rocks rose to a height of some fifteen hundred feet on both sides of the narrow gorge, which was filled to a depth of at least thirty feet with snow. . . .

. . . the scene in the cañon of the White Pass and on the summit is one of the most impressive, in its wild desolation and grandeur, that can be conceived. The beetling walls of the cañon, with its foaming torrent; the streams, here winding down a mountain-side like streaks of silver shining in the sunlight, there leaping over precip-itous ledges, and tossing a sheet of iridescent spray into the air; the awful grandeur of the summit, one mighty stretch of rugged masses of black stone, tumbled and torn into a thousand shapes, the sombreness unbroken, except by the mysterious blue lakes that fill the hollows,—all these possess the mind with a sense of dread and desolation, of magic influences and supernatural power, of astonishment and awe.[20]

Its alpine attractions notwithstanding, the White Pass earned another name during the first year of the Rush—the Dead Horse Trail. So difficult was the terrain—and so heartless were the men who traversed it in the flush of the gold-fever—that no pack animal survived the trail the first winter; the way was virtually carpeted with the corpses of dead animals, more than three thousand according to an NWMP report.[21]

Writer after writer during the Rush commented on the horrible conditions along the trail—yet thousands ignored the warnings, driving themselves to despair and their animals to death. On 19 August 1897, Wells wrote that if a "horse falls on the trail the drivers of animals behind either throw the animal from the cliff or drive, roughshod, over it. Fully fifty horses are killed or disabled every day along the trail and their packs are lost."[22]

On 25 August 1897, Adney observed an episode that has become one of the most often-repeated tales from the Rush: "Yesterday a horse walked deliberately over the face of Por-cupine Hill. Said one of the men who saw it: 'It looked to me, sir, like suicide. I believe a horse will commit suicide, and this is enough to make them; they don't mind the hills like they do these mud-holes.' He added, 'I don't know but that I'd rather commit suicide, too, than be driven by some of the men on this trail.'"23

Wells observed two old men, "gray-haired and bent," who sat "crying beside a muck hole." Their horses were caught in a bog, yet hundreds of gold-seekers passed by without offering assistance. "Not even a look of pity or sympathy was bestowed upon the unfortunates. The craze for gold has steeled the hearts of those who were once human beings." Hawthorne encountered a man who was sitting on his sled in midtrail, muttering over and over: "It's hell. It's hell." Walden saw something even more horrifying—a "dead man with the back of his head smashed in and everyone passing him and paying no attention."24

Jack London never saw the White Pass—his party had used the Chilkoot—but he had heard and read enough of its horrors that he was able to write a description of it so accurate that for a time the National Park Service reproduced it for its White Pass display at the Klondike Gold Rush National Historical Park in Skagway:

> *Freighting an outfit over the White Pass in '97 broke many a man's heart, for there was a world of reason when they gave that trail its name. The horses died like mosquitoes in the first frost, and from Skaguay to Bennett they rotted in heaps. They died at the Rocks. They were poisoned at the Summit, and they starved at the Lakes; they fell off the trail, what there was of it, or they went through it; in the river they drowned under their loads, or were smashed to pieces against the boulders; they snapped their legs in the crevices and broke their backs falling backward with their packs; in the sloughs they sank from sight or smothered in the slime, and they were disembowelled in the bogs where the corduroy logs turned end up in the mud; men shot them, worked them to death, and when they were gone, went back to the beach and bought more. Some did not bother to shoot them,—stripping the saddles off and the shoes and leaving them where they fell. Their hearts turned to stone—those which did not break—and they became beasts, the men on Dead Horse Trail.*25

In November 1897, George Brackett, a former mayor of Minneapolis, began construction of a toll road over the White Pass, but it was many months before "Brackett's Road" was completed. By 6 July 1899, the narrow-gauge White Pass and Yukon Railroad had bought out Brackett's right-of-way and had laid track, entirely by hand, along the forty miles between Skagway and Lake Bennett—a massive project begun on 29 May 1898—and the "Dead Horse Trail" was no more.[26] Today, the Klondike Highway parallels the railroad and is the principal route across the mountains; the old White Pass and Yukon is now a popular tourist attraction in Skagway.

Line 926: "Skaguay"

Only a few miles south along the Alaskan coast from Dyea, Skagway was for a year or so in stiff competition with its neighbor for the Gold Rush business. For a variety of reasons—the principal ones being its deep harbor and the construction of the White Pass and Yukon Railroad linking it with Lake Bennett—Skagway eventually supplanted Dyea as the preferred point of departure for those crossing the mountains into the Yukon. Dyea today is completely gone; Skagway remains (year-round population: 754), a terminus for the Klondike Highway, headquarters for the Klondike Gold Rush National Historical Park, and a stopping point for many Alaska cruise ships.

Although most authorities agree that the name originated with a Tlingit word (*skagua* or *skagus*) meaning "home of the north wind," Phillips argues for another Tlingit word (*sch-kawai*) meaning "end of the salt water."[27] Two visitors to the region after the Rush published varying accounts of the origin of the name, both suggesting that their stories came from authentic Tlingit legends.

In her *Cheechako in Alaska and Yukon*, Charlotte Cameron relates the following:

"Skagway!—oh, great Skagway, have mercy!" Thus implore the Indians when the Arctic wind, unleashed, hurls the blinding snows down through the Chilcoot Pass and freezes the very marrow of their bones. Skagway, or Skaguay, derived its name from an unhappy Indian princess. She was supposed to have been very beautiful, her fair face crowned with masses of Titian-red hair. Skaguay was forced to marry, without love, the son of a chief, and her husband treated her with unreasoning cruelty.

But with the patience of a martyr she endured her misery. But one day, unable to bear the burden longer, she ran screaming up the mountain-side, her glorious hair streaming in the boisterous north wind. She aroused a great fear in those of her clansmen who ran after and pursued her. Then she vanished into a great rock, and was never seen again. For many years the loyal Indians placed food for Skaguay at the foot of the rock, and to this day when the fearful storms descend on Skagway, the Indians will crave the intercession of the vanished princess.[28]

Quite a different account comes from John Scudder McLain, who says he was told the following in 1903: "An old Indian chief who lived here stood one day on shore watching his son trying to land in a canoe. The wind swept down the canyon with terrific force, but he was a strong lad and skilful [*sic*], and his father had little fear. The boy was blown around the point, however, and out of sight. A little while later his canoe was seen floating bottom up. Its occupant was never found. And so the old chief named the place Skagua, which means Home of the North Wind."[29]

The spelling of the name of the town has occasioned nearly as much controversy as its meaning. Variously rendered as "Shkagaway," "Skaguay," and "Skagawa," the town is now officially "Skagway." This would have greatly disappointed M. L. Sherpy, editor and proprietor of the *Skaguay News*, whose editorial in the 14 October 1898 issue ("Spell It with 'U'") condemned the "idiotic tendency on the part of a few people of this city to change its name from 'Skaguay' to 'Skagway.'" Sherpy saw no reason to "do away with the rythm [*sic*] of our city's name" and pointed his finger at "inconsiderate postal authorities" as the culprits.[30]

The town-site of Skagway was laid out by Captain William "Billie" Moore, who first established a camp there on 29 October 1887, gambling that prospectors would opt to use the White Pass rather than the more precipitous Chilkoot. And for a very brief while it looked as if Moore would indeed reap huge financial rewards for his prescience. But he had misjudged the impatience and independence of the Klondike stampeders—not to mention their frontier intransigence and disregard for authority. When the first ships arrived on 26 July 1897, the argonauts streamed ashore and simply ignored Moore's claims to the town-site, refused to pay for property, and set about rearranging Skagway to suit their own needs, financial and logistical. Moore even suffered the indignity of having his own house moved to a different location to accommodate the new system of streets. However, Moore was able to make a fair fortune with his wharf, and the courts eventually awarded him compensation for his property losses.[31]

When Wells visited the town in August 1897, he wrote that "all semblance of method and order has been lost" and that "nobody knows where the 'lots' begin or end." People were in such a frenzy that they occasionally committed unintentional horrors. One man tied some goats to a wharf piling, not realizing, apparently, that tides come and go. A few hours later, Hawthorne witnessed the result: "just their tails, floating around on top the water. All the rest of them was covered over."[32]

Despite the initial disorder, the town was soon booming, and on 15 October 1897, the *Skaguay News* published an impressive list of available services and businesses:

> *One bank; fifteen general merchandise stores; nineteen restaurants; four meat markets; eleven hay, grain and feed yards; twenty-six contractors; six real estate offices; six drug stores; three wharves; four transfer companies; three bath houses; three dentists; two dressmakers; one bowling alley; eleven saloons; one saw mill; six lumber yards; nine steamboat companies; three tin shops; nine hotels; five fruit dealers; four civil engineers; five hardware stores; four news stands; one book exchange; two shoemakers; seven bakeries; eight blacksmiths; eight pack trains; six cigar and tobacco stores; three furniture and mattress stores; seven doctors; six lawyers; three typewriters; one photographer; four sign painters; two barbershops; five storage houses; five wood yards; three laundries; seven lodging houses; ten grocery stores; three chop houses; four clothing and woolen goods stores; and three employment offices.*[33]

Line 927: "It was a record run. Each day for fourteen days they had averaged forty miles."

François and Perrault's fourteen-day trip was well within the range of a "record run" for the winter. Heilprin claimed in 1899 that good dog teams would be able to make the run from Bennett to Dawson in fifteen days or less. Bennett to Skagway was yet an additional day. During the Rush, various writers noted the actual record times of dog teams. Kirk wrote that the fastest trip of the winter of 1897–98 was made by Robert Insley in sixteen days. The *Daily Alaskan* published a story about a "spanking dog team" owned by J. A. Cates and Geo. Clancy that made the trip in fifteen days. And Adney wrote about a team that made the run in a mere ten days.[34]

Line 928: "threw chests"

Proud of their Dawson-to-Skagway record, François and Perrault, chests puffed out in pride, were enjoying their brief moments of fame. London uses this odd expression elsewhere, for example in his essay "The Other Animals," in which he tells about fooling his dog, Rollo. "Of course Rollo was fooled," he wrote. "But that is no call for us to throw chests about it."[35]

Lines 930–31: "Then three or four western bad men aspired to clean out the town, were riddled like pepper-boxes for their pains, and public interest turned to other idols."

It is unknown if London is referring to any specific shoot-out, but throughout the Rush, Skagway was known as a wild, lawless town. Because it was on American soil, the Northwest Mounted Police had no jurisdiction, and the U.S. authorities were ineffectual in their attempts to control the population. Virtually every visitor to the town in the early days commented upon its riotous, dangerous character. In August 1897, Adney saw that "[e]very man is armed—all with revolvers, some with repeating rifles." A few months later, Osborne observed "drunkenness, vice, and every kind of lawlessness. Crimes of violence were frequent," he continued, "and were committed with impunity. . . . In Skagway human life was cheap as dirt—much cheaper even than drink. Everyone went armed."

Price was shocked at "the lawlessness prevailing in Skaguay. . . . Strangers are frequently held up in broad daylight and openly robbed," he complained, "and a foul murder of a woman had taken place the night before our arrival, and the murderer, who was known, was walking about the place unmolested." Captain Henry Toke Munn concurred. "The six nights I slept at Skagway [early 1898]," he wrote, "there was a shooting on the street every night and at least one man was killed that I knew of, probably others. The shack I slept in had a bullet through it over my head."

In his "Annual Report to the Commissioner of the North-west Mounted Police" on 10 January 1899, Superintendent Steele characterized the town as "little better than a hell upon earth. . . . Murder and robbery were daily occurrences. . . . Men were seen frequently exchanging shots in the streets." He described one wild shoot-out, involving a half a dozen men, "in the vicinity and around the North-west Mounted Police Offices"; "bullets were passing through the buildings," he commented with typical dry understatement.[36]

The Skagway newspapers are not a good source of information about the shootings—the editors were interested in attracting, not repelling, visitors—but occasionally an item such as the following appeared: "The first shooting affray that has occurred in Skaguay for some time, took place one night last week. A one legged man named Chas. Butler, and a fellow named Bob. Larkin had some words of a personal nature in the cabin of the latter, when Butler drew his revolver and shot the other fellow through the ear. The wound is a painful but not necessarily dangerous one."[37]

The newspapers in nearby Dyea, however, gleefully reported shootings in rival Skagway. DASTARDLY MURDER shouted one headline in the *Dyea Trail*; underneath was a story of a chaotic fight in the Klondike Saloon, where "four or five men were scuffling on the floor, while Brennan was pummeling a tall man whom he had bent back over the bar. A shot was fired which killed Brennan."[38]

The "wild and woolly" nature of Skagway and Dyea was reported in newspapers all over the country. The *New York Times* quoted a letter from Governor John G. Brady of Alaska: "'News from Skaguay . . . is serious. The United States Deputy Marshal has been shot dead in discharge of his duty. Another man was killed at the same time at the same place. . . . Many [who arrive here are] gamblers, thugs, and lewd women from the worst quarters of the cities of the coast.'"[39]

In its wildest days Skagway was in the grip of Jefferson Randolph "Soapy" Smith and his band of con men, cutthroats, highwaymen, and thugs. Smith was, according to all accounts, exactly what Pierre Berton calls him in *Klondike*: the Dictator of Skagway. On 8 July 1898, however, Smith and a righteous citizen named Frank Reid exchanged shots on a Skagway dock. "Soapy" died almost immediately; Reid, wounded in the groin, lingered a few days before he expired, a hero to the law-abiding citizens of the town, who erected a marble monument with the following inscription: "He gave his life for the honor of Skagway."[40]

Jack London saw Skagway from a Chilkat canoe as he paddled by on his trip from Juneau to Dyea, but he never visited the town; his use of this incident, however, reveals quite clearly that he well knew of its violent reputation.[41]

Lines 935–39: "A Scotch half-breed took charge of him and his mates . . . for this was the mail train, carrying word from the world to the men who sought gold under the shadow of the Pole."

This unnamed character is perhaps based upon Andrew Flett, who, according to Walker, was "a Mackenzie River half-breed, [who] brought the first mail of the winter through in January [1898] with a four-dog outfit."[42] The Northland had many men of Scotch descent, some of whom had originally worked for the Hudson's Bay Company, had taken Indian wives, and had fathered children—"half-breeds," in Northland parlance, many of whom had remained in the North and worked for the Canadian government.

Lines 945–46: "the darkness fell which gave warning of dawn"

London describes this phenomenon in *Burning Daylight* "It was the darkness before dawn, never anywhere more conspicuous than on the Alaskan winter-trail."[43]

Line 946: "pitched the flies"

A fly is a primitive shelter—a simple tent. In "Where the Trail Forks," London describes it as "a sheet of canvas stretched between two trees and angling at forty-five degrees. This caught the radiating heat from the fire and flung it down upon the skin."[44]

Line 960: "the memories of his heredity"

London's idea here that instincts are "the memories of his ancestors become habits" was one that biologists had generally agreed upon in the late nineteenth century. In his book *Unconscious Memory* (1880) Samuel Butler wrote that we "possess the instincts we possess, because . . . [we] had these instincts in past generations when we were in the persons of our forefathers. . . ."[45]

Lines 964–89: Buck's vision in the fire

London was fascinated by "ancestral memories." *Before Adam*, his 1907 novel of prehistoric life, employs a similar device: An unnamed narrator, while studying evolution, realizes that the dreams he has been having are actually memories of an ancient ancestor named Big-Tooth.[46]

Line 993: "letters for the outside"

Throughout his Northland fiction, London uses "outside" and "inside"—sometimes capitalized, sometimes not—to refer to territory that is inside or outside of Alaska and the Yukon.

Lines 1005–62: Dave's suffering and death

London wrote in "The White Silence" that as long as "an animal can travel, it is not shot, and this last chance is accorded it,—the crawling into camp, if it can. . . ." But in times of crisis, such considerations were abandoned. One Klondike handbook even recommended procedures: "Shoot a dog, if you have to, behind the base of the skull; a horse between the ears, ranging downward. Press the trigger of your rifle. Don't pull it. Don't catch hold of the barrel when thirty degrees below zero is registered. Watch out against getting snow in your barrel. If you do, don't shoot it out or the gun may and probably will burst." In *Farthest North*, Nansen relates how he systematically dispatched his dogs, then fed them to other dogs in order to keep going.[47]

Line 1015: *Cassiar Bar*

Dave's struggle has been impressive: Cassiar Bar is about 340 miles from Dawson City. "Cassiar" is a corruption of the native word *Kaska*, the name given to some American Indians living in northern British Columbia and also their word for "creek." Hamilton adds that *kaska* may also mean "long moss hanging from tree" or "rags wrapped around the feet." The only certainty, he says, is that the word is of "Amerindian origin."[48]

Cassiar Bar is a large sandbar in the Yukon River, about eight miles upstream from the mouth of the Big Salmon River. In 1886, four prospectors made a small gold strike on the bar, and for a while it featured "quite a settlement," according to Heilprin, who saw it in 1898. George Dawson himself characterized it as "the richest [bar] on the river." But larger strikes elsewhere, especially on the Klondike, soon made Cassiar little more than a landmark. When Cameron passed it just prior to 1920, she noted that it was "a small deserted settlement of three or four log-cabins shrouded by Jack Pine and spruce trees."[49]

London became intimately familiar with Cassiar Bar on 3 October 1897, as Thompson's diary records: "Before coming to the Big Salmon River there is a large Bar (called Cassiar Bar) extending from the right hand bank, nearly across the river, here we should have kept the left hand bank in going down, but knowing nothing of the bar and seeing an opening on the right we were, before we knew it, in shallow water and fast on the bar, but soon got our boats off and pulled and pushed them back up the river and made a shoot across for the left hand bank passing there in safety."[50]

CHAPTER FIVE

"The Toil of Trace and Trail"

Line 1063: "the Salt Water Mail"

Mail back and forth from Dawson to the oceangoing ships departing from Skagway ("Salt Water") was neither frequent nor regular. Because Dawson was in Canada and Skagway in Alaska, international politics was an initial problem, but the difficulties were eventually resolved, and delivery commenced in the capable hands of the North-west Mounted Police.

The first post office in Skagway was opened on 10 November 1897, with William B. Sampson as postmaster. The Pacific Coast Steamship Company had the contract—their vessels, says Howard Clifford, "were considered most reliable." Service was slow, and it was "not uncommon to stand 3 or 4 hours in the cold, muddy street before one reached the postal window." The situation was no better in Dyea. Postmaster Clara H. Richards reported lines "several hundred feet long" all day. In September 1898 the *Skaguay News* announced mail departures on the first and the fifteenth every month, but noted that the mail "arrives from Yukon points at irregular intervals and not oftener than twice each month."[1]

Adney, who was in Dawson at the time, wrote that the first mail train from "Salt Water" arrived in Dawson City on 26 February 1898. Though London does not mention it here, the mail train in which Buck and his mates are laboring would have been run by the

NWMP, who did in fact hire independent drivers like the "Scotch half-breed." The last mail in Alaska to be delivered by dog team was in January 1963.[2]

Lines 1066–67: "Pike . . . had often successfully feigned a hurt leg"

Morgan warns dog-drivers not to show much affection to any animal, for "the beast will maneuver to capitalize on this partiality by faking weakness or lameness. . . ."[3]

Line 1090: "Hudson Bay dogs"

London is vague here, leaving this phrase open to two interpretations: (1) these are dogs purchased from the Hudson's Bay Company—which did sell dogs throughout the Rush, or (2) these are dogs from the Hudson Bay region, where, Charles Richard Tuttle observed, the Eskimo villages were populated with "a host of wolf-like dogs."[4]

Compounding the ambiguity is London's inconsistent spelling in his Northland writing: When referring to both the company and the bay, he sometimes writes "Hudson's Bay," sometimes "Hudson Bay." That was not uncommon: "Hudson's Bay" was an acceptable spelling for the bay until 1900 when the Geographic Board of Canada decided to make the official name "Hudson Bay."[5]

There are, however, other passages in other stories that make clear that London's reference is to the breed of dogs from the region of Hudson Bay. In "Finis," for example, he mentions "a heavy dog, half Newfoundland and half Hudson Bay. . . ."[6]

Lines 1096 and 1109: Hal, Charles, and Mercedes

Frail, feckless Mercedes was not the typical sort of woman who ventured into the Yukon during the Gold Rush—and there were many. On 14 May 1898, the *Dyea Trail* commented that "at least 100 women" had passed through, and Dawson City's *Klondike News* remarked a month earlier that "if you have an aversion to the 'new woman,' a week on the Dyea trail would change that aversion to admiration. . . ." In *Klondike Women*, Melanie J. Mayer notes that among the large numbers of "dance hall girls and 'sporting women'" were "women from all walks of life . . . poor but aspiring immigrants, professional women, socialites, wives, single women, widows, and children."[7]

The *New York Times* announced the formation of "The Women's Klondike Expedition Syndicate," whose members were among the most notable women in the city. "The women who join it," reported the *Times*, "must be physically sound and healthy, and they are expected to abide by certain prescribed regulations." In the same vein, *Leslie's Weekly* published a glowing account of the efforts of Hannah S. Gould, who was leading a group of women to the Northland.[8]

Like many of the men, however, many of the women were unprepared for the rigors of the Northland trails. The *Dyea Trail* published a notice of a woman on the Chilkoot Trail "carrying a poll parrot." And aboard the *Rosalie* bound for Dyea, Wells observed a group with many similarities to Hal, Charles, and Mercedes: ". . . Mrs. A. T. French of Seattle, proposes to accompany her husband and brother across the mountains and into the gold regions. She is a pretty, vivacious lady, apparently under 36, and is attired in a natty blue velvet costume. She wears a dainty feather in her cap and red ribbons on her hair. Mrs. French evidently believes in 'keeping up appearances' even on the rolling sea. Her husband is a little, smooth-shaved man of kindly, patient mien and wears a broad-brimmed desperado's hat that illy becomes his style and build."[9]

Mercedes is an anomaly among most of London's other Northland women, American Indian and Caucasian alike. Women characters like Frona Welse (*A Daughter of the Snows*) and Joy Gastell (*Smoke Bellew*) are in many respects the superiors of virtually all the men around them.

Lines 1098–99: "a big Colt's revolver and a hunting-knife"

Colt's is the most frequently mentioned brand name of firearm in the Northland canon of Jack London—and "big Colt's revolver" is his favored locution. Samuel Colt (1814–62) was the inventor of the revolver, and although his first patent (1836) did not result in immediate success, orders for his weapons to help prosecute the Mexican War (1846–48) propelled his company to success—and himself to enormous wealth. The Colt's Patent Fire Arms Manufacturing Company, now simply "Colt's Manufacturing," remains in the firearms business in Hartford, Connecticut, birthplace of Samuel Colt.

Hal's decision to take a side arm to the Klondike was not unusual. Although the North-west Mounted Police permitted no one to carry guns in Dawson City, pamphlets, newspapers, and books urged the gold-seekers to take weapons with them—and the manufacturers and sellers of firearms were eager to accommodate the new demand.

Early in the Rush, the *San Francisco Chronicle* published an article about the need for Northland travelers to carry weapons: "A revolver is looked upon as a necessity in the Klondyke . . . [as a] defense against the attack of either man or beast. The favorite revolver is a 44-caliber, single action, long barrel. . . . A special knife has been placed on the market for Klondyke outfits. It is larger than an ordinary hunting knife, is made extra heavy and has a double-edged point."[10]

According to one of Wells's newspaper dispatches, the stampeders were following the counsel of the periodicals and advertisers. He described passengers aboard the Alaska-bound steamer *Rosalie* out on deck with their weapons, "banging away at icebergs, seals, gulls and porpoises with a reckless disregard of the cost of ammunition." Wells added dryly that the captain had cautioned everyone "to be prudent and shoot none of the other passengers."

Not everyone was so considerate. In Skagway, bullets flew night and day. And in nearby Dyea, the *Dyea Trail* editorialized against the proliferation of firearms: "Every ruffian, crank and criminal carries his pistol or his knife. Why should decent people be put and kept at their mercy?"[11]

Line 1153: "'Rest be blanked,' said Hal"

"Blanked," a euphemism for "damned," derives from the publishing practice of substituting blank spaces for proscribed words.

Lines 1183–84: "chief thoroughfare" [of Skagway]

The main street of Skagway was—and is—Broadway, aptly named because it was eighty feet wide—twenty more than the other streets in town. Heilprin referred to "the principal thoroughfare of Skaguay, the ubiquitous Broadway . . . ," and Cameron also called Broadway "the main street." In a historical work on the city, Robert Spude described Broadway as a "wall of false-fronted, wooden buildings with bright signs, awnings, boardwalks, crates and—most likely—mud. Two church steeples towered to the northwest with the beginnings of a residential district below them."[12]

Line 1189: the Long Trail

Here, as elsewhere in his Northland writings, London is referring to the trail between Dyea (or Skagway) and Dawson City. In *White Fang*, for example, "The Long Trail" is a chapter dealing with Weedon Scott's departure from the Northland and his return to Santa Clara County.[13] But this appellation was applied to another trail in the Northland, as well: the so-called "Ashcroft Trail," from Ashcroft, British Columbia, to Telegraph Creek, northeast of Ft. Wrangell, Alaska. Hamlin Garland's novel *The Long Trail* (1907) chronicles the difficulties of the Ashcroft.

Whatever the route, "Long Trail" was an appropriate name, for all routes to the Klondike were extremely difficult. DeWindt said that the journey was "from start to finish, as fatiguing, monotonous, and generally comfortless, as it has ever fallen to the lot of the writer to accomplish." Harwood Steele's description was more pungent: "a Dantesque progress through Hell and Purgatory to Paradise."[14]

Line 1192: "'Good Lord, do you think you're travelling on a Pullman?'"

George Mortimer Pullman (1831–97) was the founder of the Pullman Palace Car Company (1867), manufacturer of luxury rail cars. Pullman's initial break in the business came when one of his cars was chosen to carry the body of President Lincoln from Chicago to Springfield, Illinois, in 1865. By the mid-1930s, Pullman had eighty-five hundred cars operating in North America and employed thirty thousand people. During the Gold Rush, a rail ticket from New York City to Seattle cost $81.50; a ride in a Pullman cost an additional $20.50.[15]

To attract some of the Gold Rush business, Pullman designed an electric sleigh featuring steam heat and electric lights and a top speed of sixty miles per hour. Charles Margeson and his party actually transported such a device to Alaska but found it "no good" and abandoned it.[16]

Line 1202: "Outside dogs"

Despite warnings from those who knew the North, people brought into the sub-Arctic world animals that simply could not survive the harsh conditions. On the streets of Dawson City, Mizner saw all sorts of dogs, "anything from a chewawa [*sic*] to a St. Bernard. . . ." And on the Chilkoot Trail, Walden observed a man who had brought along a greyhound: "One morning the short-haired dog was found frozen solid, standing up: There he stood with his tail between his legs, his back arched, and his head down."[17]

Line 1222: "Q.E.D."

This abbreviation for the Latin phrase *quod erat demonstrandum* ("which was to be shown or demonstrated") is traditionally placed at the end of mathematical proofs.

Lines 1233–34: "It took them half the night to pitch a slovenly camp, and half the morning to break that camp and get the sled loaded in fashion so slovenly"

In *Burning Daylight*, London gives an account of how a Northland camp ought to be set up. In this passage, Daylight and his American Indian companion Kama enact a brisk scene that stands in stark contrast to the farce performed by Hal, Charles, and Mercedes:

The division of labor was excellent. Each knew what he must do. With one axe Daylight chopped down the dead pine. Kama, with a snowshoe and the other axe, cleared away the two feet of snow above the Yukon ice and chopped a supply of ice for cooking purposes. A piece of dry birch bark started the fire, and Daylight went ahead with the cooking while the Indian unloaded the sled and fed the dogs their ration of dried fish. The food sacks he slung high in the trees beyond leaping-reach of the huskies. Next, he chopped down a young spruce tree and trimmed off the boughs. Close to the fire he trampled down the soft snow and covered the packed space with the boughs. On this flooring he tossed his own and Daylight's gear-bags, containing dry socks and underwear and their sleeping-robes. . . .

They worked on steadily, without speaking, losing no time. Each did whatever was needed, without thought of leaving to the other the least task that presented itself to hand. Thus, Kama saw when more ice was needed and went and got it, while a snowshoe, pushed over by the lunge of a dog, was stuck on end again by Daylight. While coffee was boiling, bacon drying and flapjacks were being mixed, Daylight found time to put on a big pot of beans. Kama came back, sat down on the edge of the spruce boughs, and in the interval of waiting, mended harness. . . . Daylight, between mouthfuls, fed chunks of ice into the tin pot, where it thawed into water. The meal finished, Kama replenished the fire, cut more wood for the morning, and returned to the spruce bough bed and his harness-mending. Daylight cut up generous chunks of bacon and dropped them in the pot of bubbling beans. The moccasins of both men were wet, and this in spite of the intense cold; so when there was no further need for them to leave the oasis of spruce boughs, they took off their moccasins and hung them on short sticks to dry before the fire, turning them about from time to time. When the beans were finally cooked, Daylight ran part of them into a bag of flour-sacking a foot and a half long and three inches in diameter. This he then laid on the snow to freeze. The remainder of the beans were left in the pot for breakfast.[18]

Line 1268: "To quarrel was the one thing they were never too weary to do."

Many visitors during the Rush commented upon the frequency of arguments all along the trail. "There is something in Alaska," wrote Mizner, "where work is not equally divided, and people are jammed together, without outside contacts, that breeds dissension." Mizner then related a tale of two partners who had known each other since boyhood, worked in the same bank, and had even married sisters. But the stress of the trail was too much, and when they divided their twenty bags of flour, "they sawed each sack in two and each took twenty halves."[19]

And Berton recounts three other odd anecdotes: "two men caught on the rocks in the middle of the Thirtymile River and, oblivious of their surroundings, fighting with their fists in white-hot anger; two more, on a lonely beach not far from the mouth of the Teslin [River], solemnly sawing their boat down the middle; and ten men at Big Salmon dividing everything up ten ways onto ten blankets, including an enormous scow, which was torn up to build ten smaller scows so that each could go his separate way in peace."[20]

Lines 1309–10: "a toothless old squaw"

Canada's Department of Indian Affairs reported that, at the end of June 1898, there were approximately two hundred American Indians in the vicinity of Selkirk, only fifty miles or so from Five Finger Rapids, where Hal and the others are struggling along. Many travelers mentioned the presence of these Indians—and commented on their impoverished condition. One argonaut characterized them in a letter home as "the most disgusting indians [*sic*] I have ever seen in my life, dirty and filthy."[21]

The American Indians in the North were certainly eager to trade. Near Lake Marsh, Wells and his party met a band of Tagish Indians who had some hardtack: "[A]fter a little dickering," wrote Wells, "I secured six of the crackers for $1."[22] Hal's exchange of a Colt's revolver for some frozen horsehide seems more plausible when, at today's prices, the one dollar Wells spent for six crackers would be about twenty-five dollars.

Lines 1312–13: "this hide . . . stripped from the starved horses of the cattlemen six months back"

London is alluding to an actual event—the slaughtering of more than two thousand cattle and horses that had been driven over the Dalton Trail, which began at Pyramid Harbor, Alaska, and ended at the mouth of the Pelly River. Although the Dalton Trail itself had sufficient grass in the summer to feed the horses of the cattlemen, the Yukon interior did not. Superintendent Constantine wrote that "owing to the scarcity of forage, most of them [horses] have been killed for dog feed." Today, Yukon River maps identify a spot near the mouth of the Pelly as "Slaughterhouse Slough."[23]

Many travelers through the area commented on the scene, including Marshall Bond, who, in his diary entry for 26 September 1897, mentions "some Indian cabins" on the banks of the river; "[t]wo scows there," he added. "They had just killed several horses wh[ich] had come over Dalton Trail, for food. . . ." And in a letter on 11 October 1897, Bond informed his mother that "Dalton [had] brought a lot of cattle over the trail, butchered them at Pelly River and rafted them down."[24]

In late October 1897, Adney saw William Perdue "just below Five Finger Rapids" butchering fifty cattle; he had lost twenty others "in the quicksands" on the trail. Thompson mentions that London's party also saw "several different parties killing and dressing beef and making rafts to carry it to Dawson. . . ."[25]

London mentions the slaughter elsewhere in his fiction, in "The League of Old Men" and "The Priestly Prerogative." In "The One Thousand Dozen" he comments more fully: "Below the Post he [David Rasmunsen] managed to buy frozen horse hide for the dogs, the horses having been slain by the Chilkat cattle men, and the scraps and offal preserved by the Indians. He tackled the hide himself, but the hair worked into the bean sores of his mouth, and was beyond endurance."[26]

Lines 1347–48: "It was dawn by three in the morning, and twilight lingered till nine at night."

Black wrote a brief description of the Yukon sun in summer: "Shortly after midnight the sun rose, revolved in spiral fashion, mounted higher and higher till it reached the zenith at noon, then sank lower and lower until it dipped below the horizon. Daytime and nighttime merged into each other so softly, so imperceptibly, that we scarcely realized the change."[27]

Lines 1359–60: "The Yukon was straining to break loose the ice that bound it down."

The Meteorological Branch of Canada's Department of Transport has calculated that the mean date for break-up between 1896 and 1958 at Dawson was 9 May; in 1898—the year that Hal, Charles, and Mercedes were on the ice—it broke on 8 May. At Whitehorse,

460 miles upriver, the ice generally breaks a week or so earlier than at Dawson.[28] Accordingly, Hal, Charles, and Mercedes—ignoring warnings—would have gone under the ice at the mouth of the White River, eighty miles upriver from Dawson, sometime during the first week of May 1898.

The break-up of the Yukon River, according to all accounts, is one of the great displays in all of nature. Mrs. Charles Black:

To this day the break-up of the Yukon is a momentous occasion. Recalling twenty or more—some came with startling and dramatic suddenness. The ice went out with a roar and navigation opened within a day. In other years there was a gradual transformation of the still silent brooding ugliness of months to a scene of wondrous ever-changing beauty. For several hours loud crackings heralded the slow breaking of the ice. As the water oozed through the cracks, the ice began to move slightly, gradually gaining momentum, to the always awesome climax of massive ice-cakes crunching, grinding, piling, like a stampede of thousands of maddened animals.

One year, Black observed quite a scene: "[S]itting on a huge ice-cake, hurtling by in mid-stream, was a bob cat, with a frantic pack of huskies in hot pursuit along the river bank. As though the poor beast had not trouble enough! The river was clearing fast."[29]

London refers to the break-up in a number of places, but nowhere more grimly than in "At the Rainbow's End," when a man named Donald has climbed a tree on a Yukon River island in the hope of escaping the ferocious forces of the break-up. But a "great wall of white flung itself upon the island. Trees, dogs, men, were blotted out, as though the hand of God had wiped the face of nature clean. This much he saw, then swayed an instant longer in his lofty perch and hurtled far out into the frozen hell."[30]

Line 1366: John Thornton

When Jack London left the Klondike in the spring of 1898, he floated down the Yukon River to the Bering Sea with two other men, one of whom was John Thorson. It is likely that London is here honoring his old Yukon companion. In another tale, "A Northland Miracle," John Thornton is falsely accused of stealing bacon and barely survives an Indian attack.[31]

Line 1367: White River

Spilling from the west into the Yukon River some eighty miles upriver from Dawson City, the White River is 177 miles long and drains 18,500 square miles. American Indian names for it included "Sand River" and "Copper River." The White was the first river prospected in the Yukon, in 1873–74, and in 1888 William Moore wrote that the "upper portion of this river is a great resort for caribou, moose, and beaver." Robert Campbell, a Hudson's Bay Company employee, named it, he wrote in his journal, because of "the color of its water."[32]

The White, loaded with glacial silt and volcanic ash, is indeed milky in color—like "thick, white cream," wrote Byron Andrews. Osborne commented wryly that if the waters of the White "carried but a little more sediment than at present, it would need no miracle to turn them into dry land." Hildebrand, passing the mouth in a canoe in the late 1980s, describes how the "silty water makes a slightly abrasive sound, like sandpaper, across the canoe's hull." Because of the sediment, the Yukon River waters are not potable from the White River to the ocean—over fourteen hundred miles.[33]

Thompson did not record anything about the White River in his diary, but because he and London arrived at the Stewart River on 9 October 1897 about three o'clock in the afternoon, they must have passed the White that same morning: It is only ten miles upriver from the Stewart.[34]

Lines 1374–75: "'They told us up above that the bottom was dropping out of the trail and that the best thing for us to do was to lay over,' Hal said"

"Up above" here means upriver, the direction from which they have come.

Because the trail was the frozen surface of the Yukon River, "the bottom dropping out" would mean breaking up. Walden, who for years drove dog-teams on the river, wrote about the hazardous conditions of spring ice travel: "The surface of the ice on the river had gradually become smoothed off, but as the water rose, the ice in the middle of the stream rose with it in a hump, the sides remaining frozen to the bank. . . . All travelling at that time was of course done in the middle of the river. . . . Later on, when the shore ice cut loose from the banks and rose to the level of the water, making a dry surface to travel on, we moved by night, when it was coldest."[35]

In "At the Rainbow's End" London provides an account of travel on a disintegrating trail:

The Yukon was growling and straining at its fetters. Long detours became necessary, for the trail had begun to fall through into the swift current beneath, while the ice, in constant unrest, was thundering apart in great gaping fissures. Through these and through countless airholes, the water began to sweep across the surface of the ice, and by the time he pulled into a woodchopper's cabin on the point of an island, the dogs were being rushed off their feet and were swimming more often than not. . . . A shrieking split, suddenly lifting itself above the general uproar on the river, drew everybody to the bank. The surface water had increased in depth, and the ice, assailed from above and below, was struggling to tear itself from the grip of the shores. Fissures reverberated into life before their eyes, and the air was filled with multitudinous crackling, crisp and sharp, like the sound that goes up on a clear day from the firing line.[36]

Line 1376: "rotten ice"

Also called "rotting ice" by a number of commentators, rotten ice is ice that is beginning to soften and break up.

Line 1395: "He exchanged the whip for the customary club."

No dog driver was without such implements. At times, they were indeed employed in awful service. On the White Pass, for example, Walden observed a scene of horror: "I saw one man who . . . got mad at his dogs, and, after beating them with a club till they were unable to go, began with the leader and pushed them all down a water-hole under the ice. He cut the traces of the last dog, leaving himself absolutely stranded with no means of locomotion. Then he sat down and cried."[37] And Margeson wrote that some drivers beat their dogs "in a most brutal manner, and it was no uncommon thing to see a dog drop dead in harness beside the trail." Nansen expressed remorse for his acts of cruelty to his own dogs: "It makes me shudder even now when I think of how we beat them mercilessly with thick ash sticks when, hardly able to move, they stopped from sheer exhaustion."[38]

Lines 1397–1400: "he had made up his mind not to get up. He had a feeling of impending doom. . . . he sensed disaster close at hand"

Young's lead dog, Voyageur, does the same: He "stopped in his tracks and deliberately lay down on the ice and snow," refusing to go on despite "the heavy whip" with which he was "most cruelly beaten." Voyageur's behavior, however, saves Young and the team, for the dog had correctly "sensed" thin ice just ahead.[39]

Line 1409: *"John Thornton sprang upon the man who wielded the club."*

Various accounts of persons interrupting the beating of an animal were published during and after the Rush. Morgan, for example, tells about an amazingly cruel beating administered by "a great hulking figure" who was kicking his dog with his "heavy, hobnailed boots." Morgan intervened, but the "hulking figure" responded in surprising fashion: "[H]e grabbed the poor creature by the tail, swung it aloft and brought the emaciated body down hard upon the frozen ground." Morgan replied with "a powerful wallop in the midriff which sent him sprawling." A brief scuffle ensued, but Morgan emerged victorious: "I gave him a final crack on the point of the jaw and he dropped like an ox."[40]

Lines 1436–38: *"They saw . . . a whole section of ice give way and dogs and humans disappear. A yawning hole was all that was to be seen. The bottom had dropped out of the trail."*

Drownings were common in the Yukon during the Rush: Inexperienced travelers tried to shoot dangerous rapids, or dared to venture out on rotten ice. On 2 November 1898, Superintendent Wood of the NWMP reported to the Parliament of Canada that twenty-two persons had drowned the previous year in the Lake Tagish district alone. A year later, a dozen more had drowned—most in Five Finger Rapids.[41] The *Dyea Press* reported one instance: "Bob. [*sic*] Wright broke through the ice on Surprise Lake in the Atlin District, and himself and dog team were drowned." And Hawthorne participated in a failed rescue attempt of two men and a team of dogs that had gone under the ice of Lake Bennett. The dogs clawed the ice desperately to keep from being pulled under by the sled, but "[f]irst the back dog went under, then the next one, and finally the lead dog was pulled back through the ice, too."[42]

In "The End of the Story," London provides more detail about an equally unfortunate team:

With a loud explosion, the ice broke asunder midway under the team. The two animals in the middle of the string went into the fissure, and the grip of the current on their bodies dragged the lead-dog backward and in. Swept down-stream under the ice, these three bodies began to drag to the edge the two whining dogs that remained. The men held back frantically on the sled, but were slowly drawn along with it. It was all over in the space of seconds. Daw slashed the wheel-dog's traces with his sheath-knife, and the animal whipped over the ice-edge and was gone.[43]

CHAPTER SIX

"For the Love of a Man"

Line 1441: "John Thornton froze his feet"

Because the gold-seekers occasionally traveled on waterways that were not always thoroughly frozen—even when they appeared to be—frozen feet were a deadly possibility in the Northland. Concealed beneath a blanket of snow could be open water. "These springs, common to most Klondike streams," wrote London, "never cease at the lowest temperatures. The water flows out from the banks and lies in pools which are cuddled from the cold by later surface-freezings and snowfalls. Thus, a man, stepping on dry snow, might break through half an inch of ice-skin and find himself up to the knees in water."[1]

The official reports of the North-west Mounted Police during the years of the Rush refer again and again to the problem: (1) two people died of "frozen limbs" in Dawson City in 1898; (2) "a civilian named Johnson had his feet frozen while prospecting . . . and was brought here [Tagish] for treatment. Dr. Bonner operated, amputating the foot." (3) "M. Skinner, frozen feet, sent to Skaguay by dog train on March 8. Died three days after arrival in Skaguay Hospital."[2]

One manual published at the time suggested that the problem of "frozen limbs" could be handled easily: "Dissolve from one quarter to one-half a pound of alum in a gallon of warm water," advised the unnamed author, "and immerse the feet or hands in it when frozen, for 10 or 15 minutes, and a cure will be effected."[3] Just how a victim of "frozen limbs" on the Yukon trail is supposed to produce a bucket, some warm water, and a half-pound of alum is not clear.

London, well aware of the prevalence of the problem, employed it as a plot device in many stories, most significantly in "To Build a Fire": The man "broke through," "wet himself halfway to the knees," and died because of his inability to build a fire. London was well aware that rapid treatment was imperative. "In five minutes, unless able to remove the wet gear," he wrote in *Smoke Bellew*, "the loss of one's feet was the penalty."[4]

Treatment began with a determination of the extent of the damage. In "The Wife of a King," Malemute Kid, treating a woman named Madeline, "stuck the point of his knife into her feet to see how far they were frozen." And in *Smoke Bellew*, when Joy Gastell broke through the ice, Smoke scrambled to save her feet in the same manner that John Thornton's partners must have scrambled to save his:

> *With his knife, Smoke cut away the lacings and leather of the moccasins. So stiff were they with ice that they snapped and crackled under the hacking and sawing. The siwash socks and heavy woolen stockings were sheaths of ice. It was as if her feet and calves were encased in corrugated iron. . . . The white skin of one foot appeared, then that of the other, to be exposed to the bite of seventy below zero, which is the equivalent of one hundred and two below freezing.*
>
> *Then came the rubbing with snow, carried on with an intensity of cruel fierceness, till she squirmed and shrank and moved her toes, and joyously complained of the hurt. He half dragged her, and she half lifted herself, nearer to the fire. He placed her feet on the blanket close to the flesh-saving flames. . . . She could now safely remove her mittens and work and manipulate her own feet, with the wisdom of the initiated being watchful that the heat of the fire was absorbed slowly.*[5]

Lines 1442–43: "to get out a raft of saw-logs for Dawson"

Because of the need for firewood and construction materials in Dawson, the lumber business was booming in the spring and summer of 1898. Kirk wrote that the demand was so great that logs had to be "drawn many miles over the snow or floated down the rivers in summer, and then dragged through the streets with horses or dogs."

Floating them downriver, as Thornton and his partners are doing, required the assembly of "cribs"—groups of logs each approximately 30 by 130 feet. The cribs were then joined to form huge rafts. One handbook asserted that "[f]our men can easily handle a raft of 500 or 600 such logs. Getting them out would be a matter of only a week or two."[6]

London and "Doc" Harvey dismantled the latter's cabin in the spring of 1898 and floated the logs seventy miles down the Yukon River to Dawson. They sold them for six hundred dollars, enabling London to buy medicine for his scurvy and to supply himself for his journey home to California.[7]

Line 1450: "Skeet and Nig"

London appropriated the names of two dogs he had actually known. Skeet, a terrier, belonged to Carrie Sterling, wife of London's good friend George Sterling. Noel remembered the dog as it "raced and barked among the cherry trees the first day London visited. . . ." Nig belonged to London's companion at Stewart River, Louis Savard. Emil Jensen, who also wintered at the river, remembered him as "lovable Nig, the short-haired, outside dog." And Charmian London quoted a letter from W. B. "Bert" Hargrave (another companion), who remembered that Nig "showed a remarkable Newfoundland strain. . . ."[8]

It is possible that Savard, a French-Canadian, had named his big, lumbering dog Nigaud (French for "fool" or "simpleton"). A less sympathetic explanation is that London's use of the name Nig for a black dog is racist. Although we find such a choice offensive, it went unchallenged by his editors at the *Saturday Evening Post* and Macmillan and no doubt went unnoticed among white readers of the plainly racist magazines and books at the turn of the century. In the summer and fall of 1897, for example, *Leslie's Illustrated Weekly* ran a series of popular cartoons about "Possumville," a community populated by the most grotesque racial stereotypes of African Americans.[9]

Lines 1452–53: "she had the doctor trait which some dogs possess"

Animal behaviorists have determined that licking among wolves and dogs is performed by the lower-status dogs upon the alpha (superior) males. Young's dog Rover I had this trait. "The instant a dog was unharnessed," Young wrote, "Rover, who was always friendly with all my dogs, would at once overhaul him and would thus quickly find the galled or wounded spots. Very gently then he licked them even if at first the dog-patient should resent his interference. . . ."[10]

Line 1545: Hans and Pete

London no doubt selected "Hans" as a representative Scandinavian name, for he has put in Hans's mouth a silly caricature of a dialect. London may have provided a glimpse of Hans in a later tale, "The Unexpected": Edith Whittlesey marries "Hans Nelson, immigrant, Swede by birth and carpenter by occupation, [who] had in him that Teutonic unrest that drives the race ever westward on its great adventure. He was a large-muscled, stolid sort of a man, in whom little imagination was coupled with immense initiative, and who possessed, withal, loyalty and affection as sturdy as his own strength."[11]

Lines 1549–50: "they swung the raft into the big eddy by the saw-mill at Dawson"

Near the spot where Joe Ladue erected his sawmill at Dawson is this eddy—an abrupt change in the current of the Yukon River. Guiding the raft of logs into the shore was not an easy proposition, as Walden recognized: "[I]t was nip and tuck how to get out of the main current into the bank eddy that swept along the shore and made tying up possible. Once you managed to get into this eddy, you were safe, but fully fifty per cent of the rafts were lost when within a few hundred feet of the shore. If you couldn't make the eddy, you were swept past down the cliff at the end of town, the raft had to be abandoned, and you had to make your way back in a tender [dinghy]." London certainly knew the eddy, for he navigated it successfully when he arrived in Dawson City on 18 October 1897.[12]

Lines 1555–57: "the head-waters of the Tanana . . . a cliff which fell away . . . three hundred feet below"

Tanana (pronounced TAN-uh-naw) is an American Indian name meaning "river trail." Schwatka identified it as "the largest tributary of the Yukon," but contemporary measurements place its 513-mile length as third, behind the Porcupine (555 miles) and the Koyukuk (554).[13]

In 1898, Webb described the river for *Century Magazine*: "This river is navigable for steamers for one hundred and fifty or two hundred miles. The water is slack for the first two hundred miles, and after that it is very swift, with mountains on the left hand from the mouth up; on the right hand the mountains are far off in the distance. The water is rough and swift, and the creeks entering it have glaciers at their sources."[14] Thornton and his partners are heading into territory that many writers had suggested might be rich in gold deposits. The Alaska Commercial Company speculated that the country near the head-waters would "prove one of the richest in all the land."[15]

London had seen only the mouth of the Tanana (14 June 1898), but he knew about the terrain near the headwaters. He knew, as well, how *Tanana* was pronounced, as evidenced by his varying spellings elsewhere: "Tana-naw" and "Tananaw."[16]

This episode at the cliff does not appear in the serialization of *The Call of the Wild* in *The Saturday Evening Post*.

Line 1569: Circle City

A Northland misnomer, Circle City, Alaska, was named because of its supposed location on the Arctic Circle, which in fact lies about fifty miles to the north. When two prospectors on Birch Creek found promising colors in their pans in the summer of 1892, they approached LeRoy Napoleon "Jack" McQuesten for a grubstake—which he willingly supplied. Then, gambling on growth, McQuesten built a store at a spot on the Yukon River called Fish Camp, sixty to eighty miles from the Birch Creek mines. But the flooding in the spring of 1894 destroyed a number of buildings in the settlement, so he moved downriver to the Circle City town-site, which had been staked out by Barney Hill and Robert English. The modest strikes on Birch Creek and its tributaries—$150,000 by the end of 1895—brought more people to Circle, and eventually it grew into a community deserving of being called a "city": By 1896 there were twelve hundred people there.[17]

Circle was not a picturesque town. Situated in a low, level area called the "Yukon Flats," the city, even in its heyday, presented a grim and gloomy appearance. Harris wrote in 1897 that it "stands on a dead-level plain, twenty feet higher than the river at the ordinary stage of water. . . . The prevailing style of architecture in this city . . . is a low, square log cabin, with wide projecting eaves and a dirt roof. The crevices between the logs are chinked with moss, which abounds everywhere." Anna Fulcomer, Circle's first teacher, characterized it as "the biggest log-house town in the world."[18]

Aesthetic qualities notwithstanding, Haskell found in the summer of 1896 quite an impressive array of businesses in Circle: There were "a theater [the Tivoli], four large warehouses, three stores, and three blacksmith shops. We counted twenty-eight saloons and eight dance halls. Back of these were log houses, interspersed with tents, laid out in fair order. . . ."[19]

When word of the strike on Bonanza Creek reached Circle over the fall and winter of

1896–97, there was some initial skepticism, but once the stampede to the Klondike began, it did not end until Circle was virtually abandoned; only those holding well-established claims remained behind. Circle's "flag-bedizened streets and glittering saloons," wrote DeWindt, became "a collection of dingy, deserted dwellings, chiefly inhabited by wandering Indians and their dogs."[20]

Later, Circle regained a bit of its size and significance when the stampeders found that the Klondike and all its tributaries had been staked, mouth to source. And, for certain types, Circle had yet another advantage over Dawson: It was lawless. In the Canadian Yukon, the North-west Mounted Police maintained strict order. Side arms were forbidden in Dawson—as were obscenity, cheating, and working on the Sabbath. But in the American city of Circle there was no official government; instead, the residents—"a very scurvy lot . . . outlaws . . . vultures," said Lynch—attempted, with occasional success, to enforce their own standards of civility. An American stampeder on his way home would stop at Circle, writes Wharton, and "have fun, get drunk and be a mite boisterous among his own people."[21]

On his own way out of the Yukon, London paused only briefly in Circle (10 June 1898); he bought some tobacco, but—according to his brief notes—found "no sugar, butter nor milk. Deserted— . . ."[22]

The 1990, the U.S. Census found only seventy-three persons living in Circle—no longer City—Alaska.[23]

Line 1570: "Black" Burton

The Klondike Gold Rush may have produced as many nicknames as nuggets. In his trip through Circle City in 1897, Webb recorded the following: Swiftwater Bill, Saltwater Jack, Big Dick, Squaw-tamer, Jimmy the Pirate, Big Aleck, Jimmy the Tough, Pete the Pig, Buckskin Miller, Old Maiden, and Shoemaker Brown. Berton adds some that are even more colorful: Mollie Fewclothes, Ethel the Moose, and the Evaporated Kid. The nickname "Black" generally indicated race. On the Stewart River, for example, was a sandbar called "Black Mike's Bar," so named, wrote Stanley, "because of the color of the man who located it. . . ."[24]

It is possible that London based this character upon "Black" Bill, an actual African American bartender in Circle, but if so, he changed his personality. Charles Hamlin remembered Bill's good qualities—most notably his largess: He "had taken many a roll of dried dog salmon as readily as gold dust for the drinks" and "was liked by all." Hamlin added, almost as an afterthought: "[W]e sometimes called him 'Nigger.' . . ."[25]

The altercation that ensues between "Black" Burton and the tenderfoot was certainly not anomalous. Fighting was common in the saloons—Roald Amundsen, after stopping in Circle City on his way home from his polar adventures, was disgusted by "the fighting and drunkenness" he witnessed. Gold Rush handbooks, however, written to encourage rather than discourage traffic northward, maintained that "the weapons are fists [so] little damage is done."[26]

Line 1571: "tenderfoot"

London's use of this word—meaning "newcomer"—is surprising here, for throughout his Northland writing he prefers the Chinook Jargon synonym, *cheechako,* which was—and is—in general use in the region. In "To Build a Fire," for instance, London identifies the man as "a newcomer in the land, a *chechaquo.* . . ." The word appeared in a wide variety of spellings in the Gold Rush era: cheecharkas, cheechawko, cheechaco, chechockoes, chechacos, and Chee Charkers. London himself once used "cheechawker."[27]

Line 1581: "a surgeon checked the bleeding"

At various times in its history, Circle City certainly had physicians among its population. Ingersoll (1897) said that there were "three or four doctors," and Fulcomer remembered a dance in 1896 "to raise money for a 'miners' hospital.'. . ." But Walden, a dog-puncher in Circle before (and during and after) the Klondike Rush, claims the town had "no sheriff, dentist, doctor, lawyer, or priest." And Hamlin remembers that the "only M.D. in camp was a horse doctor."[28]

Doctors certainly did flock to the Northland in the Rush. There may have been as many as seventy in Dawson, and there were other surgeons attached to the North-west Mounted Police. But it is unlikely that a surgeon would have been in Circle at this moment in its history. As London himself had observed in the late spring of 1898, Circle was virtually abandoned. When all the prospective patients stampeded to Dawson, the physicians would not have been far behind, and the only two NWMP surgeons in the entire region were at Dawson and the Dalton Trail posts.[29] It is of course possible that the "surgeon" was not a licensed professional but someone skilled in the frontier arts of patching and stitching.

By having a surgeon handy to save "Black" Burton's life, London is repeating a *deus ex machina* from "Bâtard": A surgeon from the tiny settlement of McQuesten travels two hundred miles "on the ice" to save the hand of a missionary who had tried to give "the soft stroke of the hand" to the vicious Bâtard.[30]

Line 1583: "a 'miners' meeting'"

In remote Alaska mining camps, and even in sizable settlements like Circle City, there was no law beyond that established and enforced by the residents themselves. When someone transgressed the tacit codes of decency or fairness—or when there was a dispute of some sort—the miners assembled to resolve the issue and to impose penalties ranging from banishment to whipping to hanging.[31]

Klondike: The Chicago Record's Book for Gold Seekers (1897) describes the process somewhat romantically:

> *A man having a dispute with another involving money or land posts in conspicuous places a notice that there will be a meeting at a given hour and place to settle a dispute between him and another, whose name is posted. At the appointed hour nearly every one crowds into the meeting; a chairman and secretary are appointed and the assembly is called to order.*
>
> *The chairman calls upon the plaintiff to state his case, and when this is done the defendant is heard from. When the principals have testified witnesses are heard from, and this evidence is heard and digested by the audience. Questions are asked by any one who cares to do this, and then motions are in order. Any one can make a motion for the disposal of the case, which, when seconded, is put to a vote, and in this way the matter is adjusted. A committee is appointed to see that the verdict is carried out, which generally is done. This seems to be the only way in which justice can be dealt out. The system seems to have had its origin in a manly desire to give every one a "fair show," but it is generally the more popular man who gets the better of it.*[32]

J. Lincoln Steffens corroborates this final point, acknowledging that the intent of the meetings was justice, but "after a while cliques are formed, which run things to suit the men who are in them, or, which is just as bad, they turn the sessions into fun." M. Webb tells about a specific instance when a prostitute was ordered to pay court costs, "including two gallons of liquor drunk by the jury." She adds that the miners had planned to "return the money in trade, [but] wiser heads prevailed before the prank could be consummated."[33]

Mizner remembered an exciting meeting occasioned by a theft near Sheep Camp. Hauled before an assembly of miners, one of the two accused—realizing a guilty verdict was imminent—"whipped out a pistol, and flourishing it, he broke from his captors and with a knife ripped a hole in the tent, and was gone." Mizner chased after him, correctly anticipating his route, and intercepted him just as a bullet ripped into the fugitive's head. "[H]e lunged into my arms, and together we plowed into the tent, a smear of blood went all over the white canvas and froze instantly."[34]

Although London employs miners' meetings in a number of other stories, most notably the long trial in *A Daughter of the Snows*, he cut it from the serialization of *The Call of the Wild*.[35]

Line 1585: Alaska

The namers thought that *Alaska* meant "great land." It comes, however, from an Aleut word, *Alaxsxaq,* which means "where the sea breaks its back."[36]

Lines 1586–1648: Buck saves John Thornton in the rapids.

Jesse's *Anecdotes of Dogs* contains a number of tales about dogs saving their owners from drowning. The following is typical: "In the immediate neighbourhood of Windsor a servant was saved from drowning by a Newfoundland dog, who seized him by the collar of his coat when he was almost exhausted, and brought him to the banks, where some of the family were assembled watching with great anxiety the exertions of the noble animal."[37]

Rescue stories occasionally appeared in newspapers of the day, as well. Early in the Rush, the *San Francisco Chronicle* published a story called "A Noble Dog Tries to Save His Master," and the *New York Times* a day earlier had another story, "Blind Man Saved by Dog," which told how a "tramp dog" had pulled a blind man out of the path of oncoming wagons in the street. The ending of the story reveals the sentimental attitudes characteristic of the era: "Joseph Kelly, one of the men who witnessed the dog's deed, raised a purse and paid for the license and handsome collar for the brute. The collar is to bear a plate inscribed with the word 'Hero.'"[38]

London employs the dog-saves-master device elsewhere in his fiction. White Fang runs for help when Weedon Scott falls from his horse, and, later, he nearly loses his life protecting the Scotts in a death struggle with Jim Hall, the escaped convict. And both Jerry (*Jerry of the Islands*) and Michael (*Michael, Brother of Jerry*) save their human masters from injury and death.[39]

London cut this episode from the serialization of *The Call of the Wild* in the *Saturday Evening Post*.

Lines 1587–89: "*the three partners were lining a long and narrow poling-boat down a bad stretch of rapids . . . snubbing with a thin Manila rope from tree to tree*"

Poling boats were popular on the Yukon River during the days of the Rush. "Poling-boats are built to an unusual length in proportion to their breadth, and are always sharp at both ends. . . . The length of these boats is ordinarily twenty-eight or thirty feet, with a breadth of from two and a half to three feet. To propel them through the water two men, each having a long pole, one standing in the bow and one in the stern, sink the poles simultaneously in the water, and then when bottom is reached throw their weight against the pole in such a way as to force the boat rapidly through the water."[40]

"Lining" and then "snubbing" a boat required a partner on shore to take a rope—or line—attached to the boat, wrap it around a tree, and control the vessel's progress in swift water. As Schwatka described it, "the long rope would be slowly allowed to play out under strong and increasing friction, or 'snubbing' as logmen call it, and this would bring the craft to a standstill in [the] water. . . ."

London knew this process well: He had done it on 19 September 1897 at Lake Lindeman, where he and his partners had built two boats for their float down to Dawson. Thompson's diary reveals that London and the others "had quite a hard time lining them down for about 2 miles. . . ."[41]

Lines 1587–88: "*a bad stretch of rapids on the Forty-Mile Creek*"

Forty-Mile Creek—now officially Fortymile River—derived its name from its distance from Fort Reliance, approximately forty miles up the Yukon. The American Indians in the region called it *Shitando* or *Chittondeg*—the "creek of the leaves." The Fortymile is fifty-six miles long and drains 6,562 square miles.[42]

Gold was first discovered on the Fortymile on 7 September 1886. In June 1887, Jack McQuesten and his partners built a trading post there, and scores of miners moved into the burgeoning settlement—from 125 to 140, according to William Moore's estimate in January 1888. The strike on the Klondike dealt Fortymile a blow from which it never recovered.[43]

During its heyday, Fortymile was populous, wild, and unprepossessing. DeWindt saw it in 1897 and later published a grim account of this "collection of eighty or ninety dismal-looking log-huts on a mud-bank. The shanties are scattered about," he observed, "without any attempt at regularity, the marshy intervening spaces being littered with wood shavings, empty tins, and other rubbish. . . ." Recalling her visit in the spring of 1897, Lyons mentions "a large store, two blacksmith shops, two restaurants, three billiard halls, rival dance-houses, opera house, cigar factory, barber shop, two bakeries, and several breweries and distilleries."[44]

The river was rough and dangerous. At least a half-dozen people drowned in it in 1887, and A. E. Ironmonger Sola, who had passed through the Klondike just before the Rush, described the notorious rapids not far from the river's mouth:

> *Eight miles up [the river] is the so-called can[y]on; it is hardly entitled to that distinctive name, being simply a crooked contraction of the river, with steep rocky banks, and on the north side there is plenty of room to walk along the beach. At the lower end of the can[y]on there is a short turn and swift water in which are some large rocks; these cannot generally be seen, and there is much danger of striking them running down in a boat. At this point several miners have been drowned by their boats being upset in collision with these rocks. It is no great distance to either shore, and one would think an ordinary swimmer would have no difficulty in reaching land; but the coldness of the water soon benumbs a man completely and renders him powerless.*[45]

On his journey out of the Yukon, London saw the mouth of the Fortymile—but not the rapids, eight miles upstream; he found the community "practically deserted" and floated on without further comment in his notes.[46]

Line 1589: "Manila rope"

Manila is the name of the fiber from the leafstalk of a banana plant, *Musa textilis*, which grows in the Philippines.

Line 1650: "totem-pole"

When Price passed through Wrangell, Alaska, early in 1898, he characterized the totem poles he saw as "a curious feature of the place." Although he was not at all sure what he was seeing, he was impressed with the "fantastic designs—human heads, goblins, birds, animals, etc." that showed "a sentiment of proportion and a sort of weird talent that is thoroughly in keeping with this strange place."[47]

But it was John Muir in his illuminating volume *Travels in Alaska* (1915) who gave one of the clearest descriptions of the appearance and significance of the poles:

The simplest of them consisted of a smooth, round post fifteen or twenty feet high and about eighteen inches in diameter, with the figure of some animal on top—a bear, porpoise, eagle, or raven, about life-size or larger. These were the totems of the families that occupied the houses in front of which they stood. Others supported the figure of a man or woman, life-size or larger, usually in a sitting posture, said to resemble the dead, whose ashes were contained in a closed cavity in the pole. The largest were thirty or forty feet high, carved from top to bottom into human and animal totem figures, one above the another, with their limbs grotesquely doubled and folded. Some of the most imposing were said to commemorate some event of an historical character. . . . The erection of a totem pole is made a grand affair, and is often talked of a year or two before hand. A feast, to which many are invited, is held, and the joyous occasion is spent in eating, dancing, and the distribution of gifts. . . . They are always planted firmly in the ground and stand fast, showing the sturdy erectness of their builders.[48]

The poles Muir saw had been carved and erected by the coastal Chilkat-Tlingit people. London would have seen very similar ones when he traveled through the Tlingit territory on his way into the Yukon—especially at Juneau. And on his journey out of the Yukon, he mentions in his notes that he had "once in a while" seen "curiously carved totem pole[s]."[49]

Ethnographers today have made extensive studies of the poles, which the Tlingit call *ka da ka dee* ("man's grave pole"). George Thornton Emmons writes that the poles were carved and erected for "the honor of the dead and glorification of the family. . . ."[50]

Line 1654: Eldorado Saloon

The saloon was the center of social activity in the Northland mining towns, from Circle City, to Fortymile, to Dawson City, and, finally, to Nome, Alaska. When Kirk arrived in Dawson on 16 October 1897, just two days before London did, he observed that the "gambling- and dance-halls in Dawson" were "thronged during the evening with miners who had practically no other place to go. . . . The most convenient place for meeting was the saloon, which in most cases had a gambling-room and a dance-hall attached." And when J. H. E. Secretan arrived on 18 June 1898—just ten days after London had begun his river journey out of the Yukon—he found that little was different: "[S]aloons were running night and day. Almost every device for gambling was in full blast, and nobody seemed to take the least interest in anybody else."[51]

In *Smoke Bellew* London provides his most thorough description of the sort of saloon where John Thornton bets on Buck:

The main room was comfortably crowded, while roaring stoves, combined with lack of ventilation, kept the big room unsanitarily warm. The click of chips and the boisterous play at the craps-table furnished a monotonous background of sound to the equally monotonous rumble of men's voices where they sat and stood about and talked in groups of twos and threes. The gold-weighers were busy at their scales, for dust was the circulating medium, and even a dollar drink of whiskey at the bar had to be paid for to the weighers.

The walls of the room were of tiered logs, the bark still on, and the chinking between the logs, plainly visible, was arctic moss. Through the open door that led to the dance-room came the rollicking strains of a Virginia reel, played by a piano and a fiddle. The drawing of the Chinese lottery had just taken place, and the luckiest player, having cashed at the scales, was drinking up his winnings with half a dozen cronies. The faro- and roulette-tables were busy and quiet. The draw-poker and stud-poker tables, each with its circle of onlookers, were equally quiet. At another table, a serious, concentrated game of Black Jack was on. Only from the craps-table came noise, as the man who played rolled the dice, full sweep, down the green amphitheater of a table in pursuit of his elusive and long-delayed point.[52]

El Dorado—the legendary City of Gold sought by the Spaniards (*dorado* means "golden" in Spanish)—is a name that appeared in a variety of ways throughout the

Klondike. Eldorado Creek, for example, a tributary of Bonanza in the Klondike region, was "the richest placer gold stream ever found anywhere in the world."[53] Initially explored and staked by some prospectors led by former Chicago newspaper reporter John Williams, the creek was so rich that a single claim on Eldorado (Number 16) paid $1,530,000 for Thomas Lippy—at a time when gold was sixteen dollars per ounce.[54]

In Dawson City proper there was not a saloon named Eldorado. Among the principal saloons were the Monte Carlo, Pavilion, Dominion, Tivoli, Orpheum, Bank Saloon and Gambling House, and the M & M. There was a well-known restaurant, however, the Eldorado House on First Avenue, which London certainly saw, perhaps patronized, and later read about in Adney's *Klondike Stampede*.[55]

There was an Eldorado Saloon, however, just across the Klondike River from Dawson in a smaller settlement called Klondike City or Lousetown—so named because the NWMP permitted prostitution there. Advertisements in the *Klondike Nugget* claimed the estab-lishment, operated by a man named Peter Sutherland, had only the "Finest Brands of Wines, Liquors and Cigars."[56]

Line 1659: "'Buck can start a thousand pounds.'"

Modern pulling records for a single dog are about two thousand pounds, so Buck's feat is a realistic accomplishment. London undoubtedly knew that a dog was capable of this feat, for Marshall Bond noted in his diary on 31 October 1897 that his dog Jack had that day pulled a "sledge and about 1000 lbs." At that time, London was camped near Bond's cabin and was a regular visitor.[57]

A few years later, London published "Husky—The Wolf-Dog of the North," an article that contains an incident remarkably similar to Buck's display of strength:

In the annals of the country may be found the history of one dog-driver who wagered a thousand dollars that his favorite husky could start a thousand pounds on a level trail. Now the steel runners of a stationary sled will quickly freeze to the surface, and by the terms of the bet he was even denied the privilege of breaking the runners loose. But it was stipulated that the dog was to have three trials. The whole camp staked its dust upon one side or the other of the issue, and on the day of trial turned out en masse. The dog was hitched to the loaded sled, and everything made ready. "Gee!" the master commanded from a distance. The dog swung obediently to the right, shrewdly throwing his whole weight upon the traces. "Haw!" The ma-

*nœuvre was duplicated on the left and the sled broken out. And then, "Mush on!"
(the vernacular for "get up!"). The dog whined softly, driving his claws into the
frozen trail, calling every muscle into play, digging away like mad. And in answer to
this tremendous exertion, the sled slowly got into motion and was dragged several
lengths. Let a man try the like and marvel. Of course it was an exceptional dog, but
creatures are often measured by their extremes.*[58]

London cut this entire episode from the serialization of *The Call of the Wild* in the
Saturday Evening Post.

Line 1661: "Matthewson, a Bonanza King"

Bonanza comes from the Spanish, meaning "fair weather and calm sea"; it also means
"prosperity." The word gradually drifted into English and came to mean a rich deposit of
ore, or great and sudden wealth or good fortune. George Carmack's original Klondike
gold discovery was on a creek the local Indians called *Tha-Tat-Dik* ("muffler creek"), but
it was known as Rabbit Creek to the miners. Once the immense value of Carmack's find
was known, the creek quickly received its new name: Bonanza.[59]

The use of the word *king* in this fashion was a Northland way to refer to someone who
had struck it rich. A "Bonanza King," then, had a rich claim on Bonanza Creek. London
uses the "king" locution throughout his Northland fiction: There are Bonanza Kings, Eldorado Kings, a Mammon King, a King of Mazy May (not an actual creek), and a Birch Creek
King. But the King of Kings is Burning Daylight, whom London refers to as "King of the
Klondike . . . Eldorado King, Bonanza King, the Lumber Baron, and the Prince of the Stampeders, not to omit the proudest appellation of all, namely, the Father of Sourdoughs. . . ."[60]

"Matthewson" could possibly be based on Sam Matthews, an actual Bonanza King
who had extracted $650,000 from Claim #8 Below and was able to employ thirty-five men
on his property.[61]

Lines 1665–66: "a sack of gold dust the size of a bologna sausage"

Because gold dust was the medium of exchange in Dawson City during the Rush,
every place of business had a scale, and every miner carried a "poke" (a sack of dust).
London became so accustomed to his poke that his wife wrote later that he "never carried
other than the slender chamois gold-dust sack that he had learned to use in the Klondike."[62]

The size and nature of the wager on Buck are not extraordinary. Black remembers wild betting during her days in Dawson—losses of twenty thousand on a single spin of the roulette wheel, a thousand on a roll of the dice, and a strange wet wager of ten thousand between "two old Sourdoughs . . . on their respective spitting accuracy—the mark being a crack in the wall."[63]

Lines 1678–79: "Jim O'Brien, a Mastodon King"

Jim O'Brien had made a rich strike on Mastodon Creek, a tributary of Birch Creek in the Circle City mining region. The Birch Creek strikes came in 1893, and Ingersoll listed Mastodon among "the most noteworthy tributaries of this rich field." The creek was named in 1894 by miners who found fossil mastodon bones in it. Schwatka said that "such remains are numerous" throughout the Yukon valley.[64]

Lines 1719–20: "a king of the Skookum Benches"

On 22 March 1897, Joseph Goldsmith named two tributaries of Bonanza "Little Skookum" and "Big Skookum." *Skookum* is a Chinook Jargon word meaning "good" or "strong" or "powerful"—all terms applicable to Skookum Jim Mason, a Tagish Indian whom Berton describes as "a giant of a man, supremely handsome with his high cheekbones, his eagle's nose, and his fiery black eyes—straight as a gun-barrel, powerfully built and known as the best hunter and trapper on the river. . . ." Skookum Jim participated in the initial Klondike discoveries, and may in fact have found the first gold in Bonanza Creek while washing a dishpan on that August day in 1896. Jim's was one of the first claims filed on the creek. When he died in 1916—the same year as Jack London—his mining properties were still earning ninety thousand dollars per year in royalties. In April 1961, the accrued interest in Skookum Jim's estate went to finance a meeting house for the native people in Whitehorse. It is unclear, however, if Goldsmith named the creeks for Skookum Jim or merely intended the Chinook Jargon word to refer to the richness of the gold deposits.[65]

A "bench" claim is one on the side or top of a hill in the bed of an ancient creek. London knew about bench claims and about the Skookum discovery. In his early essay "The Economics of the Klondike" (1900), he wrote that a "bench claim is a hillside claim as distinguished from a creek claim." He went on to tell about the Skookum strike, which "was made prior to the influx from the outside, and subsequent to it came the discovery of the French Hill and the Gold Hill benches, situated between Skookum and Eldorado."[66]

A "king of the Skookum Benches," then, was a person who had a rich bench claim on the hill above Big or Little Skookum.

Lines 1729–30: "He took his head in his two hands and rested cheek on cheek."

Blinded once in a blizzard, Young implored his lead-dog, Jack, to find the trail himself: "Thus, with my face, although it was half covered with ice and snow, close to his, I talked to Jack as a man would to a friend."[67]

Lines 1740, 1744: "'Gee! . . . Haw!'"

These are commands for draft animals that mean, respectively, "right" and "left."

CHAPTER SEVEN

"The Sounding of the Call"

Lines 1781–85: "a fabled lost mine . . . an ancient and ramshackle cabin"

Gold strikes in remote regions are invariably accompanied by rumor: In isolated mining camps, men listen greedily to legends of "lost mines"; stampedes ensue, from one creek to the next, from one valley to the next—usually without result. P. Berton tells about the Northland's legendary "Preacher's Creek," never found, where "a missionary had once seen gold by the spoonful."[1]

London employs this "lost mine" or "ancient cabin" device elsewhere. One of his first published stories, "In a Far Country," refers to an "ancient cabin" that "was one of the many mysteries which lurk in the vast recesses of the North. Built when and by whom, no man could tell. Two graves in the open, piled high with stones, perhaps contained the secret of those early wanderers. But whose hand had piled the stones?"

In another early tale, "A Northland Miracle," London's characters enter "an unexplored domain, marked vaguely on the maps, which was yet to feel the foot of the first white man. So vast and dismal was it that even animal life was scarce, and the tiny Indian tribes few and far between. For days, sometimes, they rode through the silent forest or by the rims of lonely lakes and saw no living thing, heard no sound save the sighing of the wind and the sobbing of the waters." And in a "sheltered valley" John Thornton finds "glittering particles of yellow gold"—a strike comparable in size to the one he and his partners later make in *The Call of the Wild*.[2]

In the nineteenth century, "Lost Cabin" was a fairly common name for legendary lost mines. In his *Lost Mines and Buried Treasure of the West*, Thomas Probert, for example, lists three with such a name—the earliest in 1864. Thomas Penfield includes five with the "Lost Cabin" name in his *Directory of Buried or Sunken Treasures and Lost Mines of the United States*, and other writers place "Lost Cabin" mines here and there throughout the Pacific Northwest. None, however, are in Alaska, the Yukon, or the Northwest Territories. In one of Jack London's clipping files is an undated article from the *San Francisco Sunday Examiner Magazine* titled, "The Search for the Lost Frenchman Mine"; the writer of the article refers to various lost mines, including the Lost Pegleg, Dead Horse, Buried City, and Lost Cabin.[3]

While camped at the Stewart River over the winter of 1897–98, London himself lived in an abandoned cabin that, in Thompson's judgment, had been built by Hudson's Bay Company voyageurs. He also stayed for a short time in January 1898 in a cabin near Henderson Creek—a Stewart tributary—carving on the back wall "Jack London Miner/ Author Jan. 27, 1898." The cabin was still standing in 1965 when it was located by London fan Dick North. Historians and London scholars arranged to put the cabin on display. Half is in Dawson City, half in Jack London Square, Oakland, California. To each old half a new matching half has been added.[4]

Lines 1791–93: "They sledded seventy miles up the Yukon . . . the Stewart River . . . the Mayo . . . the McQuestion . . . until the Stewart itself became a streamlet, threading the upstanding peaks"

The mouth of the Stewart is almost exactly seventy miles upstream from Dawson City, where Buck has just won the bet. The "upstanding peaks" are the Mackenzie Mountains, named for Canada's second Prime Minister, Alexander Mackenzie (1822–92). They lie approximately two hundred miles east of Dawson. In 1851 Robert Campbell named the river for his Hudson's Bay Company colleague, Robert Green Stewart—"my gallant & ever ready friend," Campbell called him in his journal. The local American Indian name was *Na-Chon-De*—also the name of the people, spelled Tutchone today. The river is 390 miles long and drains 20,500 square miles. London knew this area well, for he had arrived there on 9 October 1897—barely beating freeze-up—and had spent the winter on an island near the mouth of the Stewart.[5]

The Mayo River was named by William Ogilvie for Kentuckian Alfred Mayo, an early Yukon explorer and trader who had once been a circus acrobat. According to the notes

London kept as he left the Yukon, he met Mayo at Minook, Alaska, on 13 June 1898: "Introduced to Capt. Mayo—thirty years in country. Getting stout—very pleasant to converse with."[6]

The McQuesten River was named for LeRoy Napoleon "Jack" McQuesten (1836–1909), partner of Mayo and Arthur Harper, and generally acknowledged as "The Father of the Yukon." The founder of trading posts and the grantor of credit—and the "King of Circle City"—McQuesten was one of the most beloved men in the North. William Moore wrote on 6 January 1888 that McQuesten and Harper were "the most moderate and fair-dealing merchants they [prospectors] have ever met with in any mining camp." In 1898, J. S. Webb published the Northland consensus of opinion about McQuesten: "He has probably supported, outfitted, and grub-staked more men, and kept them through the long cold winters when they were down on their luck and unable to obtain supplies or help from any one else, than any person knows except himself and the company. . . . He has done all this from kindness of heart, without any selfish motive whatever." McQuesten married an American Indian woman and, after he retired from the Northland, moved with her to Berkeley, California. In a bizarre twist of fate, this hardy sourdough died of blood poisoning following surgery for bunions.[7]

Notes: (1) London's spelling, "McQuestion," may have come from one of his primary sources, Miner Bruce's *Alaska,* which contains the same error. (2) In his essay "Gold Hunters of the North" London claimed he had met McQuesten at Minook; his own notes, however, indicate that it was Mayo.[8]

Line 1806: "burning holes through frozen muck and gravel and washing countless pans of dirt"

Throughout the Yukon, just below the surface, is permafrost—permanently frozen sub-soil, hard as concrete and yielding only grudgingly to a miner's pick and shovel. Without the permafrost, the arid Yukon would be a desert—a fact known even in the nineteenth century.[9]

To determine if a claim had value, miners had to dig a shaft through the permafrost to bedrock—sometimes as much as one hundred feet down—where the gold, if there was any, would have settled. The miners would not know their fortune until they reached bottom. It took A. C. Dyer two months to sink his first shaft—he found nothing.[10]

Heilprin (1899) described the process for prospective Northland miners: "Over the area of the prospect shaft, whose section measures ordinarily three to four by six feet, a wood fire is built, the heat from which melts out the soil to a depth of a few inches, or at times to a foot or more. The materials of melting having been removed, a second fire is built, and the operation is repeated until the required depth has been obtained." Some prospectors sank double shafts because, according to Hawthorne, "[p]utting down two holes at a time gives you something to do while the first one is burning out."[11]

In *Burning Daylight* London credits his protagonist with the creation of this burn-and-dig method: "Here, and possibly for the first time in the history of the Yukon, wood-burning, in sinking a shaft, was tried. It was Daylight's initiative. After clearing away the moss and grass, a fire of dry spruce was built. Six hours of burning thawed eight inches of muck. Their picks drove full depth into it, and, when they had shovelled out, another fire was started. . . . Six feet of frozen muck brought them to gravel, likewise frozen. Here progress was slower. But they learned to handle their fires better, and were soon able to thaw five and six inches at a burning."[12]

Some gold-seekers were misled by the handbooks that poured in torrents from the publishing houses during the Rush. One, for example, prescribed a fairly effortless method for handling permafrost: "Take off 4 or 5 inches of earth (just a crust.) Then put a couple of bushels of lime in the space, pour water over it to slack it, and then put canvas or other covering over it, laying rocks on the canvas to keep the wind from getting underneath. In the morning the frost will be drawn for nearly three feet."[13]

The pans used by the miners were, wrote Bramble, "twelve inches in diameter at the bottom, and from fifteen to sixteen inches on the top, the sides inclining outward at an angle of about thirty degrees, and being turned over a wire around the edge to make it strong."[14] In *Burning Daylight* London reveals his familiarity with panning techniques: "He squatted over the tank and began to wash. Earth and gravel seemed to fill the pan. As he imparted to it a circular movement, the lighter, coarser particles washed out over the edge. At times he combed the surface with his fingers, raking out handfuls of gravel. The contents of the pan diminished. As it drew near to the bottom, for the purpose of fleeting and tentative examination, he gave the pan a sudden sloshing movement, emptying it of water. And the whole bottom showed as if covered with butter. Thus the yellow gold flashed up as the muddy water was flirted away."[15]

Lines 1808–9: "summer arrived, and dogs and men packed on their backs"

It was common practice among the American Indians in the Northland to use their sled-dogs as pack animals in the summer months. The load was "placed near their shoulders," wrote Harmon, "and some of these dogs, which are accustomed to it, will carry sixty or seventy pounds weight, the distance of twenty five or thirty miles a day." William Moore's son Benjamin observed similar pack trains of fifteen to twenty dogs, each carrying loads of forty to sixty pounds.[16]

Lines 1813–14: "the midnight sun"

In late June the sun is visible in the Arctic latitudes twenty-four hours a day.

Line 1815: "swarming gnats and flies"

Many accounts of Northland visits devote considerable space to descriptions of bothersome insects. Evans cursed the "black gnats [that] ferociously challenge the intrusion of their domain, visiting the intruder with indescribable and increasing torment." Hayne was similarly annoyed by gnats:

> [They] . . . have a most obnoxious habit of working half of their wretched little bodies under the skin, and as they are peculiarly vicious and poisonous, they ultimately proved a very serious source of annoyance. They get into one's blankets and clothes, and once in it is practically impossible to dislodge them. They are impervious to smoke, and even 'smudging' (smoking with fires of green wood) has no deterrent effect upon them. They have an especial affection for the ankles, wrist, neck, and under the eyes, which they cause to swell in a most alarming fashion. Nothing can be done, unless it be to gain a few moments' relief by bathing the affected parts in salt-and-water. You must simply grin and bear it—and not scratch if you can help it.[17]

Garland described the "myriads of little black flies" that attacked his horses on the trail north. "They filled the horses' ears," he wrote, "and their sting produced minute swellings all over the necks and breasts of the poor animals. Had it not been for our pennyroyal [aromatic vegetable oil] and bacon grease, the bay horse would have been eaten raw." Even the redoubtable and uncomplaining Schwatka recorded an "annoyance in bathing in Lake Marsh": large flies, which "made it necessary to keep constantly swinging a towel in the air." Any "momentary cessation" of the towel-waving, he wrote, was "punished by having a piece bitten out of one that would look like an incipient boil." He added that the flies "disabled for a week" one of their party.[18]

Lines 1815–16: "in the shadows of glaciers picked strawberries and flowers as ripe and fair as any the Southland could boast"

This apparent anomaly of lush fruit and flowers growing in "the shadows of glaciers" is in fact a well-documented Northland phenomenon. In 1879, near Wrangell, Alaska, John Muir was amazed by what he saw: "Never before in all my travels, north or south," he wrote, "had I found so lavish an abundance of berries as here. The woods and meadows are full of them. . . ." And in the Lynn Canal area near Skagway and Dyea he saw strawberries that "were as fine in size and color as any I ever saw anywhere."[19]

Wildflowers also grow in exceptional variety and size in the Northland. Muir observed near a glacier "gay multitudes of flowers, far more brilliantly colored than would be looked for in so cool and beclouded a region. . . ." Garland was reminded of "the splendor and radiance of Iowa in June."[20]

London, who left the Yukon in the early spring of 1898, had certainly seen the lushness of sub-Arctic vegetation made possible by the long hours of sunshine and warm temperatures of the Northland summer.[21]

Lines 1826–28: "a long-barrelled flint-lock . . . a Hudson Bay Company gun of the young days . . . worth its height in beaver skins packed flat"

The Hudson's Bay Company (HBC), the oldest trading company in the world, received its charter from Charles II on 2 May 1670. In the eighteenth century, the HBC began establishing trading posts in the interior of sub-Arctic North America and enjoyed a virtual monopoly on trade with the American Indians for scores of years. In 1846 the HBC ceded Oregon to the United States and in 1869 sold its vast holdings to Canada for 300,000 pounds. The HBC opened Fort Yukon and began its Yukon River trade in 1847. Although the company did not manifest a strong presence in the Klondike, their trading posts and stores throughout the Canadian North were among the most popular with the gold-seekers.

The trade items most desired by the American Indians were firearms—specifically the flintlock muskets that London mentions. Schwatka, encountering the Tagish Indians at Lake Marsh, noticed that "their only weapons" were the "stereotyped Hudson Bay Company flintlock smooth-bore musket, the only kind of gun, I believe, throwing a ball that this great trading company has ever issued since its foundation. . . . These old muskets are tolerably good at sixty to seventy yards, and even reasonably dangerous at twice that distance." There was quite an assortment of weapons traded throughout the centuries, but they would have been easily identifiable as HBC guns because of the brass serpent trademark usually affixed to the stock.[22]

The American Indians traded beaver and other animal skins at the HBC posts, satisfying the demand in England—and, later, in North America—for beaver hats and other fur products. Douglas MacKay's survey of the HBC standard of trade for 1748 provides some indication of the value of beaver skins: One to one and a half skins could purchase any one of the following items: a half pound of beads, a brass kettle, two hatchets, twenty fishhooks, two looking glasses, twelve needles, two powder horns, four spoons, one shirt, a pound of black lead, a pound and a half of powder, two pounds of brown sugar, a pound of tobacco; four skins could buy a gallon of English brandy; six could purchase a blanket. A four-foot gun cost twelve beaver skins.[23]

London's reference to a gun being worth "its height in beaver skins packed flat" was a common story in the Northland—both Munn and Stanley repeat it. But as Newman states, this is a "persistent myth." The cost was not based upon the length of the gun, for that would have resulted in "a pile of furs five feet high and consisting of about three hundred pelts," far beyond the standard price of twelve pelts or so.[24]

Line 1835: "*The gold was sacked in moose-hide bags, fifty pounds to the bag*"
Throughout the Rush, gold was sixteen dollars an ounce. At that rate, each of the fifty-pound bags "piled like so much firewood outside" was worth $12,800.

Line 1836: "*the spruce-bough lodge*"
Using the branches of evergreens—both for temporary shelters and for bedding—was common in the Northland. Schwatka saw near the mouth of Pelly "a score of the brush houses usual in this country," which he briefly described: "three main poles, one much longer than the rest, and serving as a ridge pole on which to pile evergreen brush to complete the house."[25]

Line 1836: "*Like giants they toiled*"
Although London no doubt meant to suggest here that Thornton and his partners worked extremely hard, there is another interpretation: In the late nineteenth century, a "giant" was also a large pipe used to wash ore.

Line 1871: "niggerheads"

This offensive slang term for dark clumps of Arctic vegetation was used in many Gold Rush publications.

Lines 1886–87: "timber wolf"

The adult gray wolf (*Canis lupus*) stands twenty-six to thirty-eight inches high at the shoulder, ranges in length (nose to tail) from about forty to eighty inches, and weighs from fifty-seven to one hundred thirty pounds. Packs can be anywhere from two to fifteen in number, but the usual size is four to seven. Nocturnal hunters, wolves range at speeds of up to thirty miles per hour over 100 to 260 square miles; they live from ten to eighteen years under normal conditions.[26]

As a number of biographers have pointed out, the wolf played an important role in London's personal mythology: he signed some personal letters "Wolf"; the home he built near Glen Ellen, California, was called "Wolf House"; his personal bookplate featured the image of a wolf; one of his dogs was named Brown Wolf; and, of course, wolves figure prominently in a number of London stories and in the titles of some of his works—*The Son of the Wolf*, *The Sea-Wolf* and "Brown Wolf."[27]

Line 1939: "He began to sleep out at night, staying away from the camp for days at a time"

Young wrote that he knew dogs to "wander over a hundred miles away from their homes, and to remain away for weeks." In another volume, Young mentions seeing a pack of dogs "over a hundred miles from their home."[28]

Line 1944: "he killed a large black bear, blinded by the mosquitoes"

Ursus americanus, the brown or black bear, ranges throughout North America. It stands about three feet at the shoulder, is between four and six feet long, and weighs from two hundred to six hundred pounds. Although Barry Lopez writes that a wolf "has few satisfactory meetings with bears," the blinded condition of this one would have greatly improved Buck's chances.[29]

The stampeders hunted bears relentlessly, so the creatures were quickly depleted along the Gold Rush trail to Dawson City; the North-west Mounted Police noted in an 1899 report that they were "scarce" in the Tagish District. Ten years before the Rush, however, George Dawson had commented that "black and grizzly bears roam over the entire region and are often seen along the banks of the rivers in the latter part of the summer. . . ."[30]

Virtually every Northland visitor agreed that the most unpleasant aspect of the Yukon spring was the reemergence of mosquitoes: "plague," "swarming millions," a "brown cloud," "voracious and pertinacious," a "regular hades," "an almost intolerable pest," "peerless among their kind . . . for wickedness unalloyed," "very bloodthirsty," "like smoke in the air," "ferocious and malignant," "destroyers of the soul," "known to drive men to suicide," "an unpleasant propensity for unprovoked pugnacity," "as thick as snowflakes in a snowbank," "exasperating . . . making sleep impossible."[31]

Despite his best preventative efforts, Dietz complained that whenever he made bread dough, it "would be almost black with bugs when it was taken out of the bag." And Hawthorne grumbled that the netting he wore on his head "had so much blood on the inside from them mashed-up mosquitoes I couldn't see out."[32]

Stories about the ferocity of the pests are manifold in Northland history, legend, and literature. DeWindt wrote that a Yukon "mosquito will torture a dog to death in a few hours. . . ." Price told how as he and his company were passing an island on the Yukon River, they were hailed by a man, apparently abandoned by his partners, who seemed in desperate straits. They were alarmed when they saw the man's face, "puffed and swelled by the voracious attacks of the insects to such an extent that his features were barely discernible."[33]

Schwatka's account in 1885 of a bear being blinded by mosquitoes anticipated the sort of scene that London must have been imagining: "The bear, instead of securing safety by precipitate retreat from such places, fights them, bear style, reared up on his hindquarters, until the stings near his eyes close them, and he is kept in this condition until starvation eventually causes death."[34]

London battled mosquitoes on the Yukon River as he departed the Klondike in the summer of 1898—in fact, one of the longest passages in his notes concerns the pests: "Mosquitos—One night badly bitten under netting—couldn't vouch for it but John [Thorson] watched them & said they rushed the netting in a body, one gang holding up the edge while a second gang crawled under. Charley [Taylor] swore that he has seen several of the largest ones pull the mesh apart & let a small one squeeze through. I have seen them with their proboscis bent and twisted after an assault on sheet iron stove. Bite me through overalls & heavy underwear."[35]

Line 1947: *wolverines*

Known as ferocious fighters—"perhaps the most powerful mammal for its size"—the wolverine ranges in length from about thirty-one to forty-four inches and weighs between eighteen and forty-two pounds. As London describes, wolverines are indeed carrion eaters. A report of the North-west Mounted Police called wolverines "numerous" in the Tagish District.[36]

Lines 1991–93: *ptarmigan*

The edible qualities of this pudgy bird figure in quite a few London tales. Muir wrote that the ptarmigan "has red over the eye, a white line, not conspicuous, over the red, belly white, white markings over the upper parts on ground of brown and black wings, mostly white as seen when flying, but the coverts [small feathers covering the bases of large feathers] the same as the rest of the body. Only about three inches of the folded primaries show white. The breast seems to have golden iridescent colors, white under the wings." Dietz called the bird a "fool-hen" and "a sort of morbid species of chicken."[37] The willow ptarmigan is the official state bird of Alaska.

Lines 2005–6: *"the bull [moose] tossed his great palmated antlers, branching to fourteen points and embracing seven feet within the tips"*

The largest members of the deer family, moose (*Alces americanus*) stand about six to seven feet tall at the shoulder and weigh between nine hundred and fourteen hundred pounds (females weigh, on average, about two hundred pounds less). This particular moose weighs thirteen hundred pounds—"three hundredweight more than half a ton"— well within the upper range of weight for males. Moose were plentiful in the Northland, but as the human population increased during the Rush, the numbers of moose declined precipitously in the most populous areas. The North-west Mounted Police said they were "scarce" in the Tagish District.

Contrary to London's depiction here, moose do not generally form herds in the fall of the year; nor do bulls have a "harem." Moose antlers, however, which begin growing in April, would indeed have been at their full growth about this time—although the seven-foot antler span would be larger by three inches than the largest on record. And the moose would indeed have been a "formidable antagonist." Old-timers said "they would rather face a bear than a wounded moose."[38]

Line 2010–43: "Buck proceeded to cut the bull out from the herd . . . [and] never gave it a moment's rest"

Lopez writes about this well-documented hunting strategy: "Wolves kill the largest ungulates [hoofed mammals] by running alongside them, slashing at their hams, ripping at their flanks and abdomen, tearing at the nose and head, harassing the animal until it weakens enough through loss of blood and the severing of muscles to be thrown to the ground. At this point the wolves usually rip open the abdominal cavity and begin eating, sometimes before the animal is dead."[39]

Dogs use identical hunting tactics. Mandelbaum noted that the dogs of the Plains Cree "would try to separate a buffalo calf from the herd and make the kill." And Walden saw some roving huskies in the Klondike "hamstringing" a horse; then they "tore out his throat."[40]

Lines 2065–66: "heading straight home through strange country with a certitude of direction that put man and his magnetic needle [compass] to shame"

Morris attributes such pathfinding prowess to a dog's ability to detect "subtle differences and changes in the earth's magnetic field." Elizabeth Thomas, however, is not so sure about the "innate" abilities of dogs to navigate.[41]

Line 2098: the Yeehats

There was no tribe of American Indians named "Yeehat."[42] London's decision to employ a fictitious tribe is consistent with Northland traditions, however, for it was common to hear tales of fierce people living in remote and unexplored regions of the territory. For example, on their journey through the Barrens, the Tyrrell brothers were warned that the area was "inhabited by savage tribes . . . who would undoubtedly eat us."

At the time of the Rush, there were tales about fierce people in the Mackenzie Mountains—the very region Thornton and his partners have entered. Warburton Pike repeated a story about cannibals in the mountains who had been "on the warpath during the last autumn, and had killed a party of white prospectors far down the Pelly, leaving their bodies stacked up on a gravel bar as a warning to all intruders." Stanley wrote about a tribe called the Mahoney, also (incorrectly) believed to be living far up the Stewart River: "The Mahoneys are at war with every other tribe, and with the world in general; and no one who has had the hardihood to trespass on their domains has ever returned to tell the tale. . . . These Indians, thus far, have rejected all civilizing influences and as they occupy one of nature's staunchest strongholds, located in a wilderness of frost and barricaded with ice and snow, they will probably defy the intrusion of the white man for years to come, unless subdued by the arts of some venturesome missionary."[43]

Because of the location—far up the Stewart—and because London had spent the winter at the mouth of the Stewart, it is possible that he had heard tales about the "Mahoneys" and other legendary Indians, giving him the idea to send John Thornton and his partners up the river and into what miners and American Indians alike believed was dangerous territory.

Although there were very few violent encounters with American Indians during the Rush, newspapers warned the gold-seekers about potential dangers. The *Dyea Trail*, for example, published a long article advising travelers to be able to protect themselves against "vicious Indians."[44]

There is no way to determine for certain what sort of American Indians London was imagining when he created the Yeehats. There were three groups in the Northland, each quite distinct in appearance and culture: the Eskimos were on the north and northwestern coasts of Alaska, and scattered elsewhere; various tribes collectively known as Athapaskans lived in the interior of the Yukon and Alaska and closely resembled in appearance the Plains Indians of the western United States; the Tlingit, including the Chilkat and Chilkoot, controlled the southeastern coasts of Alaska and British Columbia.

Because London refers in other stories to "savage Chilkat" and to "fierce Chilkats," it would not be inappropriate to speculate that these were the people upon whom he based the Yeehats. The Chilkat had a reputation among other Northland writers for their hostility. Schwatka had called them "the most dreaded and war-like" of the Tlingits. And Dall refers to them as "a wild and untamable people."[45]

London probably saw his first Chilkat in Juneau, where he and his party hired some to take them by canoe to Dyea, one hundred miles away. In a letter to Mabel Applegarth from Dyea on 8 August 1897 London mentioned his ride with "Indians . . . Squaws, papooses & dogs." Near Dyea, he and his party hired other Chilkat to pack their supplies over the Chilkoot Pass. And he saw evidence of Chilkat ferocity at the ruins of Fort Selkirk near the mouth of the Pelly River. Thompson's diary indicates that the London party stopped at the site for about a half an hour and "looked over the town."[46]

London saw many other American Indians on his journeys, some of whom impressed him as being "clean-limbed [and] stalwart," others of whom did not—especially a group he characterized as "sort of [a] mongrel cross of Thlinket and Esquimau."[47]

Line 2098: "dancing about the wreckage of the spruce-bough lodge"

As London left the Klondike, he and his companions witnessed American Indians dancing in a camp near the Yukon River. Out on the river, they heard "a wild chant, which rose and fell uncannily as it floated across the water." Going ashore to explore, they saw "[s]everal scores of bucks . . . giving tongue to unwritten music, evidently born when the world was very young, and still apulse with the spirit of primeval man. Urged on by the chief medicine man, the women had abandoned themselves to the religious ecstasy, their raven hair unbound and falling to their hips, while their bodies were swaying and undulating to the swing of the song."[48]

Lines 2107–8: arrows and spears

Emmons writes that common Tlingit weapons were the bow and arrow—with "leaf-shaped blades"—spear, club, and dagger. Spears were six to eight feet long, tipped with a "leaf-shaped blade of stone or metal."[49]

Line 2120: "sluice boxes"

These devices separated gold from gravel. Osborne described them in detail for his readers in *Macmillan's Magazine*:

> The [sluice] boxes are usually twelve feet long, ten inches wide at one end and twelve at the other, the two sides being about eight or ten inches high. They are fitted into each other, the small end of one being dropped into the large end of another. In the bottom of the boxes, into which the pay-dirt is to be shovelled, and for several boxes farther on, riffles are added. In the Klondike the riffle in general use consists of four or five found pieces of wood, flattened on the part that is to lie against the bottom of the sluice-box, and fastened together by a four-sided block at each end; these are wedged down firmly to keep them in place. The fall given to the sluice-boxes varies from eight to twelve inches per box, according to the amount of water obtainable. When all is ready the water is turned through the boxes, and the pay-dirt is shovelled

in, care being taken that the boxes do not choke, and then the water is allowed sufficient time to keep the top of the riffles clear of debris. The gold falls to the bottom between the poles of the riffles, and only travels a few feet; while the sand, gravel, and smaller stones are swept away by the rushing water. In one of the boxes, which is made very much wider than the others, stands a man with a fork, who throws out the heavy stones, and turns over and over the pieces of bed-rock until the gold adhering to their faces has been washed off. Every day or two the riffles are loosened, only a gentle stream of water is allowed to flow through, and by a skillful use of a bit of flat board and a whisk, most of the sand and gravel is separated from the gold, which is then scooped up, put in a pan, and thoroughly cleaned in the way already described.[50]

Lines 2178–79: "the Yeehats noted a change in the breed of timber wolves"

Wolves and dogs can breed successfully, but in the hierarchy of a wolf pack, only the "alpha," or highest-ranking, male breeds. Accordingly, the "change" noted by the Yeehats is further evidence of Buck's continuing dominance.[51]

In London's "Where the Trail Forks" a similar incident occurs. A dog named Shep returns to the wild after its masters are killed by Indians: "[T]he years were not many before the Indian hunters noted a change in the breed of timber wolves, and there were dashes of bright color and variegated markings such as no wolf bore before."[52]

Line 2181: "the Yeehats tell of a Ghost Dog"

Among the Eskimos living near the Bering Strait, Lawrence Clayton found a tale that mentions the "shades" of dogs; Clayton writes that it is "plausible" that London had heard the story "and utilized the folk belief to provide the conclusion for his story." London, however, spent most of his Yukon winter in the interior (two thousand miles from the Bering Strait), and the tale itself merely alludes to dogs and does not in any sense suggest that the Eskimo feared or revered or in any other way regarded these canine ghosts as threatening or vindictive.[53]

In another London novel, *Michael, Brother of Jerry,* Michael is so fearsome in attack that a man wonders whether "dog was real. Might it not be some terrible avenger, out of the mystery beyond life, placed to beset him and finish him finally on this road that he was convinced was surely the death-road? The dog was not real."[54]

Line 2189: "and women there are who become sad"

Alexander Mackenzie described some grieving practices of American Indian women he encountered in the northern Canadian Rockies: "[T]hey not only cut their hair, and cry and howl, but they will sometimes with the utmost deliberation, employ some sharp instrument to separate the nail from the finger, and then force back the flesh beyond the first joint, which they immediately amputate."[55]

Lines 2196–97: "he muses for a time, howling once, long and mournfully, ere he departs"

Jacobsen recorded a poignant moment when he left behind the dogs that had been with him on his long Arctic exploration: His animals were "raising their heads and howling woefully." In London's canon, the most macabre instance of a dog's howling at death occurs in *Jerry of the Islands* when Jerry howls in "woe" when he discovers the head of his recently decapitated master.[56]

Notes

INTRODUCTION

1. In a series of children's books called *Great Illustrated Classics*, Mitsu Yamamoto expands the original seven chapters into twenty-five and adds simple dialogue—for example: "'Morning, Buck. How's my big dog?' the Judge asked." Olive Price also redivides the text and adds, in direct discourse, the thoughts of Buck and the other dogs. After witnessing the death of Curly, for example, Buck thinks: "'No, I must never go down.'" The edition by Scott, Foresman and Company for eighth graders deletes all of Buck's ancestral memories of the prehistoric "hairy man" (a nod to creationists?) and removes, as well, some violence and all racial references—the Scotch half-breed becomes a Scotsman; Nig's coat, colorless.

2. Jack London, to George P. Brett, 22 November 1912, *Letters*, 1102.

3. Films were released in 1923, 1935, 1972, 1976, 1983, and 1992. See Williams, *Jack London: The Movies*, 225, 226, 229, 230, 232.

4. Haughey and Johnson, *Jack London Homes Album*, 24.

5. A cartoon in Gary Larson's "Far Side" series (17 December 1980) shows a female moose holding a telephone she has just answered. She looks over at her husband, who, beer in hoof, is slouched deeply in an easy chair in front of the TV, and announces: "It's the call of the wild."

6. Lampson, "Jack London's Titles," 4–7; and *Letters*, 954. Partridge likewise credits London for making the phrase a "firmly established" fixture in our language. See Partridge, *Dictionary of Cliches*, 40.

7. *Letters*, 351, 357, 359; George P. Brett, to Jack London, 19 March 1903, Huntington Library, San Marino, California.

8. "'The Call of the Wild,'" *Philadelphia Press*, 25 July 1903; "Reviews of New Books," *Oakland Herald*, 29 July 1903; "Best Work of Jack London," *San Francisco Chronicle*, 2 August 1903; "'The Call of the Wild,' by Jack London," *Athenaeum*, 29 August 1903, 279; Maurice, "Jack London, 'The Call of the Wild,'" 160; and "Books New and Old," 696.

9. Bosworth and Jack London, "London a Plagiarist?" 373–76. For a discussion of this issue, see Walker, *Jack London and the Klondike*, 240–42.

10. "Dogs in the Far North," *New York Times Saturday Review*, 6 December 1902, 861; the review of *A Daughter of the Snows* is on page 857; the letter from Dall, 871. London wrote to Anna Strunsky on 20 December 1902. See *Letters*, 328–30.

11. "Against Jack London," *New York Times Saturday Review*, 23 February 1907, 109; "My Dogs in the North Land," *New York Times Saturday Review*, 9 March 1907, 146; and *Letters*, 679–80. Charges of plagiarism followed London throughout his career. Charmian London defended her deceased husband in her 1921 biography, noting that he "was eternally dogged at the heels by small men at home and abroad who charged plagiarism. . . ." See C. K. London, *Book of Jack London* 2:121. For varying discussions of the plagiarism charges, see Joan London, *Jack London and His Times*, 324–26 (page references are to reprint edition); Sinclair, *Jack*, 131–33; and Kingman, *Pictorial Life*, 118–19.

12. Geismar, introduction to *Jack London: Short Stories*, ix; Walker, foreword to *"The Call of the Wild,"* xii; Labor, "Jack London's *Mondo Cane*," 2–13; Walcutt, *Seven Novelists*, 145; Rothberg, introduction to *"The Call of the Wild,"* 8; Doctorow, introduction to *The Call of the Wild*, xviii, xiii.

13. Perry, *An American Myth*, 97.

14. Arrangements for a variety of translations (into French for example, and for the blind) were underway shortly after publication of the novel in 1903. See, respectively, Macmillan Company to Jack London, 12 September 1904, Huntington Library, San Marino, California, and Macmillan Company to Jack London, 6 February 1906, Huntington Library, San Marino, California; see also Labor, *Concise Dictionary* 2:277. For a summary of the novel's publication in other languages, see Jacqueline Tavernier-Courbin, *Call of the Wild*, 28–34.

15. *Letters*, 351; George P. Brett, to Jack London, 1 April 1903, Huntington Library, San Marino, California, and C. K. London, *Jack London* 1:392. London was extremely happy with the appearance of the book, writing to Brett that he thought it "a beautiful little book . . . the most beautiful of its kind I have ever seen." See *Letters*, 375.

16. From a photocopy of Jack London's ledger, courtesy of Russ Kingman, Glen Ellen, California. The *Post* had asked London to cut five thousand words, which he did somewhat brutally, removing from his sixth chapter Buck's near-death at the cliff, the barroom fight in Circle City, the rescue of John Thornton in the rapids of the Fortymile River, and the sled-pulling wager laid in the Eldorado Saloon in Dawson City.

17. George P. Brett, to Jack London, 19 March 1903, Huntington Library, San Marino, California; *Letters*, 357. Macmillan spent between six and eight thousand dollars advertising the book, and the

publisher sent four hundred review copies to newspapers all over the country. See George P. Brett, to Jack London, 30 July 1903, Huntington Library, San Marino, California, and Herbert P. Williams, to Jack London, 15 July 1903, Huntington Library, San Marino, California.

18. Noel, *Footloose in Arcadia*, 149. See also Kingman, *Pictorial Life*, 116. Joan London wrote that the first printing was ten thousand copies—a sizable number for a writer whose first novel (*A Daughter of the Snows*, 1902) had been a failure. All ten thousand were sold on the first day of publication in July, and Brett wrote to London in late August that about eighteen thousand copies had been sold. See Joan London, *Jack London and His Times*, 254; and George P. Brett, to Jack London, 26 August 1903, Huntington Library, San Marino, California.

19. *Letters*, 352. In a letter to the author on 16 January 1993, Kingman wrote: "I had a strange caller recently. The caller said that his grandmother had the holograph *Call of the Wild* and had had it bound in leather covers. Seems that a person stole it from her home. . . . This is the first time I have ever heard that such a manuscript is or was in existence." Neither Macmillan nor the *Saturday Evening Post* has retained the typescript that London originally submitted.

20. See, for example, Joan London, *Jack London and His Times*, 252–55; Wilcox, "Jack London's Naturalism," 91–101; Labor, *Jack London*, 69–81; Sinclair, *Jack*, 91–93; James Dickey, introduction to *"The Call of the Wild,"* 7–16; Hedrick, *"The Call of the Wild,"* 94–111; and Watson Jr., "Ghost Dog."

21. Labor and Leitz, introduction to *"The Call of the Wild,"* xiii.

22. "Best Work," 32; "'Call of the Wild,'" 279; "A 'Nature' Story," 229; Doctorow, introduction to *The Call of the Wild*, xviii; Labor and Leitz, introduction to *"The Call of the Wild,"* xi–xii; Clifton Fadiman, afterword to *The Call of the Wild*, 127.

23. Stillé, "Review of *The Call of the Wild*," 7–10; Carl Sandburg, "Jack London: A Common Man." *Tomorrow* 2 (April 1906): 35–39; reprint, *The Jack London Reader* (Philadelphia, Penn.: Courage Books, 1994), 271; Tony Tanner, "The Call of the Wild," *Spectator* 215 (16 July 1965): 80; Benoit, "Jack London's *The Call of the Wild*," 247; Watson, *Novels*, 40; Nash, introduction to *The Call of the Wild*, 1; Walcutt, *Jack London*, 22; Lundquist, *Jack London*, 44; Frey, "Contradiction," 35.

24. Maurice, "Jack London," 160; "Best Work," 32; Wirzberger, "Jack London and the Goldrush," 146; Swain, afterword to *The Call of the Wild*, 107; Paulsen, introduction to *The Call of the Wild*, xi.

25. "Books," 695; Geismar, "Jack London: The Short Cut," 151.

26. Roosevelt's charges against London are in Clark, "Roosevelt," 770–74; Jack London, "Other Animals," 10–11, 25–26; *Letters*, London to Merle Maddern, 381.

See also Edward B. Clark, "Real Naturalists on Nature Faking," *Everybody's Magazine* 17 (September 1907): 423–27 and Theodore Roosevelt's article in the same issue: "'Nature Fakers,'" 427–30. John S. Burroughs's positions are in his articles "Do Animals Think?" *Harper's Monthly* 110 (February 1905): 354–58 and "The Reasonable but Unreasoning Animals," *Outlook* 87 (14 December 1907): 809–15. Burroughs does not mention London by name.

In the "nature-faking" attacks by Roosevelt and others, it was not London who was the principal target, but William J. Long, author of such popular nature books as *Beasts of the Field* (1901) and *Following the Deer* (1903). Throughout the spring and summer and on into the fall of 1907, while London was in the South Seas aboard the *Snark*, Long and Roosevelt—and their allies— hurled charges back and forth in the *New York Times*. "Roosevelt Only a Gamekiller—Long," was one headline (23 May 1907); "Roosevelt Whacks Dr. Long Once More," another (21 August 1907).

27. Doubleday, *"The Call of the Wild,"* 150 (page references are to reprint edition); Hamilton, *"Tools of My Trade,"* 8; London, "Other Animals," 238.

28. Geismar mentions "the rebirth of primitive instincts in the wilderness"; Walcutt focuses on the "primordialism" in the novel—whoever possesses the more brutish nature, writes Walcutt, is "best fitted . . . to succeed under savage conditions." Gurian characterizes it as a "perfect parable of a biologically and environmentally determined universe." Wilcox comments that London "explores the latent possibilities of his Darwinian and Spencerian views." And Doctorow adds that the novel chronicles "the failure of the human race to evolve truly from its primeval beginnings." See Geismar, "Jack London: The Short Cut," 181; Walcutt, "Jack London: Blond Beasts," 96, 104; Gurian, "Romantic Necessity," 112–14 (page references are to reprint edition); Wilcox, "Jack London's Naturalism," 181; and Doctorow, introduction to *The Call of the Wild*, xviii.

29. Flink, "Parental Metaphor," 230 (page references are to reprint edition); Flink, "Jack London's Cartharsis [sic]," 12–13; Barltrop, *Jack London: The Man*, 93; Seelye, introduction to *"White Fang" and "The Call of the Wild,"* xi.

30. *Jack London: A Sketch*, 4; Joan London, *Jack London and His Times*, 253; Walker, *Jack London and the Klondike*, 227; Sinclair, *Jack*, 93; Doctorow, introduction to *The Call of the Wild*, xvii–xviii; Giles, *"The Call of the Wild,"* 11; and Tavernier-Courbin, *Call of the Wild*, 45.

31. Joan London, *Jack London and His Times*, 252.

32. Haldeman-Julius, ed., *Life of Jack London*, 48; Watson, *Novels*, 45; McClintock, *White Logic*, 50; Mann, "Theme of the Double," 1–2; Doctorow, introduction to *The Call of the Wild*, xvii; Gair, "Doppelgänger and the Naturalist Self," 197.

33. Fusco, "On Primitivism," 76; Seelye, introduction to *"White Fang" and "The Call of the Wild,"* xvi; Lynn, "The Brain Merchant," 92.

34. For a thorough description of how Jung's theories apply to the novel, see Tavernier-Courbin, *Call of the Wild*, 63–79.

35. Geismar, "Jack London: The Short Cut," 150–51.

36. Labor, "London's *Mondo Cane*," 209–13. Elsewhere, Labor has refined his thesis. See, for example, his 1970 introduction to *Great Short Works*, xii; his 1974 volume, *Jack London*, 72–78; his 1988 essay, "Jack London," 276–78; and his 1990 introduction (with Leitz) to the Oxford University Press edition of *The Call of the Wild*, xiii–xv.

London did not read Jung until 1916, near the end of his life, so Labor is not suggesting any direct connection between London's reading and the composition of *The Call of the Wild*. But

London surely recognized something enormously useful in Jung—broad, integrative ideas and a vocabulary with which to capture the human psyche. London's copy of *Psychology of the Unconscious* has in it nearly three hundred notations, and London—"his eyes like stars"—told his wife, Charmian, that he felt, after reading Jung, that he was "standing on the edge of a world so new, so terrible, so wonderful" that he was "almost afraid to look over into it." See D. M. Hamilton, *"Tools of My Trade,"* 175 and C. K. London, *Jack London* 2:323.

37. Spinner, "Syllabus," 236; Sinclair, *Jack,* 91; Mann, "Theme of the Double," 5; Watson, *Novels,* 47; Donald Pizer, "Jack London: The Problem of Form," 166, 171; Stasz, *American Dreamers,* 106; Doctorow, introduction to *The Call of the Wild,* xvi; and Tavernier-Courbin, *Call of the Wild,* 99. Other published interpretations—minor in nature—include the notion that the novel is, in one way, a repository for the "values of love and fair play . . . that have always been respected in Western literature." See Walcutt, *Jack London,* 21. Spinner believes that London describes in the novel "an education, spiritually as well as physically, of a being suffering through the dilemma of existence of the modern world." See Spinner, "Syllabus," 234 (reprint).

I. "INTO THE PRIMITIVE"

1. John Myers O'Hara, "Atavism," *Bookman* 16 (November 1902): 229.

2. John Myers O'Hara, New York City, to Jack London, Glen Ellen, California, 7 September 1916, Huntington Library, San Marino, California; Hervey, "Life of John Myers O'Hara"; New York City Department of Records and Information Services, Municipal Archives, *Certificate of Death, No. 24385,* John Myers O'Hara, 16 November 1944.

3. *Letters,* 701. George P. Brett at Macmillan had written London on 27 March 1903 to ask that London supply a "superscription" for each chapter ("There must be something of the right kind if one could only find it. . . ."), but London replied on 10 April that he had "searched in vain." He had even tried to compose his own, but, he wrote, "not being a poet, have failed lamentably." He settled for the lone quatrain by O'Hara. See George P. Brett, to Jack London, 27 March 1903, Huntington Library, San Marino, California. See also *Letters,* 360.

4. Kingman, *Chronology,* 38, 40.

5. Hamilton, *"Tools of My Trade,"* 218.

6. Ibid., 217–18.

7. O'Hara, "Two Scrapbooks." O'Hara pasted the *Post* article in one of his scrapbooks.

8. Kingman, *Chronology,* 141; C. K. London, "Diary—1912," Huntington Library, San Marino, California.

9. "J. M. O'Hara Dies; Poet, Once Broker," *New York Times,* 17 November 1944.

10. M. Bond, "Klondike Diary," 22 July 1897.

11. *Letters,* 399; photocopy of the inscription from the collection of Russ Kingman.

12. Louis Bond, Seattle, to Jack London, Glen Ellen, California, 28 May 1906; Louis Bond, Seattle, to Jack London, Glen Ellen, California, 8 June 1906; Charmian Kittredge London, Honolulu, to Louis Bond, Goldfield, Nevada, 3 June 1907.

13. M. Bond, Jr., *Gold Hunter*, 57.

14. Ibid., 34; *Letters*, 381. "Buck," of course, is the name for the male of any number of species—deer, rabbit, goat.

15. Jack London, "Jan the Unrepentant," in *God of His Fathers*; "Flush of Gold," in *Lost Face*, 133; *Smoke Bellew*, 200.

16. Winslow, *Big Pan-Out*, 109; Bankson, *Klondike Nugget*, 19.

17. Parliament of Canada, "Annual Report; Appendix LL," 307.

18. Zaslow, *Opening of the Canadian North*, 10; Bronson and Reinhardt, *Last Grand Adventure*, 27.

19. Hunt, *North of 53*, front matter.

20. Stanley, *A Mile of Gold*, 68–69.

21. P. Berton, *Klondike*, 116. See also Brainerd, *Alaska and Klondike*. These are fourteen large scrapbooks, bulging with letters, kept by Brainerd, who headed the Chamber of Commerce.

22. "A Klondike Trip Spoiled," *New York Times*, 20 August 1897; "Missing Long Island Boys," *New York Times*, 1 August 1897.

23. "A New El Dorado," *Wave*, 9; Garland, "Ho, for the Klondike!" 454; Dall, "Alaska and the New Gold-Field," 26.

24. Spurr is quoted in "The Yukon Gold Country," *New York Times*, 8 August 1897.

25. H. Tyrrell, "Klondike Gold-fields," 106.

26. *Overland Monthly* (December 1897); Buckley, "Outfitting for the Klondike," 171.

27. "Edward Rosenberg Arrested, Manager of Klondike Transportation Company Accused of Fraud," *New York Times*, 23 February 1898; *Official Guide to the Klondyke*, 192; Harris, *Alaska and the Klondike Gold Fields*, 168–69; DeWindt, "Klondike Gold Fields," 306.

28. *Sunshine, Fruit, and Flowers*, 4; "Santa Clara: Special Edition," *San Jose Daily Mercury*, 15 May 1892.

29. M. Bond, Jr., *Judge Miller*; "Judge Bond Is Dead from Recent Injuries," *San Jose Herald*, 30 March 1906.

30. Although much of the valley had once belonged to Spain, and then to Mexico, the Judge's ranch was apparently never part of the Mexican Land Grants—called "ranchos"—although a small part of it may have been part of the "Bennett Tract," a 355.03-acre tract granted to Mary Bennett in 1845. See Sawyer, *Santa Clara County*, 341; see also Arbuckle, *Ranchos*, 14. "Santa Clara: Special Edition," *San Jose Daily Mercury*, 15 May 1892.

31. M. Bond, Jr., *Judge Miller*, 22–24.

32. "Will Teach the Filipinos," *San Jose Daily Mercury*, 16 October 1901 (this headline sits atop an

article about the doings of various important people in Santa Clara; partway down the column is this item: "Jack London, a prominent author, is the guest of Judge H. G. Bond"); *Letters*, 399. In *White Fang*, "Judge Scott's place" (Sierra Vista) also bears a strong resemblance to "Judge Miller's Place."

33. *Historical Atlas*, 12.

34. Brearley, *Book of the Pug*, 16.

35. Jack London to Marshall Bond, 17 December 1903, Huntington Library, San Marino, California.

36. Joan London, *Jack London and His Times*, 28; Atherton, *Jack London*, 22, 51–52, 207–8.

37. Jesse, *Anecdotes of Dogs*, 185.

38. Jack London, "Where the Trail Forks," in *God of His Fathers*, 192.

39. The Klondike is not a large river—only 102 miles long. See Mathews, *Yukon*, 301.

40. W. B. Hamilton, *Canadian Place Names*, 322.

41. Schwatka, "Great River of Alaska, II," 822.

42. Jack London, "A Relic of the Pliocene," in *Faith of Men*, 6.

43. "Candidates," *Oakland Enquirer*, 11 February 1893, 1; William Sturm, Librarian, Oakland History Room, Oakland Main Library, to Daniel Dyer, 14 January 1993.

44. "Manuel" appears in one of London's lengthy lists of names. See Jack London, "Names [for fictional characters]," Huntington Library, San Marino, California.

45. Culin, *Gambling Games of the Chinese*, 6–12 (page references are to reprint edition).

46. Joan London, *Jack London and His Times*, 27.

47. *Letters*, 399; "Sorosis Growers for Association," *San Jose Daily Mercury*, 16 October 1901.

48. *Sunshine, Fruit, and Flowers*, 4; *Historical Atlas*, 12.

49. M. Bond, Jr., *Gold Hunter*, 14; "Judge Bond Is Dead," *San Jose Herald*, 30 March 1906.

50. *Letters*, 399. "Garden City Athletic Club—Its House and Promoters," *San Jose Daily Mercury*, 6 October 1901; "Around the City," *San Jose Daily Mercury*, 15 October 1901; "Life Membership in Athletic Club Reduced," *San Jose Daily Mercury*, 15 October 1901; *San Jose City Directory, 1903–1904*.

51. Payne, *Santa Clara County*, 147–48; *Sunshine, Fruit, and Flowers*, 142.

52. *Standard Time Schedules*, 37; *Traveler's Official Railroad Guide*.

53. Phillips, *Alaska-Yukon*, 90; London, "Too Much Gold," in *Faith of Men*.

54. Holden, "Railroad Ferries," 13.

55. Harlan, *Ferryboats*, 17.

56. C. K. London, *Jack London* 1:100.

57. Harlan, *Ferryboats*, 109; Holden, "Railroad Ferries," 15; and Ford, *Red Trains*, 66.

58. Jack London, *Jack London on the Road*, 30.

59. *Time Schedules of Local and Express Trains; Standard Time Schedules*, 513–15.

60. Robert Hitchman, *Place Names*.

61. Dietz, *Mad Rush for Gold*, 21–22.

62. Black, *My Seventy Years*, 93–94.

63. Nichols, "Advertising and the Klondike," 21–23; Bonner, "Competition for Klondike Trade," 444.

64. *All About the Gold Fields*, 36.

65. *To the Klondike*, 4, 14.

66. "Klondike and San Francisco," *San Francisco Chronicle*, 22 August 1897.

67. Blethen, Jr., "Strange Klondike Outfits," 103; Satterfield, *Chilkoot Pass*, 46.

68. Young, *My Dogs*, 184–188, 134.

69. Morris and Morris, *Morris Dictionary*, 254; Farmer and Henley, *Slang and Its Analogues,* 360.

70. Jack London, "Bâtard," in *Faith of Men*, 202; George P. Brett, to Jack London, 1 April 1903, Huntington Library, San Marino, California; Jack London, to George P. Brett, 10 April 1903, *Letters*, 360. Brett was probably reacting to a report on the novel by one of Macmillan's readers, G. R. Carpenter, who had written in his report dated 1 April 1903 that he was concerned that the "two or three instances of profanity" would make the novel "unsuitable for children's reading." See Carpenter, "Reader's Report," 232.

71. *Dyea Trail*, 25 February 1898; and Wells, *Magnificence and Misery*, 212.

72. Parliament of Canada, "Annual Report; Appendix LL," 308.

73. Young, *My Dogs*, 125–26.

74. Jesse, *Dogs*, 134.

75. James W. Mossman, Puget Sound Maritime Historical Society, to Daniel Dyer, 11 September 1992. In a story about the sale of the yacht *Narwhal*, a local newspaper reported that the "longest cruise the yacht ever took was with the New York Yacht club, practically all her other cruising being confined to the waters around this [New London, Connecticut] harbor." See "Yacht Narwhal Sold for $25,000," *New London Day* (Connecticut), 28 March 1916. See also *Journal of a Whaling Voyage*. The whaler *Narwhal* was mentioned in a newspaper article pasted in one of London's scrapbooks from 1899–1901. See "Frozen Beside the Dead in Northern Ice," *San Francisco Examiner*, n.d., in Jack London, "Scrapbook 1, 1899–1901," Huntington Library, San Marino, California.

There is a remote possibility that London saw the yacht *Narwhal* as he was leaving New York City in July 1902 to conduct the research that would lead to *The People of the Abyss*. It was race week for the Larchmont Yacht Club (Osgood was a life member), and local newspaper accounts record that Long Island Sound was "filled with some of the finest yachts along the Atlantic Coast." Many of the larger boats were "illuminated every night with colored incandescent designs, visible for miles along the sound." It is not difficult to imagine London, an avid sailor, taking in the sights. See "Gala Days at Larchmont," *New Rochelle Pioneer*, 19 July 1902.

76. Norris, "Sailing of the 'Excelsior,'" 7.

77. Black, *My Seventy Years*, 95.

78. Roberts, *A Tramp to the Klondike*, 13, quoted in Hacking, "Great Klondike Shipping Boom," 22; Dietz, *Mad Rush for Gold*, 31–32.

79. C. K. London, *Jack London* 1: 236; Jack London, "Notebook [of short story plots, novels, and poems], 1898," Huntington Library, San Marino, California.

80. Jack London, "The One Thousand Dozen," in *Faith of Men*.

81. Newman, *Company of Adventurers* 1:20.

82. F. Palmer, *In the Klondike*, 43–44.

83. Zaslow, *Reading the Rocks*, 3.

84. Mowat, *Tundra*, 270.

85. Inglis, *Northern Vagabond*, 51.

86. Jack London, "In the Forests of the North," in *Children of the Frost*, 3.

87. W. B. Hamilton, *Canadian Place Names*, 58–59.

88. Berry, *Bushes and Berrys*, 48; Haskell, *Two Years in the Klondike*, 62; and Spurr, *Yukon Gold Diggings*, 9–10.

89. Thompson, "Diary of Yukon Experiences," 1.

90. L. McDonald, *Alaska Steam*, 15; Morgan, *God's Loaded Dice*, 31; and Dietz, *Mad Rush for Gold*, 29.

91. *Klondike and Yukon Guide*, 6.

92. Mizner, *Many Mizners*, 91; Osborne, "Impressions, Part I," 347; and Black, *My Seventy Years*, 96.

93. "A Great Demand on the Woolen Mills," *San Francisco Chronicle*, 3 August 1897; and P. Berton, *Klondike*, 117.

94. *Sunshine, Fruit and Flowers*, 4.

II. "THE LAW OF CLUB AND FANG"

1. Orth, *Alaska Place Names*, 605; Kirk, *Twelve Months in Klondike*, 20; and Mizner, *Many Mizners*, 94.

2. Phillips, *Alaska-Yukon*, 43.

3. Schwatka, *Summer in Alaska*, 58; Walden, *Dog-Puncher on the Yukon*, 3.

4. *Dyea Trail*, 18 February 1898; Price, *From Euston to Klondike*, 77.

5. "Dyea and the Chilkoot Trail," 6.

6. Thompson, "Diary of Yukon Experiences," 1.

7. "Dyea and the Chilkoot Trail," 4; Steele, *Policing the Arctic*, 20.

8. Bramble, *Klondike: A Manual*, 76.

9. Jack London, *Smoke Bellew*, 13; *Dyea Trail*, 11 March 1898; Kirk, *Twelve Months*, 25.

10. Jack London, *A Daughter of the Snows*, 7–8.

11. Thompson, "Diary of Yukon Experiences," 1–2; Jack London, "Like Argus of the Ancient Times," in *Red One*, 98.

12. Jack London, *Daughter of the Snows*, 198; Jack London, "The Gold Hunters of the North," in *Revolution and Other Essays*, 194. Somewhat earlier in *Daughter*, he mentions another clue to the store's identity. "Before the store," he writes, "by the scales, was another crowd" (page 17). It was at Healy & Wilson's that the Chilkat gathered to sell their services as packers; the scales measured the loads, and the miners paid the going rate (per pound). For other references to the store see *Smoke Bellew*, 14, and "The Night-Born," in *The Night-Born*, 23.

13. J. B. Moore, *Skagway*, 119; Spurr, *Yukon Gold Diggings*, 35; "Townsite of Dyea," 4.

14. Hart, *Encyclopedia of Dog Breeds*, 465.

15. Jacobsen, *Alaskan Voyage*, 183 (page references are to reprint edition); Schwatka, *Summer in Alaska*, 128.

16. Jack London, "Husky—The Wolf Dog of the North," 611; "Bâtard," in *Faith of Men*, 210, 212; *White Fang*, 197.

17. Nansen, *Farthest North* 1:271–72.

18. C. K. London, *Jack London* 1:251.

19. Lynch, *Three Years in the Klondike*, 14 (page references are to the reprint edition); Allan, *Gold, Men and Dogs*, 276; Adney, *Klondike Stampede*, 213; Heller, *Sourdough Sagas*, 251–52.

20. Jack London, "The White Silence," in *Son of the Wolf*, 17; "That Spot," in *Lost Face*, 113–14.

21. Darwin, *Expression of the Emotions*, 119–20 (page references are to the reprint edition); Paulsen, *Winterdance*, 137–38.

22. Adney, *Klondike Stampede*, 216–17.

23. M. Bond, "Klondike Diary," 20 October 1897.

24. Adney, *Klondike Stampede*, 24, 182; Coppinger, *World of Sled Dogs*, 40; Lyons, "American Girl's Trip, Part I," 7.

There were other designs. According to Arthur Lincoln Haydon, the sleds used by the Mounted Police were nine feet long and "turned up in front like a Norwegian snowshoe." See Haydon, *Riders of the Plains*, 212.

25. Jack London, *Burning Daylight*, 35.

26. Bramble, *Klondike: A Manual*, 279.

27. Jack London, *White Fang*, 188.

28. See, for example, Flanders, *Sled Dogs*, 68; Butler, *Wild Northland*, 82.

29. Kirk, *Twelve Months*, 192–93.

30. Nansen, *Farthest North* 1:128.

31. Young, *My Dogs*, 72–73.

32. Lynch, *Three Years in the Klondike*, 76; Osborne, "Impressions, Part I," 351.

33. Wells, *Magnificence and Misery*, 187–88.

34. C. K. London, *Jack London* 1:256.

35. Shaw, *Chinook Jargon*, 23; Pike, *Through the Subarctic Forest*, 40. "Sol-leks" and its definition appear in one of London's many typed lists of names. See "Klondike: [names]," Huntington Library, San Marino, California.

36. Young, *My Dogs*, 71, 144–45.

37. *Klondike: Chicago Record's Book*, 331.

38. Young, *My Dogs*, 77; Lynch, *Three Years in the Klondike*, 255.

39. Young, *My Dogs*, 153; Haskell, *Two Years in the Klondike*, 518; Wells, *Magnificence and Misery*, 212; Thomas, *Hidden Life of Dogs*, 102–3.

40. Jack London, "Scorn of Women," in *God of His Fathers*, 270.

41. Haskell, *Two Years in the Klondike*, 79; Price, *From Euston to Klondike*, 81.

42. Mitton, *Klondyke*, 10–11.

43. Thompson, "Diary of Yukon Experiences," 2.

44. Young, *My Dogs*, 43; Paulsen, *Winterdance*, 30–31; and Palmer, *In the Klondike*, 185.

45. Walden, *Dog-Puncher on the Yukon*, 5; Wharton, *Alaska Gold Rush*, 49.

46. Mizner, *Many Mizners*, 100; Parliament of Canada, "Annual Report of the Commissioner, 10 January 1899," *Sessional Papers*, 4.

47. Berry, *Bushes and Berrys*, 49–50.

48. Thompson, "Diary of Yukon Experiences," 3; Medill, *Klondike Diary*, 36.

49. Adney, *Klondike Stampede*, 114; Lyons, "American Girl's Trip, Part II," 21.

50. Phillips, *Alaska-Yukon*, 30; Minter, *White Pass*, 21; Davis, *Sourdough Gold*, 46; Schwatka, *Summer in Alaska*, 84.

51. Haskell, *Two Years in the Klondike*, 86.

52. Satterfield, *Chilkoot Pass*, 22–23.

53. McKeown, *Trail Led North*, 128.

54. Black, *My Seventy Years*, 105–6.

55. Thompson, "Diary of Yukon Exeriences," 3. In a letter to Mabel Applegarth from Dyea on 8 August 1897, London wrote that he would "carry 100 lbs. to the load on good trail & on the worst 75 lbs." See *Letters*, 11. Thompson records they were carrying about one hundred pounds apiece on 20 August. Chilkat packers, however, carried 3,000 pounds of the London party's supplies to the summit from Canyon City. See Thompson, "Diary of Yukon Experiences," 2.

56. Jack London, *Daughter of the Snows*, 39–40.

57. Schwatka, *Summer in Alaska*, 87; Berton, *Klondike*, 251; Dawson, "Narrative of an Exploration," 369 (page references are to the reprint edition); Spurr, *Yukon Gold Diggings*, 57–58.

58. Jack London, *Daughter of the Snows*, 40; *Smoke Bellew*, 28.

59. Coutts, *Yukon: Places and Names*, 20–21. In a letter to the author dated 7 June 1994, Jeff Leer, Alaska Native Language Center at the University of Alaska Fairbanks, translated "Kusooa."

60. Davis, *Sourdough Gold*, 70.

61. Price, *From Euston to Klondike*, 115.

62. Thompson, "Diary of Yukon Experiences," 5.

63. See Butler, *Wild Northland*, 22; Whymper, *Travel and Adventure*, 162.

64. Jack London, "The White Silence," in *Son of the Wolf*, 6. A very similar description appears in *Burning Daylight*, 49–50.

65. Parliament of Canada, "Annual Report of the Commissioner," 2 November 1898, *Sessional Papers*, 54.

66. Walden, *Dog-Puncher on the Yukon*, 35, 37.

67. Schwatka, *Summer in Alaska*, 165.

68. J. B. Moore, *Skagway*, 54.

69. Thompson, "Diary of Yukon Experiences," 6.

70. Jack London, "Through the Rapids," 40–41 (page references are to the reprint edition).

71. Jack London, *Smoke Bellew*, 44–45.

72. Jack London, "From Dawson to the Sea," 46 (page references are to the reprint edition); Schwatka, *Summer in Alaska*, 119; Dall, "Narrative," 30 (page references are to the reprint edition); J. S. Webb, "River Trip," 676.

73. Chase, *Reminiscences*, 177; Jacobsen, *Alaskan Voyage*, 94; Young, *My Dogs*, 177, 211.

74. Marshall Bond, Dawson City, Yukon, to Laura Higgins Bond, Santa Clara, California, 17 November 1897, Western Americana Collection, Beinecke Rare Book and Manuscript Library, Yale University, New Haven, Connecticut.

75. 1. W. Moore, "Report Upon Yukon Country," 499; 2. *Official Guide to the Klondike*, 283; 3. Spurr, *Yukon Gold Diggings*, 155; 4. DeWindt, *Through the Gold-Fields*, 162; 5. Haskell, *Two Years in the Klondike*, 74; 6. Palmer, *In the Klondike*, 41; 7. Edwards, *In to the Yukon*, 185; 8. Dietz, *Mad Rush for Gold*, 87; 9. Garland, *Trail of the Goldseekers*, 104.

76. Young, *My Dogs*, 192; Cody, *Apostle of the North*, 69–70; Jack London, "To Build a Fire," in *Lost Face*, 73.

77. Jack London, "Husky," 611; Young, *My Dogs*, 176.

78. Davydov, *Two Voyages*, 216 (page references are to reprint edition).

79. D. M. Hamilton, *"Tools of My Trade,"* 127; Fremont, *Memoirs of My Life* 1:98.

80. Herbert P. Williams, Macmillan Company, to Jack London, 26 June 1903, Huntington Library, San Marino, California. While London was in the Klondike, the *San Francisco Chronicle* published a story similar to the one he must have sent to Williams. With the headline "Wild Dogs at Large in a St. Louis Park," the account mentions a "tribe of wild and vicious mastiffs" that had "frequently been seen by wanderers." See "Wild Dogs at Large in St. Louis Park," *San Francisco Chronicle*, 28 August 1897.

81. Morris, *Dogwatching*, 21–22.

82. J. S. Webb, "River Trip," 672; *Skaguay News*, 30 December 1898.

III. "THE DOMINANT PRIMORDIAL BEAST"

1. Coutts, *Yukon: Places and Names*, 151; Schwatka, *Summer in Alaska*, 178. In a letter to the author on 12 April 1994, Frederica de Laguna, expert on American Indians in the North, wrote that the lake in Southern Tutchone Athabaskan is called "Flat Place Lake."

2. Service, "The Cremation of Sam McGee," in *Spell of the Yukon*, 61.

3. Thompson, "Diary of Yukon Experiences," 6.

4. Addison Clark Dyer, "Diary," 98; Schwatka, *Summer in Alaska*, 183; Walden, *Dog-Puncher on the Yukon*, 23; Magee, "To Klondike by River and Lake," 68; Thompson, "Diary of Yukon Experiences," 7.

5. Schwatka, "Great River, II," 748; Wilson, *Guide to the Yukon Gold Fields*, 31.

6. Young, *My Dogs*, 53.

7. Ibid., 54.

8. Ibid., 178.

9. C. K. London, *Jack London* 1:341. See, for example, Louis Savoy in "To the Man on Trail," in *Son of the Wolf*, 104, and French Louis in *Burning Daylight*, 2.

10. Spurr, *Yukon Gold Diggings*, 100; McKeown, *Trail Led North*, 162; Price, *From Euston to Klondike*, 143.

11. Parliament of Canada, "Appendix A, Superintendent Wood," 41.

12. Haskell, *Two Years in the Klondike*, 133; Osborne, "Impressions, Part II," 446.

13. Parliament of Canada, "Appendix A, Superintendent Wood," 54.

14. M. Bond, "Klondike Rush," 31–32; Hildebrand, *Reading the River*, 23.

15. Jack London, *Daughter of the Snows*, 304; additional references to the American Indians at Laberge are in "The Wit of Porportuk," in *Lost Face*, 215, and in *Burning Daylight*, 46.

16. Young, *My Dogs*, 55–58.

17. Hayne, *Pioneers of the Klondike*, 108; *All About Gold Fields*, 49.

18. Ingersoll, *Gold Fields of the Klondike*, 97.

19. Jack London, *Smoke Bellew*, 203–5; see also *White Fang*, 179; *The Cruise of the Dazzler*, 29–43; *The People of the Abyss*, 48; *The Iron Heel*, 326–27; and *The Scarlet Plague*, 99, for further instances of hungry people ignoring moral conventions and legal punctilios to obtain food.

20. Grinnell, *Gold Hunting in Alaska*, 45 (page references are to the reprint edition); Young, *My Dogs*, 57.

21. Jesse, *Anecdotes of Dogs*, 300.

22. Jacobsen, *Alaskan Voyage*, 94; Young, *By Canoe and Dog-Train*, 92; Whymper, *Travel and Adventure*, 151; Nansen, *Farthest North* 2:245; Ogilvie, *Early Days on the Yukon*, 147 (page references are to reprint edition); Hayne, *Pioneers of the Klondike*, 107–8; Haskell, *Two Years in the Klondike*, 165–66; Ingersoll, *Gold Fields of the Klondike*, 97; Grinnell, *Gold Hunting in Alaska*, 45.

23. Greely, *Three Years of Arctic Service* 2:18; A. D. Cameron, *New North*, 105 (page references are to the reprint edition).

24. Coutts, *Yukon: Places and Names*, 76–78. Dawson replaced Joseph Tyrrell—of Barrens expedition fame—as head of the Geological Survey of Canada.

25. Roberts, *Tramp to the Klondike*, 35; DeWindt, "Klondike Gold Fields," 307; Page, *Wild Horses and Gold*, 104

26. J. S. Webb, "River Trip," 683–84.

27. Parliament of Canada, "Annual Report, Part III, Steele," 17.

28. Jack London, "Dawson to the Sea," 42.

29. Schwatka, "Great River, I," 185.

30. Ibid., 185–86; Jack London, "Trust," in *Lost Face*, 40–41.

31. Haskell, *Two Years in the Klondike*, 510, 515–16.

32. Jack London, "The One Thousand Dozen," in *Faith of Men*, 161–62; see also "Grit of Women," in *God of His Fathers*, 172.

33. Thompson, "Diary of Yukon Experiences," 8.

34. Walden, *Dog-Puncher on the Yukon*, 81.

35. *Boater's Guide*, 24; Coutts, *Yukon: Places and Names*, 264.

36. Palmer, *In the Klondike*, 27; Thompson, "Diary of Yukon Experiences," 8.

37. Satterfield, *Exploring the Yukon River*, 64–80.

38. Coutts, *Yukon: Places and Names*, 23–24; Mathews, *Yukon*, 301; L. Berton, *I Married the Klondike*, 210.

39. P. Berton, *Drifting Home*, 95; M. Bond, "Klondike Diary," 70; *Daily Alaskan*, 23 July 1898.

40. Schwatka, *Summer in Alaska*, 195; Coutts, *Yukon: Places and Names*, 98.

41. Thompson, "Diary of Yukon Experiences," 9.

42. Jack London, *Scorn of Women*, 87.

43. Newman, *Caesars*, 45 (page references are to reprint edition); Harris, *Alaska*, 166.

44. Young, *My Dogs*, 191, 193.

45. Jack London, "An Odyssey of the North," in *Son of the Wolf*, 242; "A Northland Miracle," 814; and *Scorn of Women*, 7.

46. Newman, *Caesars*, 341–42, 342n.

47. Coutts, *Yukon: Places and Names*, 210.

48. Schwatka, *Summer in Alaska*, 203; Thompson, "Diary of Yukon Experiences," 9.

49. Thomas, *Hidden Life of Dogs*, 30, 70.

50. Young, *My Dogs*, 153.

51. Newman, *Caesars*, 45; Young, *By Canoe and Dog Train*, 96.

52. Young, *My Dogs*, 20–21; Mandelbaum, *Plains Cree*, 198.

53. Adney, *Klondike Stampede*, 210; Jack London, "The Wife of a King," in *Son of the Wolf*, 179.

54. Heilprin, *Alaska and the Klondike*, 79.

55. Jack London, *Burning Daylight*, 42; *Smoke Bellew*, 330; "A Daughter of the Aurora," in *God of His Fathers*, 220; *A Daughter of the Snows*, 187–88.

56. Phillips, *Alaska-Yukon*, 145; Coutts, *Yukon: Places and Names*, 292; M. Webb, *Last Frontier*, 2.

57. Walker, *Jack London and the Klondike*, 106.

58. Macleod, *North-West Mounted Police*, 11; Parliament of Canada, "Annual Report, Appendix LL, Constantine," 310.

59. Jack London, "The Man with the Gash," in *God of His Fathers*, 222–23; "To Build a Fire," in *Lost Face*, 64.

60. Parliament of Canada, "Annual Report, Appendix LL, Constantine," 308–9.

61. John McPhee, *Coming into the Country*, 183; Jack London, "The Story of Jees Uck," in *Faith of Men*, 243.

62. Morrison, *Showing the Flag*, 187.

63. M. Webb, *Last Frontier*, 88.

64. Haydon, *Riders of the Plains*, 191; Parliament of Canada, "Annual Report of the Commissioner of the North-west Mounted Police, 1898," *Sessional Papers*, 17.

65. Haydon, *Riders of the Plains*, 227; M. Webb, *Last Frontier*, 168–69; *Bits and Pieces* 2:105.

66. Jack London, "The League of Old Men," in *Children of the Frost*, 238–39.

67. H. Steele, *Policing the Arctic*, 55; Adney, *Klondike Stampede*, 358; *Daily Alaskan*, 11 July 1898.

68. Mathews, *Yukon*, 301; Thompson, "Diary of Yukon Experiences," 11.

69. Coutts, *Yukon: Places and Names*, 259; DeWindt, *Through the Gold-Fields*, 74; Mathews, *Yukon*, 301; Hildebrand, *Reading the River*, 21; J. B. Moore, *Skagway*, 197.

70. Pizer, Notes to *The Call of the Wild*, 101.

71. Coutts, *Yukon: Places and Names*, 238.

72. *Audubon Field Guide to Mammals*, 256.

73. Parliament of Canada, "Annual Report, 1898," 11; *Skaguay News*, 9 December 1898. By 1903 there was a NWMP detachment at Takhini. The last sled dog used by the RCMP—"Rex"—died in 1972 and, preserved and mounted, is on display at the RCMP Museum at Regina, Saskatchewan (*Bits and Pieces*, 150).

74. Young, *My Dogs*, 41; Mandelbaum, *Plains Cree*, 197; Amundsen, *North West Passage* 2:239.

75. Jesse, *Anecdotes of Dogs*, 259.

76. Darwin, *Expression of the Emotions*, 83.

77. Jack London, "The Law of Life," in *Children of the Frost*, 48.

IV. "WHO HAS WON TO MASTERSHIP"

1. Young, *My Dogs*, 168–70.

2. Jack London, "Bâtard," in *Faith of Men*, 231; "Where the Trail Forks," in *God of His Fathers*, 205; Krause, *Tlingit-Indians*, 243 (page references are to reprint edition); Davydov, *Two Voyages*, 236. In a letter to the author on 12 April 1994, Tlingit expert Frederica de Laguna confirmed that she had heard Tlingit people say "chook" to a "troublesome dog."

3. Young, *My Dogs*, 25.

4. Schwatka, *Along Alaska's Great River*, 195; Price, *From Euston to Klondike*, 155; M. Webb, *Last Frontier*, 214; Coutts, *Yukon: Places and Names*, 223; P. Berton, *Drifting Home*, 97.

5. Young, *My Dogs*, 19. Daniel Williams Harmon's glossary of Cree confirms Young; see Harmon, *Journal of Voyages*, 341. In *Two Voyages*, Davydov records *tyk* as the Tlingit word for ice. See page 237. In separate letters to the author on 12 April 1994 and 7 June 1994, respectively, Frederica de Laguna and Jeff Leer, University of Alaska Fairbanks, confirmed that *t'eex'* is Tlingit for ice.

6. Robinson, *Weather and Climate*, 129; Hayne, *Pioneers of the Klondike*, 177; Adney, *Klondike Stampede*, 203–4.

7. Phillips, *Alaska-Yukon*, 141; Stanley, *Mile of Gold*, 39; Satterfield, *Exploring the Yukon River*, 57.

8. McKeown, *Trail Led North*, 156; Davis, *Sourdough Gold*, 76–77.

9. Schwatka, *Summer in Alaska*, 166; Ingersoll, *Golden Alaska*, 52; P. Berton, *Klondike*, 272.

10. Osborne, "Impressions, Parts III and IV," 44.

11. Thompson, "Diary of Yukon Experiences," 6; Jack London, "Through the Rapids," 41–42. London's most thorough fictional description of shooting the Whitehorse is in *Smoke Bellew*, 48–53.

12. Stone, *Sailor on Horseback*, 77 (page references are to the reprint edition).

13. Winslow, *Big Pan-Out*, 135; Garst, *Jack London: Magnet for Adventure*, 101–2; P. Berton, introduction to *The Call of the Wild*, x.

14. "'Dick' Heath Breaks a Record," undated article from the *San Francisco Bulletin*, in Jack London, "Klondike" file, Huntington Library, San Marino, California.

15. Coutts, *Yukon: Places and Names*, 284–85.

16. Satterfield, *Exploring the Yukon River*, 22–23; Bruce, *Alaska*, 129; Schwatka, *Summer in Alaska*, 408–9.

17. Coutts, *Yukon: Places and Names*, 178; Kirk, *Twelve Months*, 69.

18. Phillips, *Alaska-Yukon*, 127; Lyons, "American Girl's Trip, Part III, 37.

19. Phillips, *Alaska-Yukon*, 141; Minter, *White Pass*, 25; W. Moore, "Yukon Country," 495.

20. Osborne, "Impressions, Part I," 350, 353.

21. Parliament of Canada, "Annual Report, 1898; Appendix F," *Sessional Papers*, 80.

22. Wells, *Magnificence and Misery*, 50.

23. Adney, *Klondike Stampede*, 83–84.

24. Wells, *Magnificence and Misery*, 68; McKeown, *Trail Led North*, 105; Walden, *Dog-Puncher on the Yukon*, 134.

25. Jack London, "Which Make Men Remember," in *God of His Fathers*, 79–80.

26. Cohen, *White Pass and Yukon Route*, 19, 104.

27. Phillips, *Alaska-Yukon*, 122.

28. C. Cameron, *Cheechako*, 52.

29. McLain, *Alaska and the Klondike*, 22.

30. "Spell It with a 'U,'" *Skaguay News*, 14 October 1898.

31. Minter, *White Pass*, 31, 74.

32. Wells, *Magnificence and Misery*, 31; McKeown, *Trail Led North*, 107.

33. *Skaguay News*, 15 October 1897.

34. Heilprin, *Alaska and the Klondike*, 165; Kirk, *Twelve Months*, 201; *Daily Alaskan*, 24 March 1899; Adney, *Klondike Stampede*, 463.

35. Jack London, "The Other Animals," in *Revolution and Other Essays*, 251.

36. Adney, *Klondike Stampede*, 47; Osborne, "Impressions, Part I," 347; Price, *From Euston to Klondike*, 71; Munn, *Prairie Trails*, 86; Parliament of Canada, "Annual Report, Part III, Steele," 4.

37. *Skaguay News*, 5 November 1897.

38. *Dyea Trail*, 11 March 1898.

39. "Lawlessness in Alaska," *New York Times*, 19 February 1898.

40. For an excellent account of these events, see P. Berton, *Klondike*, 320–49.

41. Thompson, "Diary of Yukon Experiences," 1.

42. Walker, *Jack London and the Klondike*, 148.

43. Jack London, *Burning Daylight*, 42.

44. Jack London, "Where the Trail Forks," in *God of His Fathers*, 186.

45. Butler, *Unconscious Memory*, 82.

46. This occasioned more charges of plagiarism from Stanley Waterloo, author of *The Story of Ab: A Tale of the Time of the Cave Man* (1897). London and Waterloo exchanged sharp letters on the subject. See *Letters*, 623–25.

47. Jack London, "The White Silence," in *Son of the Wolf*, 9; Ingersoll, *Gold Fields of the Klondike*, 91–92; Nansen, *Farthest North* 2:274–75.

48. Phillips, *Alaska-Yukon*, 27; W. B. Hamilton, *Canadian Place Names*, 46.

49. Chase, *Reminiscences*, 114; Heilprin, *Alaska and the Klondike*, 41; Dawson, "Narrative of an Exploration," 360; C. Cameron, *Cheechako*, 103.

50. Thompson, "Diary of Yukon Experiences," 8.

V. "THE TOIL OF TRACE AND TRAIL"

1. Clifford, *Skagway Story*, 36, 37; "Dyea's Postal Business," *New York Times*, 10 March 1898; *Skaguay News*, 16 September 1898.

2. Adney, *Klondike Stampede*, 357; "Mails for the Klondike," *New York Times*, 20 August 1897; *Bits and Pieces*, 36. Kirk disagrees slightly with Adney, citing 28 February as the day the first mail arrived. See Kirk, *Twelve Months*, 106–7.

3. Morgan, *God's Loaded Dice*, 143.

4. *Klondike: Chicago Record's Book*, 204; Tuttle, *Golden North*, 228.

5. Newman, *Company of Adventurers*, xxii.

6. Jack London, "Finis," in *Turtles of Tasman*, 214.

7. *Dyea Trail*, 14 May 1898; Women in the Klondike," *Klondike News* (Dawson City, Yukon), 1 April 1898; Mayer, *Klondike Women*, 4.

8. "Women for the Klondike," *New York Times*, 29 August 1897; Cahoon, "Women Sail for the Klondike,"440–41.

9. *Dyea Trail*, 21 May 1898; Wells, *Magnificence and Misery*, 12.

10. "Boom in the Trade for All Kinds of Arms," *San Francisco Chronicle*, 7 August 1897.

11. Wells, *Magnificence and Misery*, 22; *Dyea Trail*, 12 March 1898.

12. Heilprin, *Alaska and the Klondike*, 5; C. Cameron, *Cheechako*, 54; Spude, *Skagway, District of Alaska*, 77.

13. Jack London, *White Fang*, 271–78.

14. DeWindt, "Klondike Gold Fields," 306; H. Steele, *Policing the Arctic*, 17.

15. Buder, *Pullman*, 10–11; Morel, *Pullman*, 21–22; *Official Guide to the Klondike*, 237.

16. Winslow, *Big Pan-Out*, 62; Margeson, *Experiences of Gold Hunters*, 22–24.

17. Mizner, *Many Mizners*, 122; Walden, *Dog-Puncher on the Yukon*, 7.

18. Jack London, *Burning Daylight*, 40–41.

19. Mizner, *Many Mizners*, 112.

20. P. Berton, *Klondike*, 277.

21. Parliament of Canada, "Annual Report of the Department of Indian Affairs, 1898," *Sessional Papers*, 427; Charlie [?], Yukon Territory, to Mary [?], 16 June 1898, Western Americana Collection, Beinecke Rare Book and Manuscript Library, New Haven, Connecticut.

22. Wells, *Magnificence and Misery*, 186.

23. P. Berton, *Klondike*, 70; Parliament of Canada, "Annual Report, Appendix LL, Constantine," 307; Satterfield, *Exploring the Yukon River*, 87.

24. M. Bond, "Klondike Diary," 26 September 1897; Marshall Bond, to Laura Higgins Bond, 11 October 1897, Western Americana Collection, Beinecke Rare Book and Manuscript Library, Yale University, New Haven, Connecticut.

25. Adney, *Klondike Stampede*, 168; Thompson, "Diary of Yukon Experiences," 9.

26. Jack London, "The One Thousand Dozen," in *Faith of Men*, 165.

27. Black, *My Seventy Years*, 110.

28. Canada, Department of Transport, *Break-Up and Freeze-Up*, 29. These dates are confirmed by Stephens, Fountain, and Osterkamp, *Break-Up Dates*.

29. Black, *My Seventy Years*, 143.

30. Jack London, "At the Rainbow's End," in *God of His Fathers*, 251. In *A Daughter of the Snows*, London provides his most detailed account—nearly twenty pages in length—of the break-up at Split-Up Island, near the confluence of the Yukon and the Stewart, the spot where he himself had witnessed the event in the spring of 1898. See *A Daughter of the Snows*, 236–57.

31. Jack London, "A Northland Miracle," 813–14.

32. Mathews, *Yukon*, 301; Coutts, *Yukon: Places and Names*, 286; Hildebrand, *Reading the River*, 52; W. Moore, "Yukon Country," 497; Campbell, *Two Journals*, 110.

33. Andrews, *Alaska*, 15; Osborne, "Impressions, Parts III and IV," 47; Hildebrand, *Reading the River*, 52.

34. Thompson, "Diary of Yukon Experiences," 10.

35. Walden, *Dog-Puncher on the Yukon*, 79–81.

36. Jack London, "At the Rainbow's End," in *God of His Fathers*, 238–41.

37. Walden, *Dog-Puncher on the Yukon*, 134.

38. Margeson, *Gold Hunters*, 78; Nansen, *Farthest North* 2:148.

39. Young, *My Dogs*, 161–62.

40. Morgan, *God's Loaded Dice*, 50–51.

41. Parliament of Canada, "Annual Report; Appendix A, Wood, 56; "Annual Report, 1899; Part II: Yukon," *Sessional Papers*, 14.

42. *Dyea Press*, 7 November 1898; McKeown, *Trail Led North*, 147.

43. Jack London, "The End of the Story," in *Turtles of Tasman*, 236.

VI. "FOR THE LOVE OF A MAN"

1. Jack London, *Smoke Bellew*, 89–90.

2. Parliament of Canada, "Annual Report of the Commissioner," 23; "Appendix F, Strickland," 82; "Annual Report, Part II: Yukon," 15.

3. *Klondike: Graham's Guide*, 29.

4. Jack London, "To Build a Fire," in *Lost Face*, 78; *Smoke Bellew*, 90.

5. Jack London, "The Wife of a King," in *Son of the Wolf*, 167; *Smoke Bellew*, 93–94.

6. Kirk, *Twelve Months*, 102; Walden, *Dog-Puncher on the Yukon*, 181; *Klondike: Chicago Record's Book*, 32.

7. C. K. London, *Jack London* 1:243; Walker, *Jack London and the Klondike*, 161. In a 1913 letter another Yukon companion, Everett Barton, reminded London of all the difficulties he had had in this logging enterprise. See Everett Barton to Jack London, 14 May 1913, Huntington Library, San Marino, California.

8. Noel, *Footloose in Arcadia*, 246; Jensen, "Jack London at Stewart River," 4; C. K. London, *Jack London* 1:236.

9. See 1897 numbers of *Leslie's Illustrated Weekly*: 20 May, 27 May, 3 June, 10 June, 17 June, 21 October, and 9 December.

10. *A Wolf in Your Living Room*; Young, *My Dogs*, 181.

11. Jack London, "The Unexpected," in *Love of Life*, 127.

12. Walden, *Dog-Puncher on the Yukon*, 184; Thompson, "Diary of Yukon Experiences," 11.

13. Phillips, *Alaska-Yukon*, 128; Schwatka, *Summer in Alaska*, 301; Mathews, *Yukon*, 301.

14. J. S. Webb, "River Trip," 678.

15. *To the Klondike*, 32.

16. C. K. London, *Jack London* 1:251; Jack London, "The Wit of Porportuk," in *Lost Face*, 215; *Burning Daylight*, 22.

17. Hildebrand, *Reading the River*, 105; M. Webb, *Last Frontier*, 89–90; P. Berton, *Klondike*, 29.

18. Harris, *Alaska*, 215; Fulcomer, "Three R's at Circle City," 223.

19. Haskell, *Two Years in the Klondike*, 162.

20. DeWindt, "Klondike Gold Fields," 307.

21. P. Berton, *Klondike*, 308–9; Lynch, *Three Years in the Klondike*, 229; Wharton, *Alaska Gold Rush*, 169.

22. C. K. London, *Jack London* 1:249.

23. U.S. Bureau of the Census, *1990 Census*, 8.

24. J. S. Webb, "River Trip," 681; P. Berton, *Klondike*, 148; Stanley, *Mile of Gold*, 60. The most notable exception to this practice was "Nigger" Jim Daugherty, a white man with a deep Southern accent who earned his nickname with his drawl and his black-face performances in Dawson City minstrel shows. See Gates, *Gold at Fortymile Creek*, 126.

25. Hamlin, *Old Times on the Yukon*, 24.

26. Amundsen, *North West Passage* 2:143–44; *Klondike: Chicago Record's Book*, 323.

27. Jack London, "To Build a Fire," in *Lost Face*, 65; *Scorn of Women*, 6.

28. Ingersoll, *Gold Fields of the Klondike*, 101; Fulcomer, "Three R's at Circle City," 226; Walden, *Dog-Puncher on the Yukon*, 45; Hamlin, *Old Times on the Yukon*, 2.

29. Winslow, *Big Pan-Out*, 154; Parliament of Canada, "Annual Report, Part III, Steele," 9.

30. Jack London, "Bâtard," in *Faith of Men*, 206.

31. P. Berton, *Klondike*, 22.

32. *Klondike: Chicago Record's Book*, 324.

33. Steffens, "Life in the Klondike Gold Fields," 964–65; M. Webb, *Last Frontier*, 95.

34. Mizner, *Many Mizners*, 101–06.

35. Jack London, *A Daughter of the Snows*, 280–91.

36. M. Webb, *Last Frontier*, 8, 46, 319n.

37. Jesse, *Anecdotes of Dogs*, 135.

38. "A Noble Dog Tries to Save His Master," *San Francisco Chronicle*, 2 August 1897; "Blind Man Saved by Dog," *New York Times*, 1 August 1897.

39. Jack London, *White Fang*, 309–13, 319–21; *Jerry of the Islands*, 317–18; *Michael, Brother of Jerry*, 335–42.

40. Kirk, *Twelve Months*, 211–12.

41. Schwatka, *Summer in Alaska*, 140–41; Thompson, "Diary of Yukon Experiences," 5.

42. Coutts, *Yukon: Places and Names*, 103–4; Mathews, *Yukon*, 301.

43. W. Moore, "Yukon Country," 497; Coutts, *Yukon: Places and Names*, 103–4.

44. DeWindt, *Through the Gold-Fields*, 139; Lyons, "American Girl's Trip, Part V," 69.

45. Gates, *Gold at Fortymile Creek*, 38; Sola, *Klondyke: Truth and Facts*, 28.

46. C. K. London, *Jack London* 1:249.

47. Price, *From Euston to Klondike*, 65–66.

48. Muir, *Travels in Alaska*, 72–74 (page references are to reprint edition).

49. C. K. London, *Jack London* 1:253.

50. Emmons, *Tlingit Indians*, 196, 195.

51. Kirk, *Twelve Months*, 90; Secretan, *To Klondyke and Back*, 111.

52. Jack London, *Smoke Bellew*, 212–13.

53. Coutts, *Yukon: Places and Names*, 91.

54. Phillips, *Alaska-Yukon*, 45; P. Berton, *Klondike*, 54.

55. P. Berton, *Klondike*, 54, 358–75, 173; Adney, *Klondike Stampede*, 346.

56. *Klondike Nugget*, 12 November 1898; Canada, North-west Territories, Retail Sale Permit No. 6.

57. Coppinger, *World of Sled Dogs*, 284; M. Bond, "Klondike Diary," 31 October 1897.

58. Jack London, "Husky," 611.

59. Coutts, *Yukon: Places and Names*, 27.

60. Jack London, *Burning Daylight*, 112.

61. Coolidge, *Klondike and the Yukon Country*, 66.

62. C. K. London, *Jack London* 2:206.

63. Black, *My Seventy Years*, 135.

64. Ingersoll, *Golden Alaska*, 87; Orth, *Alaska Place Names*, 628; Schwatka, *Along Alaska's Great River*, 827.

65. P. Berton, *Klondike*, 40, 43, 406; *Bits and Pieces*, 19; Coutts, *Yukon: Places and Names*, 242–43.

66. Winslow, *Big Pan-Out*, 162; Jack London, "The Economics of the Klondike," *Review of Reviews* 21 (January 1900): 71. London clipped and saved a newspaper article about the Skookum

strikes. See Jack London, "Klondike" clipping file, "God Covers the Ground Around Skookum Gulch," Huntington Library, San Marino, California.

67. Young, *My Dogs*, 104.

VII. "THE SOUNDING OF THE CALL"

1. P. Berton, *Klondike*, 25.

2. Jack London, "In a Far Country," in *Son of the Wolf*, 77; "A Northland Miracle," 813. Similar passages occur in London's early essay "Gold Hunters of the North," in *Revolution*, 184; "Too Much Gold," in *Faith of Men*, 119; "The Night-Born," in *Night-Born*, 21; and *Smoke Bellew*, 119–20.

3. Probert, *Lost Mines and Buried Treasure*; Penfield, *Directory of Buried or Sunken Treasures*; Jack London, "Klondike" clipping file, Huntington Library, San Marino, California. See also Hult, *Lost Mines and Treasures*, 63–76, and Perrin, *Explorers Ltd. Guide to Lost Treasure*, 117–18.

4. Thompson, "Diary of Yukon Experiences," 10; Kingman, *Chronology*, 18; North, *Jack London's Cabin*.

5. Helen Kerfoot (Executive Secretary, Secretariat for Geographical Names, Ottawa, Ontario), to Daniel Dyer, 10 June 1993; Campbell, *Two Journals*, 86; Coutts, *Yukon: Places and Names*, 251; Mathews, *Yukon*, 301; Thompson, "Diary of Yukon Experiences," 10. For a map showing the exact location of London's camp, see D. Hamilton, *"Tools of My Trade,"* 9.

6. Coutts, *Yukon: Places and Names*, 181; M. Webb, *Last Frontier*, 59–60; C. K. London, *Jack London* 1:250.

7. Coutts, *Yukon: Places and Names*, 174–75; W. Moore, "Report Upon Yukon Country," 497; J. S. Webb, "River Trip," 683; P. Berton, *Klondike*, 12.

8. Bruce, *Alaska*, 49; "Gold Hunters of the North," in *Revolution*, 187.

9. Dall, "Alaska," 18.

10. Dyer, "Diary," 123.

11. Heilprin, *Alaska and the Klondike*, 189–90; McKeown, *Trail Led North*, 200.

12. Jack London, *Burning Daylight*, 70. A recent history of the region, Michael Gates's *Gold at Fortymile Creek*, claims that Jack McQuesten and his party of prospectors first employed the technique in 1882. See page 19 in Gates.

13. *Klondike: Graham's Guide*, 29.

14. Bramble, *Klondike: A Manual*, 207.

15. Jack London, *Burning Daylight*, 99. Immediately after reading "All-Gold Cañon," Marshall Bond wrote to London praising him for "such a perfect story." Especially did Bond—a mining

expert—appreciate the accuracy of the mining detail: "I would have detected a single false note as surely as a sailor would a misplaced line aboard his ship," wrote Bond. Marshall Bond, to Jack London, 27 October 1905, Huntington Library, San Marino, California.

16. Harmon, *Journal of Voyages*, 290; W. Moore, "Report Upon Yukon Country," 499.

17. Evans, "Story of the Yukon Valley," 339; Hayne, *Pioneers of the Klondike*, 52–53.

18. Garland, *Trail of the Goldseekers*, 84; Schwatka, *Along Alaska's Great River*, 125.

19. Muir, *Travels in Alaska*, 30, 246.

20. Williams and Williams, *Field Guide to Orchids*; Muir, *Travels in Alaska*, 224; Garland, *Trail of the Goldseekers*, 83.

21. Among some notes for a possible episode called "Chilcoot Pass," London placed an unidentified clipping from a newspaper. He underlined it as follows: "No sooner had we climbed the gently sloping banks than we *spied great bunches of red raspberries hang*ing, as thickly as they could cluster on the bushes." See Jack London, "Chilcoot Pass [note for episode]," Huntington Library, San Marino, California.

22. Schwatka, *Summer in Alaska*, 129; Gooding, "The Trade Guns of the Hudson's Bay Company," 10–17. Gooding lists ninety different manfacturers and gunsmiths who supplied muskets, in barrel lengths ranging from three to five feet, to HBC between 1674 and 1875; the annual orders throughout the eighteenth century ranged from several hundred to a high of 990 in 1731. In one of his notebooks, London quips that HBC stands for "Here Before Christ." See Jack London, "Notebook, 1898," Huntington Library, San Marino, California.

23. MacKay, *Honourable Company*, 85–86.

24. Munn, *Prairie Trails*, 55; Stanley, *Mile of Gold*, 57; Newman, *Empire of the Bay*, 62.

25. Schwatka, *Summer in Alaska*, 199–200.

26. *Audubon Field Guide to Mammals*, 539–42.

27. See, for example, Sinclair, *Jack*, 92, and Upton, "Wolf in London's Mirror," 111–18; reprint, *Casebook*, 193–201.

28. Young, *My Dogs*, 272–73; Young, *By Canoe and Dog-Train*, 92.

29. Lopez, *Of Wolves and Men*, 69.

30. Parliament of Canada, "Annual Report, Appendix A, Wood," 42; Dawson, "Narrative of an Exploration," 260.

31. In order, these quotations are from Jacobsen, *Alaskan Voyage*, 91; Hamlin, *Old Times on the Yukon*, 1; A. D. Cameron, *New North*, 48; Lynch, *Three Years in the Klondike*, 7–8; Roberts, *Tramp to the Klondike*, 31; Sola, *Klondyke: Truth and Facts*, 80; Spurr, *Yukon Gold Diggings*, 83; Dall, "Narrative," 70; Ibid., 100; C. Cameron, *Cheechako*, 155; Haskell, *Two Years in the Klondike*, 155; Ibid., 156; Wells, *Magnificence and Misery*, 221; *Klondike: Chicago Record's Book*, 284; Osborne, "Impressions, Parts III and IV," 50.

32. Dietz, *Mad Rush for Gold*, 172; McKeown, *Trail Led North*, 181.

33. DeWindt, "Klondike Gold Fields," 306–7; Price, *From Euston to Klondike*, 158–59.

34. Schwatka, "Great River of Alaska, I," 747.

35. C. K. London, *Jack London* 1:253–54.

36. *Audubon Field Guide to Mammals*, 579–81; Parliament of Canada, "Annual Report, Appendix A, Wood," 42.

37. Muir, *Travels in Alaska*, 288–89; Dietz, *Mad Rush for Gold*, 107.

38. *Audubon Field Guide to Mammals*, 656–58; Parliament of Canada, "Annual Report, Appendix A, Wood," 42; Kirk, *Twelve Months*, 246.

39. D. Morris, *Dogwatching*, 63; Lopez, *Of Wolves and Men*, 56.

40. Mandelbaum, *Plains Cree*, 197; Walden, *Dog-Puncher on the Yukon*, 73.

41. D. Morris, *Dogwatching*, 124; Thomas, *Hidden Life of Dogs*, 7–10.

42. Beryl C. Gillespie, Iowa City, Iowa, to Daniel Dyer, 8 September 1992.

43. J. W. Tyrrell, *Across the Sub-Arctics of Canada*, 77; Pike, *Through the Subarctic Forest*, 139; Stanley, *Mile of Gold*, 56–57. Haskell wrote about the same group—though he did not name them. He called them "very savage." See Haskell, *Two Years in the Klondike*, 146–47. The Mahoneys may be the Tutchone Indians, who did live along the Stewart River.

44. *Dyea Trail*, August 1897 (special monthly edition).

45. Jack London, "The One Thousand Dozen," in *Faith of Men*, 159; *A Daughter of the Snows*, 26; Schwatka, *Summer in Alaska*, 49; Dall, *Tribes of the Extreme Northwest*, 37. Dall assailed London's portrayal of American Indians in a letter to the editor of the *New York Times Saturday Review of Books and Art*, 6 December 1902. London's creations lack "verisimilitude," complained Dall; they are "unlike any Indians whatsoever . . . preposterous creatures. . . ." See *Letters*, 328–30, for London's response, the general nature of which is that "[w]e were born into the world with different eyes, that is all, & we use them differently."

46. *Letters*, 11; Thompson, "Diary of Yukon Expeiences," 10.

47. Jack London, "From Dawson to the Sea," 47.

48. Ibid., 45.

49. Emmons, *Tlingit Indians*, 337, 340.

50. Osborne, "Impressions, Parts V and VI," 150.

51. Brian Vesey-Fitzgerald notes that Aristotle referred to wolf-dog crosses in the fourth century B.C. Morris reports there is no "difficulty in crossing domestic dogs with wild wolves"; and Lopez writes that "[d]ispersing wolves and feral dogs may occasionally breed and establish hybrid packs." See Vesey-Fitzgerald, *Domestic Dog*, 10; D. Morris, *Dogwatching*, 9; Lopez, *Of Wolves and Men*, 69.

52. Jack London, "Where the Trail Forks," in *God of His Fathers*, 209.

53. Clayton, "The Ghost Dog," 158; reprint, *Casebook*, 173. For the text of the story, see Nelson, "Eskimo about Bering Strait," 488.

54. Jack London, *Michael, Brother of Jerry*, 338.

55. Mackenzie, *Voyage from Montreal*, 41 (page references are to the reprint edition).

56. Jacobsen, *Alaskan Voyage*, 186; Jack London, *Jerry of the Islands*, 220–21. This howling-over-the-dead phenomenon occasionally occurs in other London tales. After its masters were killed in "Where the Trail Forks," Shep "all the night long and a day . . . wailed the dead." See *God of His Fathers*, 209. And in "To Build a Fire," after the man had finally lost his struggle to survive, the dog "crept close to the man and caught the scent of death. This made the animal bristle and back away. A little longer it delayed, howling under the stars that leaped and danced and shone brightly in the cold sky." See *Lost Face*, 98.

Bibliography

ABBREVIATIONS:

TL	Typewritten Letter
TMs	Typewritten Manuscript
TLS	Typewritten Letter Signed
ALS	Autograph Letter Signed
AMs	Autograph Manuscript
AMsS	Autograph Manuscript Signed

I. BY JACK LONDON

Burning Daylight. New York: Macmillan, 1910.

The Call of the Wild. New York: Macmillan, 1903.

The Call of the Wild. Adapted by Olive Price. New York: Grosset and Dunlap, 1961.

The Call of the Wild. Adapted by Mitsu Yamomoto. New York: Waldman Publishing, 1989.

"The Call of the Wild." In *Explorations in Literature*, 576–639. Glenview, Ill.: Scott, Foresman, 1991.

"Chased by the Trail." *Youth's Companion*, 26 September 1907, 445–46.

"Chilcoot Pass [note for episode]." AMs. Item JL 523. Huntington Library, San Marino, Calif.

Children of the Frost. New York: Macmillan, 1902.

The Cruise of the Dazzler. New York: Century, 1902.

A Daughter of the Snows. Philadelphia: J. B. Lippincott, 1902.

"The Economics of the Klondike." *Review of Reviews* 21 (January 1900): 70–74.

"The End of the Story." In *The Turtles of Tasman*, 221–65. New York: Macmillan, 1916.

The Faith of Men and Other Stories. New York: Macmillan, 1904.

"Finis." In *The Turtles of Tasman*, 184–220. New York: Macmillan, 1916.

"From Dawson to the Sea," *Buffalo Express*, 4 June 1899. Reprint. *Jack London's Tales of Adventure*. Edited by Irving Shepard, 42–49. Garden City, N.Y.: Hanover House, 1956.

"The 'Fuzziness' of Hoockla-Heen." *Youth's Companion*, 3 July 1902, 333–34.

The God of His Fathers and Other Stories. New York: McClure, Phillips, 1901.

"The Gold Hunters of the North." *Atlantic*, July 1903, 42–49. Reprint. *Revolution and Other Essays*. New York: Macmillan, 1910.

"Housekeeping in the Klondike." *Harper's Bazar*, 15 September 1900, 1227–32.

"Husky—the Wolf-Dog of the North." *Harper's Weekly*, 30 June 1900, 611.

Inscription to Louis Bond. Presentation copy of *The Call of the Wild*. Photocopy in the collection of Russ Kingman, Glen Ellen, Calif.

Inscription to George Sterling, 23 July 1903. Presentation copy of *The Call of the Wild*. Berg Collection, New York Public Library, New York City.

Jack London on the Road: The Tramp Diary and Other Hobo Writings. Edited by Richard W. Etulain. Logan: Utah State University Press, 1979.

Jerry of the Islands. New York: Macmillan, 1917.

John Barleycorn. New York: Century, 1913.

"The King of Mazy May." *Youth's Companion*, 30 November 1899, 629–30.

"Klondike." Clipping files. Items JLE 716, 719 and 723. Huntington Library, San Marino, Calif.

"Klondike: [names]." TD. Item JL 851. Huntington Library, San Marino, Calif.

Letter to John Myers O'Hara, 27 September 1916. TL. Huntington Library, San Marino, Calif.

Letter to Marshall Bond, 17 December 1903. ALS. Huntington Library, San Marino, Calif.

The Letters of Jack London. Edited by Earle Labor, Robert C. Leitz, III, and I. Milo Shepard. 3 vols. Stanford: Stanford University Press, 1988.

"Like Argus of the Ancient Times." In *The Red One*, 89–141. New York: Macmillan, 1918.

Lost Face. New York: Macmillan, 1910.

Love of Life and Other Stories. New York: Macmillan, 1906.

Michael, Brother of Jerry. New York: Macmillan, 1917.

"Names [for fictional characters]." AMs. Item JL 975. Huntington Library, San Marino, Calif.

"The Night-Born." *Everybody's Magazine*, July 1911. Reprint. *The Night-Born*, 3–29. New York: Century, 1913.

"A Northland Miracle." *Youth's Companion*, 4 November 1926, 813–14. [This story was written in 1900 but not published until the date cited.]

"Notebook [of short story plots, novels, and poems, 1898]." Item JL 1004. Huntington Library, San Marino, Calif.

"The Other Animals." Illustrated by Boardman Robinson. *Collier's Weekly*, 5 September 1908, 10–11, 25–26. Reprint. *Revolution and Other Essays*. New York: Macmillan, 1910.

"Pluck and Pertinacity." *Youth's Companion*, 4 January 1900, 2–3.

The Road. New York: Macmillan, 1907.

The Scarlet Plague. New York: Macmillan, 1915. Reprint. New York: McKinlay, Stone & Mackenzie, n.d.

Scorn of Women. New York: Macmillan, 1906.

"Scrapbook, 1899–1901." Item JLE 715. Huntington Library, San Marino, Calif.

"The Shrinkage of the Planet." *Chautauquan* 31 (September 1900): 609–12. Reprint. *Revolution and Other Essays*, 141–57. New York: Macmillan, 1910.

Smoke Bellew. New York: Century, 1912.

The Son of the Wolf. Boston: Houghton Mifflin, 1900.

"Thanksgiving on Slav Creek." *Harper's Bazar*, 24 November 1900, 1879–84.

"Through the Rapids on the Way to the Klondike." *Home*, June 1899. Reprint. *Jack London's Tales of Adventure*. Edited by Irving Shepard, 39–42. Garden City, N.Y.: Hanover House, 1956.

"Up the Slide." *Youth's Companion*, 25 October 1906, 545.

White Fang. New York: Macmillan, 1906.

II. ABOUT JACK LONDON AND HIS WRITING

"Against Jack London." *New York Times Saturday Review of Books*, 23 February 1907, 109.

Alexander, Sidney. "Jack London's Literary Lycanthropy: A Review of *Jack London's Tales of Adventure*, ed. Irving Shepard." *Reporter* 16 (24 January 1957): 46–48.

Atherton, Frank. *Jack London in Boyhood Adventures* [ca. 1925]. TMs. Huntington Library, San Marino, Calif.

Bamford, Georgia Loring. *The Mystery of Jack London*. Oakland, Calif.: Piedmont, 1931.

Barltrop, Robert. *Jack London: The Man, the Writer, the Rebel*. London: Pluto, 1976.

Barton, Everett, to Jack London, 14 May 1913. TLS. Huntington Library, San Marino, Calif.

Benoit, Raymond. "Jack London's *The Call of the Wild*." *American Quarterly* 20 (Summer 1968): 246–48.

Berton, Pierre. Introduction to *The Call of the Wild*, by Jack London. Los Angeles: Ward Ritchie, 1960.

"Best Work of Jack London." *San Francisco Chronicle*, 2 August 1903.

Bond, Louis B., Goldfield, Nev., to Jack London, Calif., 15 August 1905. TLS. Huntington Library, San Marino, Calif.

———, Seattle, to Jack London, Glen Ellen, Calif., 28 May 1906. TLS. Huntington Library, San Marino, Calif.

———, Seattle, to Jack London, Glen Ellen, Calif., 8 June 1906. TLS. Huntington Library, San Marino, Calif.

Bond, Marshall, Santa Clara, Calif., to Jack London, 27 October 1905. ALS. Huntington Library, San Marino, Calif.

Bond, Marshall, Jr. *Judge Miller of Jack London's "The Call of the Wild."* Santa Barbara, Calif.: Privately printed, 1980.

———. "To the Klondike with a Big Dog Who Met Jack London." *American West* 6 (January 1969): 44–48.

"Books New and Old." *Atlantic Monthly*, November 1903, 693–98.

Bosworth, L. A. M., and Jack London. "Is Jack London a Plagiarist?" *Independent* 62 (14 February 1907): 373–76.

Brett, George P., President, The Macmillan Company, to Jack London, 3 December 1902. TLS. Item JL 2974. Huntington Library, San Marino, Calif.

———, to Jack London, 19 February 1903. TLS. Item JL 2981. Huntington Library, San Marino, Calif.

———, to Jack London, 19 March 1903. TLS. Item JL 2986. Huntington Library, San Marino, Calif.

———, to Jack London, 26 March 1903. TLS. Item JL 2987. Huntington Library, San Marino, Calif.

———, to Jack London, 27 March 1903. TLS. Item JL 2988. Huntington Library, San Marino, Calif.

———, to Jack London, 1 April 1903. TLS. Item JL 2990. Huntington Library, San Marino, Calif.

———, to Jack London, 21 April 1903. TLS. Item JL 2992. Huntington Library, San Marino, Calif.

———, to Jack London, 15 July 1903. TLS. Item JL 2997. Huntington Library, San Marino, Calif.

———, to Jack London, 30 July 1903. TLS. Item JL 2999. Huntington Library, San Marino, Calif.

———, to Jack London, 26 August 1903. TLS. Item JL 3000. Huntington Library, San Marino, Calif.

Calder-Marshall, Arthur. *Lone Wolf: The Story of Jack London.* New York: Duell, Sloan and Pearce, 1961.

"'The Call of the Wild,' by Jack London." *Athenaeum* 3957 (29 August 1903): 279.

"The Call of the Wild." *Philadelphia Press*, 25 July 1903.

Carpenter, G. R. "A Reader's Report for *The Call of the Wild.*" *Jack London Journal* 1 (Fall 1994): 231–32.

Clark, Edward B. "Real Naturalists on Nature Faking, *Everybody's Magazine*, September 1907, 423–27.

———. "Roosevelt on the Nature Fakirs," *Everybody's Magazine*, June 1907, 770–74.

Clayton, Lawrence. "The Ghost Dog, A Motif in *The Call of the Wild.*" *Jack London Newsletter* 5 (September–December 1972): 158. Reprint. *"The Call of the Wild" by Jack London: A Casebook.* Edited by Earl J. Wilcox, 172–73. Chicago: Nelson-Hall, 1980.

Dall, William H. "Jack London's 'Local Color.'" Letter to the Editor. *New York Times Saturday Review of Books and Art*, 6 September 1902, 871.

Dickey, James. Introduction to *"The Call of the Wild," "White Fang," and Other Stories*, by Jack London. Edited by Andrew Sinclair, 7–16. New York: Penguin, 1981.

Doctorow, E. L. Introduction to *The Call of the Wild*, by Jack London. Edited by Donald Pizer, xi–xviii. New York: Vintage/Library of America, 1990.

"Dogs in the Far North." *New York Times Saturday Review of Books and Art*, 6 December 1902, 861.

Doubleday, J. Stewart. *"The Call of the Wild."* *Reader* 2 (September 1903): 408–9. Reprint. *"The Call of the Wild" by Jack London: A Casebook.* Edited by Earl J. Wilcox, 150–51. Chicago: Nelson-Hall, 1980.

Fadiman, Clifton. Afterword to *The Call of the Wild*, by Jack London, 127–28. New York: Macmillan, 1963.

Flink, Andrew. *"Call of the Wild:* Jack London's Cartharsis [*sic*]." *Jack London Newsletter* 11 (January–April 1978): 12–19.

———. "'Call of the Wild': Parental Metaphor." *Jack London Newsletter* 7 (May–August 1974): 58–61. Reprint. *"The Call of the Wild" by Jack London: A Casebook.* Edited by Earl J. Wilcox, 229–33. Chicago: Nelson-Hall, 1980.

Franchere, Ruth. *Jack London: The Pursuit of a Dream.* New York: Thomas Y. Crowell, 1962.

Frey, Charles. "Contradiction in *The Call of the Wild.*" *Jack London Newsletter* 12 (January 1979): 35–37.

Fusco, Richard. "On Primitivism in *The Call of the Wild.*" *American Literary Realism* 20 (Fall 1987): 76–80.

Gair, Christopher. "The Doppelgänger and the Naturalist Self: *The Call of the Wild.*" *Jack London Journal* 1 (Fall 1994): 193–214.

Garst, Shannon. *Jack London: Magnet for Adventure.* New York: Julian Messner, 1944.

Geismar, Maxwell. Introduction to *Jack London: Short Stories,* ix–xx. New York: Hill & Wang, 1960.

———. "Jack London: The Short Cut." In *Rebels and Ancestors: The American Novel, 1890–1915,* 139–216. Boston: Houghton Mifflin, 1953.

Giles, James R. "*The Call of the Wild*: Jack London's Novel of Personal Liberation." Paper presented at the annual meeting of the Popular Culture Association, Chicago, 8 April 1994.

Gurian, Jay. "The Romantic Necessity in Literary Naturalism: Jack London." *American Literature* 38 (March 1966): 112–14. Reprint. *"The Call of the Wild" by Jack London: A Casebook.* Edited by Earl J. Wilcox, 174–77. Chicago: Nelson-Hall, 1980.

Haldeman-Julius, E., ed. *Life of Jack London.* Ten Cent Pocket Series No. 183. Girard, Kans.: Haldeman-Julius, 1923.

Hamilton, David Mike. *"The Tools of My Trade": Annotated Books in Jack London's Library.* Seattle: University of Washington Press, 1986.

Haughey, Homer L., and Connie Kale Johnson. *Jack London Homes Album.* Stockton, Calif.: Heritage, 1987.

Hedrick, Joan D. *"The Call of the Wild."* In *Solitary Comrade: Jack London and His Work,* 94–111. Chapel Hill: University of North Carolina Press, 1982.

Jack London: His Life and Work. New York: Macmillan, 1907.

Jack London: A Sketch of His Life and Work. New York: Macmillan 1905.

"Jack London's Explanations." *New York World,* 29 April 1906.

Jensen, Emil. "Jack London at Stewart River, 13 November 1926." TMs. Huntington Library, San Marino, Calif.

Kingman, Russ. *Jack London: A Definitive Chronology.* Middletown, Calif.: David Rejl, 1992.

———. *A Pictorial Life of Jack London.* New York: Crown, 1979.

———, Jack London Bookstore, Glen Ellen, Calif., to Daniel Dyer, 16 January 1993.

———, to Daniel Dyer, 1 February 1993.

Koenig, Jacqueline. "Jack London's *The Call of the Wild.*" *Jack London Newsletter* 9 (September–December 1976): 127–29.

Labor, Earle. Introduction to *Great Short Works of Jack London,* vii–xvii. New York: Harper & Row, 1965, 1970.

———. *Jack London.* New York: Twayne, 1974.

———. "Jack London." In *The Concise Dictionary of American Literary Biography.* Vol. 2, *Realism, Naturalism, and Local Color, 1865–1917,* 270–91. Detroit: Gale Research, 1988.

———. "Jack London's *Mondo Cane*: 'Bâtard,' *The Call of the Wild*, and *White Fang*." In *Critical Essays on Jack London*. Edited by Jacqueline Tavernier-Courbin, 114–30. Boston: G. K. Hall, 1983. Reprint. *"The Call of the Wild" by Jack London: A Casebook*. Edited by Earl J. Wilcox, 202–16. Chicago: Nelson-Hall, 1980.

———. "Jack London's Symbolic Wilderness: Four Versions." *Nineteenth Century Fiction* 17 (September 1962): 149–61. Reprint. *Jack London: Essays in Criticism*. Edited by Ray Wilson Ownbey, 31–42. Santa Barbara, Calif.: Peregrine Smith, 1978.

Labor, Earle, and Robert C. Leitz, III. Introduction to *"The Call of the Wild," "White Fang," and Other Stories*, by Jack London, ix–xxi. New York: Oxford University Press, 1990.

Labor, Earle, and Jean Campbell Reesman. *Jack London*. Rev. ed. New York: Twayne, 1994.

Lampson, Robin. "Some Sources of Jack London's Titles." *Pacific Historian* 20 (Spring 1976): 4–7.

Lane, Rose Wilder. "Life and Jack London, Part I." *Sunset, the Pacific Magazine* 39 (October 1917): 17–20, 72–73.

———. "Life and Jack London, Part II." *Sunset* 39 (November 1917): 29–32, 64–66.

———. "Life and Jack London, Part III." *Sunset* 39 (December 1917): 21–23, 60, 62, 64, 66–68.

———. "Life and Jack London, Part IV." *Sunset* 40 (January 1918): 34–37, 62–64.

———. "Life and Jack London, Part V." *Sunset* 40 (February 1918): 30–34, 67–68.

———. "Life and Jack London, Part VI." *Sunset* 40 (March 1918): 27–30, 64–66.

———. "Life and Jack London, Part VII." *Sunset* 40 (April 1918): 21–25, 60, 62.

———. "Life and Jack London, Part VIII." *Sunset* 40 (May 1918): 28–32, 60, 62, 64, 66, 68, 70, 72.

London, Charmian Kittredge. *The Book of Jack London*. 2 vols. New York: Century, 1921.

———. "Diary—1912." Item JL 226. AMs. Huntington Library, San Marino, Calif.

———, Honolulu, to Louis Bond, Goldfield, Nev., 3 June 1907. ALS. Bancroft Library, University of California Berkeley.

———, Glen Ellen, Calif., to John Myers O'Hara, New York City, 19 May 1921. TL. Huntington Library, San Marino, Calif.

London, Joan. *Jack London and His Daughters*. Berkeley, Calif.: Heydey, 1990.

———. *Jack London and His Times: An Unconventional Biography*. Garden City, N.Y.: Doubleday, 1939. Reprint. Seattle: University of Washington Press, 1968.

Lundquist, James. *Jack London: Adventures, Ideas, and Fiction*. New York: Ungar, 1987.

Lynn, Kenneth S. "Jack London: The Brain Merchant." In *The Dream of Success: A Study of the Modern American Imagination*, 75–118. Boston: Little, Brown, 1955.

McClintock, James I. *White Logic: Jack London's Short Stories*. Grand Rapids, Mich.: Wolf House, 1975.

Macmillan Company, New York, to Jack London, Oakland, Calif., 12 September 1904. TL. Huntington Library, San Marino, Calif.

———, to Jack London, Glen Ellen, Calif., 6 February 1906. TL. Huntington Library, San Marino, Calif.

Mann, John S. "The Theme of the Double in *The Call of the Wild*." *Markham Review* 8 (Fall 1978): 1–5.

Martin, Stoddard. "The Novels of Jack London." *Jack London Newsletter* 14 (May–August 1981): 48–71.

Maurice, Arthur Bartlett. "Jack London, 'The Call of the Wild.'" *Bookman* 18 (October 1903): 159–60.

Mitchill, Theodore C. Introduction to *The Call of the Wild*, by Jack London, vii–xxxi. New York: Macmillan, 1928.

Mott, Frank Luther. Introduction to *The Call of the Wild*, by Jack London, v–xxxi. New York: Macmillan, 1928.

Nash, Roderick. Introduction to *The Call of the Wild, 1900–1916*. Edited by Roderick Nash, 1–15. New York: George Braziller, 1970.

"A 'Nature' Story—*The Call of the Wild* by Jack London." *Literary World* 34 (September 1903): 229. Reprint. *"The Call of the Wild" by Jack London: A Casebook*. Edited by Earl J. Wilcox, 149. Chicago: Nelson-Hall, 1980.

Noel, Joseph. *Footloose in Arcadia: A Personal Record of Jack London, George Sterling, Ambrose Bierce*. New York: Carrick & Evans, 1940.

North, Dick. *Jack London's Cabin*. Whitehorse, Yukon: Willow, 1986.

Noto, Sal. "Jack London and the College Park Station." *San Jose Historical Association News* (January 1987): 7.

O'Connor, Richard. *Jack London: A Biography*. Boston: Little, Brown, 1964.

O'Hara, John Myers, New York City, to Jack London, Glen Ellen, Calif., 11 August 1907. ALS. Huntington Library, San Marino, Calif.

———, to Jack London, Glen Ellen, Calif., 4 September 1910. ALS. Huntington Library, San Marino, Calif.

———, to Jack London, Glen Ellen, Calif., 27 March 1911. ALS. Huntington Library, San Marino, Calif.

———, to Jack London, Glen Ellen, Calif., 25 April 1911. ALS. Huntington Library, San Marino, Calif.

———, to Jack London, Glen Ellen, Calif., 24 September 1911. ALS. Huntington Library, San Marino, Calif.

———, to Jack London, c/o The Macmillan Company, New York City, 11 January 1912. ALS. Huntington Library, San Marino, Calif.

———, to Jack London, Glen Ellen, Calif., 7 September 1916. ALS. Huntington Library, San Marino, Calif.

———, to Charmian Kittredge London, Glen Ellen, Calif., 27 February 1935. ALS. Huntington Library, San Marino, Calif.

———, to Charmian Kittredge London, Glen Ellen, Calif., 8 [?] March 1935. ALS. Huntington Library, San Marino, Calif.

Paulsen, Gary. Introduction to *The Call of the Wild*, by Jack London, ix–xi. New York: Macmillan, 1994.

Perry, John. *Jack London: An American Myth*. Chicago: Nelson-Hall, 1981.

Pizer, Donald. "Jack London: The Problem of Form." *Studies in the Literary Imagination* 16 (Fall 1983): 107–15. Reprint. Pizer, Donald. *Realism and Naturalism in Nineteenth Century American Literature*, 166–79. Rev. ed. Carbondale: Southern Illinois Press, 1984.

———. Notes to *The Call of the Wild*, by Jack London, 101–02. New York: Vintage/Library of America, 1990.

Reed, A. Paul. "Running with the Pack: Jack London's *The Call of the Wild* and Jesse Stuart's *Mongrel Mettle*." *Jack London Newsletter* 18 (September–December 1985): 96–98.

Reimers, Johannes. "Jack London's Book *The Call of the Wild:* It Is More Than a Rattling Good Dog Story—It Is an Allegory of Human Struggles and Aspirations." *Stockton Evening Mail* (California), 30 September 1903, 4.

"Reviews of New Books." *Oakland Herald*, 29 July 1903.

Roosevelt, Theodore. "Nature Fakers." *Everybody's Magazine*, September 1907, 427–30.

Rothberg, Abraham. Introduction to *"The Call of the Wild" and "White Fang,"* by Jack London, 1–17. New York: Bantam, 1981.

Sandburg, Carl. "Jack London: A Common Man." *Tomorrow* 2 (April 1906): 35–39. Reprint. *The Jack London Reader*, 268–72. Philadelphia: Courage Books, 1994.

Seelye, John. Introduction to *"White Fang" and "The Call of the Wild,"* by Jack London, vii–xviii. New York: Signet, 1991.

Shivers, Samuel A. "The Demoniacs in Jack London." *American Book Collector* 12 (September 1961): 11–14.

Sinclair, Andrew. *Jack: A Biography of Jack London.* New York: Harper & Row, 1977.

"Singular Similarity of a Story Written by Jack London and One Printed Four Years Before a New Literary Puzzle." *New York World*, 25 March 1906.

Solensten, John. "Richard Harding Davis' Rejection of 'The Call of the Wild.'" *Jack London Newsletter* 4 (May–August 1971): 122–23.

Spinner, Jonathan H. "A Syllabus for the 20th Century: Jack London's 'The Call of the Wild.'" *Jack London Newsletter* 7 (May–August 1974): 73–78. Reprint. *"The Call of the Wild" by Jack London: A Casebook.* Edited by Earl J. Wilcox, 234–42. Chicago: Nelson-Hall, 1980.

Stasz, Clarice. *American Dreamers: Charmian and Jack London.* New York: St. Martin's, 1988.

Stillé, Kate B. "Review of *The Call of the Wild*." *Book News Monthly* 22 (September 1903): 7–10. Reprint. *"The Call of the Wild" by Jack London: A Casebook.* Edited by Earl J. Wilcox, 157–60. Chicago: Nelson-Hall, 1980.

Stone, Irving. *Sailor on Horseback: The Biography of Jack London.* Boston: Houghton Mifflin, 1938. Reprint. New York: Signet, 1969.

Swain, Dwight. Afterword to *The Call of the Wild*, by Jack London, 107–14. New York: Aerie, 1986.

Tanner, Tony. "The Call of the Wild." *The Spectator* 215 (16 July 1965): 80–81.

Tavernier-Courbin, Jacqueline. *The Call of the Wild: A Naturalistic Romance.* New York: Twayne, 1994.

Thompson, Fred. "Diary of Yukon Experiences with Jack London, Mr. Shepard, Merritt Sloper, Jim Goodman, July–October 1897." TMs. Huntington Library, San Marino, Calif.

Upton, Ann. "The Wolf in London's Mirror." *Jack London Newsletter* 6 (September–December 1973): 111–18. Reprint. *"The Call of the Wild" by Jack London: A Casebook.* Edited by Earl J. Wilcox, 193–201. Chicago: Nelson-Hall, 1980.

Walcutt, Charles Child. *Jack London.* University of Minnesota Pamphlets on American Writers, No. 57. Minneapolis: University of Minnesota Press, 1966.

———. "Jack London." In *Seven Novelists in the American Naturalist Tradition: An Introduction.* Edited by Charles Child Walcutt, 131–67. Minneapolis: University of Minnesota Press, 1974.

———. "Jack London: Blond Beasts and Supermen." In *American Literary Naturalism, A Divided Stream,* 87–113. Minneapolis: University of Minnesota Press, 1956.

Walker, Franklin. Foreword to *"The Call of the Wild" and Selected Stories,* by Jack London, vii–xii. New York: Signet, 1960.

———. *Jack London and the Klondike: The Genesis of an American Writer.* San Marino, Calif.: Huntington Library, 1966.

Watson, Charles N., Jr. *The Novels of Jack London: A Reappraisal.* Madison: University of Wisconsin Press, 1983.

Wilcox, Earl J. "Jack London's Naturalism: The Example of *The Call of the Wild.*" *Jack London Newsletter* 20 (December 1969): 91–101. Reprint. *"The Call of the Wild" by Jack London: A Casebook.* Edited by Earl J. Wilcox, 178–92. Chicago: Nelson-Hall, 1980.

Williams, Herbert P., Macmillan Company, New York, to Jack London, Piedmont, Calif., 21 April 1903. ALS. Huntington Library, San Marino, Calif.

———, to Jack London, Piedmont, Calif., 26 June 1903. ALS. Huntington Library, San Marino, Calif.

———, to Jack London, Piedmont, Calif., 15 July 1903. ALS. Huntington Library, San Marino, Calif.

Williams, Tony. *Jack London: The Movies.* Los Angeles, Calif.: David Rejl, 1992.

Wirzberger, Karl-Heinz. "Jack London and the Goldrush." Translated by Ruby Susan Woodbridge. *Jack London Newsletter* 6 (September–December 1973): 146–47.

III. THE NORTHLAND: ALASKA, THE YUKON, AND THE GOLD RUSH

Adney, Edwin Tappan. *The Klondike Stampede.* New York: Harper & Brothers, 1900.

All About the Gold Fields of Alaska, Yukon River, and Its Tributaries. Chicago: North American Transportation and Trading Company, 1897[?].

Allan, A. A. ("Scotty"). *Gold, Men and Dogs.* New York: G. P. Putnam's Sons, 1931.

Amundsen, Roald. *The North West Passage.* 2 vols. London: Archibald Constable, 1908.

Andrews, Bryon. *Alaska and Its Gold Fields and How to Get There.* Washington, D.C.: National Tribune, 1897.

Bankson, Russell A. *The Klondike Nugget.* Caldwell, Idaho: Caxton, 1935.

Berry, Alice Edna. *The Bushes and the Berrys.* Los Angeles: Ward Ritchie, 1941. Reprint. San Francisco: Lawton Kennedy, 1978.

Berton, Laura Beatrice. *I Married the Klondike.* Boston: Little, Brown, 1954.

Berton, Pierre. *Drifting Home.* New York: Alfred A. Knopf, 1974.

———. *Klondike: The Last Great Gold Rush, 1896–1899.* Rev. ed. Toronto: McClelland and Stewart, 1985.

———. *The Klondike Quest.* Boston: Little, Brown, 1983.

Bits and Pieces of Alaskan History. Vol. 2, *1960–1974.* Anchorage: Alaska Northwest, 1982.

Black, Mrs. George [Martha Louise Munger]. *My Seventy Years.* As told to Elizabeth Bailey Price. London: Thomas Nelson and Sons, 1938.

Blethen, A. J., Jr. "Strange Klondike Outfits." *Leslie's Weekly* 86 (17 February 1898): 103.

A Boater's Guide to the Upper Yukon River. Rev. ed. Anchorage: Alaska Northwest, 1976.

Bolotin, Norm. *Klondike Lost: A Decade of Photographs by Kinsey & Kinsey.* Anchorage: Alaska Northwest, 1980.

Bond, Marshall. "Klondike Diary." AMs. Western Americana Collection, Beinecke Rare Book and Manuscript Library, Yale University, New Haven, Conn.

———. "The Klondike Rush of 1897." TMs. Western Americana Collection, Beinecke Rare Book and Manuscript Library, Yale University, New Haven, Conn.

———, Yukon Territory, to Laura Higgins Bond, Santa Clara, Calif., 11 October 1897. ALS. Western Americana Collection, Beinecke Rare Book and Manuscript Library, Yale University, New Haven, Conn.

———, Yukon Territory, to Laura Higgins Bond, Santa Clara, Calif., 17 November 1897. ALS. Western Americana Collection, Beinecke Rare Book and Manuscript Library, Yale University, New Haven, Conn.

Bond, Marshall, Jr. *Gold Hunter: The Adventures of Marshall Bond.* Albuquerque: University of New Mexico Press, 1969.

Bonner, John. "At the Gates of Klondike." *Leslie's Weekly* 85 (30 September 1897): 215.

———. "The Competition for the Klondike Trade." *Leslie's Weekly* 85 (30 December 1897): 444.

———. "Klondike at the Birth of Winter." *Leslie's Weekly* 85 (4 November 1897): 298.

———. "The New El Dorado at Klondike." *Leslie's Weekly* 85 (12 August 1897): 107.

Brainerd, Erastus. *Alaska and Klondike Collection, 1868–1898.* 14 vols. Manuscripts Division, Library of Congress, Washington, D.C.

Bramble, Charles A. *Klondike: A Manual for Goldseekers.* New York: R. F. Fenno, 1897.

Bronson, William, and Richard Reinhardt. *The Last Grand Adventure: The Story of the Klondike Gold Rush and the Opening of Alaska.* New York: McGraw-Hill, 1977.

Bruce, Miner Wait. *Alaska: Its History and Resources, Gold Fields, Routes and Scenery.* Seattle: Lowman & Hanford, 1895.

Buckley, L. W. "Outfitting for the Klondike." *Overland Monthly* 31 (February 1898): 171–74.

Butler, William Francis. *The Wild Northland: Being the Story of a Winter Journey, with Dogs, Across Northern North America.* Philadelphia: Porter and Coates, 1874. Reprint. New York: Allerton, 1922.

Cahoon, Haryot Holt. "Women Sail for the Klondike; What They Propose to Do." *Leslie's Weekly* 85 (30 December 1897): 440–41.

Cameron, Agnes Deans. *The New North: An Account of a Woman's 1908 Journey Through Canada to the Arctic.* New York: D. Appleton, 1909. Reprint. Rev. ed. Edited by David R. Richeson. Lincoln: University of Nebraska Press, 1986.

Cameron, Charlotte. *A Cheechako in Alaska and Yukon.* London: T. Fisher Unwin, 1920.

"The Camp at Skaguay." *Leslie's Weekly* 85 (23 September 1897): 203.

Campbell, Robert. *Two Journals of Robert Campbell, 1808–1851.* Edited by John W. Todd, Jr. Seattle: Privately printed, 1958.

Canada. Department of Transport. Meteorological Branch. *Break-Up and Freeze-Up Dates in Canada.* Report prepared by W. T. R. Allen. Circular 4116. 1 October 1964.

———. *Break-Up and Freeze-Up Dates of Rivers and Lakes in Canada.* Circular 3156. 30 January 1959.

———. North-west Territories. Retail Sale Permit No. 6, Eldorado Saloon. 3 May 1898. White-horse, Yukon: Yukon Archives.

Carmack, George W. *My Experiences in the Yukon.* Privately printed, 1933.

Chapman, George. "Mining on the Klondike." *Overland Monthly* 30 (September 1897): 262–72.

Charlie [?], Yukon Territory, to Mary [?], 16 June 1898. ALS. Western Americana Collection, Beinecke Rare Book and Manuscript Library, Yale University, New Haven, Conn.

Chase, Will H. *Reminiscences of Captain Billie Moore.* Kansas City, Mo.: Burton, 1947.

Clements, J. I. *The Klondyke: A Complete Guide to the Gold Fields.* Edited by G. Wharton James. Los Angeles: B. R. Baumgardt, 1897.

Clifford, Howard. *The Skagway Story.* Anchorage: Alaska Northwest, 1975.

Coates, Ken S., and William R. Morrison. *Land of the Midnight Sun: A History of the Yukon.* Edmonton, Alberta: Hurtig, 1988.

Cody, H. A. *An Apostle of the North: Memoirs of the Right Reverend William Carpenter Bompas.* Toronto: Musson, [1908?].

Cohen, Stan. *The Streets Were Paved with Gold: A Pictorial History of the Klondike Gold Rush.* Missoula, Mont.: Pictorial Histories, 1977.

———. *The White Pass and Yukon Route: A Pictorial History.* Missoula, Mont.: Pictorial Histories, 1980.

Coolidge, L. A. *Klondike and the Yukon Country: A Description of Our Alaskan Land of Gold.* Philadelphia: Henry Altemus, 1897.

Coutts, R. C. *Yukon: Places and Names.* Sidney, British Columbia: Gray's, 1980.

Craft, Mabel C. "Horrors of the Skagway Trail." *Leslie's Weekly* 85 (16 December 1897): 395.

Crane, Alice Rollins, ed. *Smiles and Tears from the Klondyke: A Collection of Stories and Sketches.* New York: Doxey's, 1901.

Curtis, Edward S. "The Rush to the Klondike Over the Mountain Passes." *Century* 55 (March 1898): 692–97.

Dall, William H. "Alaska and the New Gold-Field." *Forum* 24 (September 1897): 16–26.

———. "The Narrative of W. H. Dall, Leader of the Expedition to Alaska in 1866–1868." In *The Yukon Territory*, 1–242. London: Downey, 1898. Reprint. New York: AMS, 1975.

———. *Tribes of the Extreme Northwest.* Washington, D.C.: Government Printing Office, 1877.

Daniells, Roy. *Alexander Mackenzie and the North West.* New York: Barnes & Noble, 1969.

Davidson, George. "Alaska." *Overland Monthly* 30 (November 1897): 429–39.

Davis, Mary Lee. *Sourdough Gold: The Log of a Yukon Adventure.* Boston: W. A. Wilde, 1933.

Davydov, G. I. *Dvukratnoe Puteshestvie v Ameriku.* Compiled by Aleksandr Semenovich Shohkov. St. Petersburg: Pechashano in Morskoi Tipograffi, 1810, 1812. Reprint. *Two Voyages to Russian America, 1802, 1807.* Translated by Colin Bearne. Kingston, Ontario: Limestone, 1977.

Dawson, George M. "The Narrative of an Exploration Made in 1887 in the Yukon District." In *The Yukon Territory*, 243–381. London: Downey, 1898. Reprint. New York: AMS, 1975.

DeLaguna, Frederica. "Tlingit." In *Handbook of North American Indians.* Vol. 7, *Northwest Coast*, edited by Wayne Suttles, 203–28. Washington, D.C.: Smithsonian Institution, 1990.

———, Bryn Mawr University, to Daniel Dyer, 12 April 1994.

DeWindt, Harry. "The Klondike Gold Fields." *Contemporary Review* 72 (September 1897): 305–11.

———. *Through the Gold-Fields of Alaska to Bering Straits.* New York: Harper and Brothers, 1898.

Dictionary of the Chinook Jargon, or, Indian Trade Language of the North Pacific Coast. Seattle: Shorey, 1964, 1977.

Dietz, Arthur Arnold. *Mad Rush for Gold in Frozen North.* Los Angeles: Times-Mirror, 1914.

D'Orsay, Peggy, Librarian, Yukon Archives, Whitehorse, Yukon, to Daniel Dyer, 28 May 1993.

"Dyea and the Chilkoot Trail." Unpublished monograph. Dyea, Alaska, Society for Industrial Archaeology. Fall 1990 Study Tour. Skagway, Alaska: Klondike Gold Rush National Historical Park, 20 August 1990.

Dyer, Addison Clark. "Diary: 14 March 1898 to 20 October 1899." AMs. Personal collection of the author.

"Editorial." *Wave* 16 (31 July 1897): 3.

Edwards, William Seymour. *In to the Yukon.* Cincinnati: Robert Clarke, 1904.

Emmons, George Thornton. *The Tlingit Indians.* Edited by Frederica de Laguna. Seattle: University of Washington Press, 1991.

Evans, Taliesin. "The Story of the Yukon Valley." *Overland Monthly* 30 (October 1897): 330–40.

Facts for Klondiekrs [*sic*]. Seattle: Yukon Publishing, [1897?].

Fetherstonhaugh, R[obert] C[ollier]. *The Royal Canadian Mounted Police.* New York: Carrick & Evans, 1938.

Fountain, Andrew G., and Bruce H. Vaughn. *Yukon River: Freeze-Up Data (1883–1975).* Report prepared for the U.S. Department of the Interior, Geological Survey. Washington, D.C.: Government Printing Office, 1984.

Fulcomer, Anna. "The Three R's at Circle City." *Century* 56 (June 1898): 223–29.

Garland, Hamlin. "Ho, for the Klondike!" *McClure's Magazine* 10 (March 1898): 443–54.

———. *The Long Trail.* New York: Harper & Brothers, 1907.

———. *The Trail of the Goldseekers: A Record of Travel in Prose and Verse.* New York: Macmillan, 1899.

Gates, Michael. *Gold at Fortymile Creek: Early Days in the Yukon.* Vancouver: University of British Columbia Press, 1994.

Gilette, Edward. "The All-American Route to the Klondike." *Century* 59 (May 1900): 149–52.

Gillespie, Beryl, Iowa City, Iowa, to Daniel Dyer, 8 September 1992.

Gillespie, C. B., comp. *Souvenir Edition of the Norwich Evening Record.* Norwich, Conn.: Cleworth & Pullen, 1894. Reprint. Norwich: Franklin Impressions, 1992.

Gooding, S. J. "HBC Trade Guns." *Beaver* (December 1951): 30–31.

———. "The Trade Guns of the Hudson's Bay Company." In *Indian Trade Guns*, edited by T. M. Hamilton, 1–17. Union City, Tenn.: Pioneer, 1982.

Gordon, Eliott. *Klondike Cattle Drive: The Journal of Norman Lee.* Vancouver, B.C.: Mitchell, 1960.

Greely, A[dolphus] W[ashington]. *Three Years of Arctic Service: An Account of the Lady Franklin Bay Expedition of 1881–1884, and the Attainment of the Farthest North.* 2 vols. New York: Charles Scribner's Sons, 1886.

Green, Lewis. *The Gold Hustlers.* Anchorage: Alaska Northwest, 1977.

Grinnell, Joseph. *Gold Hunting in Alaska.* Edited by Elizabeth Grinnell. Chicago: David C. Cook, 1901. Reprint. Anchorage: Alaska Northwest, 1983.

Gurcke, Karl (Resource Management Specialist), Klondike Gold Rush National Historical Park, Skagway, Alaska, to Daniel Dyer, 22 February 1993.

———, to Daniel Dyer, 9 March 1993.

Hacking, Norman. "The Great Klondike Shipping Boom, 1897–1898." *Sea Chest* 17 (September 1983): 18–37.

Hamilton, Walter R. *The Yukon Story.* Vancouver, B.C.: Mitchell, 1964.

Hamilton, William B. *The Macmillan Book of Canadian Place Names.* Toronto: Macmillan, 1978.

———. *The Macmillan Book of Canadian Place Names.* 2nd ed. Toronto: Macmillan, 1983.

Hamlin, Charles Simeon. *Old Times on the Yukon: Decline of Circle City, Romances of the Klondyke.* Los Angeles: Wetzel, 1928.

Harmon, Daniel Williams. *A Journal of Voyages and Travels in the Interior of North America.* New York: A. S. Barnes, 1903.

Harris, A. C. *Alaska and the Klondike Gold Fields.* Chicago: Monroe, 1897.

Haskell, William B. *Two Years in the Klondike and Alaskan Gold Fields.* Hartford, Conn.: Hartford Publishing, 1898.

Haydon, Arthur Lincoln. *The Riders of the Plains: A Record of the Royal North-West Mounted Police of Canada, 1873–1910.* Chicago: A. C. McClurg, 1910.

Hayne, M. H. E. *The Pioneers of the Klondike: Being an Account of Two Years Police Service on the Yukon.* London: Sampson Low, Marston, 1897.

Heilprin, Angelo. *Alaska and the Klondike: A Journey to the New Eldorado, with Hints to the Traveller.* New York: D. Appleton, 1899.

Heller, Herbert L., ed. *Sourdough Sagas: The Journals, Memoirs, Tales and Recollections of the Earliest Alaskan Gold Miners, 1883–1923.* Cleveland: World, 1967.

"The Heroine of the Klondike." *Leslie's Weekly* 85 (9 September 1897): 171.

Hildebrand, John. *Reading the River: A Voyage Down the Yukon.* Boston: Houghton Mifflin, 1988.

Hinton, A. Cherry, and Philip H. Godsell. *The Yukon.* Philadelphia: Macrae Smith, [1955?].

Hult, Ruby El. *Lost Mines and Treasures of the Pacific Northwest.* 4th ed. Portland, Ore.: Thomas Binford, 1974.

Hunt, William R. *North of 53: The Wild Days of the Alaska-Yukon Mining Frontier, 1870–1914.* New York: Macmillan, 1974.

Ingersoll, Ernest. *Golden Alaska: A Complete Account to Date of the Yukon Valley; Its History, Geography, Mineral and Other Resources, Opportunities and Means of Access.* Chicago: Rand McNally, 1897.

———. *Gold Fields of the Klondike and the Wonders of Alaska.* New Haven, Conn.: Edgewood Publishing, 1897.

Inglis, Alex. *Northern Vagabond: The Life and Career of J. B. Tyrrell.* Toronto: McClelland and Stewart, 1978.

Jacobsen, Johan Adrian. *Captain Jacobsen's Reise an der nordwestkuste Amerikas, 1881–1883.* Leipzig: Max Spohr, 1884. Reprint. *Alaskan Voyage: 1881–1883.* Translated by Erna Gunther. Chicago: University of Chicago Press, 1977.

Kerfoot, Helen, Executive Secretary, Secretariat for Geographical Names, Ottawa, Ontario, to Daniel Dyer, 10 June 1993.

Kirk, Robert C. *Twelve Months in Klondike.* London: William Heinemann, 1899.

Klondike and All About It. New York: Excelsior, 1897.

Klondike and Yukon Guide. [Pamphlet.] Seattle: Seattle-Alaska General Supply Co., 1898.

Klondike: The Chicago Record's Book for Gold Seekers. Chicago: Chicago Record Co., 1897.

"The Klondike Excitement." *Leslie's Weekly* 85 (12 August 1897): 82.

"The Klondike Gold Rush." *Beaver* (March 1928): 164–65.

Klondike: Graham's Alaska Gold Fields Guide. Chicago: Lamas, 1897.

"A Klondike Hunter's Gold Mine." *Leslie's Weekly* 86 (27 January 1898): 55.

Krause, Aurel. *Die Tlinkit-Indianer* [The Tlingit Indians]. Jena, Germany: H. Costenoble, 1885. Reprint. Translated by Erna Gunther. Seattle: University of Washington Press, 1956.

Ladue, Joseph. *Klondyke Facts: Being a Complete Guide Book to the Gold Regions of the Great Canadian Northwest Territories and Alaska.* New York: American Technical, 1897.

———. *Klondyke Nuggets: A Brief Description of the Great Gold Regions in the Northwest Territories and Alaska.* New York: American Technical, 1897.

La Roche, F. *En Route to the Klondike.* Chicago: W. B. Conkley, [1898].

Leer, Jeff, Alaska Native Language Center, University of Alaska Fairbanks, to Daniel Dyer, 7 June 1994.

Leonard, John William. *The Gold Fields of the Klondike: Fortune Seekers' Guide to the Yukon Region of Alaska & British America.* Chicago: A. N. Marquis, 1897.

Lindsay, Matthew J. *Yukon and Klondike Gold Fields of Alaska.* San Francisco: Privately printed, 1897.

Lynch, Jeremiah. *Three Years in the Klondike.* London: Edward Arnold, 1904. Reprint. Edited by Dale L. Morgan. Chicago: Lakeside, 1967.

Lyons, Esther. "An American Girl's Trip to the Klondike. Part I: From Seattle to Sheep Camp." *Leslie's Weekly* 86 (6 January 1898): 5, 7.

————. "Part II: From Sheep Camp to Lake Bennett." *Leslie's Weekly* 86 (13 January 1898): 21, 23.

————. "Part III: From Lake Bennett to Lake Lebarge." *Leslie's Weekly* 86 (20 January 1898): 37, 39.

————. "Part IV: Lake Lebarge to Dawson City." *Leslie's Weekly* 86 (27 January 1898): 53, 55.

————. "Part V: Dawson City to Fort Yukon." *Leslie's Weekly* 86 (3 February 1898): 69, 71.

————. *Glimpses of Alaska: A Collection of Views of the Interior of Alaska and the Klondike District from Photographs by Veazie Wilson.* Chicago: Rand McNally, 1897.

McCourt, Edward. *The Yukon and Northwest Territories.* New York: St. Martin's, 1969.

McDonald, Lucile. *Alaska Steam: A Pictorial History of the Alaska Steamship Company.* Anchorage: Alaska Geographical Society, 1984.

MacDonald, Malcolm. *Down North: A View of Northwest Canada.* New York: Farrar & Rinehart, 1943.

MacKay, Douglas. *The Honourable Company: A History of the Hudson's Bay Company.* Indianapolis: Bobbs-Merrill, 1936.

Mackenzie, Alexander. *Voyage from Montreal on the River St. Laurence, Through the Continent of North America, to the Frozen and Pacific Oceans: In the Years 1789 and 1793.* London: T. Cadell, Jr., and W. Davies, 1801. Reprint. Chicago: Lakeside, 1931.

McKeown, Martha Ferguson. *The Trail Led North: Mont Hawthorne's Story.* New York: Macmillan, 1948.

McLain, John Scudder. *Alaska and the Klondike.* New York: McClure, Phillips, 1905.

Macleod, R. C. *The North-West Mounted Police, 1873–1919.* Canadian Historical Association Booklets, No. 31. Ottawa: Love, 1978.

McPhee, John. *Coming into the Country.* New York: Farrar, Straus and Giroux, 1976, 1977.

Magee, Thomas. "To Klondike by River and Lake." *Overland Monthly* 31 (January 1898): 66–72.

Mandelbaum, David Goodman. *The Plains Cree.* Anthropological Papers of the American Museum of Natural History. Vol. 37, Part II. New York: American Museum of Natural History, 1940.

Margeson, Charles A. *Experiences of Gold Hunters in Alaska.* Hornellsville, N.Y., 1899.

Marvin, Frederick R. *The Yukon Overland: The Poor Man's Route to the Gold Fields.* Cincinnati: Editor, 1898.

Mathews, Richard. *The Yukon.* New York: Holt, Rinehart and Winston, 1968.

Mayer, Melanie J. *Klondike Women: True Tales of the 1897–1898 Gold Rush.* Athens: Ohio University Press, 1989.

Medill, Robert B. *Klondike Diary: True Account of the Klondike Rush of 1897–1898.* Portland, Oreg.: Beattie, 1949.

Miller, Joaquin. "Stampedes on the Klondike: How I Missed Being a Millionaire." *Overland Monthly* 30 (December 1897): 519–27.

Minter, Roy. *The White Pass: Gateway to the Klondike.* Fairbanks: University of Alaska Press, 1987.

Mitchell, C. E. "Overland to the Yukon." *Overland Monthly* 31 (March 1898): 206–13.

Mitton, H. Eustace. *Klondyke: How to Get There, When to Go, and What to Take.* London: Samuel Deacon, n.d.

Mizner, Addison. *The Many Mizners.* New York: Sears, 1932.

Moore, J. Bernard. *Skagway in Days Primeval.* New York: Vantage, 1968.

Moore, William. "Report Upon Yukon Country, 6 January 1888." *British Columbia Sessional Papers*, 495–501. Victoria, B.C.: Government Printing Office, 1888.

Morgan, Edward E. P. *God's Loaded Dice: Alaska, 1897–1930.* Edited by Henry F. Woods. Caldwell, Idaho: Caxton, 1948.

Morrison, William R. *Showing the Flag: The Mounted Police and Canadian Sovereignty in the North, 1894–1925.* Vancouver: University of British Columbia Press, 1985.

Mowat, Farley. *Tundra.* Vol. 3, *Top of the World.* Toronto: McClelland and Stewart, 1973.

Muir, John. *Travels in Alaska.* Boston: Houghton Mifflin, 1915. Reprint. Boston: Houghton Mifflin, 1979.

Munn, Captain Henry Toke. *Prairie Trails and Arctic By-Ways.* London: Hurst and Blackett, 1932.

Nansen, Fridtjof. *Farthest North: Being the Record of a Voyage of Exploration of the Ship "Fram" 1893–96 and of a Fifteen Months' Sleigh Journey by Dr. Nansen and Lieut. Johansen.* 2 vols. New York: Harper & Brothers, 1897.

Nelson, Edward William. "The Eskimo about Bering Strait." In *Eighteenth Annual Report of the Bureau of American Ethnology to the Smithsonian Institution, 1896–1897, Part I*, edited by J. W. Powell. Washington, D.C.: Government Printing Office, 1899.

"A New El Dorado." *Wave* 16 (24 July 1897): 9.

Newell, Gordon, ed. *The H. W. McCurdy Marine History of the Pacific Northwest.* Seattle: Superior, 1966.

Newman, Peter C. *Caesars of the Wilderness.* Vol. 2, *Company of Adventurers: The Story of the Hudson's Bay Company.* Markham, Ontario: Penguin, 1987. Reprint. New York: Penguin, 1988.

———. *Company of Adventurers.* Vol. 1, *Company of Adventurers: The Story of the Hudson's Bay Company.* Markham, Ontario: Penguin, 1985. Reprint. New York: Penguin, 1987.

———. *Empire of the Bay: An Illustrated History of the Hudson's Bay Company.* Markham, Ontario: Penguin, 1989.

Nichols, Jeannette Paddock. "Advertising and the Klondike." *Washington Historical Quarterly* 13 (January 1922): 20–26.

Norris, Frank. "A Miner Interviewed." In *Frank Norris of "The Wave,"* 198–201. San Francisco: Westgate, 1931. Originally published in *Wave*, 24 July 1897.

———. "Sailing of the 'Excelsior.'" *Wave* 16 (31 July 1897): 7.

The Official Guide to the Klondyke Country and Gold Fields of Alaska. Chicago: W. B. Conkey, 1897.

Ogilvie, William. *Early Days on the Yukon.* London: John Lane, 1913. Reprint. New York: Arno, 1974.

———. "Extracts from the Report of an Exploration Made in 1896–1897." In *The Yukon Territory*, 385–423. London: Downey, 1898. Reprint. New York: AMS, 1975.

————. *The Klondike Official Guide: Canada's Great Gold Field, the Yukon District.* Buffalo, N.Y.: Matthews-Northrup, 1898.

Orth, Donald J. *Dictionary of Alaska Place Names.* Washington, D.C.: Government Printing Office, 1967.

Osborne, Charles C. "Impressions of Klondike, Part I." *Macmillan's Magazine* 82 (September 1900): 347–53.

————. "Impressions of Klondike, Part II." *Macmillan's Magazine* 82 (October 1900): 442–47.

————. "Impressions of Klondike, Parts III and IV." *Macmillan's Magazine* 83 (November 1900): 43–50.

————. "Impressions of Klondike, Parts V and VI." *Macmillan's Magazine* 83 (December 1900): 143–51.

Overland to Klondike Via the Spokane Route. Spokane, Wash.: Pigott-Greenburg, [1897?].

Page, Elizabeth. *Wild Horses and Gold: From Wyoming to the Yukon.* New York: Farrar & Rinehart, 1932.

Palmer, Frederick. *In the Klondike: Including an Account of a Winter's Journey to Dawson.* New York: Charles Scribner's Sons, 1899.

Palmer, Joel. *Journal of Travels Over the Rocky Mountains.* Cincinnati: J. A. and U. P. James, 1847. Reprint. Ann Arbor, Mich.: University Microfilms, 1966.

Parliament of Canada. "Annual Report of the Commissioner of the North-west Mounted Police, 1897." *Sessional Papers.* Ottawa: Printer to the Queen's Most Excellent Majesty, 1898.

————. "Annual Report of the Commissioner of the North-west Mounted Police, 1897; Appendix LL: Annual Report of Superintendent C. Constantine, Commanding Yukon District, 18 January 1898." *Sessional Papers.* Ottawa: Printer to the Queen's Most Excellent Majesty, 1898.

————. "Annual Report of the Commissioner of the North-west Mounted Police, 1897; Appendix MM: Annual Report of Acting Assistant Surgeon, W. A. Richardson, Yukon District, 1897." *Sessional Papers.* Ottawa: Printer to the Queen's Most Excellent Majesty, 1898.

————. "Annual Report of the Commissioner of the North-west Mounted Police, 1898." *Sessional Papers.* Ottawa: Printer to the Queen's Most Excellent Majesty, 1899.

————. "Annual Report of the Commissioner of the North-west Mounted Police, 1898; Part III: Yukon Territory, Report of Superintendent S. B. Steele, Commanding, North-west Mounted Police in the Yukon Territory, Dawson, 10 January 1899." *Sessional Papers.* Ottawa: Printer to the Queen's Most Excellent Majesty, 1899.

————. "Annual Report of the Commissioner of the North-west Mounted Police, 1898; Appendix A: Annual Report of Superintendent Z. T. Wood, Tagish, 2 November 1898." *Sessional Papers.* Ottawa: Printer to the Queen's Most Excellent Majesty, 1899.

————. "Annual Report of the Commissioner of the North-west Mounted Police, 1898; Appendix D: Annual Report of Inspector F. Harper, Fort Herchmer, Dawson, 29 December 1898." *Sessional Papers.* Ottawa: Printer to the Queen's Most Excellent Majesty, 1899.

————. "Annual Report of the Commissioner of the North-west Mounted Police, 1898; Appendix F: Annual Report of D'A. E. Strickland, Tagish, 1 November 1898." *Sessional Papers.* Ottawa: Printer to the Queen's Most Excellent Majesty, 1899.

———. "Annual Report of the Commissioner of the North-west Mounted Police, 1898; Appendix H: Annual Report of Inspector A. M. Jarvis, Tagish, 31 October 1898." *Sessional Papers.* Ottawa: Printer to the Queen's Most Excellent Majesty, 1899.

———. "Annual Report of the Department of Indian Affairs for the Year Ended 30th June, 1898." *Sessional Papers.* Ottawa: Printer to the Queen's Most Excellent Majesty, 1899.

———. "Annual Report of the Commissioner of the North-west Mounted Police, 1899; Part II: Yukon Territory." *Sessional Papers.* Ottawa: Printer to the Queen's Most Excellent Majesty, 1900.

Paulsen, Gary. *Winterdance: The Fine Madness of Running the Iditarod.* New York: Harcourt, Brace, 1994.

Penfield, Thomas. *Directory of Buried or Sunken Treasures and Lost Mines of the United States.* Conroe, Tex.: True Treasure, 1971.

Perrin, Rosemarie D. *Explorers Ltd. Guide to Lost Treasure in the United States and Canada.* Harrisburg, Penn.: Stackpole, 1977.

Phillips, James W. *Alaska-Yukon Place Names.* Seattle: University of Washington Press, 1973.

Piers, Sir Charles. "Fire-Arms of the Hudson's Bay Company." *Beaver* (March 1934): 10–12, 62–63.

Pike, Warburton. *Through the Subarctic Forest.* London: Edward Arnold, 1896.

Placer Mining: A Hand-Book for Klondike and Other Miners and Prospectors. Scranton, Pa.: Colliery Engineer, 1897.

Plempel, Charles Alexander. *The Klondyke Gold Fields: Their Discovery, Development, and Future Possibilities.* [Pamphlet.] Baltimore: Maryland Publishing, 1897.

Price, Julius M. *From Euston to Klondike: The Narrative of a Journey Through British Columbia and the North-West Territory in the Summer of 1898.* London: Sampson Low, Marston, 1898.

Probert, Thomas. *Lost Mines and Buried Treasure of the West.* Berkeley: University of California Press, 1977.

Rich, E. E. *Hudson's Bay Company.* 3 vols. New York: Macmillan, 1961.

Richardson, Sir John. *Arctic Searching Expedition: A Journal of a Boat Voyage Through Rupert's Land and the Arctic Sea, in Search of the Discovery Ships under Command of Sir John Franklin.* 2 vols. London: Longman, Brown, Green and Longmans, 1851.

Rikard, T. A. *Through the Yukon and Alaska.* San Francisco: Mining and Scientific, 1909.

Roberts, R. W. *A Tramp to the Klondike; Or How I Reached the Goldfields of Alaska.* Vaughnsville, Ohio: Privately printed, 1898.

Robinson, J. Lewis. *Weather and Climate of the Northwest Territories.* Reprint. *Canadian Geographical Journal.* March 1946.

Rodney, William. *Joe Boyle: King of the Klondike.* Toronto: McGraw-Hill Ryerson, 1974.

Ross, Alexander. *Adventures of the First Settlers on the Columbia River.* London, 1849. Reprint. Ann Arbor, Mich.: University Microfilms, 1966.

Russell, Carl P. "Trade Muskets and Rifles Supplied to the Indians." In *Guns on the Early*

Frontiers: A History of Firearms from Colonial Times Through the Years of the Western Fur Trade. Berkeley: University of California Press, 1957.

Sackett, Russell. *The Chilkat Tlingit: A General Overview.* Anthropology and Historic Preservation, Cooperative Park Studies Unit, Occasional Paper No. 23. Fairbanks: University of Alaska, November 1979.

Satterfield, Archie. *Chilkoot Pass: The Most Famous Trail in the North.* Rev. ed. Anchorage: Alaska Northwest, 1978.

———. *Exploring the Yukon River.* Seattle: Mountaineers, 1979.

Schwatka, Frederick. *Along Alaska's Great River.* New York: Cassell & Company, 1885.

———. "The Great River of Alaska, I." *Century.* September 1885, 738–51.

———. "The Great River of Alaska, II." *Century.* October 1885, 819–29.

———. *A Summer in Alaska.* St. Louis: J. W. Henry, 1894. [This is a popular account of *Along Alaska's Great River*, 1885]

Secretan, J[ames] H[enry] E[dward]. *To Klondyke and Back: A Journey down the Yukon from Its Source to Its Mouth.* London: Hurst and Blackett, 1898.

Service, Robert. "The Cremation of Sam McGee." In *The Spell of the Yukon and Other Verses.* New York: Barse & Hopkins, 1907.

Shaw, George Coombs. *The Chinook Jargon and How to Use It: A Complete and Exhaustive Lexicon of the Oldest Trade Language of the American Continent.* Seattle: Rainier Printing, 1909.

Sleicher, John A. "The Original King of the Klondike." *Leslie's Weekly* 85 (16 September 1897): 186.

Sola, A. E. Ironmonger. *Klondyke: Truth and Facts of the New El Dorado.* London: Mining and Geographical Institute, 1897.

Spude, Robert L. S. *Skagway, District of Alaska: Building the Gateway to the Klondike.* Anthropology and Historic Preservation, Cooperative Park Studies Unit, Occasional Paper No. 36. Fairbanks: University of Alaska, 1983.

Spurr, Josiah Edward. *Through the Yukon Gold Diggings.* Boston: Eastern, 1900.

Stacey, John F., and Mrs. John A. Davis. *To Alaska for Gold.* Worcester, Mass.: Privately printed, 1916.

Stanley, William M. *A Mile of Gold: Strange Adventures on the Yukon.* Chicago: Laird & Lee, 1898.

Stansbury, Charles Frederick. *Klondike: The Land of Gold.* New York: F. Tennyson Neely, 1897.

Starr, Walter A. *My Adventures in the Klondike and Alaska, 1898–1900.* Lawton Kennedy, 1960.

Steele, Harwood. *Policing the Arctic: The Story of the Conquest of the Arctic by the Royal Canadian (Formerly North-West) Mounted Police.* London: Jarrolds, 1936.

Steele, Capt. James. *The Klondike: The New Gold Fields of Alaska and the Far North-West.* Chicago: Steele Publishing, 1897.

Steele, S[amuel] B[enfield]. *Forty Years in Canada: Reminiscences of the Great North-West, with Some Account of His Service in South Africa.* New York: Dodd, Mead, 1915.

Steffens, J. Lincoln. "Life in the Klondike Gold Fields: Personal Observations of the Founder of Dawson." *McClure's Magazine* 9 (September 1897): 956–67.

Stephens, C. A., A. G. Fountain, and T. E. Osterkamp. *Break-up Dates for the Yukon River:*

I. Rampart to Whitehorse, 1896–1978. Fairbanks: Geophysical Institute, University of Alaska, April 1979.

Stewart, Elihu. *Down the Mackenzie and up the Yukon in 1906.* London: John Lane, 1913.

Suttles, Wayne, ed. *Northwest Coast. Handbook of North American Indians.* Vol. 7. Washington, D.C.: Smithsonian Institution, 1990.

Thomas, Edward Harper. *Chinook: A History and Dictionary of the Northwest Trade Jargon.* 2nd ed. Portland, Oreg.: Binfords & Mort, 1970.

To the Klondike and Alaska Gold Fields. San Francisco: Alaska Commercial, 1898.

"Townsite of Dyea" Unpublished monograph. Skagway, Alaska: Klondike Gold Rush National Historical Park, n.d.

Treadgold, A. N. C. *Report on the Goldfields of the Klondike.* Toronto: George N. Morang, 1899.

Tuttle, Charles Richard. *The Golden North: A Vast Country of Inexhaustible Gold Fields, and a Land of Illimitable Cereal and Stock Raising Capabilities.* Chicago: Rand McNally, 1897.

Tyrrell, Henry. "The Klondike Gold-fields and Alaskan Exploration." *Leslie's Weekly* 85 (12 August 1897): 106–7.

Tyrrell, James Williams. *Across the Sub-Arctics of Canada: A Journey of 3,200 Miles by Canoe and Snow-Shoe Through the Barren Lands.* New York: Dodd, Mead, 1898.

U.S. Bureau of the Census. *1990 Census of Population and Housing: Summary Social, Economic, and Housing Characteristics—Alaska.* Washington, D.C.: Government Printing Office, April 1992.

Walbran, John T. *British Columbia Coast Names, 1592–1906, to Which Are Added a Few Names in Adjacent United States Territory, Their Origin and History.* Ottawa: Government Printing Bureau, 1909.

Walden, Arthur Treadwell. *A Dog-Puncher on the Yukon.* Boston: Houghton Mifflin, 1928.

———. *Leading a Dog's Life.* Boston: Houghton Mifflin, 1931.

Webb, John Sidney. "The River Trip to the Klondike." *Century* 55 (March 1898): 672–91.

Webb, Melody. *The Last Frontier: A History of the Yukon Basin of Canada and Alaska.* Albuquerque, N.Mex.: University of New Mexico Press, 1985.

Wells, E. Hazard. *Magnificence and Misery: A First-Hand Account of the 1897 Klondike Gold Rush.* Edited by Randall M. Dodd. Garden City, N.Y.: Doubleday, 1984.

Wharton, David. *The Alaska Gold Rush.* Bloomington: Indiana University Press, 1972.

Whymper, Frederick. *Travel and Adventure in the Territory of Alaska.* London: John Murray, 1868.

Williams, John G. *A Forty-Niner's Experience in the Klondike.* Boston: Privately printed, 1897.

Wilson, Clifford A. *Campbell of the Yukon.* Toronto: Macmillan, 1970.

Wilson, V[eazie]. *Guide to the Yukon Gold Fields: Where They Are and How to Reach Them.* Seattle: Calvert, 1895.

Winslow, Kathryn. *Big Pan-Out.* New York: W. W. Norton, 1951.

"Women in the Klondike." *Klondike News* (Dawson City, Yukon), 1 April 1898.

Wright, Allen A. *Prelude to Bonanza: The Discovery and Exploration of the Yukon.* Sidney, B.C.: Gray's, 1976.

Young, Egerton R. *By Canoe and Dog-Train Among the Cree and Salteaux Indians*. New York: Eaton and Mains, 1891.

——. *My Dogs in the Northland*. New York: Fleming H. Revell, 1902.

——. "My Dogs in the North Land." *New York Times Saturday Review of Books*, 9 March 1907, 146.

Zaslow, Morris. *The Opening of the Canadian North, 1870–1914*. Toronto: McClelland and Stewart, 1971.

——. *Reading the Rocks: The Story of the Geological Survey of Canada, 1842–1972*. Toronto: Macmillan, 1975.

IV. GENERAL REFERENCE

Beebe, Lucius. *Mr. Pullman's Elegant Palace Car*. Garden City, N.Y.: Doubleday, 1961.

Bender, Eric J. *Tickets to Fortune: The Story of Sweepstakes, Lotteries, and Contests*. New York: Modern Age, 1938.

Binns, Archie. *Northwest Gateway: The Story of the Port of Seattle*. Garden City, N.Y.: Doubleday, Doran, 1941.

Bockstoce, John R. *Steam Whaling in the Western Arctic*. New Bedford, Mass.: New Bedford Whaling Museum, 1977.

Buder, Stanley. *Pullman: An Experiment in Industrial Order and Community Planning, 1880–1930*. New York: Oxford University Press, 1967.

Budlong, Philip L., Associate Curator of Collections, Mystic Seaport Museum, Mystic, Conn., to Daniel Dyer, 20 April 1993, 29 April 1993.

Butler, Samuel. *Unconscious Memory*. London: David Bogue, 1880.

Chapman, Robert L. *American Slang*. New York: Harper & Row, 1987.

Culin, Stewart. *The Gambling Games of the Chinese in America*. Philadelphia: Publications of the University of Pennsylvania Series in Literature and Archaeology, Vol. 1, No. 4, 1891. Reprint. Las Vegas: Gambler's Book Club, 1972.

Duke, Donald. *Southern Pacific Steam Locomotives*. 2nd ed. San Marino, Calif.: Golden West, 1962.

[Ely, Richard T.]. "Pullman: A Social Study." *Harper's Monthly* 70 (February 1885), 452–66.

Ewig, Rick, Manager of Reference Services, American Heritage Center, University of Wyoming, to Daniel Dyer, 18 October 1993.

Farmer, J. S., and W. E. Henley. *Slang and Its Analogues*. 7 vols. London: T. Poulter, 1890–1904. Reprint. New York: Arno Press, 1970.

Hervey, John. "Life of John Myers O'Hara [1939]." TMs. Special Collections. Newberry Library, Chicago.

Hitchman, Robert. *Place Names in Washington*. Tacoma: Washington State Historical Society, 1985.

Jones, Nard. *Seattle*. Garden City, N.Y.: Doubleday, 1972.

Journal of a Whaling Voyage to the Arctic Ocean and Return, by James A. Tilton, Master of the Steamer "Narwhal," 9 March 1897 to 8 November 1898. AMs [microform]. Item #93A. New Bedford, Mass.: Old Dartmouth Society Whaling Museum.

Lewis, Oscar. "Introduction." In *Frank Norris of "The Wave,"* 1–15. San Francisco: Westgate, 1931.

Leyendecker, Liston Edgington. *Palace Car Prince: A Biography of George Mortimer Pullman.* Niwot: University Press of Colorado, 1992.

Malone, Dumas, ed. *Dictionary of American Biography.* 20 vols. New York: Charles Scribner's Sons, 1933.

Mathews, Mitford M., ed. *A Dictionary of Americanisms on Historical Principles.* Chicago: University of Chicago Press, 1951.

Morel, Julian. *Pullman: The Pullman Car Company—Its Services, Cars, and Traditions.* London: David & Charles, 1983.

Morris, William, and Mary Morris. *Morris Dictionary of Word and Phrase Origins.* New York: Harper & Row, 1977.

Mossman, James, Puget Sound Maritime Historical Society, Seattle, Wash., to Daniel Dyer, 11, 17 September 1992, 22 February 1993.

New York, N. Y., Department of Records and Information Services, Municipal Archives. *Certificate of Death, No. 24385.* John Myers O'Hara. 16 November 1944.

O'Hara, John Myers. "Atavism." *Bookman* 16 (November 1902): 229.

———. "Comments of Press and Critics on Books by John Myers O'Hara, 1937." Scrapbook, Case Collection, Special Collections, Newberry Library, Chicago.

———. *Papers of John Myers O'Hara.* AMsS. Manuscripts Division, Library of Congress, Washington, D.C.

———. "Scrapbook, 1929–1944." Case Collection, Special Collections, Newberry Library, Chicago.

———. *Songs of the Open.* Portland, Maine: Smith and Sale, 1909.

———. "Two Scrapbooks, 1909–1944." Case Collection, Special Collections, Newberry Library, Chicago.

Partridge, Eric. *A Dictionary of Cliches.* 4th ed. New York: Macmillan, 1966.

———. *A Dictionary of Slang and Unconventional English.* 8th ed. Edited by Paul Beale. New York: Macmillan, 1984.

Robinson, Sinclair, and Donald Smith. *Practical Handbook of Quebec and Acadian French.* Toronto: Anasi, 1984.

Sale, Roger. *Seattle, Past and Present.* Seattle: University of Washington Press, 1976.

Smith, William George. *The Oxford Dictionary of English Proverbs.* 2nd ed. Revised by Sir Paul Harvey. London: Oxford University Press, 1948.

Spears, Richard A. *NTC's Dictionary of American Slang and Colloquial Expressions.* Lincolnwood, Ill.: National Textbook, 1989.

"Vessel Information Reply, *Narwhal.*" Mystic Seaport Museum. January 1993.

Wallace, W. Stewart. *A Dictionary of American Authors Deceased Before 1950.* Toronto: Ryerson, 1951.

Wentworth, Harold, and Stuart Berg Flexner. *Dictionary of American Slang.* 2nd. ed. New York: Thomas Y. Crowell, 1975.

Wilson, R.L. *The Colt Heritage: The Official History of Colt Firearms from 1836 to the Present.* New York: Simon and Schuster, 1979.

V. NEWSPAPERS

Daily Alaskan (Skagway), 1898–99, scattered issues.
Dyea Press, 1898, scattered weekly issues.
Dyea Trail, 1898, scattered weekly issues.
Klondike Nugget (Dawson City, Yukon), 12 November 1898.
New London Day (Connecticut), 28 March 1916.
New Rochelle Pioneer (New York), 19 July 1902.
New York Times.
Norwich Bulletin (Connecticut), 11 November 1924.
Oakland Enquirer, 11 February 1893.
San Francisco Chronicle.
San Jose Daily Mercury, 1892, 1897–98, 1901.
San Jose Herald, 30 March 1906.
San Jose Mercury Herald.
San Jose Mercury News.
San Jose News.
Skaguay News, 1897–98, scattered weekly issues.

VI. CALIFORNIA HISTORY AND GEOGRAPHY

Arbuckle, Clyde. *Santa Clara County Ranchos.* San Jose, Calif.: Harlan-Young, 1968.
"Around the City." *San Jose Daily Mercury*, 15 October 1901.
Beck, Warren A., and Ynez D. Haase, *Historical Atlas of California.* Norman: University of Oklahoma Press, 1974.
Butler, Phyllis Filiberti. *The Valley of Santa Clara: Historic Buildings, 1792–1920.* San Jose: Junior League of San Jose, 1975.
California Gazetteer. Wilmington, Del.: American Historical Publications, 1985.
California Place Names: A Geographical Dictionary. Berkeley: University of California Press, 1949.
Ford, Robert S. *Red Trains in the East Bay: The History of the Southern Pacific Transbay Train and Ferry System.* Glendale, Calif.: Interurbans, 1977.
Fremont, John Charles. *Memoirs of My Life.* Vol. 1. Chicago: Belford, Clarke, 1887.
"Garden City Athletic Club—Its House and Promoters." *San Jose Daily Mercury*, 6 October 1901.
Gudde, Erwin Gustav. *California Place Names.* Berkeley: University of California Press, 1960.
Harlan, George H. *San Francisco Bay Ferryboats.* Berkeley: Howell-North, 1967.
Historical Atlas Map of Santa Clara County, California. San Francisco: Thompson and West, 1876.
Holden, James. "93 Years of Railroad Ferries on San Francisco Bay." *Railroad* (January 1965): 13–17.

Jones, Herbert C. "Recollections of College Park in the 90's." *Trailblazer* 8 (Summer 1968): n.p.

Kemble, John Haskell. *San Francisco Bay: A Pictorial Maritime History*. Cambridge, Md.: Cornell Maritime Press, 1957.

"Life Membership Fee in Athletic Club Reduced." *San Jose Daily Mercury*, 15 October 1901.

Ma, L. Eve Armentrout, and Jeong Huei Ma. *The Chinese of Oakland: Unsung Builders*. Edited by Forrest Gok. Oakland: Oakland Chinese History Research Committee, 1982.

Men of California, 1900–1902. San Francisco: Pacific Art Company, 1902[?].

Munday, Jerome, Archives Researcher, San Jose Historical Museum, San Jose, Calif., to Daniel Dyer, 15 February 1993.

Payne, Stephen M. *Santa Clara County: Harvest of Change*. Northridge, Calif.: Windsor, 1987.

Peterson, Martin Severin. *Joaquin Miller: Literary Frontiersman*. Stanford: Stanford University Press, 1937.

Riegel, Martin P. *Historic Ships of California*. San Clemente, Calif.: Riegel, 1988.

San Jose City Directory, 1903–1904. San Jose, Calif.: Nusted, 1904.

Sawyer, Eugene T. *History of Santa Clara County*. Los Angeles: Historic Record Co., 1922.

Schwendinger, Robert J. *International Port of Call: An Illustrated Maritime History of the Golden Gate*. Woodland Hills, Calif.: Windsor, 1984.

Standard Time Schedules. San Francisco: Time Schedules Co., May 1897.

Sturm, William, Oakland History Room, Oakland Main Library, Oakland, Calif., to Daniel Dyer, 14 January 1993.

Sunshine, Fruit, and Flowers. Santa Clara County, California. San Jose, Calif.: *San Jose Mercury*, 1896.

Time Schedules of Local and Express Trains on the Lines in Oregon. San Francisco: Southern Pacific Company, 1 May 1897.

Traveler's Official Railroad Guide. 27 December 1897.

Wood, Raymond, F. *The Saints of the California Landscape*. Eagle Rock, Calif.: Prosperity, 1987.

VII. FLORA AND FAUNA

The Audubon Society Field Guide to North American Fishes, Whales, and Dolphins. New York: Alfred A. Knopf, 1983.

The Audubon Society Field Guide to North American Insects and Spiders. New York: Alfred A. Knopf, 1980.

The Audubon Society Field Guide to North American Mammals. New York: Alfred A. Knopf, 1980.

Darwin, Charles. *The Expression of the Emotions in Man and Animals*. London: J. Murray, 1872. Reprint. Chicago: University of Chicago Press, 1965.

Grolier's Field Guide to North American Trees. Rev. ed. Danbury, Conn.: Grolier Book Clubs, 1989.

Lopez, Barry Holstun. *Of Wolves and Men*. New York: Charles Scribner's Sons, 1978.

National Geographic Society Field Guide to the Birds of North America. 2nd ed. Washington, D.C.: National Geographic Society, 1987.

Peterson Field Guides: Western Trees. Boston: Houghton Mifflin, 1992.

Roberts, Charles George Douglas. "The Animal Story." In *The Kindred of the Wild*, 15–29. Boston: L. C. Page, 1902.

Sage, Brian. *The Arctic and Its Wildlife.* New York: Facts on File Publications, 1986.

White, Helen A., and Maxcine Williams, eds. *The Alaska-Yukon Wild Flowers Guide.* Anchorage: Northwest, 1974.

Williams, John G., and Andrew E. Williams. *Field Guide to Orchids of North America.* New York: Universe, 1983.

VIII.   DOGS

Brearley, Joan McDonald. *The Book of the Pug.* Neptune, N.J.: T. F. H. Publications, 1980.

Caldwell, Elsie Noble. *Alaska Trail Dogs.* New York: Richard R. Smith, 1945.

Coppinger, Lorna. *The World of Sled Dogs.* New York: Howell Book House, 1977.

Denlinger, Milo, Albert Heim, Mrs. Henry H. Hubble, Gerda Umlauff, and Joe Stetson. *The New Complete Saint Bernard.* Edited and expanded by E. Georgean Raulston and Rex Roberts. N.Y.: Howell Book House, 1973.

Drury, Mrs. Maynard K., ed. *This Is the Newfoundland.* Neptune City, N.J.: T. F. H. Publications, 1978.

Flanders, Noel K. *The Joy of Running Sled Dogs.* Loveland, Colo.: Alpine, 1989.

Hart, Ernest H. *Encyclopedia of Dog Breeds.* Neptune City, N.J.: T. F. H. Publications, 1968.

Jesse, Edward. *Anecdotes of Dogs.* London: Henry G. Bohn, 1858.

Morris, Desmond. *Dogwatching.* New York: Crown, 1986.

Thomas, Elizabeth Marshall. *The Hidden Life of Dogs.* Boston: Houghton Mifflin, 1993.

Vesey-Fitzgerald, Brian. *The Domestic Dog: An Introduction to Its History.* London: Routledge and Kegan Paul, 1957.

"A Wolf in Your Living Room." Written and directed by Mike Beynon. Narrated by Desmond Morris. Discovery Channel, 3 January 1993.

Index

Boldface indicates London's text; lightface, the Reader's Companion. (Because Buck's name appears on virtually every page of the text, the only reference to his name is for the Reader's Companion.)

PLACE-NAMES

CHARACTERS